Civilization's End

Song of the King's Heart

Book Three

Nicole Sallak Anderson

Literary Wanderlust | Denver, Colorado

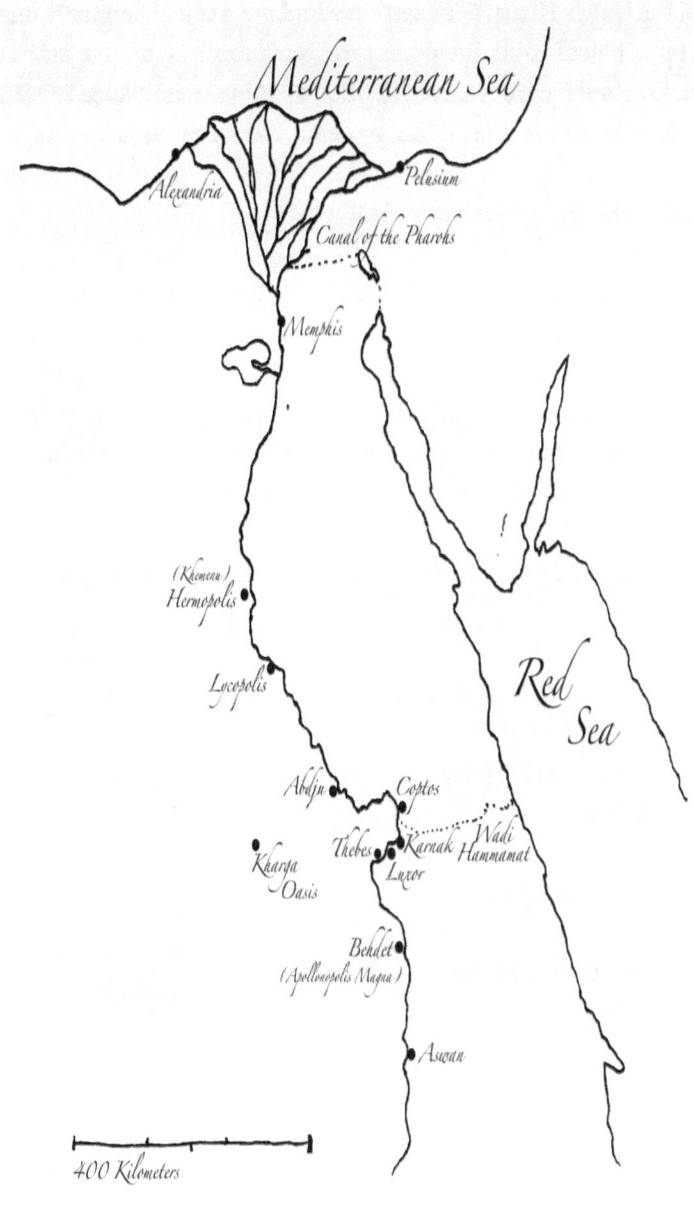

Mediterranean Sea
Alexandria
Pelusium
Canal of the Pharohs
Memphis
(Khemenu)
Hermopolis
Lycopolis
Red Sea
Abdju
Coptos
Thebes
Karnak
Wadi Hammamat
Luxor
Kharga Oasis
Behdet
(Apollonopolis Magna)
Aswan
400 Kilometers

Published in the United States by Literary Wanderlust LLC, Denver, Colorado.

https//www.LiteraryWanderlust.com

ISBN Print: 978-1-942856-90-1
ISBN Digital: 978-1-942856-91-7

Cover design: Pozo Mitsuma

Printed in the United States of America

Acknowledgments

What started as a Twitter pitch, turned into a five-year project and I'm forever grateful to Kylee Howells for "liking" the story about the Rebel King of Egypt and granting me the chance to share it with the world. Thanks also to Susan Brooks and Literary Wanderlust for investing in me as an author.

To my loved ones, cheerleaders, sons, and patron (that's you Walter): thanks for giving me the courage and the space to be a novelist.

Lastly, I want to thank the reviewers and the readers. You're the ones who share Ankhmakis with others and have enabled this forgotten man to be known once again among mortals. I hope you enjoyed this story and I appreciate your continued support and encouragement. Without you, there is no writer's life.

Dear Reader

Here we are, at the end of the tale. If you've read the other two novels in the Song of the King's Heart trilogy, you know that a Wikipedia entry is what inspired this story. As with the other two novels, I've had very few historical facts to go on, but there are a handful I've chosen to use in this story, and I wanted to point them out.

Records, what's left of them, suggest Ankhwenefer was crowned in Thebes in 199 BCE and then Ptolemy V was crowned in Thebes shortly after. Ankhwenefer was crowned again in 196 BCE and arrested in 185 BCE when Ptolemy V was crowned again. There is some evidence that perhaps Ankhwenefer lost the crown in Thebes for a few years, or at least wasn't in residence for his whole reign. Given Theban records suggest he held the crown for eleven straight years, I decided that he never lost control of the Upper Kingdom but did leave the city to expand his kingdom south, taking advantage of the alliances with Nubia and Kush. There's some evidence this might be true, and I went with it.

Given the Ptolemys reigned until 54 CE when they fell to Rome, they're the ones who wrote the final chapter of ancient Egypt's history. There is clear evidenfce in their telling that Ankhwenefer was arrested by the Greek General Conanus in 185 BCE near Thebes and that the priests had been behind it. Moreover, the priests of Memphis were rewarded for crowning Ptolemy V Pharaoh in Lower Egypt in 196 BCE with a stele that would later be known as the Rosetta Stone. That would suggest they too were behind the downfall but would have needed Theban priests to declare Ptolemy V Pharaoh of Upper Egypt in order for the arrest to happen. Since all other records of Ankhwenefer's reign were destroyed, we'll never know exactly how this came to be, but given Chanax's and Isidor's parts in the novels so far, betrayal has always been in the cards.

One question has always bothered me: Why did Ankhwenefer stop at Lycopolis? Why didn't he go all the way north, to Memphis, and then finally to Alexandria? Why split the kingdom for over a decade? For answers to both this question and the priest's deception, I let Natasa and Chanax show me the way.

I hope you find this as satisfying an end as I did.

Sincerely,
Nicole Sallak Anderson

For Lord Ankhwenefer, Good Being of Isis and Rebel King of Egypt.

PART ONE

EXILE

*"**G**rief is part of the human experience because you have forgotten your divine essence, and thus you create grief. You feel abandoned in your grief, but nothing is further from the truth.*

At the point when you are darkest, when you are saddest, where you are alone and separated from every other person on Earth, you are in the heart of what it means to be human. For when humanity bonded with death and destruction in order to die, grief was the result.

Animals feel sadness, remorse, and loneliness, but they cannot cry, and therefore cannot grieve. Only humans can do this. Tears are the gift of the gods. For when you decided to become human, you decided to know grief and the gods took pity upon you and gave you the ability to cry.

And through your tears, you will pass through the eye of the needle, and all that will remain is your light."

~ "Our Lady of Sorrows," by Finnian, Scribe of the North

1

Ten Thousand Voices

For three thousand years, the Wadi Hammamat was the major trading road between Thebes and the Red Sea, and hence was the gateway to the Silk Road. In the days of the Great Egyptian Revolt, the desert road was also the main escape for refugees, both Greek and Egyptian, as the two sides fought for control of the treasured trade route.

~Wadi Hammamat, Egypt, 199 BCE

The desert caravan traveled at a snail's pace. Crowds of refugees made the trek on foot, all victims of the civil war. At the moment, Egyptians were heading to Quseir, hoping to find work and safety, but months before the Greeks were the ones fleeing along the desert route.

The sandy road stretched out before Natasa, winding between craggy rock canyons and cliffs. The longer they traveled, the more rolling sandstone hills they encountered. Long ago, before men walked these lands, an ancient river had carved its way through the earth, leaving behind a path between the Nile and the sea, and a way to flee Egypt. The desolate, sandy landscape was more than her path to safety; it had become her world.

Just because Natasa was silent didn't mean her mind was quiet. No, to be Natasa was to hear voices—thousands of them—whispering horrible truths.

"Whore."

"Self-indulgent."

"Sinner."

"Careless."

"Failure."

"Murderer."

Over and over they taunted her. Every living moment of her life was a nightmare.

"You should be dead."

Truth. They spoke the truth.

The moment she tried to connect with her Ka, the voices would start. There was no place to hide. They attacked from all directions. Her soul was naked before their taunts.

"You murdered your child. There is no mercy for you."

Truth. Her child had died for her sins. Yet somewhere beyond the cruel cacophony was her lover, Ankhmakis. She sensed him calling her, and she wanted to answer.

"You don't deserve the prince. He never loved you. It was all for nothing."

It was impossible to hide from the truth, and in those moments when she was about to scream from the madness of it all, she'd focus on the wind, or the sands, or the rocking hips of the camel sauntering in front of her along the desert road, and Natasa would detach from her humanity, surrendering to their perfect, non-human, emotionless harmony, far removed from her own defiled existence. The elements, plants, and animals were her refuge, and she no longer existed in her body. Her own skin felt foreign; dead and cold like stone.

Days turned into weeks. Weeks turned into months. The desert crawled by. Wind whipped the linens wrapped around her head about her face. The sun god Ra dried her lips with his hot kiss. She constantly thirsted, yet no water could quench her need. Sometimes she walked, other times she rode in a wagon. There were settlements made of low brick houses in which she stayed to rest. Sleep was elusive, and when she did drift into her dreams, the voices often woke her up, forcing her to seek refuge from her mind.

"*Indulgent whore.*"

"*Murderer.*"

"*Filth.*"

Truth. She was a murderer and a whore. Before she could remember why, she'd seek a place between the other travelers by the evening fire and stare into the flames, connecting to the form of the flickering element of fire, vanishing from the voices in her head and all who were around her. Sometimes her mother and father talked about her in concerned, hushed tones, but the firelight was safer than human interaction. It was a quiet abyss, a place where the voices couldn't find her. By the time they arrived at the Red Sea, she was disconnected from humanity, and from her very own life force.

Natasa now lived within the life force of the Earth herself, where no humans, or emotions, or voices, could find her. In time, she would come to know this place as the Void—the place between the physical world and the world of light. For now, it was a shelter from the storm of endless taunts within her mind.

☥

Hundreds of miles in the other direction, Pharaoh Ankhwenefer and his army marched through their own desert wasteland. His route didn't have hills or canyons for shelter. No river had ever graced this vast sea of sand. Endless horizons and rolling, golden waves blazing under the blistering gaze of the sun surrounded them. The skin on his strong hands was cracked and blistered. The inside of his throat and nose were raw from the sand he inhaled at a constant pace. He'd lost men and animals. The trip was taking its toll on them all.

Wrapped in linens from head to knee to keep the sun from scorching his skin further, he rode in silence beside Khaleme for most of the trip. The general respected his mood, speaking only when spoken to. As Ankhwenefer looked out ahead of him, he remembered how he'd taken Natasa on rides out to the western sands. She had been so afraid of the desert and clung to his body like a child in fear, and now he'd sent her out there without him. His head fell to his chest, and he hid behind his long dark hair as he swallowed his tears.

"Why do fight your tears, Pharaoh Ankhwenefer?" Khaleme asked, his voice a low murmur.

"I don't want to worry the men," he replied. His new name sounded strange to his ears.

"They know your child was murdered and your lover has fled," Khaleme answered, turning his face to the sky. "Even the gods cry, my lord."

"I wish Natasa would answer my call," Ankhwenefer said, remembering how easy it used to be to connect with her in the astral realm before Helena's murder. They'd been one mind. Now when he searched for her, he met a cold emptiness, as if she were dead. "Perhaps I'm doing it wrong? I don't know. She was the gifted magician, and I nothing more than her adoring fan."

Khaleme shook his head. "I think Natasa is deep within."

"Deep within?"

"Gone from the Earth, but still alive."

"What will happen to her?"

"It is up to her."

Ankhwenefer recalled the last time he'd seen Natasa, tears pouring down her cheeks, begging him to stay. Their parting had been hard on both of them.

"I should have run away with her and Helena," he said, staring out at the bright horizon as a gust of wind swirled the sand around his horse's legs. "Rode to the west and then to the south to live with your people."

"Why?"

"Because I love Natasa, I need her by my side, and Helena would still be alive if I had taken them when I had the chance. I don't love the war, but I love those two more than life itself."

"Do you love Egypt?"

Ankhwenefer thought about it. "I did until my mother killed Helena. Now, I'm not so sure. Natasa is safe but wounded, and every step I make takes me farther from her side. There isn't much left of Egypt for me but war and pain."

"Lord Ankhwenefer, you are the true, native pharaoh of Egypt," Khaleme replied, his eyes narrowed upon his dark face. "Don't be the last."

"What do you mean?"

"If you don't finish this, your son will not inherit the throne. Your failure is the end of the line of Egypt's true kings. You cannot let that happen."

Ankhwenefer's shoulders curled forward. The burden of carrying his nation was too great. Perhaps he'd die in battle—that would end things nicely, wouldn't it? However, if he died, Natasa would have nothing left in this world, and he couldn't abandon her. He had to succeed so the war would end and Natasa could come home. It was this mission that gave him the strength to go forward.

"Great men are forged in the fires of suffering," Khaleme continued. "Yet greatness does not ensure victory."

Ankhwenefer raised his chin to look at the man, throwing back the wrap from his face. "I must win, Khaleme. It is my only purpose."

Khaleme met his gaze and paused for a moment. The Kushman's eyes were black and fathomless in the glaring sun. In spite of the desert heat, Ankhwenefer felt a chill run across his skin as his dear friend spoke, "The man who clings to what he has lost cannot see what matters most."

"Your Majesty," a captain called out as he approached from behind, "another horse has fallen. The animals tire and the men do as well. We will not find success in Lycopolis if we arrive in this state."

The pharaoh turned to address the man. "I agree, which is why when we arrive at the Kharga oasis tomorrow morning, we will take it under our control and remain there until we are ready to fight. Tell the men we will rest now until evening. Pitch the tents for relief from the heat. We ride out at sunset. Khons's silver boat is full tonight, and it's easier for the horses to travel under the cover of the night sky."

"Yes sir," the captain replied as he cantered off to deliver the update.

Ankhwenefer extended his Ka once more in all directions, searching for Natasa, and felt nothing. "How do we know she's not dead?"

"We don't know, but my heart says she still lives. If she dies, you will find out, one way or another," Khaleme answered.

"Natasa," Ankhwenefer whispered her name as if it were a prayer, his gaze turned to the clear blue desert sky, lips tugging and cracking as he pleaded. "Please come back. I need you."

2

The White Harbor

Queen Hatshepsut sponsored the most famous expedition through Quseir in 1493 BCE to the fabled land of Punt. The legend is recorded in her temple on the west bank of Luxor. It is said Punt was a wealthy country, and to this land, Hatshepsut had sent her general Senenmet to acquire goods for the temples, such as myrrh, frankincense, ebony, and ivory. While Punt is mentioned in many Egyptian temples as the Land of the Gods, no modern man has ever found it.

~ Quseir, Egypt, 199 BCE

"Well," Hecataeus declared, "Pistias says it's time to head out." Neferu stood on her balcony overlooking the Red Sea. The harbor was impressive and many tall-masted ships sailed along the water. One of those would be hers. She'd never been in such a large craft before. She glanced at Natasa, who sat in a chair and stared out at the sea, her green eyes still vacant. They'd survived the Wadi Hammamat, taking turns watching her at night to make sure she didn't walk off into the desert to be eaten by jackals. Here in the city of Quseir, a coastal town dappled with palm trees, gardens, and low mud and brick houses where they'd been hiding for months, Natasa had remained in their apartment, preferring to sit on the balcony like a statue as the water birds screeched overhead.

She still wasn't speaking.

"What's the rush?" Neferu asked as she turned to face Hecataeus. "Why not wait here for Ankhwenefer's sign?"

"Do you like it here in Quseir?" he asked.

"Yes, I do," she replied. "It reminds me of Behdet, and yet I like the sea much better than the Nile. And the food is wonderful. What do they call that dish I like so much?"

"Eggplant," he answered.

"Yes," she replied, rubbing her belly. "Eggplant and all the shellfish. Mussels, crabs, and oysters—so many things we don't have at home. And I like the light-colored wine."

"It's good here, I agree." He smiled.

Neferu's stomach tightened. Hecataeus looked like Adonis when he smiled. At first, the events in Behdet had cloaked him in grief. All of them had suffered, but he'd also lost his wife. However, as they traveled farther from Egypt, he grew more youthful, as if casting off the cares of his years as vizier. She still sometimes heard him weeping in his rooms about Corinna, and he spoke of his shame for failing her and Helena. Each day he fretted about leaving Eleni behind, telling Neferu about his plans to get her back once they got to safety, but Hecataeus was resilient, and in his resiliency, Neferu found herself falling for him, just as she had when he'd first arrived in Behdet, decades ago. Why had she ever let him go? The reasons weren't so clear now.

She picked up a pitcher and poured him some of the clear wine they made in Quseir. "Here, have some. It's so refreshing."

He took the glass from her hand. "Problem is, Neffa, this is still Egypt," he said, gesturing his arms out over the bay. "The Ptolemies won't give up terrorizing the Egyptians in this town until Ankhwenefer takes back Coptos and sends a cleanup crew here. We're not safe. We have to keep moving."

"I see." She sighed, finishing her wine, and allowing herself to enjoy the slight tingling she now felt in her legs. "When do we head out?"

"Tomorrow morning. Would you like to go dancing tonight?"

"Dancing?" She raised an eyebrow. She'd danced her whole life in the temples, but never for fun.

"Yes," he said, his cheeks turning red. "Greek dancing. Pistias says the musicians are outstanding. They even sing songs about the Great Revolt of Egypt."

"They've written songs about it?"

"Of course," Hecataeus said, now dancing himself around the room to a tune only he could hear in his head. "Some of the truest commentary of the war is sung by the rhapsodists in the taverns."

"Well." Neferu hesitated. "If you think Natasa will be okay."

He glanced at his daughter and quieted, his smile now a soft frown. "She'll sit in silence at the table. Can't do her much harm."

They both looked to Natasa for some sort of sign of life. The girl breathed, her chest rising and falling like the waves on the beach. She blinked and wrapped her yellow scarf closer to her body. These things proved her heart was still beating, but Natasa continued to stare ahead, not making eye contact, and not giving them any indication of her needs.

"She has started bathing herself," Neferu said.

"When?"

"Last night," she answered. "I think she likes the big, tile tub. I filled it with water, lit the fires below to heat it up, and she floated in it for hours, washed her own hair, toweled off, and dressed herself."

"That's an improvement." He exhaled a short breath. "Are you up for dancing? Pistias would love to take us out."

"Yes," Neferu agreed. "Let's do it."

Later that evening, the small family walked down the main street toward the harbor. The sounds of drums, tambourines, panduras, lyres, and harps filled the air. Men were singing at the top of their lungs, yelling, and calling out tunes. They entered the busy tavern and found their guide, Pistias, hired by Ankhwenefer to take them to Pelusium, and his men at a large table in the corner of the room. Men and women of every color, age, and ethnicity danced, ate, gambled, and laughed. Pistias rose from his seat, Belladonna the mongoose on his shoulder, grinning as he greeted them, his golden tooth shining in the candlelight. He wiggled close as he hugged Neferu, giving Hecataeus a wink, and gestured for them to sit. They guided Natasa to take a seat near the wall, her eyes wide as she trembled like a rabbit stalked by a jackal, head swiveling as if searching to find an escape. Pistias put a large candle in front of the girl, and her breathing relaxed as her eyes slowed from darting around the room to focus on the candle flame before fading into her usual deadened look.

"I've noticed she's more settled when she has fire to look at," the sailor explained.

"Thank you for taking such good care of her," Neferu replied. "I'm sorry she's so silent."

"Still in shock, I guess," Pistias replied, picking up a clay pitcher. "Now, here's some of that white wine you like so much."

"White wine?" she asked.

"Yes, they take the skins from the grapes before fermenting them, makes it nice and clear," he explained. "They call it white. It's also why they call the harbor 'The White Harbor,' because the water is so clear, like the wine."

"Yes, please," she said, reaching out to take the mug. She took a deep sip and swished it around in her mouth before swallowing it down. "It's very, very good."

Plates piled with grapes, cooked collard greens, olive leaves stuffed with fish, mussels in broth, raw oysters, rice, pilafs, lentils, and bread covered the tabletop. The wine flowed and the musicians played. Less than a half an hour later, Neferu found herself in Pistias's arms dancing a Greek circle with thirteen other people. They shimmied to the left, to the right, and then holding hands, spun all the way around. They repeated the entire sequence, moving faster and faster each round. She hadn't had so much fun in years. It seemed that work and dread had filled every waking hour of her life the moment the war had started, and now she was free. Spinning in time to the drums, she snuck a glance at Hecataeus, who stood in the corner, leaning against a post, smiling. He toasted her his drink when she caught his eye. Her heart melted.

After all these years, Neferu still loved him.

The night wore on, and soon Hecataeus was dancing as well. The crowd was wild, throwing drachma at the musicians and calling out for more. A song about the war was requested, one detailing the recent fall of Thebes to the Greeks. The rhapsodist rose from his place and sang at the top of his voice.

The soldiers ran into the palace, to capture the rebel king. They found him dead, in his very own bed, crown stolen as well as his ring.

Confused they searched high and low, wondering who had stolen from the pharaoh.

When suddenly Haronnophris, whom they'd thought was dead, rose and clung to the side of his bed.

"You won't find the crown," he whispered like a ghost. "My son now wears it, and he heads toward the coast."

Then the rebel king fell, all life now truly spent, and the soldiers realized their master wouldn't be content.

The rebel's son now wears the crown, and Ptolemy can't rest until Chaonnophris is taken down.

Halfway through the song, Neferu and Hecataeus stopped dancing, instead standing still in the middle of the dance floor as others spun around them, listening to the story, and taking in what they heard. It was heartbreaking to hear how Horwenefer had died.

"I'm glad he died that way," Hecataeus whispered in her ear. "It's befitting of him."

She looked up in his gaze, her heart fluttering—from wine or the nearness of him, she wasn't quite sure. To her surprise, Hecataeus leaned in and kissed her. Neferu lost track of time and place.

"Sing the one about the rebel king and his lover," a voice called out, causing Neferu to jump out of Hecataeus's embrace.

"The one they sing in the south," another suggested. "About the golden eagle and the little hawk."

A knot tightened in Neferu's belly, and she whipped her head to Natasa, who was still staring at the flame, oblivious to the world around her.

"Ah," the rhapsodist said, his voice soft now, "that's a beautiful and honorable song. Not one to be sung in low places such as this."

"Come on," the bartender bellowed. "I want to hear it."

Hecataeus drew Neferu closer as if to protect her from the mood of the room. They inched their way toward Natasa as the rhapsodist plucked his lyre, the melancholic notes setting the tone.

"They say he's come to save the land, to take Egypt back into his hands. They say he has Nubia and Kush under his command, and yet the golden eagle king is the loneliest man..."

The notes sailed upon the air and into each heart. The room was silent. Neferu's throat constricted.

"He lived in the south, this prince of the sun, and fell in love with a girl when he was quite young.

She pleased him and blessed him with love and foresight, and he grew into a man as they made love through the night.

Theirs was the sun and the moon and the stars, until that fateful day, when envy smote them from afar.

She was taken from his side and thrown to the wind.

The law of the land decreed their love forbidden.

Yet she knew the secrets of time and immortality, and she turned them into birds that were finally free.

To fly unto the night and make love under the stars, he a golden eagle and she the little hawk.

And to this day the rebel king has no peace, except when the moon rises and he sails the desert seas, to fly with his lover and finally be free."

"My word," Hecataeus whispered into Neferu's hair, "they did make a song about her."

Neferu gazed into his tear-filled eyes. He drew her close to embrace her and she glanced over his shoulder toward their daughter, who was no longer looking at the candle flame. Instead, Natasa stared at the rhapsodist, tears tracing lines down her dusty cheeks.

"If only she could have turned them into birds," Neferu said. "Then all three of them would still be together."

"Our daughter is magical," Hecataeus replied, turning to look at Natasa himself, "but even that is beyond her."

"*And to this day,*" the rhapsodist finished, "*the rebel king has no peace. Only in his lover's arms will he ever be free.*"

Natasa rose from her place and walked to the door. Neferu and Hecataeus followed her out into the night, holding hands and making sure she made it to their home. When Natasa was tucked into bed, Neferu left their room and found Hecataeus on the balcony, his big, brown eyes shining under the moonlight.

"Stay with me tonight," he begged. "I need you."

She held out her hand. "Yes."

His hand felt warm in hers, and she led him down the hall to his bed to make love for the first time in over twenty years. As they climaxed in one another's arms, Neferu felt as though no time had passed at all.

3

Belladonna

Animals were revered in Ancient Egypt, often mummified, and buried in the tombs with their masters.

The Red Sea, Egypt, 199 BCE

"The *world knows you're a whore."*

Natasa shook her head, rattling her brain. After a week on the sea, the voices were back. She attempted to bond to the wind or the powerful waves of the sea as they crashed upon the boat but found that path blocked. The Void was closed, and she was trapped in her mind. Hateful words filled her every thought.

"They sing and laugh about you in their taverns and call you the prince's concubine. The lowest of women."

Hidden deep within the boat in her small quarters, she slammed her head into the wooden panels that made up the walls.

"Soon they will sing the real truth…

She hit her head upon the wall again, relishing the pleasure of the pain and the warmth of blood as it dripped from the cut along her hairline.

"…and everyone will know how you murdered your own child."

Natasa rose and screamed. She ran toward the opposite wall and drove her forehead into it.

"Natasa," Pistias said, barking at her like a dog. He stood in the doorway, the mongoose on his shoulder shaking as she gripped her master's hair. "What are you doing?"

He strode into the cabin, yanking her from the floor and into his embrace, tightening his grip as she struggled to break free. Had he heard the voices? Did he agree with them? Of course, he did because they spoke the truth. She was filth, and Pistias knew it. He put up with her because he owed her father a debt. Pistias walked her out of the cabin and up to the deck. The sunlight blinded her, and she searched for anything to connect to. Wind, water, birds, livestock, anything but a human. Yet nothing returned her gesture. She was open and raw, and the madness was tearing away at her soul. The flapping of wind in the sails above her head drove the beat of chaos deeper into her mind.

"The prince's whore shall die for her sins."

Natasa struggled against Pistias's strong hands. He countered her escape attempt with an even firmer hold. As he led her to the bench near the prow, her heart raced even faster. Not out here, she thought. She wanted to beg Pistias to take her back down below where she could hide from the accusing glares of the crewmen, but spoken words evaded her. For to speak would mean to scream out loud the vile musings of her tainted mind.

"Shameless, dirty whore."

"Natasa, be still." Pistias sat her down on a bench to inspect her head, brushing back her hair and wiping the blood away. "You have cuts and bruises on your forehead. How long have you been abusing yourself this way?"

She wanted to tell him since they'd stepped on the boat when she'd lost the Void. Instead, she stared out beyond him, gaze vacant, and saw the form of his fear and revulsion as it swelled around him.

"Everyone hates you, even Pistias. You failed to protect your child. You're a whore and a murderer."

Rather than answer Pistias, she rose from her place and looked over the edge of the boat. The sunlight danced like diamonds on the waves, and she wanted nothing more than to give in and let the water take her away to the very end of life. Natasa leaned closer to the edge and gripped the railing. She was a jump away from relief when the mongoose sprung from Pistias's shoulder and landed on her chest. As the beast burrowed under her chin, Natasa felt the animal reach out to her with its own, pure Ka. No words, only the harmony of animal nature. Natasa clung to the small creature and allowed herself to fall into the perfect energetic form. She clutched the mongoose closer and rubbed her cheek upon the soft fur.

"*I know you,*" the animal said within her heart.

For a moment she hesitated, recalling her precious, dead child and how she could speak to the animals, but Natasa allowed the mongoose to fill her consciousness, and at long last, the voices stopped. Her mind calmed.

"Well, what do you know?" Pistias said, putting his hands on his hips and puffing out his chest. "It appears Belladonna likes you."

Natasa held the mongoose closer and closed her eyes, drifting deeper into the Void. It was blessed, blessed peace.

"Fine, Bella," Pistias continued, "you can stay with Natasa. She needs you more than I."

The sailor turned and left the two clutching one another on the bench, the sea air blowing their hair and fur and caressing their skins. Natasa stopped trembling, and Belladonna held herself across Natasa, allowing her to cradle the animal like a child. They remained together for the rest of the trip up the Red Sea, through the Suez Canal, and to the Great Bitter Lake, where they stayed for several days to give their sea legs a rest. That area of the world was beautiful, busy, and vibrant, yet Natasa saw none of it. Till her dying day, she couldn't recall the passage, as if it had never happened. But she never forgot Belladonna.

After a year on the run, they sailed out along the Canal of the Pharaohs, back toward the Nile, and onward to Pelusium, an Egyptian port town along the Mare Nostrum where they would launch the final leg of their journey, leaving Egypt behind forever, as well as Belladonna, for Pistias wasn't taking them across the sea. After sending a message to Ankhwenefer, Hecataeus took Natasa into his arms and led her aboard the new ship. Natasa fell into her father's embrace, hiding her eyes so he wouldn't see her madness. Without Belladonna the mongoose, she was once more struggling to find a place of peace. What her father mistook for fear of the high seas was the insanity of her own mind, torturing her very broken soul.

"*Selfish, indulgent whore*," the voices whispered as the ship disembarked. "*You should be dead.*"

She tugged her wrap closer as her father drew her deeper into his arms. *Yes*, she thought, *I should be dead.*

4

What Must Be Done

"From the time of the revolt of Chaonnophris, it happened that most of the farmers were killed and the land had gone dry. When, therefore, as is customary, the land which did not have owners was registered among the ownerless land, some of the survivors encroached on the land bordering their own and got hold of more than was allowed."

~ SB XXIV 15972, Greek Papyrus dated 186 BCE

The Nile River, South of Lycopolis, Egypt, 198 BCE

The taking of Lycopolis had been more of a struggle than Ankhwenefer had planned. Unable to breach the city for months, he changed tactics and left for the south, making his way back toward Thebes, this time along the Nile. He left two thousand men behind, surrounding Lycopolis and cutting the Greeks off from all trade and supplies from the north. He'd starve them out if he had to. The rest of his army followed him on his desperate quest to finish this never-ending military campaign. They left a path of destruction in their wake.

As had been predicted, the Greeks had advanced most of their forces southward, to hold Coptos and Thebes, never thinking Ankhwenefer would come from behind. The area between Lycopolis and Abdju had been a warzone for seven years now, and they needed to take away the attraction of this part of the Nile Valley. At every turn, Ankhwenefer and his troops destroyed the farmland, burning the crops and tearing down the irrigation systems, rendering them dry and useless after the next Inundation. Farmers were either killed or driven off the land. Stored grain was torched, as well as animals and livestock. Greeks fled from their homes; Egyptians were offered a place in the pharaoh's army. Greek temples were destroyed and looted, the gold taken to pay for the troops and the war. It was a bloodbath, and yet it had to be done. The Upper Kingdom needed a buffer between them and the Ptolemaic kingdom. Rendering the land from Lycopolis to Abdju empty and useless was the only way.

Over many months, they made their way to Abdju, finding little or no resistance. The work was in the destruction of the infrastructure. However, when the Greek army realized they were surrounded, they sent some of their troops north, and the battles began at full force. Ankhwenefer tore Abdju from their hands in a bloody skirmish that left many dead on either side, but the city was returned to Egyptian control.

After the battle, Ankhwenefer set his troops and the remaining citizens of Abdju to the task of repairing the wrecked city. Tents were erected for the soldiers. The palace was cleared out for Ankhwenefer and his staff. The farmlands in Abdju were spared, and refugees were given amnesty, even Greeks, as long as they pledge allegiance to Ankhwenefer. One night, after things had calmed in the city, Ankhwenefer found a moment to recall the temple of Seti I.

"Min," he said one evening, "join me, I have something I need to look into."

"Of course, Your Majesty," the soldier replied.

The two strolled under the moonlight, each exhausted by the campaign. They spoke little as they took stock of the situation. The city was a mess. Irrigation walls needed to be rebuilt and sanitation implemented. Everywhere they looked, there was work to do. Yet they couldn't stay long; they had Coptos to take back before moving onward to the real prize—Thebes.

"Here," Ankhwenefer said, pointing a torch toward a ruined

temple entrance. He crossed the crumbling threshold of the complex and held out a map he'd taken from Hecataeus's little house in the city. "According to this, there's a room under this temple so old, no one knows when it was made."

"Then how do we know about it?" Min asked.

"Builders uncovered it centuries ago when building Seti I's temple," he explained. "They changed the architectural plans to accommodate it. They named it the Osirian. Natasa claims it is the legendary Resurrection Bath, where the kings of old bathed in the power of Osiris to extend their lives and grant them their military power."

"Sounds like a legend all right." Min laughed. "Like the songs they sing about you in the taverns."

"Those songs are exaggerated, I agree." Ankhwenefer frowned. "However, they also give us clues. This is something they taught me in the temple Min, that all myths and symbols hold hidden truths. You have to have the eyes to see."

He stepped forward into the dark tunnel and followed the path deeper below the temple. The two walked out of the passageway out into a circular room that smelled of the sea and ancient dust. In the center sparkled a well, about ten feet deep and ten feet in diameter. Steps had been built to walk down inside the well to bathe. It was supplied by an eternal spring and a small trench led the overflow out of the room and into a wall. Above the trench was an enormous Flower of Life, carved into the stone with perfect precision. Ankhwenefer shivered in the chill. It was a cool as a tomb.

"My lord," Min whispered. "Why are we here?"

Ankhwenefer stepped forward, put his hands in the water, and placed a finger to his lips. "It's salty."

"Salty?" Min asked. "There isn't any sea near here."

"Not now, there isn't," Ankhwenefer replied. "Who knows where this spring originates? No one."

He looked into the pool and recalled what Natasa had said about the Wands of Horus and their ability to renew his Ka and grant him the power to manifest the end of the war. They were still in Behdet where she'd left them, but he'd vowed to use them in the Osirion. He doubted he'd have the power to make them work. This was a job for Natasa, and he would do all he could to secure Egypt so she could return to fulfill her divine duty.

He rose and spoke in a hushed tone, "Now that I've seen it, I understand Natasa a bit more."

"Natasa?" Min frowned. "How so?"

"She is the key," Ankhwenefer replied. "She's always been the key, and I will escort her here to this well, Min, and with her, end this war."

Min cocked his head to the side, but the pharaoh didn't try to explain. He needed to secure her safe passage back to his side much sooner than they'd planned. Perhaps he didn't have to wait until all of Egypt was his. It was too important that she work with the wands in the Osirion. Once he had Thebes back in his hands, he would call her home and they could finish their work together. The thought scared him. After what had happened to Helena, the idea of Natasa suffering any punishment at Greek hands was unbearable. Yet he feared the death of the nation if she didn't return.

Out of habit, he extended his Ka toward her and found nothing. He looked to Min and nodded. "Come. We're done here, for now."

The next day he received word that Lycopolis had surrendered and was under Egyptian control. He penned a letter to Hecataeus, informing him of his victories and asking him to stay a bit longer in Pelusium.

I might have Thebes by the start of Akhet, and if I do, I want Natasa sent back to my side. I no longer wish to wait until the war is over to call her home. Instead, she must return once the Upper Kingdom is secure. Remain in Pelusium with my beloved until you receive further word from me.

Ankhwenefer prayed his missive would not be too late.

5

Massilia

Legend has it Massilia was founded in 600 BCE by Protis, a Greek trader from Phocaea, who had been searching for new trading outposts in the Mediterranean Sea. When he happened upon the cove of Lacydon, Gaul, he was met by the king, Nannus, who invited him to a banquet, where his daughter, Gyptis, was to choose a spouse among the guests that night. To everyone's surprise, Gyptis forsook her Celtic brethren and chose Protis. As a wedding gift, the king gave the couple the land by the sea, and together they founded the city of Massilia.

Massilia, Gaul, 198 BCE

By late spring, the small family arrived in Massilia, greeted by sheets of rain pouring from a gray sky. Neferu had seen such rains before in her life, but never this frigid. From the moment they'd stepped on the boat, the air had grown colder and colder until the point where Neferu thought she could no longer feel her skin. She'd covered both herself and Natasa in the scratchy woolen dresses and stockings Hecataeus had purchased in Pelusium and thrown their dark blue wool cloaks over their bodies, yet still, they shivered. The cold was bone-deep, and the freezing rain didn't help the situation one bit.

As the harbor approached, Neferu felt a sense of relief wash over her. The journey across the sea had been terrifying. Waves higher than the deck and several storms had been encountered. She'd vomited more times than she cared to recall. Natasa wasn't much better. Still unresponsive, she'd spent most of her time locked away in her room. Neferu wasn't sure what she did in there, but from time to time she'd stand outside her daughter's door and listen. Pistias had warned her of the way he'd found her striking her head against the wall when traveling the Red Sea, but on this journey, all had been quiet in Natasa's room—too quiet.

Neferu held her distant daughter close and smiled, trying to muster some enthusiasm. "We're here."

The harbor was simple with rows of wooden docks and slips. The same merchant ships she'd seen in Pelusium lined these shores. Beside the docks rose the city, fashioned in Greek style and familiar. Beyond the city lay something she'd never seen in her life—mountains, rising from the earth, covered in lush green with a carpet of trees at their feet. How could there be so many trees in one place?

"Look at the trees," she exclaimed to Natasa. "Those mountains are bigger than our pyramids."

To Neferu's surprise, Natasa looked up and sneezed. This weather was going to make them sick.

"We're here," Hecataeus called out, tugging them both into his embrace. "Welcome to Massilia."

He turned and led them to the bow, where they waited for the ship to be tacked. Once the plank was lowered, the three were ushered off in the crowd, all eager to get out of the wet weather and into a warm inn or home, where food and fire awaited them. A wagon with a decent cover approached, and Hecataeus flagged down the driver.

"Taran," he yelled.

The driver stopped and jumped from the seat, landing on the ground in a muddy splash. The two men embraced, Taran even larger than Hecataeus. From under his hooded cloak, Neferu could see a full beard the color of fire. Red hair was rare in Egypt—even the Greeks didn't have it. This man was as red as could be. Neferu drew her daughter closer and wiped the rain from her own brow. It would take hours before they were dry.

The men noticed the drenched women, and Taran waved his arms. "Come, dear ladies," he said, speaking in Greek but with an accent neither Greek nor Egyptian, rather something else, with a lilt on the vowels. "Your chariot awaits you."

Neferu followed him, and he lifted her and Natasa into the wagon. The covering provided a bit of respite from the downpour as the men hefted their trunks in the back of the wagon. Soon Hecataeus climbed into the front of the cab, and Taran took his seat behind the horses, whipping them into action as they rode over the bumpy, muddy road toward town.

"We'll spend the evening in my home in the city," he explained. "Tomorrow I will escort you to a cottage in the woods. It's small, but the best I could arrange for you right now. Hecataeus was clear he didn't want to live in the city."

"Why can't we live in the city?" Neferu asked.

"Because, I've been living in noisy, dirty cities for decades. I need a change."

Neferu crossed her arms across her chest. "You never asked me what I wanted."

He shrugged. "I'm sorry, Neffa. I thought you'd need some peace and quiet as well. It's been an exhausting seven years or so, don't you think?"

"Yes," Taran spoke from up front. "War will break your soul. We've recently finished one here as well."

"You've been at war?" Neferu asked. She'd had no idea. "Who were you fighting? Is it safe to be here?"

"Oh," Taran answered in his low yet musical voice, "we Massilians weren't at war. The Romans were, with Carthage. We supplied the Legion a port full of ships. Many of our finest sailors never made it back, and while many Romans still remain here, the war itself has ended."

"Who won?" she asked.

"The Romans," he said, his gaiety fading into a scowl. "Which is a shame after the inspiring strategy and efforts by the Hannibal the

Great. He attacked Rome from the north, taking his elephants over the Alps in northern Italia in the snow."

"Elephants in the snow?" Neferu's eyebrows lifted as she considered the image. "What does that mean?"

Taran turned to look over his shoulder, laughing. "You don't know the story? It's legend on this side of the Mare Nostrum."

"She doesn't even know what snow is," Hecataeus explained.

"Oh," Taran replied. "Ice falls from the sky here. We call it snow. Makes for a slippery mess when riding elephants. They say he had to put wooden skis on their feet. Just imagine it."

"I can't imagine it," Neferu said, her teeth chattering as she gazed up at the clouds. She didn't like the idea of ice falling from the sky. It was already so cold. "Does it snow here in Massilia?"

"Sometimes," he replied. "Up in the mountains, there's snow all year round. It can be sunny and hot along the shore and when you look back at land, you see the white caps."

She shook her head. "I'm not looking forward to experiencing this thing you call snow."

"Don't worry madame," he said. "It will be at least nine moons before snow is even a possibility. Summer is on her way. Besides, we mostly get rain down by the sea."

"It's raining now."

"These are the spring rains," Taran explained. "Much warmer than our winter rains."

"That's not any better to my ears." She exhaled, her lips vibrating like a bird's wings flapping.

Hecataeus reached back to ruffle her hair. "That's what I love about you, Neffa." He laughed. "Always looking at the bright side."

She brushed his hand away and glanced at Natasa, who was shivering so hard, her teeth were chattering. "Are we close to your home? Natasa needs to get out of these soaking wet clothes."

"As you wish," Taran replied, turning down a narrow street and stopping minutes later in front of a home made from yellowish stone. The wooden front door had a brass knocker in the middle of it, shaped like a pair of snakes. Taran leaped from his seat, splashing in the puddles, and helped Natasa out of the wagon. He escorted them inside a warm entryway, and Neferu let out a long-held breath. An elder female servant arrived and offered to take their wet cloaks and boots.

"This way." Taran beckoned them to follow through the low-ceilinged room, past the kitchen, and into a bedroom in the back of the house heated by a blazing fire and wooden tub full of steaming water.

"Please, wash up," he said. "You'll want the warmth. Your trunks and dry clothes will be delivered soon."

"Thank you," Neferu said. There were two beds in the room. All three of them would sleep together that night. Looked like she wasn't going to have a private moment with her lover until they moved out to their cottage.

Natasa tugged the wet clothes from her own body, leaving them in a mushy pile on the floor. Natasa turned her back on her mother and climbed into the tub on her own, wrapping her arms around her torso and refusing any help. Without words, she gestured that she wanted to be alone. Neferu shrugged and took herself back into the front room, where Taran stood stoking the fire.

"I don't want to be a bother, but Natasa won't let me share her tub," she said.

"There's a second bath being drawn in my quarters," he offered. "Please, use that."

"Thank you," Neferu replied.

"I will send a servant up to help you," he continued. "There are plenty of women's clothes in there, choose whatever you'd like."

"Shouldn't I wait for the lady of the house to put something out for me? They're her clothes after all."

Taran looked up from the fire, and now that his cloak was off, Neferu was able to see him. His long red hair was braided into leather strips and hung down to his middle back. Along his arms were strange, dark black tattoos that looked like ribbons and knots. Around his neck, he wore a silver pendant, also in the shape of a knot around a large red stone in the center. She looked into his bearded face and saw he was frowning.

"I'm sorry," he replied in a low voice, "but the lady of the house is no longer with us. I lost my wife years ago to a cough."

Neferu clutched her heart. "I'm sorry," she began, but he held up a hand.

"Brida would have been honored to share her clothes with a high priestess from Egypt. Please, take as much as you need for both you and Natasa. One of my servants will fit the two of you. Trust me, you won't be wearing your white tunics and golden collars here in Gaul, my lady."

He called in a servant, and the young girl took Neferu into Taran's quarters. Neferu stripped off her wet clothes and slid into the wooden tub, thankful for the steamy, soapy water as its heat penetrated her flesh and warmed her for the first time since she'd left Egypt.

6

Closer

The Romans originally used the term Mare Nostrum to describe the western part of the Mediterranean Sea during their conquest of Sicily, Sardinia, and Corsica during the Punic Wars. As their empire grew, eventually the entire Mediterranean would go by this name. The Second Punic War had just ended as Hecataeus and his family embarked from Pelusium, but that didn't mean this area of the world was at peace. War waged along all of the Mare Nostrum's shores.

Coptos, Egypt, 198 BCE

Ankhwenefer scowled, his head throbbing as he read Hecataeus's letter.

My dear friend,

We have made it to Massilia in one piece. Neferu isn't a fan of the cold, rainy weather, but the greening of nature during the springtime is quite refreshing after decades of sand and hot sun. No offense, my lord, but I'm glad to be here. Natasa still doesn't speak and while she can take care of herself, remains more dead than alive in spirit. Yet I have hope that the end of our travels will help. We leave the city today and make our home in the forest. Please send any correspondence to Taran the Druid in Massilia, and we will receive it. I wish you luck and await your reply.

Yours,

Hecataeus

Ankhwenefer tore the letter to pieces, cast them to the floor, and stomped to the window overlooking the harbor. He'd taken back Coptos and what had felt like a victory moments before now felt too little too late. "He took her all the way to Gaul."

"Gaul?" Min exclaimed. "That's even farther than Carthage."

"It's over two thousand miles from here." Ankhwenefer paced before the window. "How will she travel back alone?"

"Hecataeus will return with her when you request it," Min replied.

"I'm not so sure." Ankhwenefer shook his head. "He's no longer in my service."

"He is in the service of Natasa," Min reminded him. "Besides, he'll want to gather Eleni eventually, won't he? Use the younger daughter as a means to draw him back with Natasa when the time is right."

"If the time is ever right. We may have Coptos, but now ten thousand Greeks stand between us and Silus's army in the south. After holding the line for well over a year, my brother has begun advancing forward as we strike from the other direction. Yet they outnumber us by at least three thousand men, I had to leave so many in Lycopolis. Until we take Thebes, we have not yet succeeded."

"I'm sorry this campaign has taken so long," Min agreed. "I want to get to Thebes as well."

"Have you any word about Maharet and your son?" Ankhwenefer asked. He was so involved in his own worries, he often forgot about Min's wife and young child in Thebes.

"Yes," he answered. "They made it to their family estate in the south before the Greeks took Thebes."

"You too know what it's like to keep your loved ones in hiding." The young pharaoh bit his lip. Everyone suffered while he tarried in his duties.

"Your Majesty, my dear Maharet is close by, not in Gaul."

"And alive."

"What do you mean? Natasa is still alive."

"Yes, but weak. I'm not sure she'd survive the return trip. From what Hecataeus writes, she hasn't spoken since the night of Helena's death."

Min clasped his hands behind his back and lowered his gaze. A knock on the door ended the conversation.

"Lord Ankhwenefer," the guard announced. "Your chariot awaits you."

Ankhwenefer put on the blue Khepresh crown of Thebes and pharaoh's collar. It was time for a victory parade.

"Ride by my side," he said to Min. "It should be my queen, but right now, I don't have a queen in my residence. Let it be my best friend instead."

"My lord," Min said, eyes glassy with unshed tears. "I'm so sorry I failed you in Behdet."

"Even if Helena's life had been spared, Natasa would still be in Gaul because it was always the plan to let Hecataeus take them out of the country."

"Yes," Min replied, "but if Helena were by her side, Natasa would be whole, and the two of you still connected, doing that thing you did."

"Astral travel?" he asked.

"Yes," Min answered. "Astral travel. She was your eyes on the battlefield, remember?"

"I do. I'll never forget it. More than my eyes, we also made love in the astral plane. We were together that way the night they killed Helena. It's how I knew something was wrong long before Iu-Amon sent for me."

Min's jaw dropped. "I can't believe it."

"Min, what is it?" Ankhwenefer asked.

"My lord," Min said, "the songs about Natasa are true."

"What songs about Natasa?" he asked, now protective of her.

"The songs about the two of you and your love," Min explained. "Haven't you heard them?"

"No," Ankhwenefer answered, crossing his arms. "I've been busy fighting a war. How is it you've heard them?"

"The men sing them after you retire for the night, sir."

"What do these songs say?"

"That you and Natasa turn into birds in order to meet in the desert and make love."

Ankhwenefer pondered this. It was a very strange coincidence. "What sort of birds?"

"You are the golden eagle," Min answered, "and she is the red kite, or little hawk, depending on the version of the song."

"Well, astral travel is similar to flying over the sands of time, so yes, there's a truth hidden within the legend. If only I still had the joy of meeting her in spirit. I wouldn't be alone right now."

"You miss her, don't you?"

"More than anything. Come, we have to ride out before the people and force them to acknowledge me as their pharaoh."

"Only Thebes left, my lord," Min smiled, "and then she will be home."

Ankhwenefer grabbed his hook and flail and left the room. As he rode about the streets, people threw palm leaves and lotus flowers before his chariot. They cheered from the broken, war-torn walls and chanted his name. He was king of yet another ruined city in need of repair, and all he could think of was that just over a year ago, as he fought his way through the desert toward Lycopolis, Natasa had been here, in Coptos, fleeing upon the desert road and out of his country.

He nodded to the roaring crowds, his painted face serious like the statues in his temples, and Ankhwenefer feared her flight had taken Natasa from his life for good.

7

Finnian

Leto was one of the many beautiful maidens seduced by Zeus, the Greek father god of all. When his jealous wife, Hera, discovered the maiden was pregnant, she cursed Leto such that nowhere under the sun would she find shelter to birth her children. Zeus took pity on his lover and turned her into a bird. She flew to the island of Delos and gave birth to the goddess Artemis, who helped her mother give birth to her brother, Apollo, the golden god of the sun, music, and poetry.

Massilia, Gaul, 198 BCE

Spring had turned into summer, and though the air was warmer, the change of seasons still hadn't stopped the rains, which continued to grace this green world at odd times, even on an otherwise sunny day. Natasa sat in the lush garden outside her cabin in the woods. Trees like stairways to heaven surrounded her, water still dripping from their leaves after the latest summer rainstorm. They had trapped her in their woody cage, and Natasa longed to see the horizon. She couldn't unite with these trees to escape the voices in her head. Their energy was too powerful and old—the giants were more human than plant.

Natasa was again under attack by her mind and there was only one way to stop it. She yanked up the sleeve of her coarse, gray dress revealing the various marks, some white scars, other scabbed over wounds crisscrossing along her dark arms.

She shivered. She was cold. Always so cold.

"*Whore.*"

The voices were constant companions. She rubbed her fist into her temple to try and quiet them.

"*You should be dead.*"

Truth. Tucking her now shoulder-length hair behind her ears, she slipped a hand into her boot and removed her knife, the only possession she'd managed to bring from Behdet, other than the little blue paper flower. For some reason she'd pinned the delicate thing on her tunic before going to bed on the evening she'd killed her daughter. It now lay buried in her trunk, for the voices hated the blue flower and tortured her, even more, when she touched it.

Natasa looked at the blade as it sparkled under Ra's demanding gaze, peeking through the trees. Ankhmakis had given it to her to protect Helena. She'd been wearing it the night they killed her but hadn't used it.

"*Failure.*"

How much time had passed since she'd killed her daughter? She looked around and forgot where she was. In a dense, green forest. Far from home.

"*You have no home. No one wants you.*"

Natasa placed the knife against her skin and sliced down deep, her lips curling into a slight smile as she did so. She dug deeper and then drew the blade across her flesh, biting her lower lip as she cut through. The pain soothed her, and the thin trail of blood made her feel alive.

"*You should be dead.*"

Truth. She continued to cut lines across the top of her forearm, and for a moment, the voices stopped. She slid the knife into her skin and the world fell quiet. Blessed quiet. She turned her arm over and touched her wrist, caressing the gentle pulsing of the veins spreading out below her palm. They reminded her of the Nile Delta, light blue against her skin.

"*You should die.*"

Yes, that would be nice. Death would mean forgetting. Death would be sweet.

"You should bleed, like Helena."

Bleed she must. Just like Helena. Her mind's eye replayed the moment when her tiny daughter fell from Pontius's arms and landed at his feet in a pool of her innocent blood. Red droplets splattered against his legs as he turned to flee the room. Natasa closed her eyes and with motion as quick as lightening, sliced her veins. Her eyes flew open as blood oozed from her wrist. This was more dangerous than anything she'd done before. This was crossing over to a new place. As her blood pooled in her lap, she became dizzy. It dripped from her wrist, staining her boots, yet her body was frozen, and she was unable to call for help.

"What are you doing?" a low voice asked.

Natasa looked up and discovered a young man racing toward her. His skin was as pale as the clouds, and a mane of thick blond hair glimmered in the morning sunlight. He shone as if kissed by Ra himself, and Natasa thought he was the god Apollo, come to take her to the Halls of Amenti.

"Cutting," she spoke for the first time in over a year, her voice strained from disuse.

"Stop," he commanded, taking the knife from her hand and casting it to the ground. He tore a thick strip of cloth from the green, woolen robe he wore, and wrapped it around her open wound.

She gazed at his beautiful face as he shoved the fabric on her wrist. He had a pure energy, something she hadn't experienced since Helena. The form of concern shimmered around him, and Natasa felt her own Ka approach his with the form of grief. Her vision blurred.

"I can see you," she whispered, touching his cheek. "I can see you."

"My lady," the young man asked as he looked over her abused arms and took in the results of months of self-torture. He traced his finger along one of the longest scars, and Natasa felt the shiver of life course through her very being. "Why are you doing this?"

"To stop the voices," she croaked. "To bleed like my daughter."

Neferu rushed out of the cabin. "What's going on?" she yelled as she approached, the color draining from her face when she saw the bloody knife in the grass. "Natasa," she exclaimed as she beheld her daughter's bare arms.

"It's okay, Mama," Natasa answered, her throat tight as she choked out her words. "It's okay. I can see."

Neferu placed her hands on either side of her head, her dark eyes wide. "You're speaking."

Natasa pointed to the tall, golden boy. "I can see him. It's been so long, but I can see."

Her voice faded and she fainted into her mother's arms.

☥

When she woke, Natasa lay in her bed by the fire, and her mother, father, and the young man stood in the far corner of the room. The stranger wore a dark green hooded cape, the color of the wet summer leaves, and carried a leather satchel strapped across his chest.

"Who are you?" she called out from across the room.

All of their heads whipped her way. The golden boy strode toward her and got down on one knee before her bed. "I'm Finnian, son of Atticus and Taran's scribe. He sent me to help out. Said you folks aren't too good at household chores."

Natasa saw her parents smile as they too approached her bed. She searched for the horrible, shaming voices in her head, but found none. Where had they gone? "Thank you. We do need help."

Hecataeus patted Finnian on the back. "Well, if you can get Natasa to talk, you're welcome anytime," he said in a cracked voice.

Natasa glanced at her bandaged arms, traces of blood visible through the cloth. The image of Helena trembling in Pontius's grip flooded her mind. The knife cutting through the child's throat. She tried to block the memory but couldn't. She looked at Hecataeus as the tears flooded her eyes.

"Papa," she exclaimed. "Why did they kill her?"

Hecataeus took her into his arms, and Natasa sobbed for the first time since the day the royals of Behdet had killed her precious Helena. Her grief built within her, tears welling up in her eyes first like the Nile during Inundation, then pouring out and streaming down her cheeks as she wailed like a storm upon the Mare Nostrum. When she could cry no more, she lay down and fell into a deep sleep.

She awoke to the sun shining through the window, casting rays of light across the wooden floor. Natasa looked around, seeing her new home for the first time. The cottage was one large room, in which sat her bed by the stone fireplace, a long wooden table with six chairs around it, a larder, and what looked like a cooking stove and table in the corner. Near the stone fireplace was a door leading to a back room, and near the cooking stove, a second door hung open to the outside, allowing a sweet summer breeze to drift inside the cabin. Herbs hung from the ceiling and sounds of laughter filled the air. Her mother, sleeves rolled up to her elbows, was chopping vegetables at the table. The golden boy named Finnian was instructing her.

"Yes," Neferu said. "You must show me how to cook rabbit. I need to feed my family."

"Cooking is easy," Finnian replied. "It's the hunting and growing of food that's hard."

"Good thing I have Hecataeus." Neferu laughed. "He can do anything he sets his mind to."

Natasa rose from the bed and crossed the floor, her steps hesitant upon the wooden boards beneath her bare feet. Both Neferu and Finnian looked up—her mother's face unreadable, but Finnian smiled.

"I can help too," Natasa offered. "Just show me what to do."

Neferu dropped her knife and ran to Natasa, grabbing her close and sobbing into her hair. Natasa wrapped her bandaged arms around her mother, and the woman hugged her even harder. She looked over Neferu's shoulder at the young man, his hair glowing in the sunlight. He gazed at them, hands folded behind his back.

"Would you like some nettles tea?" he asked, nodding to the kettle.

"Yes, thank you," Natasa replied. Her mother drew away, wiping her eyes with the apron she was wearing, and then took her place next to the young man, who handed Natasa a steaming mug.

Hecataeus bounded into the cabin and stopped mid-step, looking at Natasa and wearing the same stony face as her mother had. A wave of guilt squeezed Natasa's heart, she'd been distant for so long, yet the words still weren't ready to be said. She needed time to figure out what had happened, so she could explain herself.

"A letter from Ankhwenefer," her father said as he made his way to the table, holding up a scroll.

"Ankhwenefer?" Natasa asked, the name was unfamiliar.

"Ankhmakis, dear," her mother replied. "He's been crowned pharaoh, and that's his new name."

"The pharaoh of Egypt sends you letters?" Finnian's eyes widened. "You *are* a special family."

Natasa slammed her mug on the table, pointed at Hecataeus, and begged, "Read it. Read it *now*."

"Yes, yes, let me sit," he grumbled, finding a chair by the fireplace, which was now empty and cold. Already the summer heat had warmed the house. Hecataeus sliced the seal bearing the pharaoh's signet and unrolled the scroll. Clearing his throat, he read aloud.

Dear Hecataeus,

Thank you for your correspondence. It arrived the very day I took Coptos under my control. We now have the entire Greek army surrounded in and around Thebes. My men in the north still hold Lycopolis, preventing reinforcements. Yet the Greeks outnumber us and hold us back, far from the city. I'm working to discover how I might break them with the least number of Egyptian deaths.

More men come from Nubia and Kush as I write, which will help. I tell you this because though it's still not safe for Natasa to be by my side, I want you to begin to figure out how to return her. I know you recently arrived in Gaul, but I need her here. I no longer feel the war must be won for her to join me in this quest. I need only to secure Thebes and take the entire Upper Kingdom, from Lycopolis to Aswan, under my control. I'm so close, Hecataeus, so very close.

Tell Natasa I love her, I miss her, and I need her. Every day I search for her, hoping she has awakened, and every day I am still alone. I need my spiritual companion and true queen by my side. Until she wakes up, don't bother writing back. Let it be she who contacts me next.

In gratitude,

Ankhwenefer, Pharaoh of Upper Egypt

Natasa's heart pounded beneath her chest. She stepped forward and grabbed the letter from her father's hands, reading it and re-reading it. Each word was like fine wine and nourishment to her soul. Ankhmakis was pharaoh of Upper Egypt. He wanted her home. The thought both scared and delighted her. She turned to Hecataeus.

"Do you have any more letters from him?" she asked.

"Yes." He nodded, rising from his seat. "I will get them for you."

He gave her mother a glance from under his thick brows. Of course, they didn't want her to leave, and she wouldn't, not yet. She didn't feel strong enough to go back to the place where she'd lost Helena. Natasa felt a sudden darkness in her soul and fell forward, catching herself on the tabletop, fearing the voices were back.

"You're betrothed to the pharaoh of Egypt?" Finnian asked, interrupting her anxiety attack. Natasa had forgotten he was there. She gazed at his face and golden hair and gasped. His eyes were the brightest of blue, even bluer than Helena's. As clear as the White Sea in Quseir. She shook her head to focus.

"What does 'betrothed' mean?" she asked.

"It means promised to be married," he explained. He glanced away and out the window as if to avoid her gaze.

"Oh," she replied, feeling a bit shy about the conversation, "I've never considered it that way."

"Why not?" Finnian asked. Neferu had stopped chopping and was watching Natasa.

"Because, I'm not of the royal line," Natasa explained, "so I can't be his queen. Yet I was his spiritual companion and mother of his child."

Her thoughts trailed off. What was she to Ankhmakis? His lover? His wife-to-be?

His whore?

Natasa cringed at the word whore as it echoed through her mind. She looked Neferu, unsteady as if the floor was slipping from beneath her feet.

"In our country," Neferu answered, her head held high, "the king has a queen, often his sister, to produce pure-blooded heirs. He is also granted a spiritual companion, the bride of his heart, who teaches him of divine love and bliss. This is the holiest of partnerships the king can have. Natasa has been Lord Ankhwenefer's spiritual companion for over eight years. He sent her from Egypt for her safety and when he has secured his nation, he will call her home to return to his side."

Natasa gripped the table with both of her hands, gasping for air as she fought off the voices. *The bride of his heart. The bride of his heart. The bride of his heart.* She repeated the words inside of her mind, trying to erase the fear that she was nothing more than a discarded concubine.

"Now that Ankhwenefer is pharaoh," Neferu continued, walking over and placing her arms around her daughter, "it appears he also has plans to make her his second queen as well. She *is* betrothed to the pharaoh of Upper Egypt, and I'm very happy."

Natasa's heart slowed and she exhaled, grateful for her mother's support. She placed the letter on the table and grabbed her mug as Hecataeus re-entered the room, a pile of scrolls in his arms.

"I think this is all of them. Nothing much in here but a lot of boring war talk, but I think you'll like the parts where he asks about you."

"Thank you, Father," she said as she sat to read them. "When I'm finished, I should like to write him a letter as well."

"Of course, dear," Hecataeus replied. "It appears a letter from you would make all the difference in the world. Finnian, how about you come help me build that fence? Now that Natasa has started speaking, I think we need to make her an herb garden."

"Papa," she said, looking up from her letters, "I don't even know what sort of plants grow in such a wet, cold place."

"That's no problem," Finnian said, smiling in a way that sent a flush of heat racing along her skin, followed in almost the same moment by the sting of shame in her throat. No one but Ankhmakis should make her feel that way. "I have a friend I know who would be willing to help you. Do you know a lot about herbs?"

"Of course she does," Neferu replied. "She is a priestess of Isis, as well as one of the most gifted healers of Behdet."

Finnian raised an eyebrow. "Impressive. I know Aurelia would help a priestess. In exchange for your wisdom of Egyptian herbology, she can teach you all there is to know about our plant allies here in Gaul."

The golden boy bowed and then grabbed a hat, flipping it onto his lion's mane of hair. Natasa picked up a letter, drawn to the sight of her lover's handwriting. She turned away from Finnian, but not before noticing the way his shoulders slumped as he followed her father out of the room.

8

Simple Joys

Where is the king's green-eyed girl? Why does she fly away? The black-eyed cobra attacked her, they say, and her terrible sorrow has led her astray.

~ The Lament of the Golden Eagle King, 194 BCE

Coptos, Egypt, 198 BCE

My Dearest Ankhmakis,

It is I, Natasa. I'm sorry I've been away so long from your heart. I lost my way in darkness and suffered much. No worse than you, I imagine, but you're the more resilient one.

May I still call you Ankhmakis? Your new name and title seem foreign to me. I've never met that man, but I know I love Prince Ankhmakis dearly, thus I shall call you that if you don't mind.

I have lost my connection to the All-One. Taran, father's druid friend, says it's because we're too far apart and our energetic connection was part of the land of Egypt. I fear I'm no longer granted access due to the fact that I lived in the Void for so long in order to cope with the loss of our child. The Void will grant you relief from pain and grief, but also tears your Ka into pieces. I'll have to tell you how I left the Earth's plane, but not right now. It still hurts to think about.

Life in Massilia is very different from Egypt—so green and wet. There are trees in the forest so tall they stretch to heaven, and farther inland, mountains bigger than the pyramids. It rains all year. The people are as diverse as Alexandria, but Father got us a house in the country away from the noise of the busy harbor city. You should see Mother try to do chores—she's hopeless. I shouldn't tease her. If I hadn't spent years with Iu-Amon, I wouldn't know how to clean either.

I'm working on a garden. A witch named Aurelia with long gray hair, blue eyes, and skin so pale you can see her veins comes by to show me which plants are good in this climate. In return for her efforts, I tell her about our medicines. The scribe, Finnian, a young man who's at most sixteen years of age, takes down our conversations. Finnian also helps Papa around the house. He's such a golden boy, I thought he was Apollo when I first met him. He is pure sweetness.

Yet even with these blessings, you and Helena aren't here, and thus I am never at peace.

I love you and long for your response,

Natasa

Ankhwenefer read the letter for the third time that day, drinking his wine and pacing his makeshift chambers. Natasa had written him. He couldn't believe it. He hugged the letter to his heart and bounced on the balls of his feet. The paper on which it was written was strange and waxy in nature, but the Greek letters were in her writing, and it was pure bliss—the first bit of joy he'd felt in a long, long time.

Min entered the room, his brow furrowed. "My lord, the Greeks are advancing north. They've sent several troops in an attempt to take back Coptos."

"Send a runner to Silus and have him deploy five small, swift megau units to follow them at a distance as they progress. Take them out at night." The megau units, the king's elite company of archers, would respond quickly.

"Sneaky," Min answered. He raised his chin to the letter in Ankhwenefer's grip. "What do you have there?"

Ankhwenefer held the letter in the air and waved it like a victory banner. "A letter from Natasa, written in her own hand. It arrived yesterday, and all I can do is read it whenever I'm alone. I want to keep it near me. I'm so grateful she's alive and writing to me."

"Why hasn't she contacted you in that other way?"

"Astrally? She says she can't anymore."

"That's terrible," Min answered. "I know that connection means so much to you."

"Your Majesty, Pharaoh Ankhwenefer," a guard called from the doorway. "I have a message for you."

"Thank you," Ankhwenefer replied, and as he took it into his hand, he recognized Hecataeus's seal. "Another letter?" he wondered aloud as he peeled off the wax and read it.

My Dearest Ankhmakis,

I know I just sent you a message, but now that I can write you, I find myself with all sorts of things to say. Father says we have the money, thanks to you, to send as many letters as I want, so I shall. What good is a pharaoh's coin if not spent on letters between lovers?

I visited the harbor today, staring at the Mare Nostrum for hours, a sea so big, it covers the horizon. I realized that you are on the other side of that sea, so far I cannot see you, and grief washed over me. I haven't been able to shake it.

On a brighter note, I've begun writing a book. The goddess herself has asked me to document what I learned while using the wands in Behdet. Finnian, the young scribe, writes what I speak. We had our first lesson today. It's humbling and scary, but I must do it—for some reason, it feels urgent.

How I love you and hope you will call me home soon.

Always,

Natasa

"Well," Min chuckled, "I guess letters can be efficient if you have the pharaoh's coin supporting you."

Ankhwenefer grabbed Min and hugged him close. "This is so good Min, so good. Is there anything else you had to tell me?"

"No, sir, that's it. You wish me to instruct Silus to sneak up on the Greeks and rain arrows down upon them while they're sleeping?"

"Yes. Better yet, after the megau take them out, have our men occupy the Greek camp to form a blockade. The closer we keep them near Thebes, cut off from their supplies and the rest of their troops, the better."

"Yes, sir," Min replied.

After the soldier left him, Ankhwenefer read both letters a second time. He was still happy about Natasa's improvement, but now concern had begun to creep into his mind. Who was this young Finnian, the scribe spending hours at Natasa's side, documenting her work, and hanging on her every word? He recalled how he'd fallen in love with her in Alexandria, listening to her speak about the mysteries of life. Natasa was intoxicating when in her power. All this time, Ankhwenefer hadn't considered she could love someone other than him. Her vow of celibacy had been a relief, knowing no other man could touch her, but now she was far away in Gaul and no such vows, other than his offer of marriage, kept her from other men. She couldn't marry him and become his second queen if he couldn't get her home.

Damn the Greeks. He needed Thebes under his control now.

9

The Book

"A few meters from the edge of the Vieux Port de Marseille, a large bronze plaque has been set into the concrete. It reads, "Here around 600 BCE Greek sailors arrived from Phocaea, a Greek city in Asia Minor. They founded Marseille, from where civilization spread to the west."
~ The Extraordinary Voyage of Pytheas the Greek 2002 CE

Massilia, Gaul, 198 BCE

Dearest Love,

Nothing makes me happier than knowing you have awakened. I have missed you so much. The war progresses by degrees, yet we have taken Lycopolis as well as Coptos, and Silus still holds the line to the south. We now attack our enemy each day from either direction, hacking away at their control. As soon as I have Thebes under my control, I will send for you. Now that I am pharaoh, nothing stands in our way. I wish I'd taken the crown from my family sooner. They are inferior to us, and their envy has hurt you so much, but they have paid for their sins. I banished Chanax, Bithiah, and my mother. Nefermaat is dead by my own hand.

Of course, you can still call me Ankhmakis. It sounded so perfect upon your lips. How I wish I could kiss them. Your arms are my refuge. Please send me as many letters as you wish. I want to know all about Gaul and the people you meet. It is much more interesting to read your words than to focus on the things I'm forced to think about here in Coptos.

Love,

Ankhmakis

"What a relief." Natasa laughed as she sneezed. "I'm so glad he doesn't mind all the letters, for I've sent at least eight more since the first two, and now I've heard back from him."

She sat with her mother in their herb garden, finishing up the last of the harvest efforts. The weather was turning colder, and the leaves of the trees had changed from greens to golds, reds, browns, and ambers. It was stunning, even if the chill air did make her sneeze.

"Are you okay?" Neferu asked her, a look of concern on her face.

"I'm fine," Natasa replied, wrapping her knit blanket over the goosebumps forming on her skin. "Aurelia thinks it's a reaction to the changing of the seasons. We've never experienced autumn before."

"Yes, but I'm not weak," Neferu said.

Natasa frowned. "I'm not weak either, though I do tire quicker than you."

Her mother raised her eyebrow, and Natasa ignored it. She'd received her first letter from Ankhmakis, and Finnian was due any minute for the day's writing. She wasn't going to let her mother spoil the day.

"Don't overdo it today," her mother continued.

"I thought you supported this work."

"I do. If the goddess has asked you to write down what you know about the All-One, you must do it. Just take it easy that's all. Sometimes these channelings make you very tired."

"I've noticed," Natasa agreed, drawing her shawl tighter still around her shoulders. "Which is strange, because when I worked with the wands in the apiary, I would end those sessions more energetic than when I started."

"Yes," Neferu replied, "I remember. That's what concerns me."

"Maybe it's because I spent too much time in the Void."

"Have you written about the Void yet?"

"No, I haven't."

"Can you tell me about it?"

Natasa bit her lip and tucked her hair behind her ear. The topic was so complex, she was unsure of where to begin. She raised her gaze to the sky, noting the puffy clouds as they drifted above in the crisp autumn air. Exhaling, she spoke, "You know how we live in a body here on Earth?"

"Yes, in our Khat, the physical plane."

"Next, there's the energetic plane, where we can sense one another's emotions as forms and send information between us and all living things. The plane where our Ka lives."

Her mother nodded.

"On the next level, we have the astral plane where our thoughts, feelings, desires, and motivations reside. The realm where all ideas are born. Also our passions and where we spend all our time when in a state of bliss with our lovers."

"Of course."

"Well, when I worked with the wands, I traveled through all those planes to something else—to the All-One, where all potential exists, the realm of streaming light I call the Way. There, everything is happening all at once. There's more information than in the Great Library of Alexandria, all of human endeavors, past, present, and future are accessible in that realm—and anyone can connect to it and learn. Being there was a bliss all of its own."

"Yes, I was reading Finnian's notes the other day on how you would access events and information within that plane. It's a place I've never been."

"Well the Void is none of those things," Natasa said, her shoulders falling. A pain throbbed in her stomach as she considered her next words. "Like the realm of light, it's the world behind the world, but while the realm of light is where all action begins, nothing happens at all in the Void. It's darkness, no energy pulses there. This enabled me to escape the madness in my mind. Nothing exists there. No love, no ideas, no passion, no laughter. I could follow the life force of non-human entities to the Void because they don't belong to the astral plane, since they don't have desire or passion. They have a body and Ka, but their spirit, their Ba, is united with the All-One at all times. Unlike us, who like the stars in the sky have our own individual light source, the elements, plants, and animals connect right into the Way, skipping the astral realm, where my pain was. Instead of the astral, non-human life has the Void. The voices lived in the astral, but nothing is in the Void. Connect to a flame and if you allow yourself to merge with its energy, soon it will take you to empty space."

"I'm not sure that makes sense." Neferu twisted her mouth. "Yet why wouldn't there be a cosmic force where nothing happens in order to balance out the rest of the energies and actions in the universe?"

"That is the Void."

"I don't think you've lost your connection to Ankhmakis because you spent too much time in the Void," her mother continued. "I think you fear the astral plane where your connection resides because the voices of your pain, grief, and shame also reside there. Let go of those wounds, and the two of you will reunite in spirit. You'll see."

Finnian arrived, carrying his satchel over one shoulder and a basket full of goods from town over the other. Neferu sprung from her seat and rushed over to greet him.

"Hecataeus sent you shopping?" Neferu asked as she took the basket from him.

"Of course, madam," he replied, wearing a grin as wide as the brim upon his floppy hat. Natasa felt her spirits rise. He had such magic about him.

"Well, stop in before you go. I need to pay you," Neferu said.

"Thank you." Finnian nodded and walked to the place in the garden Natasa had set out for them. "Good afternoon, my lady," he said as he approached. "How are you today?"

"Just fine, Finnian. Yourself?"

"Wonderful. What's in your lap?"

"Oh," Natasa answered, rolling the scroll closed, "a letter from Ankhmakis."

"He wrote you?" Finnian exclaimed. "How wonderful. May I see it? The Egyptian papyrus method of papermaking has long fascinated me. He uses a reed to write, doesn't he?"

"It's private," she replied as she hid the letter behind her back. For some reason, she didn't want him to read it. Finnian's smile faded, but he didn't push the matter. He took out his writing supplies.

"Well," he said when he'd set up his writing station, "let's get started then, shall we?"

Finnian drew a beautiful piece of waxy parchment paper from his satchel as well as his stylus made of bone. He'd trained as a scribe in the court at Massilia, and his equipment was of the finest quality. He rolled up his sleeves and gazed at her with his big, blue eyes, his golden hair tied back in a black ribbon, making him look very scholarly. A simple, black tattoo on his inner wrist caught her attention. It was a beautiful form, wrapping around itself three times inside a circle. She leaned forward to touch it, running her finger around the knotted figure just as Finnian had run his fingers down her scars when they'd first met.

"What is this?" she asked.

He swallowed hard and wrenched his arm away, cradling it near his chest. "It's a trinity knot."

"A trinity knot?" She'd never heard of it.

"Yes, a sacred symbol of the Celts," he explained. "It represents the triune nature of our goddess."

"Triune nature?" she murmured, grasping hold of his arm to get another look. When he didn't resist, she drew it toward her to examine the tattoo as she spoke. "Your goddess has more than one face?"

"Yes," Finnian said, his torso drawing back as he spoke. "She has three faces—maiden, mother, crone. The maiden is known as Coventia, the spring goddess, the mother is Brigid, the fertility goddess, and the crone is Nemetona, the goddess of the dark night. She shows us these faces throughout the months, years, and phases of our lives."

Natasa nodded, letting go of his arm. He exhaled and his face softened.

"Aurelia is like the crone?" she asked.

"Yes." Finnian laughed. "Your mother would be Brigid and you are the maiden, Coventia."

A pain seared between her ribs as if she'd been stabbed. "No, Finnian, I'm not the maiden. Your goddess is missing a face. What's the face of the childless mother? The one who has given birth and then lost the person most precious in her life?"

Finnian placed his hand on his forehead. "My lady, I'm so sorry. I forgot."

Natasa rubbed the scars on her wrist and arms. They were white against her dark skin. What would Ankhmakis think about what she'd done to herself? Would he judge her, or would he understand she'd been out of her mind?

"What was she like?" Finnian asked, interrupting her thoughts.

"Who?"

"Your child? What was she like?"

Natasa recalled one of her last moments with Helena, braiding her long dark hair, the girl struggling to get away. She'd wanted to play with Senui, who had stopped by their house to fetch her. Natasa closed her eyes and breathed, taking the air deep within her abdomen. She could imagine Helena's thick hair under her fingers and smell the musty scent of horses and hay that emanated from her soft skin, no matter how much Natasa had scrubbed the child.

She opened her eyes and gazed into Finnian's bright blue ones, swallowing back her tears. "Helena was a wild thing. Of me, and yet not. She was a child of the stars."

They looked at one another for some time before he spoke. "How old was she when she died?"

"Almost seven. I was your age, turning eighteen when I became her mother."

"My age?" he asked. "Truly you jest, my lady. I'm twenty-two."

"That old?" she said, unable to hide the surprise in her voice. "Why I'm now twenty-five myself. I thought I was so much older than you."

"Well, you are older, at least in terms of experience. You've had a child and studied the mysteries of the temple of Isis. I've grown up here in Massilia, writing for the druids and the men of the court, but they do not share their mysteries with me."

"I've lost a child as well," she said, "and that will age a woman faster than anything."

She reached out to touch his tattoo and traced her finger along it. He trembled, but he didn't resist this time. "The triune goddess. Maiden, mother, and crone. Yet you don't have a form for the childless mother."

"No," he answered, his voice shaky. "Not that I know of."

"Then I shall give her a name," Natasa replied. "For I know this face of the goddess very well. She lives deep within my heart and comforts me. The childless mother shall be called, Our Lady of Sorrows, for her heart is always pierced by a sword."

Finnian wiped his eyes with the back of his hand, and it made her want to cry, but instead, Natasa nodded toward his writing supplies. "Perhaps we will start today with Our Lady of Sorrows," she suggested as she made herself comfortable. "She has something to say about grief, and she'd like you to write it down."

Natasa leaned back in the oaken day bed her father had made her and covered herself with a woven blanket. The late autumn sun beat down upon her face. She glanced at Finnian, who sat upright at attention, stylus in hand, ready to write. She connected her mind to her heart, and within the blink of an eye, the goddess spoke through her.

10

The Tears of Isis

It's said that when Set killed her husband, Osiris, Isis cried tears of sorrow. Her pain consumed her, and in her tears, the Nile River was born. Each year, Isis cries in remembrance of the death of her beloved, causing the Inundation and ushering in the season of Akhet.

Coptos, Egypt, 197 BCE

My dear Ankhmakis,

They have four seasons here in Gaul. Like Egypt, they have a planting season, a growing season, and a harvesting season, but my love, they also have a season of death. Nothing grows. Everything dies. The trees lose their leaves, the birds abandon us for warmer climates, and all animals bury themselves in the ground. It's terribly cold, and without fire, even the humans die. Worse, ice falls from the sky. Yesterday, when I woke, everything was covered in a blanket of white. Finnian says snow is unusual in Massilia, this ice on the ground is just a dusting, and if I want to, he can take me farther west, to the mountains, to see real snow. Father wants to join him, but I refuse to go to such a place. I'm not sure I could survive it. On quiet, moonless nights, this season reminds me of the Void. They call it winter.

During the solitude of these silent, cold evenings I've begun to remember the last months before Helena's death. So much happened, so much I regret. Yet one mistake stands out that I must tell you—when you were in Aswan, I learned a great secret. Chanax is not Hugronaphor's son. Your mother conceived him with Isidor. She pretended reconciliation with your father in order to cover up her crime.

I grew angry when I learned of this news and confronted Chanax. I'd thought I could buy us some time by holding this information over him. I underestimated his power, and in the end, I am sure this is the real reason he betrayed us—to kill you for the throne, and me so no one would know he's not a prince of Behdet, but a queen's bastard.

He didn't kill either of us, did he? Instead, they punished our beloved child. I'm sorry, my dear, for failing you. I understand if you never want to speak to me again.

Natasa

Ankhwenefer gripped the letter in his hands, crumpling it within his fists. Chanax was Isidor's son? How could this be? He looked up at the men in his room who awaited his command. Silus stood front and center, shoulders thrown back, his chest armor glistening in the torch light. Should he tell Silus this information? Would it help, or add more confusion to an already precarious situation? What about his father's memory? To reveal his mother's affair would be an embarrassment to the throne of Behdet. He didn't doubt Natasa believed this to be true, and from Chanax's response of trying to get them both killed, Chanax must also believe Isidor is his real father.

There was one person left in the kingdom he could ask—Keket— and he'd banished her to the south. Once he had Thebes under his control, he'd send for her and get to the bottom of this. The sooner the better, for he needed Natasa by his side. How could she ever think he didn't want her? Goddess, he missed her more than anything, and here she was, having adventures with this Finnian fellow far away in a snowy land. Two long years, and still she was out of his reach.

Ankhwenefer looked at his maps and traced the path of his troops with his finger. They encircled Thebes in all directions and had begun the careful art of advanced guerilla warfare. He had small troops infiltrating the city, poisoning the wells, destroying weapons, sabotaging infrastructure, and setting fire to food stores. Many of his men were caught and killed, but not before the damage had been done. The Inundation had begun, and with it, great floods. It seemed this year Isis was mourning more than usual. This was both a blessing and a curse. A blessing because it held the Greeks in Thebes, which was overcrowded due to the thousands of troops forced to remain there. A curse because it also made Ankhwenefer's own movement up and down the Nile impossible.

"Take out their irrigation," he said.

General Khaleme, Min, and Silus all stood taller at his orders.

"What?" Silus asked. It was the first time they'd seen each other since Silus had fallen to the Greeks at the beginning of the surge. Ankhwenefer recalled Natasa's letter and thought of Chanax. If her information was correct, Ankhwenefer wasn't the middle son, but rather the youngest, making his position with his eldest brother even more uncertain.

"They've drawn back to the city during the Inundation, leaving their farms open. They must assume we won't surge against them during the flooding. They're correct, but that doesn't mean we can't do damage. Tear down the farm walls along the Nile that channel the river into the fields," Ankhwenefer replied.

"That will flood the city," Silus continued.

"It will," Ankhwenefer nodded, "and make for a miserable Akhet filled with pestilence and unsanitary conditions. Furthermore, when the Nile recedes, the act will leave the farmland dry, as we did to the north. Without any place to grow crops, they will run out of food and be starving this time next year."

"And forced to surrender," Khaleme finished.

He looked to his men. It was a destructive thing to do. Many innocent inhabitants would starve to death. Conditions in the city would be inhumane.

"What will we do when we take the city back into our own hands?" Silus asked.

"You, brother, will go back to Behdet when Thebes is mine," Ankhwenefer answered. "You've fought long and hard and deserve time away from battle. We all do."

Silus nodded, his mouth drawn into a tight line. "I agree."

"From there, you will manage the training of soldiers in Behdet. Even though we'll have Thebes, this war won't be over, and troops are needed until we take back all of Egypt. I'll also need you and Ruia to send grain from our fields in the south to Thebes to feed the people and the court until we've reconstructed the city and irrigation system once more."

Silus jutted out his chin and glared at his brother from under his narrow, heavy-lidded eyes.

"Do you agree with this?" Ankhwenefer asked his elder brother.

"Yes, Lord Pharaoh," the eldest brother answered, crossing his arms across his armored chest.

"Silus," Ankhwenefer continued, rising from his seat, "do you bow to me as pharaoh?"

"You stole the crown," Silus replied, dropping his arms to his sides, fists now clenched. "I'm the rightful heir to Behdet."

"Which is why I have given the city to you and will name you King of Behdet upon your return."

Silus stormed closer, standing inches from Ankhwenefer's face. Their breast plates touched. "I have something to say."

Ankhwenefer raised an eyebrow. "Go on, brother."

"I hate you," Silus continued, "yet I admire you for the way you took the Greek Surge and used it to our advantage. Your plan was risky but brilliant. Time and again we've come across obstacles, and each time you've found a solution. I may despise you for taking the throne out from under me, but I will bow to you as pharaoh, for we need you to win this war. If we lose, we all will burn. Tearing Egypt from the hands of the Greeks matters more than your betrayal in this matter."

"Do agree to follow my orders until your dying day?" Ankhwenefer demanded.

"Yes," Silus promised through gritted teeth. "Though that is hard for me to admit."

Ankhwenefer held out a hand and Silus shook it. Then he tugged his brother into his arms. As Silus squeezed Ankhwenefer closer, the pharaoh felt his brother's body relax.

"Chanax was an ass," Silus said as he extracted himself from the embrace. "Good riddance. Memphis can have him. He was different from us somehow."

If you only knew, Ankhwenefer thought as he slapped his brother on the back and forced a grin. "When this war is over, we should spend time sparring in the ring, brother. Those are some of my best memories of childhood."

"Ha." Silus laughed. "Do you remember the day when we caught Chanax in the trees with the little temple maidens?"

Ankhwenefer cocked his head, trying to recall it. "There were many times he and his friends threw things at us from the fig tree in the royal gardens."

"Yes," Silus answered, "but on this occasion, Natasa herself threw a fig right at the center of my forehead. I'll never forget it. She was so fierce, like a little lioness. I thought her ridiculous, but you, the look on your face was priceless. I think you already loved her, even though she was nothing more than a dirty playmate of our stupid little brother at the time."

Ankhwenefer smiled at the memory. "Yes. I remember." He turned to the rest of his men in the room. "I need her back. She can't stay in Gaul much longer. One winter there is too long. Which is why we must destroy the irrigation walls along the Nile to the north and south of Thebes, killing all their farmers as well. They will fight as we do it, so damage as much as possible before discovered, and then repeat. Kill them as you must, for they won't send full troops at first. Ambush at night, under the cover of the dark sky, from all directions at once. Keep them guessing where the next attack will be. Is this clear?"

"Yes, sir," Silus and Min replied.

Khaleme bowed. "I will see it done."

"Thank you," the pharaoh said. He looked down at the waxy parchment from Natasa and picked up his reed, moving maps around and searching for a blank piece of papyrus. "Now leave me. I have a love letter to write."

11

Solstice

In the northern countries, the winter solstice is a high holy night. More moon than sun, the longest night was seen as the birth of the Sun King. Each day after the solstice, more and more light would shine upon the earth, melting the snow and ice, and ushering the great out-breath of spring.

Massilia, Gaul, 197 BCE

Dearest One,

My latest plan should have Thebes under my control by your next summer. I'd like it to be sooner, but circumstances require yet another drawn-out effort at gaining control of the city. I'm not on the battlefield risking my life, and this form of war is frustrating. I'd rather be fighting the bastards face-to-face, instead of destroying their infrastructure, but what must be done, must be done. Besides, I hear the summers are warm in Gaul, so you won't suffer too much.

I'm still not sure how best to approach your revelation of my younger brother's true parentage. I've banished both him and Mother from the kingdom for now. I will have to attend to the matter when Thebes is mine. Please don't think you had anything to do with our daughter's death. It was my fault. I failed to do the one thing a man should do for his family—keep them safe.

Natasa, I yearn for you, and yet I wonder, when you return, will you still love me? So much has changed. As always, I feel that a part of me is dying inside as the war progresses, and somehow you've become more of a goddess. While I've spent years killing, you have healed the ill, worked with the wands in the All-One, and now are writing a book about our mysteries in a strange land surrounded by mountains and snow and other things I can't even envision.

I want you here by my side. Please, don't ever stop loving me.

Love,

Ankhmakis

Natasa shivered in her bed by the fire, a cough rattling her lungs while reading her lover's words, hating Chanax even more for his lies and treachery. How could Ankhmakis think she'd ever stop loving him? A knock pounded at the door, startling her. It was barely dawn. She grabbed a warm cloak and wrapped herself in it as she walked across the room to open it.

"Coming," she called.

Aurelia, the old witch, stood outside, wet from the morning rain falling in chunks upon the doorstep. The old woman entered in a swirl of freezing air.

"What is that?" Natasa asked, pointing to the icy, gray clumps forming on her entryway. It wasn't snow, but it also wasn't liquid.

"Hail," the old woman answered as she hobbled to the fireplace. Natasa slammed the door and coughed. Aurelia eyed her up and down. "How long have you been coughing?"

Natasa shrugged, her voice an octave lower due to the constant irritation in her throat. "Off and on since the autumn. Why are you here at this hour? My parents are still asleep."

"I'm here to discuss the solstice celebration this evening," the witch replied, tossing her coat upon the drying rack by the fire. She dragged a chair up to the fireplace and stoked the wood. "And yes, I'd love some tea. With cinnamon."

"Of course, Aurelia." Natasa hung a black pot over the embers still glowing from the night before. "Let's get this fire going, shall we?"

Aurelia placed a few logs on the dying embers, muttered several Gaelic words Natasa didn't understand, pulled a handful of herbs from a pouch around her waist, and threw them at the coals, causing a roaring fire to come to life.

"Nice." Natasa smiled. "I like your magic. Much more helpful than making requests in the realm of light."

Aurelia nodded. "This is why we call it practical magic. What you do is esoteric magic. Both are needed."

Natasa shrugged, not wanting to discuss it further. Her own magic felt so distant these days. "You came to discuss solstice, the longest night of the year. We celebrate it in Egypt, for it is the god Horus's birthday."

"Yes. Here, it is the birth of the Horned God, Cernunnos, the Stag King, the god who leads us from the hearth of our homes to Tor itself."

"Tor?" Neferu asked. Natasa and Aurelia looked up from the fire to see her approaching them, wrapped in a shawl, dragging her own chair to escape the chill of the dawn.

"Tor," Aurelia continued, scooching over to make room for Neferu, "our blessed hill, the gateway to Tir-na-og, the realm of the fairies, gods, and goddesses. We travel there and become one with them."

"Does it exist?" Neferu frowned as she plunked down in her chair.

"Yes, in Avalon, a fair city far to the north in Briton. We celebrate here in Massilia with an evening of ceremony, culminating in a meditative experience of Tor, and then dancing and drinking until the sun rises."

"Sounds wonderful," Neferu replied.

"It's tonight," Aurelia said, her pale blue eyes shifting between mother and daughter. "Both of you have been invited. The people in our coven feel you are the representatives of The Goddess of the South, and desire for Natasa to be the consort of the Stag King this evening."

"The consort of the Stag King? What is required?" Natasa asked.

"The goddess mates with the Stag King," the old woman explained, "and gives birth to the sun at dawn."

"Mates?" Natasa gasped, her mouth dropping open. What in the world was this woman suggesting?

"Yes," Aurelia answered, smiling as she noted the look on Natasa's face, "but don't worry, you act the part. The actual sex magic ceremony is held in private between Taran, the high priest, and our high priestess, Latharna. We send them off with a blessing at the beginning of the evening, and then the re-enactment begins, where a young man chosen to be the Stag King for the year, and a young maiden chosen to be the goddess, play the roles. There are narrators and musicians. All you'll have to do is follow. After the goddess blesses our Stag King, we enter into silence and connect to Tor and the All-One. When the ceremony is complete, the party begins and continues until the true sunrise, at which point we will all gather for a final prayer and blessing before stumbling home drunk and merry into our warm beds."

Natasa chewed on the inside of her mouth. "I'm not sure if I can do it."

Her mother put a hand on her leg. "Yes, you can. They have seen your goddess nature, it's your duty to oblige."

"Who will play the part of the Stag King?" Natasa asked.

Aurelia gave her a toothless smile. "Finnian, of course."

☥

Later that evening, Natasa stood to the side of the busy town hall as Aurelia and her fellow coveners dressed her in a thin, see-through white dress. Over her shoulders, they placed a beautiful, navy blue hooded robe, and in her hair, they wove holly and mistletoe. She and her mother were the only brown-skinned people in the room; the rest were brilliant in their whiteness, hair colors ranging from light brown, like her father, who stood in the corner kissing her mother's neck, to golden blonde with a fiery redhead mixed in here and there. They all wore dark capes and necklaces crafted in various sorts of silver and stone pendants. In Natasa's hands, the old woman placed a small wooden wand.

"Rowan," Aurelia said, her voice low and soft, "our most blessed tree. Keep it as our gift."

The old woman nodded to an even older man standing next to a large red curtain and a quartet of musicians. "Do whatever he tells you, and you'll be fine."

The music started and the people in the room knelt as the master of ceremonies raised his arms.

"Welcome," he said in Greek. They'd agreed to use the language, rather than their local Gaelic, for the sake of their visiting Goddess of the South. "Tonight, we celebrate the winter solstice, the longest night, and the birth of Cernunnos, the Horned One, and the god of the sun."

The curtain parted and out stepped Taran and Latharna, dressed in ceremonial robes of crimson. They bowed and the crowd lowered their heads.

"Tonight, while we travel together, the lord and lady of our coven will take ceremony and lie together, in hopes of birthing the sun back into the world and ensuring prosperity and health to all in our community."

The high priest and priestess of the coven danced to a sensual rhythm while the rest of the coveners sat in silent reverence. When the song came to an end, Taran took the lady's hand and bowed to the crowd.

"It is my pleasure to spend my evening in the arms of the goddess."

"As it is mine to bestow love upon the people of this land," Latharna replied, her red lips parted, and she drew him in for a lingering kiss.

Natasa's face flushed as she recalled the ceremony with Ankhmakis. This couple would raise their serpents together. As she considered this, the serpents in her own body trembled alive as if awakening from a long slumber. Her breasts ached, and a tickle ran up her spine.

The next moment, a pair of acolytes escorted the couple out of the room, and the old man continued the story: "The time has come to welcome our Stag King, as he is born and reborn to us this night."

Finnian appeared from behind the curtain. He was shirtless,

wearing nothing but a pair of tight leather pants and a set of antlers on his head. His lean, muscular chest glowed pale in the firelight and his long, golden hair framed his handsome face. He sauntered around the large fire blazing in the center of the room, throwing branches of mistletoe into the audience. Natasa's passion swirled through her body as he turned and gestured in time to the music and the words. He was both man and animal, the Stag King of the forests come alive, and he wove his way through the audience with a sexual confidence she'd never seen in him before. Gone was the studious scribe. Instead, before her stood Finnian, the man.

"Cernunnos, born of the sun, escorts us to Tor this evening. He guides us to our hearts and shows us the way to the fey. The Great Horned One comes and he goes, but first, he mates with the goddess herself, in order that we might live after he dies."

Finnian turned to Natasa, all traces of his boyhood gone. Instead, his pale gaze penetrated hers, hard yet glittering, and her heart skipped several beats. He took her hand, one corner of his mouth turned up, chin held high, his antler crown giving him the regal appearance of a king. She'd seen that look of power in a man's eye before, and the desire to kiss his arrogant grin swept through her body. How could he make her feel this way?

"The Horned One loves the goddess, for she is the light of his heart. He knows that only in her arms can we find our truest selves. At Beltane, he takes his beloved to the fires of desire where they mate and become one."

Finnian led her toward the fire and then removed her cloak. She stood before the people in her thin dress, her body trembling, not from the cold, but from the heat of lust sweeping the room. Finnian put his arms around her from behind and kissed her neck. Her unfulfilled sexual need penetrated her soul, and for the first time in years, her blood rushed through her veins. The crowd bowed low, palms together over their chests, eyes wide, and Natasa considered the striking contrast of the dark Goddess of the South against the pale beauty of their Stag King.

Finnian lowered to one knee and the old man continued. "After their mating, the goddess blesses him with her wand of Rowan, giving him dominion over life, death, karma, and rebirth until his own death on the longest day of the year."

Natasa knew this was her cue and raised the rowan wand, placing it on Finnian's shoulder. A surge of energy pulsed through her and the wand as she gazed into his perfect face.

"May you hold humanity in your strong embrace," she said in a voice much too low to be her own. "May you protect the goddess, for it is your destiny to aid her in her work for all of time."

Finnian never took his gaze from hers, and Natasa felt her knees go weak as the master of ceremonies continued, "The White Stag becomes the Stag King and rules over human life and death until the summer solstice, when he lays down and dies, giving humanity into the arms of the moon and her wisdom."

A young girl handed Finnian a sword, which he took, rising from his knees. He strode before the blazing fire and beckoned Natasa to his side as an acolyte handed them a chalice of red wine. Finnian drank from it before putting it in her hands. A shock of electricity pulsed through her as their fingertips brushed. Natasa drank down what was left and gave the empty cup to the server. Finnian took her hand and raised his sword to the crowd.

"Have mercy on us, oh Lord of the Sun, Horned One, King of the Forest, Stag King, Cernunnos," the master of ceremonies sang in a haunting melody. "Guide us to Tor, to the nemeton of our hearts. Open our inner vision to our needs and our pain. Allow the goddess to enter us and make us holier as yet another year spins around the wheel of time."

Natasa breathed out and felt the serpents rising in her spine. They shimmied up and around her chakras. Every cell in her body hummed. The next instant, Natasa saw herself standing on a large green hill. Finnian stood to one side of her, Ankhmakis on the other. She bathed in their love—one so fair and golden and the other dark and delightful, she in the center, the center of the world and the heart of the universe. She entered the All-One, dancing, spinning, and turning in the streams of light with the people of Gaul. She sensed their fears, and they knew hers—shame, guilt, anger, and betrayal. They'd all felt them, each and every one. To be human was to swim in the sea of dark and light. To be human was to love in spite of the pain.

She had no idea how long they stayed in this place together before the music called her and each person in the room back into their bodies; she had never group meditated before. All had gone to Tor and experienced their true, divine nature. All had seen the face of the god and goddess.

"We love you, Lord and Lady of Creation. Let us begin a new year."

Natasa opened her eyes, the crowd before her still on their knees. Some were crying, others wore dazed looks of ecstasy, and one by one, they popped up from the floor to embrace each other, their laughter and cries—musical in their own right. Natasa turned to Finnian and found him gazing at her, the forms of love and desire surrounding him so strongly now she could taste them. To her surprise, her own desire twirled with his. She hadn't experienced these forms in so long, she'd forgotten them.

The band struck up a jig, and wine and food were ushered into the room. Finnian sheathed his ceremonial sword and smiled. "What do you think of our ceremony?"

"I love it because it's not only about the priests and priestesses, but everyone gathered together, seeking Tir-na-og as a community."

He nodded, now wearing the regular boyish grin she was used to. He reached into her hair and took one of the flowers as he whispered into her ear, "Mistletoe. Deadly poisonous if you eat it, but when placed in a doorway or your front porch it is a sign you forgive anyone who comes to your house of any wrong they may have done in the past."

"Any wrong?" she asked, unable to stop herself from gazing into his sparkling, blue eyes.

"Yes," he continued as he stood nearer, his naked chest now brushing her own clothed one, and placed the mistletoe branch back into her thick black hair. She shivered at his touch. "Complete reconciliation, to the point you could kiss them."

"I don't like the idea of kissing someone who has wronged me." She thought Chanax's betrayal, and her heart pounded.

"No," Finnian shook his head. "I imagine not. How about kissing someone whom you have blessed?"

He leaned in close and placed his lips upon hers, and her toes began to tingle. She knew she should resist, but Finnian's kiss was soft and quick—over too quickly to protest.

"Now, my lady." He grinned, his face very flushed. "It's customary for the Stag King and his bride to lead the first dance. May I have the honor?"

"Of course, my lord."

She clasped his hands and danced the night away in his arms, swirling, twirling, drinking wine, and remaining in the state of bliss only the merriment of the winter solstice could bestow. As the sun rose in the pink dawn sky, the group gathered outside in silence, watching the great solar being as it poured the new year's sun across the cold, frozen land.

Natasa sneezed, and Finnian covered her in her cloak. After celebrating all night, she was tired. "Have you seen my family?"

Finnian shook his head. "I'll take you home."

They gathered their things, and Natasa gave her costume to Aurelia. "Well," the gray witch said. "What did you think?"

"It's not Egypt," Natasa replied, looking around her and taking it all in, "but I think Gaul isn't so bad after all. Even if you do have winter."

The woman smiled and pinched Natasa's cheek. "Winter is horrible. That's why we throw such a big party."

Finnian arrived on his horse, his stag crown now gone, and his body wrapped in a heavy, green cloak. Natasa sat behind him wrapping her arms around his torso. They rode home in silence as the forest grew brighter each moment. She burrowed into him; the dawn was cold, and the heat of the night still emanated from his body. When they arrived at her little cabin in the woods, she smiled at how inviting it looked. For the first time, it felt like a home. Smoke billowed from the chimney; her father had arrived before her to get it warm. Finnian stopped the horse and dismounted, holding out his arms. She fell into them and landed in his firm, steady embrace. Something about this man grounded her, for he was the one who had saved her from the brink of madness.

"You know," she murmured, gazing up into his charming face, stunned by his beauty. "You are my savior."

He drew her closer, wrapping them in his cloak like a cocoon for two, and she tilted her face toward his. He kissed her, and she didn't refuse, allowing herself to feel his need and responding with her own. Later, when the wine wore off, she'd regret it and feel guilty, but she'd also regret it if she stopped him now. Finnian's kiss made her feel alive and whole.

They continued to kiss one another, their hands exploring the other under the cover of his cloak, unaware Hecataeus and Neferu were watching them through the window.

☥

"Well," Neferu said, folding her arms over her chest, "it appears your plan with Aurelia worked. Our daughter is now falling for Finnian."

"Is that so bad?" Hecataeus asked. "Aurelia said the ceremony tonight was the most powerful she'd experienced, and that old lady's been around a long time."

"To be in love with two men isn't a good thing." Neferu sighed, shaking her head. "I wouldn't wish it on anyone, even my worst enemy."

"Neffa, Ankhmakis offers her nothing more than a world of war, death, and fear. She will be in danger at his side. We both know this. He needs to let her go so she can start her new life here in Gaul. I can gather Eleni, and we'll be a family. Finnian loves Natasa and would give her a wonderful home. He makes a good living as a scribe, and they can live in the city, write books together, make babies, and do the things new lovers do. She's still young. Can't you see this is what's best?"

"My dear," Neferu replied, placing a hand on his cheek, "all you say is true, and yet she also belongs by Ankhmakis's side. She'll never stop loving him. Unless he dies or releases her from her proposal, she will choose him over Finnian and break the younger man's heart."

"Then somehow I must get the pharaoh to break his proposal," Hecataeus answered, hands on his hips, turning to peek once more at his daughter through the window.

"And break her heart?"

"Finnian will cure her, trust me."

Neferu also stole a glance at her daughter and the Stag King's sweet embrace. Finnian was a good man, and Neferu couldn't deny the way her daughter lit up whenever he visited. He'd healed her from the shock of Helena's death, yet for some reason, this made Neferu sadder. "I only want her to be happy."

"I know, Neffa. That's all I want as well."

12

War Everywhere

The second of Ptolemy V's regents, General Tlepolemus, proved weak with time and was removed from his service to the young boy king. His army managed to put out the rebellions in the Delta, but Upper Egypt still remained under rebel control. While part of the Ptolemaic army was under siege in Thebes fighting Ankhwenefer, two other Macedonian kings, Antiochus III the Great and Philip V of Macedon, agreed to conquer and split the Ptolemaic possessions overseas, leaving the Ptolemaic dynasty unable to send more troops to Thebes, and instead forcing them to fight two wars at once— finding themselves strangled in the middle.

Memphis, Egypt, 197 BCE

"We can't continue like this," the high priest of Memphis, Metakryon, declared.

He paced his chambers, hands clasped behind his back as Isidor lounged on a couch by the fireplace, stroking the large black panther seated at his side. The animal's yellow eyes followed Metakryon as he continued to walk back and forth, back and forth, his black robes swirling around his feet. The priest was in obvious distress and for good reason, the war was taking way too long, and with Ankhwenefer's rise to the throne, all their plans were now in disarray.

Isidor didn't mind. He raised an eyebrow and shrugged, taking a sip of his wine and then a puff of opium. In his opinion, they could remain like this forever. Life was good in Memphis.

The ancient priest continued to complain. "Thebes is starving. The bastard rebel king destroyed their fields during the Inundation, and now they have no food to feed the army living in and around the city. The citizens are starting to revolt. The mayor has been commanded to hold out, but the generals claim there's no hope of victory."

"If they surrender, what will happen?" Isidor asked.

"The priests of Thebes will crown Ankhwenefer pharaoh a second time, and he will control an empire vastly larger than Ptolemy V."

"The boy king won't know the difference until he's older," Isidor replied. "I suggest we let the rebels take Thebes, negotiate safe transport of the troops back north, and focus on the Syrian peninsula. Antiochus III is slaughtering us, and if he takes possession of all our overseas lands, he will invade Egypt itself. Better to save the border."

"Must we divide our country?" Metakryon asked as he fell into his seat and grabbed a goblet from the side table.

"For now. Let Epiphanes grow up to be a man, and then we can strike."

"What about Chanax?" Metakryon replied. "The plan had been to destroy the Ptolemies and put Chanax on the throne. Why the sudden change of heart?"

"Two reasons," Isidor answered. "First, the original plan failed. Horwenefer was supposed to win the war eight years ago and after we crowned him pharaoh of Egypt, we were to kill him and crown Chanax, a loyal priest of Set."

"Yes," Metakryon agreed. "That was the plan. We worked so hard to make it happen. Why did we fail?"

"Horwenefer's court," Isidor spat, "and Neferu-ankh-maat. Between the horrible way Queen Keket and her children behaved, and the high priestess's ability to thwart the Invisible Hands, many things got in the way."

"Well, they're all gone now."

"Yes, but Ankhwenefer is against us. He hates the Cult of Set, and no one here in Memphis will support him."

"That's your fault, Isidor," Metakryon said, glaring at Isidor with pinched eyebrows, taking a sip from his cup. Isidor shivered at the bright red stains left on the ancient man's teeth.

"How so?"

"You never should have killed his child."

"You should thank me," Isidor said, his voice rising. "I saw the future. Had she lived, Set would have been driven out of Egypt. Yes, the Stewards of Behdet would have won the war and taken all of Egypt back into native hands, but our form of magic would have been banished. Worse, the girl would have obliterated us, and even you wouldn't have survived."

"I have no doubt the Golden Child had to die," Metakryon admitted. "However, her murder happened too soon. You gave her father a reason to hate us when instead we might have found an ally in him and salvaged the plan. Now we run the risk of being stuck in the middle of two very dangerous wars."

"Epiphanes is thirteen. Let him rule Lower Egypt while he grows up," Isidor repeated. "Give Ankhwenefer Thebes."

"You still haven't answered my question. Why are you accepting Ankhwenefer as pharaoh, rather than Chanax?"

"Chanax is ruined," Isidor admitted, exhaling. It broke his heart to speak of his student this way. "Unstable. I've watched him for years. Yes, he's the reason it's taking so long for Ankhwenefer to take Thebes. He and the Invisible Hands work non-stop, cursing Ankhwenefer's operation, and it works. If it weren't for Chanax, Ankhwenefer would have Alexandria in his pocket right now."

"Then what's the problem?"

"He's too powerful to be the pharaoh," Isidor said, pausing for a moment to consider his negligence with Chanax. He'd set out to make the prince a great magician yet had failed to see the eventual outcome. "If someone like Chanax were to rise to the throne, the priesthood would never stand a chance. I trained him too well, I see this now. We must make him think we still want him to rule so he'll continue his invaluable work for us, but if he wore the crown, I fear for what would become of Egypt."

Metakryon slurped from his cup, finishing the drink, and wiped his mouth.

"Was that human blood, sir?" Isidor asked, one eyebrow raised.

"Young human blood. The secret to my long life." Metakryon smiled, his bloodied teeth glowing in the firelight. "You should drink it more often, even outside of ceremony."

Isidor made a face and shook his head. He had his own methods but wasn't going to share them with a priest as powerful as this one.

Metakryon continued, "If I advise the Ptolemaic generals to retreat from Thebes and give it to Ankhwenefer, we will need to show our support here in Memphis. We'll have to crown the boy king our pharaoh and Ptah once and for all."

"Yes," Isidor pressed his lips together, "we will."

Metakryon took a long drag from the opium pipe and remained silent as the drug filtered through his mouth into his mind. Isidor did the same.

Isidor continued, coughing, "In a decade, maybe less, when Ptolemy V is a warrior himself, has fought off his Macedonian enemies to the north, and created a loyal army, we can advise him to attack the Upper Kingdom, and conquer Ankhwenefer once and for all."

Metakryon hesitated. "There is a risk Ankhwenefer grows prosperous, and his own sons grow strong."

"As all things in war, timing will be everything. Cut him down before his son is old enough to take the throne. A common play in our book, don't you think?"

Metakryon laughed. "Indeed. Can the Invisible Hands kill him from afar, the way you did Philopater?"

Isidor shook his head. "No, I still can't attach an energetic cord. Chanax has failed as well. The child is dead, but I can't get inside Ankhwenefer. Something still protects him and blocks us from doing any energetic manipulations."

"Could it be his lover?"

"It pains me to admit this, but even after all these years, I still have no idea."

"Well, you'd best figure this out," Metakryon demanded, "because we'll need all the help we can get when the time comes."

"Believe me," Isidor drawled as an opium cloud danced around his head, "I'm well aware."

13

Beltane

The dance of spring. Love is in the air and all the maidens seek the Stag King, as he chooses one with which to mate, ensuring that all might live again.

Massilia, Gaul, 197 BCE

My dearest Natasa,

Thebes is starving. The city overflows with refuse, the water is poisoned, the civilians die, and their troops are surrounded. Yet still, they don't surrender. I will write no more about it—some dark force works against me.

Your father has requested that I withdraw my offer of marriage. He doesn't want you to return to Egypt and says it will be too hard for you. Is this true? Please tell me it's not. Please tell me you will return when I call you home.

Please tell me you still love me.

Love,

Ankhmakis

Natasa clutched the letter to her breast, clenching her jaw, her lower lip trembling as tears formed. What was her father thinking? How dare he put such an idea in Ankhmakis's head? She ran into the garden, searching for Hecataeus, but he wasn't there. Nor was her mother. Panting from her efforts, she sat on her wooden divan and re-read the letter.

Of course, she loved Ankhmakis, more than anything in the world. True, Finnian had kissed her, but nothing else had become of it. When he arrived to scribe a few weeks later, he'd pretended like nothing had happened between them. Finnian might make her stomach turn butterflies with his dazzling smile, but it was clear he had no interest in her beyond their professional relationship.

The sounds of the wagon riding through the woods echoed off the trees, causing her to look up from her beloved's words. Her parents were laughing and talking from their places in the wagon. Finnian rode his horse beside them. All three were deep in conversation and didn't notice her. She ran into the house and washed her face to hide her tears, running her fingers through her hair. Finnian might not be interested in her, but for some reason, it still mattered that he find her attractive.

"Hello?" Hecataeus called out as he entered the room, his heavy footsteps pounding on the wooden floor. He carried a basket full of food and wine. Her mother and Finnian followed behind.

"Hello," Natasa replied, swallowing down the harsh words she had for Hecataeus, gripping the letter behind her back. She didn't want to talk about it in front of Finnian. "I'm here."

"You're not going to wear that, are you?" her mother asked.

"What?" Natasa asked, glancing at her brown linen dress and leather boots. "What's wrong with what I'm wearing?"

"It's Beltane," Neferu answered, looking at Finnian, who was now blushing.

"Beltane?"

"I told you about it yesterday. Today is the first day of May, and a spring fertility ritual is planned," Neferu continued. She smiled as she looked at Natasa out of the corner of her eye. "Finnian's been telling me all about it."

"Ah, yes," Finnian said, giving Natasa his own sideways glance. "I must be going. The event is held not too far from here, deep in the forest. Will I see you there?"

Natasa forced a smile on her face. It wasn't Finnian's fault her father was meddling in her life. "Of course, I love to celebrate the seasons."

"Well, goodbye." Finnian nodded, tipping his hat, and running from the house as if it were on fire.

As the door shut behind the boy, Natasa rounded on her father, gaze narrowed. "How dare you?"

"What?" He took a step back, startled.

She slapped the opened letter on her father's chest. "Ankhmakis wrote me. He told me how you asked him to drop his offer of marriage and leave me stranded in Gaul."

Neferu glanced at Hecataeus. "You didn't."

Hecataeus shrugged. Neferu rolled her eyes and walked to the table where she unpacked the basket, shaking her head as she muttered, "Men."

"Natasa," Hecataeus began, holding out his arms, "I thought that after the way you and Finnian were at the solstice celebration, perhaps there was a better life for you here than in Egypt."

"Nothing is more important than returning to Ankhmakis. I love him, Father, and I need him."

"What about Finnian?"

"What about him? He has nothing to do with Ankhmakis."

"If Ankhmakis died tomorrow, would you go back to Egypt?"

"No. Of course not."

"If you remained here, would you marry Finnian?"

Natasa choked. "Finnian? Why would he want to marry me?"

"Because, child, he loves you. Can't you see that?"

Natasa backed away from her father, fists clenched, shaking her head. He didn't make any sense. "No, he kissed me at the solstice, but that's because I was his goddess for the night. It was a ceremony of theirs, but not love. Are you out of your mind?"

"Why do you think he comes here so often?" A crooked smile

tugged at Hecataeus's mouth.

"Because you pay him."

"Darling, we don't need his help anymore. It's been a year since we arrived, and the three of us have this whole living-without-royal-slaves thing pretty well managed."

Natasa gulped, unable to speak.

"He *is* interested in documenting what you say," Neferu chimed in, "but he's also interested in you. "

Natasa couldn't believe what was happening. Was her attraction to Finnian so obvious? Was he interested in her? He acted so politely and detached, perhaps he too was hiding his true feelings behind his guilt? She often daydreamed about their kiss. It had been so sweet, and the memory still left her breathless. She couldn't admit her desire—this attraction she had for the young man was wrong. Ankhmakis needed her.

"Tell me, dear," Hecataeus said, a knowing look upon his face, "if Ankhmakis were to die, and you remained here, could you see yourself marrying and growing old with Finnian?"

Panicking, Natasa wagged her finger at Hecataeus. "Don't speak such things. Ankhmakis will not die, and I shall return to his side. You don't want me to go back because it's dangerous."

Hecataeus slammed the letter on the table. "Fine. You've got me. I don't want you to go back. We're happy here. There's no war, no Weret, no temple life, no dying soldiers, and no crisis. Here we're all safe and together, we have new friends and a new way of celebrating life. It's good here, Natasa. Why would you want to leave it?"

"Because," she said, her voice rising to match the form of anger now surrounding them, "I promised him I'd return. I can't break any more vows, Father. I owe it to him, and Helena. Now please, let me be."

She turned her back on them to storm out of the house, her fists still clenched, whole body trembling, but her mother stepped forward and stopped her with a comforting hand. "Will you at least join us at Beltane? I think you'll find it interesting. The Stag King has a role, but don't worry, you only have to partake if you feel called."

Natasa paused. The entire conversation left her confused and unsure. She'd loved Ankhmakis for most of her life, yet she also found Finnian very attractive and looked forward to the time she spent in his company. If he was going to be at the festival, she wanted to be there as well. She took several deep breaths to calm herself. Perhaps another ceremony was what she needed. Unlike Winter Solstice, she hadn't been asked to play a part. "Fine, but I need to pen Ankhmakis a letter first, telling him I still accept his offer of marriage and will come as soon as he thinks it's safe."

"Until he takes Memphis and Alexandria, you'll never be safe," Hecataeus frowned, his forehead wrinkled. "You'll be a target at his side, and should he fail, the Greeks will torture you in the most heinous of ways to punish him."

Natasa turned on her father and yelled at the top of her lungs, "He will not fail!"

Her father stepped forward, clenching his fists, mouth opening to counter her.

"Let it be, Hecataeus," Neferu interrupted as she walked to a basket and took out a lightly spun linen dress. It was pale green with clasps running down the bodice and long sleeves with yellow ties at the wrists. She held it up to Natasa. "Yes, I think this will be perfect."

☥

A few hours later they rode through the forest for a mile before arriving at the grandest picnic Natasa had ever seen. At the center of a meadow that stretched across the valley floor there roared a bonfire taller than her cottage. Mountains rose in the distance, surrounding the valley as if watching over the event. Blankets spread out all around the fire, musicians played, and dancing had already begun. Wooden casks of beer and wine were stationed near the entrance, and a long table covered in food had been set out. Neferu walked to the table and placed their offering of sweet cakes. Then she took Natasa's hand and put a goblet of wine in it.

"Drink and be merry, daughter."

Neferu drank from her cup, and Natasa sensed strange energy in the air. It was one of desire and lust mixed with recklessness.

"Mother," she said, now unsure she wanted to be there. "Did you say this was a fertility festival?"

"Yes," Neferu replied.

"Well, what happens?"

"For the most part, it's a party. Soon there will be some sort of dance around that tree." She pointed to a gnarled oak tree large enough for the crowd to dance around, standing alone in the meadow. It looked forlorn, so far from the rest of the forest.

"After the dance, married couples go off into the woods and make love," she continued, her face now flushed. "They don't have to choose their spouses. This is one night a year where they can mate with someone else if they choose."

Natasa stepped away from her mother. "What will you and Father do?"

"I've convinced him to give it a try." She shrugged, blushing deeper. "He's had his eye on a woman in town for a few months and, well, I fancy a roll in the forest with Taran."

"Mother," Natasa said, slapping her hand to her own cheek.

"Oh, Natasa, you know sex is different than love," Neferu said, flicking her hand. "I've loved your father for over thirty years. We've each had several different mates during our courtship. Sometimes a little variety can make a relationship more exciting, hence Beltane."

Natasa rolled her eyes as she drank the rest of her wine. "What do the rest of us do?"

"That's where the Stag King comes in. He'll arrive and lead a group dance. When the dance ends, all the maidens, or unmarried women, go and hide in the woods. He chases and mates with the women of his choice, and the rest can spend the night dancing around the tree."

"Excuse me?"

"You heard me." Neferu poured more wine into Natasa's cup. "You don't have to do it. You can stay around the fire and dance or take one of the horses and go home. You know the way, it's one mile down the main road."

"Let me guess, Finnian is the Stag King once more?"

Neferu smiled like a child caught stealing sweets from the royal kitchens. "Yes. He's the Stag King until midsummer's eve when he pretends to die before the coven, and a different young man takes his place next winter solstice."

"Of course," Natasa replied as she thrust her cup into her mother's empty hand. "Why in the world didn't I see this coming? This was your plan all the long, wasn't it? I'm going home. Good night."

Natasa turned her back on her mother and stormed away, leaving the party behind. Her heart begged her to stay—if she did, Finnian might choose her, and part of her wanted that more than anything. Yet Ankhmakis and his needs rushed through her entire being. She had to focus on her twin flame, he was her duty. She'd made a promise. She glanced around the party and noted dozens of young women, all bright-eyed and round-breasted. Finnian was in good company. Ankhmakis however, was alone, fighting for his life. As she made her way to the corral to fetch her horse, someone grabbed her arm and yanked her behind a tree.

"Finnian. What are you—?"

He put a finger over her lips. "Shhh."

"Are you okay?" she asked. She gazed into his face, eyes wide and mouth trembling, and saw his need. She struggled under his grip, she had to get away.

He shook his head and squeezed her arms. "No, I'm not okay. I'm nervous."

"Nervous? Why?"

"Didn't your mother explain my role tonight?" She nodded. "Well, I'm nervous. I've never, you know..." His voice drifted off, his gaze wild like the wind.

She frowned. "You've never made love before?"

"No." He blushed.

"In my country, you would have been given first rites by now." She laughed. "Let me go ask my mother if she'll do the honors." She pretended to walk away, but he jerked her back.

"Natasa, please. Don't be cruel."

She chanced another glace at his face, biting her lip. Goddess, he was as stunning as the rising sun. She surrounded him with her Ka and understood what he wanted. "You want me to give you your first rites?"

"Yes, I want it to be you."

She looked to her feet and then to the sky. Ra was beginning to set, and thoughts of Ankhmakis filled her mind. Would he ever call her home? How long was she to live in limbo like this? She turned to face Finnian, and her legs felt like jelly. If she didn't leave soon, she would give in. "Finnian, I can't. I'm sorry."

"Why not? Because of your king?" he asked, a different sort of fire now burning in his gaze. "Natasa, why do you wait for him?"

"Because he asks it of me," she said.

"So? I'm asking you now as well."

"Finnian, how could you?"

"This festival is about sex and love, not about promises. Just tonight. Please, I won't ask more of you. I don't want any of the rest of the women here. It's you I dream of. It's you who I love. I beg of you, make me a man this evening."

The pounding in her heart made it hard to breathe. As the high priestess in Thebes, it would be her duty to teach the younger men Anit-Shadya as they came of age—Ankhmakis's sons included. She swallowed hard, now drowning in her fear and desire as she considered doing the same for Finnian. She hadn't felt a man's touch in so long.

She placed a hand upon his warm cheek, and his gaze shone upon her like a blessing.

"Just this night," he begged, "be the goddess for me. Please."

He drew her close and kissed her. She fell into his sweet, pure embrace.

"Yes." With one word, she surrendered. "Yes, Finnian, if you want this."

"More than anything," he said as he continued to kiss her neck.

"Then it would be my honor," Natasa replied, her voice low.

"Hide near that tree," he instructed, pointing over her shoulder to a maple in the distance.

"What if you stumble upon a different maiden first?"

"I'm allowed to keep running until I've chosen. It's my right."

The music played a new, rowdier tune, and he drew away from her. "It's time to begin. Just follow my lead."

"And then you shall follow mine," she replied, feeling the passion rise from the base of her spine and into her mind.

As Finnian sauntered away, she considered what Ankhmakis would say about all this, and ran to the table where the wine flowed. He'd been with plenty of women, both before and when they were together, yet it didn't drive them apart. Giving Finnian his first rites shouldn't either. She'd often made love to Ankhmakis mere hours after he'd been with Weret, but still, Natasa was scared. Did she even remember how to make love? It had been so long since she'd felt the goddess's blessing. She found Finnian in the crowd, who stared at her from his place across the circle forming around the giant, ancient tree. Natasa shivered. What had she done?

Yet as she drank down her wine, a rush of energy flowed through her. This was her true self, the one who worked with the Way of the universe. Her muscles pulsed and her skin glowed. A worthy young man, one who had spent a year in her service penning her words, had asked her to show him the Way of the Goddess. This is what she was born to do, and she was tired of hiding, of waiting, of being stripped of her titles while others, including her own mother, did as they wished. She strode to the circle of dancers around the old oak tree, her hips swaying to the erotic rhythms of the drums, her body light as a feather as if she were floating on the wind.

She and the goddess became one—Natasa had come home.

She tossed her hair over her shoulder and took her place across from Finnian to join in the dance. As the drums beat, she let her Ka connect to Finnian's, allowing her desire to cascade over him in waves, causing him to dance even more sensuously and thus arousing the rest of the participants as well. Natasa held the space and stirred their passions. She could see how many young girls wanted Finnian, but moreover, she saw the energetic connections between the married couples, eyeing each other, asking, begging for a night in the arms of someone other than their spouses. Many of them waited all year to be together for this one night. The sexual tension built as the musicians played louder, and the men and women began to howl. Natasa shimmied her hips, causing ripples of her energy to intermingle and dance among the others. She beamed at Finnian, who tossed his golden hair behind his shoulders, his lips parted and eyes set upon her like an archer before his target. Natasa sensed Neferu and received her encouragement. The high priestess had handed down the title.

When the music stopped, the Stag King called out, "Run, maidens, run. Into the forest you go. Will you be the one for me? If I catch you, you will know."

At least a dozen young women between the ages of sixteen and twenty sped into the forest. Natasa stood panting, her heart pounding in her head. Finnian remained still, gaze sparkling. The crowd was watching, waiting for the dark maiden's choice. Would she partake, or would she remain behind?

"*Go,*" he begged.

She bowed and ran off to the place he'd specified. There was no stopping this now. As she ran, she kicked off her shoes and tore the ribbons out of her hair. She unclasped her dress. Finnian was hot on her tail. She could hear his footsteps behind her, and she fell into freedom and bliss as she hid behind the tree, awaiting the Stag King's arrival. Within moments Finnian was there, and she was in his arms, kissing him, allowing her hands to wander over his chest, back, and bottom. He was so young and carefree, so beautiful and true. He'd saved her the day he found her cutting herself, and yet he still loved her, even in her brokenness. She held his warm hands against her naked breasts.

"Come," she whispered. "Let me show you the way."

14

The Golden Boy and the Dark King

A thing of beauty is never perfect.
~ Ancient Egyptian Proverb

Massilia, Gaul, 197 BCE

The next day was rather awkward for everyone in the house. Neferu and Hecataeus danced around one another, speaking in short, curt sentences. Natasa knew her father was very traditional, and while he'd enjoyed Beltane's pleasures, he also felt jealous of Neferu's own adventure with Taran. Natasa's own heart alternated between joy and guilt at regular intervals, one minute wishing Finnian would call on her, the next fearing she had destroyed her love for Ankhmakis. As the day wore on, something else became clear—Natasa was still one with the goddess. She glowed and felt the connection between her Ka and everything around her. The trees that once seemed cold now spoke volumes, and she bathed in their ancient song. Many things had come to pass in these woods, and the story of creation was written in their twisty, knotted trunks and branches. It was glorious to be one with the vital élan of the earth once more. How was it she found her way back to herself in Finnian's arms?

Natasa thought of the golden young man and his earnest, gentle touch as she did her chores, first milking the goats, then tending to the chickens, and last, weeding the garden. He'd been awkward at first, but after his first climax, he'd relaxed and let her teach him the ways of pleasure. Her groin ached as she considered his eagerness to learn how to grant her bliss. Unlike Ankhmakis, who'd had many, many lovers, Finnian had never seen a naked female before. He'd never felt a nipple grow hard in his mouth, nor experienced a woman's mystery. Natasa had given him permission to explore her body, and he'd done so for hours, touching and tasting every part of her with the zeal only a twenty-something man is capable of.

Ankhmakis had taught her about the pleasures of her body from a place of experience, but last night, she had been the expert and Finnian the innocent one. Over and over they took turns pleasing each other, and as the sun rose, they'd been able to enter into ecstasy at the same time. It had been strange to be in the sacred space after all these years, and yet it had felt natural. When she'd performed ceremony with Silus years ago, Natasa had closed her eyes and pretended she was somewhere else. Last night, she'd embraced Finnian and found union, and her future had never been clearer.

She'd sent a letter to Ankhmakis before Beltane assuring him she still wanted to return to his side. That letter was now traveling to the king, and she couldn't take it back, even if she wanted to, which she didn't. But it wasn't a marriage proposal she wanted from her twin flame. There was work for her in Egypt, she knew this now. The time had come for her to take up the Wands of Horus and reignite the magic of the Old Kings, but what in the world was she going to do about these feelings for Finnian? She drove all thoughts of the boy from her mind as she sent Ankhmakis a second letter, this time from a place of power rather than fear.

A few days later, Finnian still hadn't come to call on her, and Natasa decided to go to town with her father as he did his business. She had to get out of the house, waiting for Finnian was driving her crazy. Natasa walked the market, looking for a new pair of shoes for the summer. As she strolled down the stone street, she listened to the sounds around her—humans laughing and negotiating, chickens clucking, dogs barking, donkeys braying, birds screeching overhead, pots clanking, and children giggling as they chased each other through the crowded streets. The scents of cooked meat and warm bread mixed with the salty air from the sea taunted her grumbling, hungry stomach. She turned a corner on her way to the market and bumped into Finnian, of all people.

"Natasa," he exclaimed, holding out his hand as she tumbled into him. "I was looking for you. Your father said you'd be at the market."

She found herself speechless and giddy in his presence, yet also embarrassed.

"Why haven't you visited?" she demanded. "It's been days."

"I've been busy," he replied. "Come, I have much to tell you."

He held out his arm, and she took it, but she was worried. For some reason, she feared he was ending their relationship, even though she'd only promised him one evening.

"Well," she continued as he led her toward the harbor, her mind getting the best of her. "What is it?"

"Finnian," a tall, brown-haired man with a matching thick beard called out.

They turned and greeted a small group of men and women, each near Finnian's age.

"Maedoc," Finnian replied. "Good to see you. I hope you're enjoying this fine afternoon."

"Yes," Maedoc said, eyeing Natasa, a twinkle in his gaze, "and the new lovebirds as well."

Natasa felt a wave of heat flush through her body. Lovebirds? Finnian gave her a hard look before turning to smile at Maedoc, lips pressed, looking more like a statue than a man.

"Yes," Finnian replied. "Natasa and I are enjoying this day."

"Then it's true," a younger girl exclaimed. "You *are* courting one another."

Natasa froze. She wanted to speak out, to clarify that Anit-Shadya wasn't a promise of marriage. She looked at Finnian's face and felt a wave of communication from him as if he too could speak heart-to-heart.

He wanted her to remain silent.

"Well," Maedoc said, grinning like he knew something no one else did, "we never thought you'd settle down, Finnian. Always the girls have chased you. Isn't that right, Ceana?"

The young girl named Ceana pouted and eyed Natasa up and down as if she were merchandise in one of the market stalls. The woman's disappointment reminded Natasa of Weret, only without the power of the crown behind it.

"Good to see you all," Finnian answered as he led Natasa away. "Natasa and I must be going now. We are very busy."

As soon as they were out of earshot, Natasa began hounding him. "Finnian, we're not courting. We agreed only one evening, remember?" He looked out at the harbor before them, his gaze squinting at the bright sun on the water. Or was he trying to hide his tears?

He led her to a little bench near an empty slip. Tall merchant ships made their way in and out of the harbor and the noises of the men, boats, bells, waves sloshing on the dock, and sea birds filled the air. Finnian settled on the bench, placed his hands in his lap, and stared at them.

Natasa sat beside him and put her hand upon his. "Finnian? What's going on?"

He gazed out from beneath his long, blond eyelashes, the corners of his mouth slowly turning. A wave of desire passed through her, and she knew he was thinking about their time together in one another's arms.

"First," he said, his voice cracking a bit, "I want to thank you. Beltane was wonderful."

She felt her cheeks grow warm and opened her mouth to speak when he raised his hand.

"Second," he continued, "I ask for your forgiveness. I haven't told anyone we were courting, but I also haven't denied it. People started talking after they saw me run after you at Beltane. It is the tradition the Stag King chooses the maiden he wishes to marry, so everyone assumes that's the case now. They don't know about your king. They think you're a beautiful, exotic woman I've fallen in love with—and they'd be right, you know, I do love you."

"Finnian—"

"No, let me finish. I was going to correct them, but then I realized it was best to let them think we're courting. I mean, we've been spending hours a week together for a year now, haven't we?"

His shoulders slumped as he turned his face to the sea. There was so much going on within him and Natasa wished she could read his mind, but she couldn't, so she waited in silence until he was ready to speak.

"It's a relief for them to think I'm taken," he admitted, gaze still focusing on the harbor. "Natasa, you don't know how frustrating it is to be me. Fathers seek me out to marry their daughters. It began happening before you arrived. I was over twenty, and everyone expected me to take a wife. Yet none of the maidens of Massilia call to me. Now that everyone thinks I'm taken, I no longer have to keep turning them down, or trying to explain I'm not interested in their daughters. Trust me, men are insulted if you don't want their darling girl. They'd even begun to call me a homosexual, like so many of the Greek sailors seem to be, and since my line of work allows me much contact with the sailors, well you can see why the rumor caught fire. I sometimes think they made me the Stag King to cure me of anything unnatural."

Natasa laughed. "You are anything but that."

He turned and blushed. "I love women, just not all women." She gulped as she recalled him inside her, and a wave of heat passed over her skin as he continued, "Can you see why it's better for me to let them think we're to marry? Besides, it protects your honor. We may have Beltane once a year, but the rest of the time, sexual purity is expected. You'd be seen as loose, and I don't want these people to think such things. You're not loose, you're the goddess herself."

She looked into his eyes and inhaled, allowing herself to feel the passion and love now stirring around them. "Finnian," she whispered, "I must leave when Ankhmakis calls for me."

"I know," he replied, taking her hand into his. "Until then, can't you be mine?"

"No." She shook her head. "I can't give to you like I did on Beltane."

"I understand," he answered. "No sex. Even if we were courting, there wouldn't be any sex between us until the night of our handfasting. Like I told you, Beltane is a special exception."

"Handfasting?"

"Yes," he explained. "Our Celtic wedding ceremony, when we tie our hands together in a vow to live together and love one another."

"But I don't know when Ankhmakis will call me home. He hopes this summer, but it could be longer. I have no idea."

"That's fine," he replied. "I'm not in a hurry."

"What will you do when I leave?"

"Taran wants to relocate to Briton and has asked me to join him when he goes next spring. He's sending me to Avalon tomorrow to deliver his plans to the community. I'll be gone a month, which was my real reason for seeking you out. I won't be able to visit for a while, and I didn't want you to worry."

"I see," Natasa replied, her heart falling. Here she was, alive and in her power once more, yet her heart was torn. She gazed out upon the sea and let the waves carry her mind for a moment. As she merged with the sea, the truth became clearer—she loved them both. The realization caused pain as if a giant had punched her in the gut, and she sucked in her breath, tears trickling from her eyes.

"Natasa," Finnian said, "I know what I ask might feel wrong to you, but is it so bad to pretend to love me for the duration of your stay?"

He was blurry through her tears. "Finnian, it's not pretend. I do love you." His eyes grew wider. "I've loved you since the moment you saved me from taking my own life, I didn't allow myself to feel it before now."

"What about your king?"

"I love him as well." She sobbed, burying her head in her hands. "What am I to do?"

He placed an arm around her and drew her close. "Do you love him more than me?" he asked.

"No, but I loved him first. Ankhmakis is my twin flame. We never should have been separated." She picked at her fingernails, stuttering as she choked on her words. "I wasn't expecting to find anything to love about Gaul, but it turns out there's much to love."

He took her jittery hands into his and brushed her windswept hair out of her face. Her heart fluttered at the touch of his fingertips. "Why must you return to a place where so much is wrong?"

"Because I promised him," she admitted, swallowing down a gulp of her guilt. "He needs me. He wouldn't call for me otherwise."

"What if I need you?" Finnian asked.

"You don't," she answered, tugging her hands into her lap, unable to listen anymore. "Not like Ankhmakis. He and I have unfinished business, while you still have the world at your door. If you mean it, if you want to let everyone think we're courting until I leave, I shall do it. However, I will leave you, Finnian, when my king calls me back."

His lower lip trembled as he nodded.

"You deserve a beautiful life, Natasa," Finnian whispered, running his finger down her cheek, "and I shall give you that until you set sail for your home." He leaned in and kissed her upon the lips.

Natasa couldn't resist him.

"Besides," he said, pausing his kiss and wiping his own eyes. "It'll keep the folks here from saying I prefer men. You can be my cover."

She laughed. "And we have to finish the book. We're almost done, I can feel it."

"Yes." He smiled and patted his satchel. "I'm working on a surprise for you."

"You are?"

"I think you're going to like it," he said, leaning in for another kiss.

Natasa returned the kiss, enjoying the warmth of his lips upon hers. Many would consider a woman lucky to be loved by two men, and they'd be right—yet the price was very high. For the rest of time, she would be missing one of them, no matter where she was in the world.

15

Victory at Hand

The pyramids of Giza and the Nile Delta were the tombs of the rulers of the Old Kingdom. Centuries later, the New Kingdom pharaohs desired to be closer to their original dynastic roots, and for five hundred years built their crypts in the barren valley west of Luxor. They called this place "the Valley of the Kings."

The Valley of the Kings, outside of Luxor and Thebes, Egypt, 197 BCE

My dearest Ankhmakis,

Do I fear returning? It would be a lie to deny it. I fear living in the world where Helena was brutally torn from my side and slaughtered by our brother. I disdain Weret and her petty nature. She is a lesser woman, and my time here in Gaul, amongst common folk who are not a part of the court, has shown me how unsatisfying the arrangement is.

I fear the war. Who wouldn't?

When I was in darkness, I wondered if I could be the woman the pharaoh of Egypt deserves, but now I know I can and will serve you until my dying day. I do not wish to be your second queen, for that would put me under the thumb of the high

queen. Nor do I seek the role of the high priestess of Behdet, for I no longer wish to teach Anit-Shadya. I long to continue my work with the Wands of Horus in the Resurrection Bath of Abdju. Let Alexa have the temple in Behdet and make me the high priestess of the Osirion that I might uncover the secrets of our people and help you restore our kingdom to its glorious splendor. I am a wand bearer, and I promise to teach you the wisdom I discover in my role by your side.

Do not tarry any longer. I am ready.

Love,

Natasa

Ankhwenefer stood, sword and shield in hand, at the base of colossus statues, built by his ancestors long ago. Far above him rose the forms of Horus, Isis, Osiris, and Hathor, carved into the side of the orange, desert cliffs. He was a mere insect at the base of their toes, gazing up at their majesty. The desert hills surrounded him, casting shadows on his camp. He turned and looked down the Nile to the southwest. Thebes was visible in the distance; only the desert lay between them. The fires from the Greek army were burning strong, but Ankhwenefer knew they were weak. The time had come to attack.

His own army was preparing for battle around the base of the tombs. Everywhere he turned, there was evidence of greatness. For five hundred years, his ancestors had tended this place. It had long ago fallen into ruin, but tonight of all nights it felt right that a native Egyptian king made camp at their feet. He bowed low to these kings of old, and asked for their blessing in destroying their enemy, driving them out of the country.

He would hit Thebes like a sandstorm the size of the Mare Nostrum. Phalanxes and chariots would clash in the Valley of the Kings, and there would be no rest until the city fell into his hands.

Ankhwenefer thought about Natasa's letter, so grateful to have received it before heading out on this campaign. Hecataeus's demand to let her go had infuriated him and had the man still lived in Egypt, the pharaoh would have cut him down. How dare the fool suggest such a thing?

He was grateful she promised to return, yet sensed trepidation in her words. Her time in Gaul had changed her. Somehow, Ankhwenefer knew that even though he was the pharaoh and king of Upper Egypt, the life he offered Natasa might be inferior to the one in which she now found herself. He couldn't fathom the difference, but something in her tone suggested she wouldn't be as accepting of court politics, nor Weret as the high queen, as she had in the past. There wasn't much Ankhwenefer could do about Weret's position in the court; she'd born him two sons, and he needed those boys to secure Egypt, thus stripping Weret of her titles wouldn't do much good for anyone.

The point remained—Natasa had spent more than two years from his side, seen a new world, and no longer wished to be his spiritual companion, in the official sense, nor did she want to be his queen. She sought autonomy in her request to become the wand bearer for their nation. While this scared him, for in that role she owed him nothing but to show him the wisdom of the Old Kings, he knew it was her destiny.

He glanced up once more at the giant statues and felt a shiver run through him as he asked the kings of old if they agreed. A breeze blew upon his face. He took that as a yes.

The pharaoh made his way to his tent. Battle was at hand.

It would be the Greeks who launched their attack at sunrise, but Ankhwenefer had been expecting them. He rode Biriq toward the city, the wind in his hair and his heart pounding, leading the cavalry down the center, behind the main phalanx. His energy flowed through him, it had been so long since the battle at Lycopolis, and he longed to clash swords with the invaders. The Ptolemaic army was trapped— the Nile behind them, where Silus would be leading an army from the south, from the north, along the river, Khaleme was sailing a second army from Coptos, and Ankhwenefer's troops charged before them, showering the Valley of the Kings in their dusty wake.

The enemy's archers shot from the front of their line and caused Ankhwenefer's army much damage, but the king drove his men over their fallen comrades toward the Greek phalanx where the two armies met with the clanging of swords and screams of rage. Ankhwenefer sliced his khopesh at the neck of a Greek warrior, sending the soldier's head flying into his fellow countrymen. The pharaoh launched himself from Biriq's back into the swarms of bloodied men, fighting and thrashing, deep in the throes of battle fury. Yanking a xyston from an enemy's dying grip, he thrust it into the chest of the man in front of him. He sent his Ka out in waves, outward from the battle and toward the city, sensing every man's grief, fear, and bloodlust. This was where Ankhwenefer ruled, spinning and turning, taking life and forcing his way toward the gates of the city. They loomed in front of him, golden and barred. Behind him, seven of his strongest horses lugged the cart carrying an enormous, wooden battering ram. They would take this city without mercy. For too long his enemy had held him at bay. No longer. He wanted this done. He wanted rest. He wanted Thebes.

Above all, Ankhwenefer wanted Natasa at his side once more.

His men forced the Greeks back toward the city as they approached the main gates, where many more soldiers waited atop the walls, firing arrows that rained down upon the shields they held above their heads for protection. Silus was on the far side of the city, waging a similar battle as his men rode across the makeshift bridges Khaleme's men had constructed. They would tighten the noose and end this war.

"Megau," Ankhwenefer called. "To the city walls."

He fell in with the group as they roared past, sheathing his sword and drawing his bow from his back. He connected his Ka to the space between him and each of his targets. Taking count, he sensed several hundred archers atop the city walls, many more waiting down below. He had over three hundred megau archers of his own. He drew an arrow, lined it up with the young Greek boy standing at the top of the keep, and fired. Before the boy hit the ground, Ankhwenefer had yet another arrow ready. He would mow them down.

As he fought, the pharaoh of Egypt felt a power stir deep within his heart, filling him with energy. He drew an arrow and fired, swiftly turning after its release to avoid the Greek arrow heading for his chest. It flew by his shoulder and lodged itself in the ground. Battle was a dangerous dance, but one in which he excelled. While he and his men thinned the numbers of the soldiers guarding the gate, a large group of Ethiopians from Khaleme's army arrived carrying the huge battering ram. The muscular, war-painted men slammed the great tree trunk against the gates, screaming their wild battle chants to the rhythm of their weapon as it pounded against the golden structure. The sun god Ra set behind the temples of Thebes, and the city appeared to be burning. The Valley of the Kings blazed brilliant orange as well.

"Soon," Ankhwenefer whispered to the hot wind caressing his sweaty, bloodied face. He licked his lips and could taste their surrender. "Very soon."

16

A Woman's Heart

The Ka is the life force of the body. A strong Ka is vital for health. If the Ka is weak, it must be strengthened, either with foods, medicines, movement, or meditation. Anit-Shadya is a superior form of Ka renewal. So are the Wands of Horus. Unfortunately, Natasa had access to neither.

Massilia, Gaul 197 BCE

Spring turned to summer, and the days became long and hot. Natasa welcomed the heat, but Finnian found it unbearable. Often the couple would ride his horse deep into the woods for a picnic in the shade, spending hours working on the book, kissing, or sleeping off the heat of the day in one another's arms. When she was close to Finnian this way, Natasa would feel an unbearable flame of desire, but he was always a gentleman and never crossed any lines. Natasa was grateful. Leaving him was going to be hard enough without the extra bond of Anit-Shadya between them.

Just after the feast of Lammas honoring the first harvest of the grains, when the summer heat was at its peak, they finished the book and began spending their days courting like a normal couple, walking along the sea, gathering in the city for dinner parties, and participating in community activities within the coven. Natasa spent hours in

Finnian's room above an apothecary in the city helping him with work. As Taran's scribe, he was responsible for coven documentation as well as correspondence with other covens in the country and Briton.

One afternoon in late August, as the summer heat flamed and the vines dripped with berries, Natasa awoke in Finnian's arms under the familiar beautiful green canopy of the forest. She gazed down and beheld him sleeping, his chest rising and falling with each soft breath. A cool whisper of a breeze stirred a golden lock of his hair across his cheek, and she sighed at his beauty. Finnian was a perfect being, not only handsome, but also free of the brokenness of most people, as if grief, shame, and pain had never touched him. Natasa's heart ached when she considered how selfish she was, letting him grow more in love with her each day. If Finnian loved her the way he claimed, he would soon know grief when she broke his heart in a cruel and horrible way and returned to Ankhmakis. The hot sting of tears formed in her throat, ushering in a coughing fit.

Finnian's eyes fluttered open. "Natasa," he whispered, "why do you weep?"

"Because I am hurting you."

"Hurting me?" he replied. "How so? I've never felt better than I do in this moment."

"Finnian, how can you say that when I'm so cruel? What will you do when I leave you?"

"Natasa," he answered, now wide awake and sitting up, "we've been over this. I know what I'm doing. You've always been honest with me, and I've accepted you will go to your king when he calls. Until then, I've promised to give you the most beautiful life I can offer."

"What about you?"

"Well, you could change your mind and marry me."

"Finnian, after all of this, you'd still marry me?"

"Of course, Natasa. I love you."

Somewhere deep within her soul, she felt a tug of longing.

"I brought you a gift," the young man said, changing the subject. "I hope you like it."

He opened his satchel and retrieved something in his hands

Natasa had never seen—a set of papers, bound in a leather cover. He placed it on her lap, and she ran her fingers along its front. Burned into the leather were the words *The Goddess of the South* curved over a trinity knot.

She opened the cover and inside were dozens upon dozens of papyrus sheets, not rolled into scrolls as she was used to, but stacked on top of one another, filled with writing and pictures in various colors of ink. They were her words, organized into themes such as Love, Grief, Energy, Health, Force, Nature, Light, Earth, Fire, and so on. Twenty-two sections in total— beautiful drawings accompanied each theme. She'd never seen anything like it.

"Is this the book?" she asked.

"Yes," he answered. "It is."

Natasa hugged it to her chest and smelled the leather and the pages.

"How did you get the papyrus?"

"We live in Massilia, the great Greek outpost of Gaul. I can buy anything I want. Reeds, papyrus, ink. I bought the leather when I was in Avalon. I didn't want to create one huge scroll because that seemed cumbersome, and twenty-two scrolls would risk parts separating. I wanted to be able to carry the book in my satchel. I've seen a few works bound in leather like this—Taran has one in his study—but they're rare and not something most scribes do. I find it easier to use, so I made it this way."

Natasa traced her fingers over the symbols that filled the pages. "You were inspired by the goddess," she whispered.

He tucked her hair behind her ears. "I was inspired by you, so I guess that's true."

She bit her lip. "I'm not the goddess, Finnian."

"To me you are."

She coughed into her hand and gazed down at the book, admiring its beauty and craftmanship. "It's perfect."

"You can take it with you to Egypt," Finnian offered.

"No," she replied. "You must keep it. This wisdom belongs here, in Gaul."

"That way you'll have something to remember me," he answered.

She placed his hand on her heart and squeezed it. "I'll always remember you here."

Finnian drew her into his strong arms, and she coughed into his chest. Would her throat ever stop this nonsense?

"Don't worry about me," he begged her, kissing the top of her head. "When your king demands your return, I'll face my pain. Until then, I prefer to live in this moment, with you."

He kissed her, his lips soft and full. She returned his kiss and fell into his arms, lying down once more under the trees. Natasa didn't dare tell him the real truth she held in her heart—of how lately she dreamed of staying in Gaul, marrying him, and having his children in safety. This was the future she now wanted—one in which she was nothing more than the woman of Finnian's home and his beloved without question, not the high priestess of Egypt who shared her lover with not only a jealous queen but an entire kingdom. It would be so peaceful to grow old in Gaul beside Finnian instead of returning to Egypt where her life would be in constant danger.

Later, after Finnian had dropped her back at her little cabin in the woods, Natasa found herself alone and very much torn. Her parents were still in town and as the sun set behind the trees, Natasa wandered their gardens, marveling at how much they'd managed to accomplish in a few years. Life in Egypt felt like a lifetime ago. She plucked a plum from the tree and ate it, wiping at the warm juices running down her chin. A sultry breeze blew past her and she leaned against the tree. Tears fell from her eyes, and she didn't stop them.

She loved Finnian, and with each breath, it became clearer she didn't want to leave him. No, if Natasa listened to her heart, it no longer sang only Ankhmakis's name, for now, Finnian had a role in her song. There was no removing his melody from her soul, nor her desire to remain in Gaul at his side. She allowed herself to see such a future and saw children, more than one, with creamy dark skin and light eyes, like Eleni, laughing and playing in the garden. These were her children, and no one would threaten them—she would mother them in safety and watch them grow and have children of their own.

How could she refuse this path? Why would she instead follow the one of pain and war? From the moment of Helena's brutal murder, Egypt was no longer home—she was exiled. Natasa loved Ankhmakis, and always would, but returning to her Twin Flame would mean denying her own peace of mind and wellbeing. Egypt meant dealing with Weret and politics, and never having another child, for Ankhmakis was now the pharaoh of a country at war with many enemies. How could she ever feel safe being the mother of his children after what had happened to Helena? It was impossible.

The image of her precious daughter chasing the old mares in the stable spread out before her and Natasa fell to the ground, tearing at the soil, choking on her pain. She longed for Helena so much the memory took her breath away. She'd give anything, even her own life, to hold her child again. The pain of her loss was too much to bear. She couldn't return to the world that murdered her precious child. Her father was right; the time had come to let Ankhmakis go and start over in Gaul. The full moon was rising above the trees, and she wailed to the goddess in agony.

"What do you want from me? Why can't you tell me what I must do? Do I stay or do I go? My lady, please give me a sign, for I can't make this decision on my own."

The deep silence of the balmy summer night surrounded her, yet all she could see was Ankhmakis's face when they were young, before the war, long before his family had betrayed them. She remembered him on the deck of the ship on the way back from Alexandria, twenty years old and singing her song as Ra rose in the eastern sky. He had once been sweet and pure, like Finnian, but that Ankhmakis was long gone, and he was now a king, fighting an important war, hardened and distant, yet still in love with her.

Egypt needed her pharaoh, and he needed his spiritual companion. She was the wand bearer and must return to the Osirion. Another vision flashed before her mind—she stood before Ankhmakis, granting him the power of the wands, of the All-One, and of the universe. He couldn't do this without her.

Gazing at the sky, hands clasped above her breast, Natasa

whispered, her voice quivering, "My lady, I offer myself to you. I will return to Ankhmakis and take up my work with the wands, even if it means I must give up my future with Finnian. Please, have my king call me home soon, for I'm not sure how much longer I can stand to be here in heaven, knowing I must leave it."

☥

Time marched forward; the summer days turned shorter, the air crisper, and soon the apple trees were bursting with fruit. The cold of autumn took hold of the weather, yet Ankhmakis still didn't call her home. It became clearer with each day that the goddess hadn't heard her plea, and Natasa would indeed spend another winter in Gaul.

With the arrival of the season of death, a new sort of cough settled upon Natasa that she couldn't shake. Her lungs rattled and her body shook, and with each passing day, she grew weaker. No matter what herbal remedy Aurelia or her mother gave her, she was soon feverish and bedridden.

Natasa's life force was fading, and no one knew what to do.

17

The Golden Eagle King

In the seventh year of his reign, when he was twelve years of age, the priests in Memphis declared Ptolemy V the divine ruler of Egypt and established a cult in his honor. This happened months after the Greek surrender in Thebes in 196 BCE. Ptolemy V had the decree inscribed in a stele in three languages—Greek, Egyptian Hieroglyph, and Demotic. The stele was placed in a temple in Sais, but eventually found its way to Rosetta, in the Nile Delta. Thus, when discovered in 1799 CE during a Napoleonic expedition, they named the stele the Rosetta Stone.

Thebes, Egypt, 196 BCE

My dearest love,

I am sick. Very, very, very sick. The witch Aurelia gives me herbs and steams. Mother prays and does ceremony. They both lay their hands on me, but I'm exhausted, and a cough seems to have infected my lungs. I received your letter of victory, but I can't travel to you until I'm well. Father says we can't leave until the winter has passed anyway when the sea is safer to cross. So perhaps all is as it should be and I shall spend yet another winter here in Gaul, but this time asleep. I pray time passes with all haste, and that in the spring I will be ready to take the ship to your shores.

I'm so proud of you, Lord Ankhwenefer, the Good Being of Isis and Pharaoh of Upper Egypt. You are a great man and a great king.

Love,

Natasa

Ankhwenefer stood in temple vestibule, outside the great hall in Thebes. The city was a wreck, for the Greeks had left it in disarray, but it was his wreck. The Theban priests lined up before him, High Priest Setep carrying the blue Khepresh crown of the pharaoh. Ankhwenefer wore his collar bearing the phoenix on his bare chest, and a crisp, white skirt. His sword hung at his waist and golden cuffs shone upon his wrists. His eyes were lined in dark charcoal, lids painted green—the color of Natasa's eyes. He was as magnificent as the statuary surrounding him.

As had become custom, Min stood at his side.

"Ah," Ankhwenefer said to his friend, whispering so the priests couldn't hear him, "here we are, you, standing guard, while I get all the glory."

Min laughed. "I enjoy playing the part of the queen. I could get used to this."

Ankhwenefer nodded, slapping his friend's back. "You're a much better queen than Weret," he said, still trying to keep a low voice while the priests began their ceremony. He'd wait in the alcove until he was called.

"When will you relocate the court here?" Min asked.

"As soon as the streets are cleared of the rubble, the palace repaired, and the sanitation functioning."

"Several months?"

"Maybe longer." He sighed. "Silus and I sail to Lycopolis tomorrow to negotiate the final peace treaty. In time, I'll return to Behdet to fetch the court."

He wasn't looking forward to the return trip to Behdet. He hadn't been there since Helena's murder. There was no one there he wanted to see, other than Ankhmaat and his younger son, Khenefer. He'd be a toddler now, yet they'd never met.

"When does Natasa arrive?"

The pharaoh thought about the letter he'd received the day before. He couldn't believe Natasa was ill. It scared him, for he could sense her energy weakening. After three years of waiting for his call, why had she fallen ill the moment he'd succeeded? It was unthinkable.

"It's winter there," he said to Min, not wanting to tell him about her illness. "The sea is too dangerous to cross right now."

"Ah, so she'll arrive when Thebes is beautiful enough for such a creature as she," Min replied with a squeeze of the shoulder.

"Yes." Ankhwenefer agreed, nodding his head as he imagined greeting Natasa at the docks, his city shining and gleaming in the sun. He didn't want her to see the mess it was now. "That's the spirit. The palace will be beautiful and worthy of her by then. I'm building her a wing of her own and royal quarters. I've selected an artist to decorate her bath with scenes from the *Song of Isis* in honor of the Osirian, where she will do her great work in service of our kingdom."

"Welcome, people of Thebes," High Priest Setep called out to the throng. It was the pharaoh's cue. Ankhwenefer and Min stood at attention. "Men of the south, nobles from Aswan, the kings of Kush and Nubia. You are here today to witness the crowning of your pharaoh."

"This is it, my lord," Min whispered. "After many years, you will have your day."

Ankhwenefer stepped from the alcove and strode to the dais, shoulders down and head held high that all might see strength in the man they now called pharaoh. Hundreds of allies, some since birth, and others more recent crowded the temple hall. Khaleme stood beside a large group of heavily painted Kushmen, all holding their xystons and dressed in bright-colored celebratory robes. There was a scattering of ladies and noblewomen of Thebes as well. Ankhwenefer, however, stood alone. Just as in the songs they sung about him, the golden eagle king was without his hawk. He bowed low to the crowd to address them.

"My friends, this has been a long time coming. While my father took Thebes easily at the start of the war, it took me three years to make it my own and I now rule Upper Egypt. We control the Nile to the south and the Wadi Hammamat trade route. We control the Valley of the Kings, Luxor, and Karnak, our great cities of old. We have alliances with Nubia and Kush and control trade between them and Alexandria. This is no small feat, and as Ptolemy V is beaten down in Syria, we will grow stronger. Upper Egypt will become the greater nation, and she will thrive under the rule of her native peoples once more."

The crowd cheered. Their screams were like the howls of furious wildcats. Their nationalism was at its peak, and all he needed to do was stoke it to earn their fealty. He turned to the high priest, who held the crown over his head. The white columns of the temple soared above them, and Ankhwenefer gazed at the hieroglyph-covered walls. In spite of the war, the temple was in pristine condition. All around him were golden statues of gods and goddesses. Animals and other brightly painted forms graced the walls. His flag bearing the phoenix flew high in the wind. Everyone in the room dropped to their knees as their king approached Setep.

"By the power invested in me," the priest called out, "on this day, the fourth month of Perit, the eleventh day, in the third year of your holy reign, I re-crown you Lord and Pharaoh Ankhwenefer, the Good Being of Isis, Golden Eagle King, protector of our lands and Horus himself. May Amon-Re protect you and our people as we rebuild our nation. Egypt shall reign in glory until the end of time."

Setep placed the heavy crown on Ankhwenefer's head. A second priest handed him the hook and flail. He gripped them tightly as he crossed his chest with his arms and, turning to the crowd once more, gazed down upon them.

"My people," he called, "I pledge myself to you."

The sun poured in from the windows and shone upon Pharaoh's face, and the people rose from the floor and clapped. To those in the room, their new king looked like the statues of Horus himself. Ankhwenefer was master of his domain—young, strong, intelligent, and wise. He'd fought hard for many years and won. The priestesses sang as he walked past and out to the courtyard where the commoners flooded the area, crying and tossing palm branches and lotus flowers at his feet. His entourage followed behind him, leading a procession of dancing, music, and singing, toward the palace where a feast awaited them. Tomorrow, the next phase of his reign would begin—creating peace with the Lower Kingdom, rebuilding the cities destroyed by the war, and most importantly, establishing a court in Thebes, with his sons, and Natasa, at his side.

Ra shone above the large outer wall of the grand temple and the white marble glistened and glowed. The colossal forms of Horus and Osiris cast long shadows across the courtyard and beckoned to the new pharaoh. Ankhwenefer thought back to the day the war had first begun, and how on the eve of his departure, he'd made love to Natasa for hours in his chambers, exploring every inch of her beautiful body. He'd been so young, twenty-two, and she even younger, a woman of eighteen. Helena had just been born, and no thought of ever being parted by such a distance crossed their youthful, innocent minds. He'd been one with her then, one with himself, and one with the entire world.

When the processional passed the statue of Isis, Ankhwenefer bowed and placed a hand on her golden foot. "I miss her," he said under his breath. "Please, my lady, return her to me."

18

The Primal Wound

Just as a child shares a physical body with her mother while she grows in the womb, a child also shares her mother's Ka body until the age of seven, when she has created her own life force. If a mother dies while her children are young, they carry a wound in their Ka for the rest of their lives. The same is true for a mother—she never recovers from the death of her young child. Within her Ka, there is a scar nothing can heal. This is called the Primal Wound. When the child is murdered, the Primal Wound cuts doubly deep, for the darkness of such a crime festers within the mother's life force, and never sets her free.

Massilia, Gaul, 196 BCE

Finnian sat beside Natasa's bed, watching her chest rise and fall. She was so pale, her skin no longer a dark bronzed color, but faded and dull, her lips cracked like a dry seabed. He leaned over and rubbed calendula paste on them, no longer feeling the shock of desire when he did so. Instead, his heart ached with each beat—she was terribly weak as if she no longer lived in her body. Her lungs rattled like the winds through a ship's sail.

Dying of cough wasn't unusual in Massilia. It happened every year during the winter and early spring. Finnian had lost his own mother to it when he was a teen, which was why Taran, whose wife also died of the same disease, took him under his wing. Everyone feels sorry for the motherless child.

Now his dear, childless mother lay dying before him, and there was nothing he could do. He picked up the book, opened it to the chapter called The Star, and read aloud.

"The birth of a child is a miracle of the highest order. It is a piece of the light of the cosmos pouring itself into matter. It physically grows within the mother's body first. Then it grows within her energy, nurtured by her vital élan. Finally, the child grows within the community, soaking up its customs, emotions, and songs until one day it steps forth and takes up its service, its calling, and its place in humanity.

The birth of a human being and its progress is no small thing, for it is the act of a star, coming to know itself."

He looked at his beloved and felt his throat swell up as he whispered, "Do you remember when you told me this, my love? We were in the garden in late spring. Just after Beltane. I'll never forget that moment."

He ran his finger over the drawing he'd created to go with the words, a picture of a woman dancing naked beneath a huge star in the sky. He looked back at Natasa, surprised to see her eyes were open.

"Finnian," she whispered, "you're always by my side."

"Not always." He smiled. "But as often as I can."

"Finnian," Natasa croaked, "I love you. Please don't forget that."

"Natasa, you must get better. Your king awaits you."

She had a look similar to the one she wore when channeling the goddess's words. Natasa was no longer fully in this world.

"I need you to write one last letter for me," she said, her voice so soft he had to lean forward to hear her.

He leaped up to get his writing tools. When he returned, her eyes had closed again. He sighed and made to put down his paper and stylus.

"No," she mumbled, startling him. "I need you to write this down and make sure it gets to Ankhmakis. Please?"

He swallowed hard and nodded. It was such a great effort to speak, she took several breaks between passages, but he penned every word.

My love, the winter skies of Gaul weep constantly, building up fluid in my lungs. I can't seem to swim out of this. Aurelia says I'm too weak to shake this infection. I'm too weak to even write this letter myself. Since Samhain in late autumn, I fall in and out of fever, in and out of the Void. I fear this might be the last time I open my eyes, so I must tell you, Ankhmakis, I love you. I'm so sorry my love for you killed our child, and I didn't defend her. Worse, I'm sorry I can't fight for my own life now. If you receive this, I'm no longer coming home to you. I've been living for you these past years, but I now realize that isn't enough because I stopped living for myself the moment they ripped Helena from my arms. I bear a wound from which I can never recover. I regret abandoning you in this way, but I must go to our daughter, for she calls to me and I cannot refuse. You must go on without me. Use the wands in my stead and you will succeed. Forever I am you, and you are me.

She uttered her last word on an exhale and coughed, her entire body shaking. Finnian set the letter on the table and crawled into the bed, cradling her in his arms, easing warm water into her mouth. The fit ended with a bit of blood, and he wiped it away from her beautiful face.

"Deliver it after I die," she said, her eyelids fluttering shut as she dropped her head to his chest.

"Don't die," he replied, tears stinging in his throat. He caressed the nape of her neck. "There's so much to live for."

"I loved her more than anything in the world, Finnian," she murmured. "Helena was the star of my soul. The Golden Child of my universe. She calls me home to Amenti."

"There will be more children if you stay here with me," he begged, gripping her closer as if he could drag her back from the abyss, as he'd done when they first met. If returning to Ankhmakis wasn't enough, perhaps a life with him could give her the will to live?

She raised her head at his words, a glow returning in her gaze as she placed a cold fingertip to his cheek. "I saw them once, our children.

In a vision, I saw our lives as husband and wife, and our children and grandchildren played at our feet."

"Then see them again, Natasa, it's not too late," Finnian's heart pounded louder with each word. "I want nothing more than to father your children."

Natasa's lower lip began to tremble and her breathing quickened. She wove her fingers into his thick, golden hair and drew his forehead to hers as she spoke, "I've made a grave mistake Finnian. I should have accepted your proposal. How could I be so foolish?" Her voice was raw as if her coughing had torn her vocal cords. "I would be a mother now, and a wife, warm in your bed. I'm so, so sorry. Finnian, please forgive me."

He kissed her forehead and cheeks, her tears salty upon his lips. "Natasa, don't say such things."

"It's true," she sobbed, rubbing her forehead against his rough, woolen collar. He snuggled closer into her thin body, running his hands along her side. He could feel every one of her ribs, there was almost nothing left of her. A lump formed in his own throat, as if he'd swallowed a ball of holly leaves, pointed and sharp. He choked down the screams of anguish now building within and unfurled her hands from his hair to hold them in his own clammy palms, kissing each finger.

"Natasa," he whispered, the words stung as he spoke them, "I will always love you."

"Don't make the same mistake I did," she said, rolling out of his embrace to face him. "Promise me you will find love again."

"Natasa—" he began, but she placed a finger on his lips.

"You'll be a wonderful husband and father. Please promise that when your heart is healed you will not deny the love that is sure to come."

How could he promise such a thing? How could she ask it?

"I want *you* to live and be my wife. It's not too late."

Her eyes were glossy, head sweating, each breath gurgling as if she were drowning. In spite of his words, he knew she was dying and his love couldn't save her.

"I love both you and Ankhmakis, my golden boy and the dark king. Our hearts are capable of great devotion and mustn't be denied. Please, listen to yours and say yes when love calls."

His whole body began to tremble. She asked the impossible of him, and yet she'd given him so much. How could he wallow in sadness for the rest of his life? He might not ever love again, but he could be grateful for what they'd shared.

"I promise to live my life to the fullest," he said, kissing her lips, knowing it would be the last time.

She closed her eyelids, but her faint breath still stirred from her lungs. Finnian laid her down on the bed and arranged her pillows and blankets. He curled up beside her and placed his hand on her forehead. She was feverish and trembled like a willow in the breeze. He nuzzled the top of her head.

"Tell my golden eagle king I'm sorry," she murmured. The gurgling noises of her breath sputtered to a stop and she grew still. He stared at her face, her eyelashes dark against her pale skin, mouth slightly open, as the silence between them grew and spread out across the universe. He wanted nothing more than to follow her, but her soul had flown to a place he couldn't go. He closed his eyes and wiped the tears streaming down his face.

Natasa was dead.

Not long after, her parents entered the room, soaked from the winter rains, which had been pouring without mercy for days. Neferu threw off her wet cloak and ran to the bedside, elbowing him out of the way as he rose from the bed to give her space. Hecataeus remained in the doorway.

Neferu cradled Natasa and screamed. Her moans filled the cabin, and Finnian's chest burned. Hecataeus drew Finnian into his embrace, and Finnian felt the older man's sobs as they wrapped their arms around each other. Finnian loved Natasa so much, and while he'd known she'd leave him, he'd envisioned their parting with a kiss on the docks in Massilia, waving goodbye and completely heartbroken, but knowing she'd live on and take up her mantle as The Goddess of the South for all her long life.

Natasa didn't sail home to Egypt. Instead, she chose to join her daughter and take her place among the stars in the sky.

19

The Parting of Ways

Celtic burials were simple. They dressed the body in a death shirt and laid it out in the home for seven days, surrounded by candles and loved ones, and then buried the corpse, either in a cemetery or on one's own property. Sometimes games were held in the departed's honor, especially if he or she were a public official. Natasa's body was laid out in her garden beneath the canopy of trees and honored by the many people she'd met in her short time in Gaul. Hecataeus buried her in Taran's family cemetery, outside of the city walls of Massilia. In her grave were three things—the rowan wand the Celts had given her, the little blue paper flower from Ankhmakis, and Finnian's bone stylus, with which he'd written her book.

Massilia, Gaul, 196 BCE

Neferu stood at the harbor beside Hecataeus, body wrapped in her blue cloak, the hood hanging heavily down her back. Spring winds blew strands of graying hair across her face. Her heart was heavy, but she stood tall, back straight and stiff. Life hurt her over and over, and yet, there she was, ready to get back on the horse and ride.

"Are you sure about this, son?" Taran asked Finnian.

The young man was different. Where once there was eternal optimism in his gaze, now his eyes were lined with wrinkles, peering out from beneath a heavier brow. Neferu often wondered if he would have suffered less if Natasa had left him for Ankhmakis rather than death. It was hard to tell; the boy was doomed the moment he'd met her.

"Yes," he said, tugging his dark green cloak around himself. He patted his satchel. "I'm a scribe and courier, Taran, this is my line of work. I've never been to Egypt, but I'm sure it can't be harder to deliver a message there than it is to get one to the settlement near Avalon."

"It's a lot farther away and filled with war," Hecataeus said, his voice thick. "We can find someone else to deliver the message to the pharaoh."

"No," Finnian said, shaking his head. "I must go. I need to meet him."

Neferu admired him for his courage but thought him foolish just the same. She placed a hand on his shoulder and asked, "Will you join us in Avalon when you've completed your mission?"

Taran gave her a hard look. It was a touchy subject. Until Natasa's death, it had been the plan that Finnian be the one to accompany Taran to the settlement in Avalon, but now everything had changed.

"We'll see," Finnian said, shrugging. "I'm not sure what I'll do after I'm done in Egypt."

"I want you in Avalon son," Taran replied. "I need you."

Finnian raised his gaze to his master and gave a slight nod. "I understand. After I've delivered the news to Ankhmakis about Natasa, I'll be in touch. Who knows? I might fall in love with Egypt and want to stay."

"I doubt that very much," Neferu said.

"Why?" he asked.

"Because even though you hurt right now about Natasa, you are much too lighthearted and fair for such a place. Perhaps in the days of old, when our kings were great monument builders and seers, but now we struggle to keep our dignity and darkness fills the lands. No, Finnian, Egypt is no place for someone as pure as you."

"She's right," Hecataeus agreed. "It was no place for someone as pure as Natasa either, which is why I took her away."

"Yet she wanted to return," Finnian noted, his voice fading as he spoke.

"Natasa was true to her heart," Neferu answered, "even if it didn't make sense to the rest of us."

The four stood still in silence, and Neferu swallowed the lump in her throat. She missed her daughter.

Finnian spoke. "My ship is leaving. I must board it. Thank you, Taran, and I will come to you when my heart is ready. I promise."

He hugged Taran, who patted Finnian on the back while speaking. "By the way, son, we didn't make you the Stag King to cure you of anything unnatural. We did it because you are the best of men, and as such, a true representation of our godlike nature."

Finnian gave Taran a crooked smile, and Neferu couldn't help smiling back. The young man turned to Hecataeus. "You sure you don't want to join me?"

"Not yet," Hecataeus replied, crossing his arms over his barrel chest. "I have unfinished business in Athens, and then I will head to Thebes to collect Eleni. Ankhwenefer must learn of Natasa's death sooner than later, so thank you for doing this."

"Yes, sir." Finnian nodded, giving the Greek a strong hug.

"I'm sorry Finnian," Hecataeus added. "I never thought she'd die like that."

Neferu felt herself trembling, and Finnian noticed. He grabbed her and hugged her tight.

"I didn't think she'd die either," he whispered. "She was doing so well."

"Yes," Neferu said, "but she never recovered from the trauma of losing her child so brutally. Thanks to you, her spirit reawakened in spite of the grief, and her last two years were spent in joy."

"Me?" Finnian asked, tears now forming in his eyes.

"Yes," Neferu said, running her hands through his hair. "You reminded her of the goddess within, and I will always be grateful."

He rubbed his nose. "Do you have the book?"

"Yes," she replied. "Are you sure you want us to take it to Avalon?"

"Please do. I know they long for this information." He patted his satchel. "I still have the original notes. I'm thinking about creating a second one, this time with even more beautiful artwork." Finnian stood taller and bowed to them, "Goodbye, my friends. We will meet again. If not in this lifetime, in another, I'm sure."

Finnian, son of Atticus and scribe to the high druid Taran, turned and strode across the dock toward the ship headed to Alexandria. In his satchel, he carried the original manuscript from his days in the garden with Natasa and two letters for Lord Ankhwenefer, Pharaoh of the Upper Kingdom of Egypt; one from Natasa, and one from Hecataeus. The golden boy turned to wave to them one last time and then disappeared into the crowd gathering upon the ship's deck.

"Well, there goes one fine man." Hecataeus sniffled. "I, too, must board my own ship to Athens."

"Why won't you come with us?" Neferu begged.

"Why won't you come with me?"

"Because my heart calls me to Avalon, not Greece, so do what you must in Athens and hurry to Eleni before it's too late. Perhaps then you'll join us?"

He eyed her and Taran and shook his head. "I'm not a priest, Neffa. I'm a cleric, a sailor, and a man of the sea. I can't live on Tor and pray all day, hoping to find the way into mystical other worlds. You know this."

She was conflicted and yet understood. She needed to dive into the cult of the Tor and learn the secrets of Tir-na-og. It was time to understand the magic of the north and meet the Lady of the Lake. Hecataeus wouldn't fit in such an environment.

"I understand, my love," she replied. She stepped forward and kissed him before whispering in his ear, "We almost had it all."

He grunted and drew away, wiping his eyes with the back of his hand. "Goodbye, Neffa, and thank you for asking me to be the father of your daughter all those years ago."

Neferu's heart burst into a thousand pieces, and she grabbed him one more time. He held her close for what seemed like an eternity before he shrugged her off and turned to shake Taran's hand. "Thank you for everything you've done for me, my friend. Take care of this woman, she's one of a kind."

Hecataeus grabbed his bag from the dock, slung it over his shoulder, and turned to make his way to his ship. Unlike Finnian, he didn't stop one last time to wave. Instead, Hecataeus faded into the crowds along the harbor, and out of Neferu's sight forever.

She turned to Taran, and he drew her close to his side.

"What now, Taran?"

"It's time to head north," he answered. "Though there is something I wish to discuss with you.

"What?" Neferu asked, sensing an uncomfortable conversation.

"This book of Finnian's," he began, "I don't think it's wise to take it to Avalon."

"Why not?"

"Because I've met the Lady of the Lake," Taran answered, shifting back and forth between his feet, "and she isn't as open to outside wisdom as one would think."

"We promised him and Natasa."

"Natasa wanted Finnian to have the book as a remembrance of her. It's Finnian who thinks Avalon would be interested, and I don't think marching into the Tor armed with your own holy book is wise. You're already challenging the Lady of the Lake as a high priestess yourself. I think it's best to share the wisdom orally as the situation presents itself."

Neferu considered his words. How would she have felt if the Lady of Avalon arrived in Behdet with a book she swore was from the goddess herself? Would Neferu be open to its teachings? She'd like to think so, but pride and ego were often strongest in the leaders of any religion.

"How about you leave it behind in a safe place?" Taran suggested. "If the politics works out, and the Lady of Avalon is open to receiving the gift, we can come back to get it. I'm sure we'll have reason to return to Massilia quite often."

"Yes," she agreed. "I can protect it under Natasa's grave with enchantments, and we will retrieve it when the time is right."

"Wonderful. Now, my lady Neferu-ankh-maat, High Priestess of

Isis," Taran proclaimed. "Are you ready to meet the Lady of Avalon?"

She turned her face to the brilliant blue sky, recalling that all her children were now gone and only she remained. "Yes, I am. Like Natasa, I'm now a childless mother, and as she showed me, only in the goddess's arms will I find peace."

20

The Messenger

During the Great Revolt, the crowning of the pharaohs by the priests of Thebes and Memphis were handled very differently. In Memphis, they held out, not proclaiming any pharaoh once Philopater died, instead biding their time and finally crowning Ptolemy V Epiphanes Ptah of the land after Thebes fell to the rebels in 196 BCE. In Thebes, the crown proceeded from Philopater, to Epiphanes, to Haronnophris, to Chaonnophris, to Epiphanes, and back to Chaonnophris in 196 BCE. With each crowning, the king in Thebes was not named Ptah, but Amun-Re. It has been suggested this is evidence of the desire of Theban priests to aid the rebellion, and restore an Egyptian king to the throne, for Amun-Re had always been the god of Upper Egypt, where Ptah was the guardian of Lower Egypt. The forming of two nations, as in the days of old, was inevitable.

Thebes, Egypt, 196 BCE

From the moment he arrived in Egypt, Finnian's confidence began to decline. The port of Alexandria was the most splendid city he'd ever set eyes upon, and he'd taken the liberty of spending days in the Great Library before buying safe passage upon a barge down the Nile. When he arrived in Giza, Finnian delivered a few messages he'd picked up along the way—work had a way of finding a scribe—and then spent time near the Sphinx and the Great Pyramid. As he stood in front of the grand monuments, the sands swirled around his feet, and he was both at one with the world and very much out of place. Everywhere he turned, there was nothing but desert sands, and Finnian longed for something green. Yet, when he stared at the architectural wonders before him, he marveled at what sort of humans could build such treasures, and so long ago. His Natasa had been one of these people. How could he have ever thought she'd choose him over the king of such a land?

Finnian continued up the Nile, meeting cordial and intelligent, yet distant people. This was a nation at odds with itself and very much at war. It was obvious the strife was affecting them. In the north, those fair like himself owned dark slaves and yet lived under Egyptian customs. When he arrived in Lycopolis, however, the dark ones roamed freely, and there were very few of his skin tone. He showed his scribe credentials several times to gain passage. When his boat parked at the docks in Lycopolis, several Egyptian soldiers boarded and searched the ship.

"Whom are these letters for?" they demanded.

"Various people living in Thebes, two of which belong to the pharaoh of the Upper Kingdom himself, Lord Ankhwenefer."

The men inspected the waxy parchment and noted the seals upon each, which were Egyptian in origin and bore the vizier of Behdet's seal as well as Natasa's phoenix seal. "Fine, you may continue."

Finnian spent several more days on the boat, gazing at Egyptian majesty as they sailed upriver toward Thebes. The signs of war were everywhere, and the farmland lay dry and barren, but the pyramids, towers, obelisks, and ancient stone promenades still stood, taunting him, and telling him of his foolishness, of the plainness of the world in which he lived, as well as his looks and his life. For Natasa, Massilia must have seemed like a swamp compared to this, and yet she'd said she was torn. Natasa claimed she'd grown to love the trees and the greenery of his world in Gaul, but perhaps in the pain of her daughter's death, she'd forgotten Egypt's glory?

On the final day of his trip down the Nile, Thebes appeared around the river's bend. Pyramids, temples, and statuary taller than the trees in the great forests of Gaul peppered the golden sea of sand stretching in every direction.

"You see those statues?" said a dark, old man standing nearby. He pointed to the north, at the colossal monuments carved into ancient desert hills. "They call it the Valley of the Kings."

The monuments rose from the sands like giant sentinels, endlessly guarding buildings with steps larger than most ships.

"Tombs of old," the man continued. "Our pharaoh, Lord Ankhwenefer, the Good Being of Isis, battled on those grounds and reclaimed them for Egypt." Finnian turned to the dark, wrinkled man. "You're a foreigner," the man explained. "I thought I'd tell you. These are glorious days for Egypt, my son."

They rounded a turn in the river and entered the harbor at Thebes. Flags bearing the phoenix, similar to the one on Natasa's seal, hung from the promenade at the docks. Finnian's heart strummed like a hummingbird's wings. It was time to meet Natasa's king. He disembarked from the ship and discovered directions to the palace as well as a few of the other locations in which he needed to deliver messages. He did those assignments first, learning the lay of the land, taking inventory of the state of the city, and finding an inn in which to stay. Thebes was busy with construction; new buildings and statues popping up in every direction he turned. Workers carved the image of the pharaoh out of an alabaster block in the courtyard outside of an administrative building. A library rose from its foundation as well. Everywhere, beautiful white marble buildings glowed in the sun. He'd long ago sold his green cloak to someone going north, trading it in for a simple white tunic, sandals, and a headscarf. His pale skin had turned a copper color during the trip, and he'd allowed his golden beard to grow in. He was sure he wouldn't be recognizable to anyone at home.

After delivering his other messages and freshening up at the inn, he decided to visit the king. Normally a courier delivering a message needing no immediate reply would deliver his message to a guard who would take the message to the king, but Finnian wanted to meet Lord

Ankhwenefer. It was important. Finnian stopped in the market for a drink of ale to calm his nerves and then made his way to the palace. Dozens of guards secured the entry. He rose to his full height, swung back his shoulders, and raised his chin.

"I come with a message for Pharaoh Ankhwenefer, lord of these lands," Finnian declared as they crossed their xystons to block his path.

"Give it to us and we will deliver it," the main guard replied.

"I have specific instructions to deliver it myself," he answered, a sheen of sweat forming upon his brow. He was about to lose his nerve.

"The pharaoh hasn't approved any guests for the evening."

"Tell him the Lady Natasa has sent me," Finnian answered with as much authority as he could muster.

The guard shrugged to his mates and strode inside the palace. Finnian gazed about the courtyard, noting the gilded statues, fountains, and lush gardens. Dark, beautiful women, golden bangles upon their arms, laughed in the shade while servants fanned them. Elegant men, their long, thick black hair in braids and woven in golden strands, walked past, deep in discussion. Everything was decadent and surreal. This was a king he was visiting, and Natasa had been his betrothed. Again, Finnian wondered how he, a mere scribe from the north, could ever have competed against this.

He was grateful he hadn't understood the world a noble of Egypt inhabited, for if he knew, he'd never have begged Natasa to give him first rites at Beltane, nor courted her afterward. A wave of heat passed through his body, and his heart ached as he remembered her kiss and the look in her eyes when she'd shown him the Way of the Goddess under the deep canopy of the forest. She'd made him a man that night and given him the sweetest gift he'd ever receive. Their months of courting afterward had been the best days of his life. No, he thought as he looked around the courtyard, though he felt the fool now, he was grateful he'd had no idea of the opulent life led by the pharaoh of Egypt. Thanks to his innocent ignorance, Finnian now knew the taste of love.

"The pharaoh will see you," the guard announced, startling him back to the present.

Finnian sucked in a breath and followed a pair of guards inside. If he'd thought the courtyards and exterior of the Egyptian buildings were magnificent, the interior of the palace was even more so. He'd studied Egyptian hieroglyphs at the court in Massilia, so a few of the inscriptions were familiar. Every drawing on the walls was more beautiful than anything he'd ever done himself. Perhaps he could convince the king to let him stay and study them? The scribe in him yearned to copy their designs and add them to the manuscript he carried in his satchel.

The guards led him to a pair of huge golden doors, and another set of guards opened them as they approached. Finnian gulped and clutched his messenger's bag to his side, crossing the threshold to meet Natasa's king.

☥

Ankhwenefer's head snapped toward the door when the stranger entered his study, but the king remained seated at his desk, covered in maps, figurines, and scrolls, fingering his lapis ring as he considered the man Natasa had sent. Ankhwenefer's men gathered around a second table beside the large window overlooking the royal gardens, playing a game that involved carved, ivory pieces they tossed onto a board. Their golden goblets filled with wine and food piled high on plates before them, oblivious to the disturbance in the room. The group laughed and the stranger flinched as his shockingly blue eyes darted around the study. Ankhwenefer wondered if the man regretted his request to deliver the correspondence himself. The messenger was the sole pale man in the room.

"What is your name, scribe, who comes in the name of Lady Natasa?" Ankhwenefer demanded. At his words, the room grew silent, and all the men turned to stare at the tall, blond man at the door.

The stranger crossed the room, bowed, and then rose to look the Ankhwenefer in the eye. He was an inch taller than Ankhwenefer, and the king had to glance up to meet the messenger's gaze. Already, he hated this man, this intruder.

"I am Finnian, son of Atticus, and scribe of the druid high priest, Taran of Massilia," he replied, never taking his eyes from Ankhwenefer's face. "I come to deliver two messages directly unto Lord Ankhwenefer's hands."

Ankhwenefer's mouth went dry as placed his hand over his heart. "Is she on her way?"

"No, Your Majesty," Finnian replied, opening his satchel, taking out two letters, and holding them out before him.

Ankhwenefer ripped the scrolls from Finnian's hands.

"Sir," Finnian said, pointing to the scrolls, "only one is from Lady Natasa. The other is from her father."

"Well, scribe," Ankhwenefer asked, clicking his tongue. "Which one is which?"

"Hers bears the symbol of the phoenix."

Ankhwenefer looked closer and nodded. Hecataeus used the stamp of the royal family of Behdet, but Natasa had begun using one of her own, bearing Ankhwenefer's signet. His heartbeat throbbed in his ears as he thought of all her letters throughout the years. Why had she sent a messenger this time?

"Yes," the pharaoh murmured, running his finger along the raised, waxen form. "She's been using this seal for a while. I'm sorry, I'd forgotten."

"She requested I make it for her, when we first met," Finnian replied, rising up even taller and tossing his long, golden hair over his shoulder.

Ankhwenefer glanced up at the messenger, gaze narrowing, jaw clenching, a painful, stabbing sensation building in his gut. "What did you say your name was?"

"Finnian, Your Majesty."

Ankhwenefer took a step closer, noting the messenger's age. He was young, younger than Natasa even, his hair and skin as golden as the sun. She'd called him Apollo in one of her letters. Ankhwenefer's pulse raced as he considered Natasa spending time in this man's company.

"She's mentioned you," Ankhwenefer said, turning away, unable to look at the boy. Ankhwenefer's palms were now sweaty, and the gnawing in his gut was turning into a constant throb. He placed Hecataeus's scroll on his desk and slipped open Natasa's letter. His comrades stood at attention, all eyes upon their pharaoh. As he read her words to himself, his vision darkened. The words grew blurry. He blinked.

My love, the winter skies of Gaul weep constantly, building up fluid in my lungs. I can't seem to swim out of this. Aurelia says I'm too weak to shake this infection. I'm too weak to even write this letter myself...

Ankhwenefer let his arm drop to his side, the ache in his abdomen had spread to his chest, and he felt as if someone had put a cover over his head to suffocate him. Still clutching the waxy paper, he looked to Finnian, "What is the meaning of this?"

"It's her final letter to you, Your Majesty. She asked me to pen it in her last moments of life."

Heart pounding, room spinning, Ankhwenefer glanced down again at the parchment.

...I bear a wound from which I can never recover. I regret abandoning you in this way, but I must go to our daughter, for she calls to me and I cannot refuse. You must go on without me...

Khaleme raced to his king's side and placed a hand on Ankhwenefer's shoulder. "My lord, I'm so sorry."

Ankhwenefer slapped the parchment into his general's chest and tore open Hecataeus's letter. This one, he read aloud.

Dear Pharaoh,

Congratulations on your victories. The merchants tell me Alexandria is shaking with fear and strives to keep news of the success of your rebellion from Macedonian, Syrian, and Roman ears. This is impossible of course, given the way merchants trade gossip as they trade goods. Yet the Ptolemy leadership has managed to hide the extent of your domination from their Macedonian counterparts, so be careful. What may seem like a peace treaty between the

Lower and Upper Kingdoms is a pause while Ptolemy V grows older and a solution is found with the Seleucids. The generals know that without a true king, they will continue to fail. As you are the fully grown and more powerful pharaoh, use this time wisely.

But it is for other reasons I write you. Natasa died of a cough this winter, and we buried her in the Celtic cemetery, in a place of honor. Taran says it's the least they could do, given the wisdom she left them. Neffa claims a new stream of consciousness has been born, that out of the merging of the Celtic and Egyptian wisdom will rise a new form of devotion. I have no idea what she means, but perhaps it means something to you, and grants you some sort of joy in this dark moment. Maybe Natasa and Helena will live on in these new teachings, and our efforts will amount to something? I cannot say, for my failure to keep them alive is still too painful.

Neffa will remain in Gaul with Taran. I make for Athens to settle a family debt and request to meet you in Thebes at the end of the year, to fetch Eleni.

I'm sorry, my lord. I failed to do the one thing you asked—to keep your family safe.

Your Servant,

Hecataeus

Ankhwenefer dropped the scroll to the floor and collapsed as his knees gave out. He slammed his hands on the ground, fingers clutching at the woven carpet, and screamed like a hawk about to attack. He felt his men around him, stroking his head, his back, and his hair.

Ankhwenefer's chest seared with pain as if Set himself had lodged a fist inside of him and the god of chaos was tearing his heart, bit by bit, into strips of agony. Natasa, his twin flame, his love, his true queen, was dead. The words passed before his mind's eye, but something within him refused to accept them. She wasn't supposed to die. He pounded his fist on the hard, stone floor like a defiant child. Natasa was to return to his side and ride with him to victory. How dare the gods keep her from his side for years, in a foreign land surrounded by strangers, only to take her life and send this man-child from the north to him instead?

The pharaoh raised his head, pointing his finger at the messenger. "You are *Finnian*," he screamed. He rose to attack, but his men held him back. He wanted the boy dead and could make it so. The king's word was law. Ankhwenefer was about to command his guards to arrest the stranger when he caught Finnian's eye and noticed tears the messenger held back.

"You were there when she died, weren't you?" Ankhwenefer asked, trembling like a caged animal within his friends' grips.

"Yes, Your Majesty," Finnian replied, his voice cracking. "I was by her side."

"You two were close, weren't you?" the king accused.

"Yes, we were."

Ankhwenefer tugged at Khaleme and Min, trying to get out of their grip to strike out at Finnian, but his friend's nails dug into his bicep as Khaleme tightened his grip.

"Tell me, scribe," the pharaoh begged, "did she mention me when she died?"

"Yes," Finnian whispered, "she did."

"What did she say?"

"She said," Finnian began, before pausing, pressing his mouth into a thin line.

In the silence that followed, Ankhwenefer felt a darkness settle deep within him. It cut through his heart down to a place where only his raw emotions existed. What if she'd forgotten him in her dying moments?

"What did she say?" Ankhwenefer yelled, his words echoing off his granite walls.

"She said to tell her golden eagle king she was sorry."

Ankhwenefer roared like a wounded dog and fell again to his

knees, sobbing and pounding at the floor as if he could break it and fall through into the center of the earth.

"*Get out,*" he wailed.

Finnian fled from the room, the golden doors slamming behind him, leaving Ankhwenefer to his agony.

21

Common Ground

"If you are a leader of peace, listen to the discourse of the petitioner. Be not abrupt with him; that would trouble him."
~Ptah-Hotep

Thebes, Egypt, 196 BCE

Finnian awoke in the middle of the night to the sound of someone pounding on his door.

"Open, Finnian of the North. Pharaoh Ankhwenefer calls upon you."

He made his way to the door, rubbing the sleep from his eyes as he opened it. Two of the men who had consoled the king earlier stood at attention. It was the Ethiopian who caught Finnian's gaze—no one in his world looked so savage and yet so wise.

"It is late," Finnian said, fighting a yawn. "Can the pharaoh not call in the morning?"

"Who are you to deny the pharaoh?" the smaller man demanded.

"Min," the Ethiopian admonished, "no need to be so harsh. He has a point."

The man called Min dropped his shoulders and looked to Finnian, shrugging. "Can we come in, sir?"

Finnian was surprised but nodded. "Of course," he said, opening the door wider so that the massive Ethiopian could fit through. As they entered, the king himself appeared from behind the Ethiopian, and the three men stood by the window, none looking quite like they knew what to do.

"I'm sorry, I have nowhere for you to sit," Finnian said, now wide awake and nervous. He couldn't believe the pharaoh of Upper Egypt was in his room.

The dark king sat on the floor, and the other two followed his lead.

Finnian scratched his bushy, blond head. "What is it I can do for you?"

Ankhwenefer threw back the hood of his cloak hiding him from those still awake in the inn. His once kohl-lined eyes were now raw and bloodshot.

"I'm sorry to disturb you, Finnian," the pharaoh began, his voice hoarse and thick. "These are my friends and companions, Min, Captain of my Guard, and Khaleme, General of Kush. Now, I need some more answers from you."

"I understand sir, but couldn't it have waited until morning?" Finnian asked.

"No," the royal answered, his lips drawn into a tight line. "Do you think I can sleep after the news you delivered today? Tell me, boy, have you ever lost someone you loved?"

Finnian looked the pharaoh in the eye. "Yes, twice."

Ankhwenefer raised his chin. "Have you ever lost the love of your life?"

"Yes," Finnian replied, clenching his fists. What was this man up to?

Ankhwenefer stood, tossed his cloak on Finnian's bed, and began to pace the room. He wore a simple white tunic and his sword at his waist. "How long did you know Natasa?"

"Two years."

"What was this book you two were writing?"

Finnian frowned. Natasa *had* mentioned their relationship in her letters. How much had she confessed? "She would channel the goddess, and I wrote down what she said."

"What did she say?"

Finnian felt a surge of energy flow through him. This was what Natasa would have wanted. He eyed Ankhwenefer and saw what she had loved—he was the male version of her. The way he held his head and gestured his arms while talking was familiar. He was curious and demanding, as was she. Natasa had been kinder, and yet the pair were complements. Finnian crossed the room and opened his satchel.

"I have the entire manuscript here, sir," he replied, "but I don't think we could finish it tonight. It took us over a year to write."

"When must you return to the north?" Ankhwenefer asked.

"Never," Finnian admitted. "I'm free to go as I please. I'm a scribe, I can make money anywhere."

Ankhwenefer sat on Finnian's bed, patted the space beside him, and said, his voice now low and soft, "Read part of it to me. Please."

Finnian shuffled his stack of loose papers. He hadn't bound the original copies, and on the top of the stack was the page called "The Lovers." He looked to Ankhwenefer and shrugged. "Fine. Let's start here." Finnian cleared his throat and then began.

"Throughout the ages, from era to era and eon to eon and every second of your life, once you realize you are not whole, you search for the one who will complete you. You do not search in vain, for the one to complete you is real, and the path to your other half is inside your heart—where you live together for all time. You are never apart and therefore you are already whole.

Your other half does indeed have a physical manifestation, and you long to meet. The way to experience this reunion of souls on Earth is the freedom to be open to love, yet you make rules about love, marriage, who you can or can't marry, and why. Promises lasting until death. Arranging love as if it could be controlled. This is misguided, for in these rules you often prevent yourself from the freedom of union with your other half in the physical realm.

Make no mistake, regardless of whom you do or don't share your bed with, in spirit you are with your beloved—in the heart you are together. One flame in two bodies.

The perfect male. The perfect female."

Finnian stopped reading and the room hung with a heavy silence. Ankhwenefer let his head hang low upon his chest.

"She was the perfect female," he choked, "but I am not the perfect male." The pharaoh faced Finnian. "Perhaps you're the perfect male?"

"No," Finnian replied, his jaw tight. "You're trying to figure out my role in her life."

"I am."

"I'll be honest, I love her," Finnian said, and Pharaoh's glittering gaze narrowed. Finnian swallowed, found his courage, and continued. "The first time I laid eyes upon her, I found her trying to kill herself with her knife, grieving the loss of her child."

"She wanted to take her own life?" Ankhwenefer gasped and rose from his seat, his hand going to the hilt of his sword. His fingers hesitated for a moment above the gleaming weapon, shaking like spider's legs before forming into a fist, catching himself before he drew his weapon, and instead sitting back down on the bed.

"Yes," Finnian replied, "so great was her grief she didn't speak for over a year after Helena's murder, blaming herself and stewing in her despair. One day, I stumbled upon her and found her cutting her arms and wrists. I stopped her…"

He paused as he remembered the terror he'd felt the day he'd first approached the cabin on his horse, per the request of Taran, to help the family. How shocked he'd been to find such a beautiful, yet broken creature. He recalled the blood pouring from her wrist and the wild look in her shocking green eyes when she'd first spoken.

"Yet," Finnian continued, looking at the pharaoh's pale face, "she rose from her pain and became whole. Yes, I love her very much, and I asked her to refuse you and marry me instead, but she denied me my wish. If she hadn't become sick, she would be here before you, not I. The death of her child haunted her. She once told me the childless mother felt as if a sword were piercing her heart at all times. She never recovered from her loss, and she couldn't live upon the Earth any longer, regardless of how much you or I love her, or how much she loved us."

Ankhwenefer groaned and dropped his head in his hands. "My

family killed our Helena. Natasa blamed herself, but I never should have been her lover when it was forbidden. My goddess, it was so hard to be near her and not make love."

Finnian shifted in discomfort; having spent months courting Natasa in purity while knowing the pleasure of her body, he understood the king's words. Denying his pleasure had been excruciating. Ankhwenefer noticed Finnian's expression and grabbed his forearm.

"You understand then, that after years without her, against my own wishes, I had to know her touch. We were mated in the holy temple when we were both so young. She was my source of power, and I hers. This is the way of Anit-Shadya. To be denied our love was painful."

Finnian regarded the manuscript in his lap. "The goddess says such laws are wrong," he noted, pointing to the line that said so. "That we should be open to love and not stop it."

"Yes," Ankhwenefer said, wiping his eyes with the back of his hand, "but my mother and father, the king and queen, disagreed with such sentiments and made our love a crime, punishable by death."

"The death of a child, my lord?" Finnian frowned. "I don't understand why Helena paid for your crime."

"The punishment for our crime was death to both of us, and we'd agreed together that the price was worth it. Natasa and I never thought they'd use our child as a proxy for my part in the act, but they did, as was their right, under the law."

Finnian drew away from the king. Now everything made sense. He was grateful to be a regular man of no importance, a man for whom no one would use a child in such a way to keep alive.

"Trust me," Pharaoh said, the tension in his body beginning to ease, "if we'd known they'd kill her instead, we never would have indulged in our pleasure."

Ankhwenefer stared off into space, and Finnian glanced at his companions. They sat, legs folded in their places, staring without blinking, or so it seemed.

"You knew her?" he asked them.

"Yes," the man named Min replied, "I grew up with her. She was a wonderful woman."

"I met her briefly," Khaleme answered in a low, thick voice. "She was a most powerful magician."

Finnian nodded. "Yes, she was. Natasa was the goddess herself."

Ankhwenefer made to stand. He looked down at Finnian, defeated yet proud, like the etchings on his temple walls. Finnian shivered under his cold gaze. "I agree with you, Finnian, she was the goddess. Min, Khaleme, please escort me to the palace."

The two men rose from the floor and walked to the pharaoh's side. Ankhwenefer turned to Finnian. "Come tomorrow to the palace and read to me. I'll have a room made up for you, and you can stay at my court until you have read me the whole book. I want to know what she told you."

Finnian fought back a grimace. He had no choice but to obey the king. It was the way of the world, and yet...

"I will do as you ask, my lord, but in return, I wish to study and copy the hieroglyphs of your palace and temples. I think I will need them in the future."

Ankhwenefer shrugged. "Fine with me. Report at midday."

"Yes, my lord."

22

Homecoming

The Greeks, in exchange for safe passage of their soldiers from Thebes to the north, had promised a temporary halt to the war. The troops were needed to fight off the Seleucids in Syria. Many were stationed north of Lycopolis to ensure Ankhwenefer abided by the treaty and didn't attempt to take Memphis while the Macedonians were so weak. Ankhwenefer constructed a fortress south of Lycopolis, in order that he might begin to establish the official boundary of the Upper Kingdom. Two kingdoms of Egypt, two pharaohs, and Lycopolis in between.

Thebes and Behdet, Egypt, 196 BCE

Ankhwenefer found the scribe in the temple, discussing a stele with the Theban priests. They hadn't wanted to share the space with the foreigner, claiming their secrets couldn't be divulged to a northerner, but the pharaoh no longer cared what the priests thought. Years of worshiping the gods had granted him nothing but grief. Besides, this was part of the deal he'd made with the young man—a few temple secrets for the opportunity to hear Natasa speak from beyond the grave. It was worth it. Ankhwenefer wasn't sure what the priests were so concerned about—if he himself didn't understand half of what was written on the ancient walls, how could the light-skinned man of the north understand it?

"Finnian," he called out.

The younger man turned and smiled at Ankhwenefer. The sunlight shone through the window upon his golden hair, which he wore tied back in a neat, scholarly ribbon. When Finnian arrived in Thebes a few months prior, he'd worn a beard, which he shaved once he began spending more time in the court. It had been a funny sight at first, for the bottom half of his face was so much paler than the top. A few days under the rays of Ra cured him of the odd condition, and now he was no longer as white as marble but sported a rather deep, rich tan, which was quite striking with his golden hair and bright blue eyes. Ankhwenefer's chest still squeezed tight every time he looked at Finnian—Natasa had called him pure sweetness in one of her letters. After spending time getting to know Finnian, Ankhwenefer had to agree with her, the scribe was sweet as well as kind, intelligent, and interesting. Why then, had she turned down the boy's proposal? Had she done so out of love for Ankhwenefer, or duty toward her kingdom? It was a question that haunted Ankhwenefer whenever he was in Finnian's company.

"Yes, Your Majesty," Finnian replied, bowing low.

"We have finished the book," Ankhwenefer said.

"Yes, my lord. I've read it to you three times now. I have also made you your very own copy to read whenever you wish."

"Then I think we have finished our business together," Ankhwenefer replied. "I head to Behdet for the first time since my daughter's murder to collect my court and escort them here, to Thebes."

"Your court?" Finnian asked.

"Yes, my queen, sons, musicians, priests, and priestesses. I have a vizier as well, and I need to relocate my best healers, that I might integrate them with the Houses of Healing here."

"Queen," Finnian said, eyebrows pinched. "Yes, I remember Natasa mentioning the queen."

Ankhwenefer shifted in his place under the scrutiny of the boy's pale eyes.

"I can't imagine wanting more than one wife. Not with a woman like Natasa at my side," Finnian answered, rising to his full height.

Many words crossed his mind, but Ankhwenefer swallowed them down. He didn't want his time with Finnian to end on a bad note. "Trust me," he said in a low growl, "it is not about what I want. Nothing in my life, with the exception of taking Natasa as my spiritual companion, has ever been about what I want."

Finnian's face flushed and he looked away. "I'm sorry, my lord, my words were uncalled for."

"Don't let it bother you," Ankhwenefer continued, placing his hand on the young man's shoulder. "I leave tomorrow. If you wish, you can join me on this trip and see where Natasa grew up."

Finnian stepped back, his eyes glittering as tears formed. Ankhwenefer grimaced. Finnian wore his love for Natasa so openly.

"No, thank you," Finnian answered, waving his hand. "I don't need to see any more of her life. I appreciate you letting me stay in Thebes a bit longer. There's one more stele I wish to copy, and then I'll be on my way."

"Where will you go?" Ankhwenefer asked. While Finnian's relationship with Natasa made him uncomfortable, he didn't want the young man to leave. Being near him gave Ankhwenefer a sense of her final years on Earth. Finnian had not only shared Natasa's last great work for the goddess, but also many stories about her life in Gaul. It was obvious Natasa's life in the north had been full of love, laughter, and adventure. After what he and his family had put her through, it comforted Ankhwenefer to know Natasa experienced joy before she died.

He also knew Finnian left out a few events from his stories, and from the glow in his blue eyes and the flush of his cheeks when he spoke of her, Ankhwenefer could guess Finnian had known Natasa's kiss. How much of her the young man had known, Ankhwenefer didn't want to ask. It pained him to consider the pair might have been lovers, and while he'd spent their separation covered in blood and death, she'd fallen in love with another man. He'd rather not know.

"To Syria and then on to the Indo-Greek kingdom in Punjab," Finnian replied. "It is an area I've longed to see, but first, I want to spend time in Alexandria. The Great Library is amazing, and I desire to spend many long weeks in it."

"Natasa also loved the Great Library of Alexandria," Ankhwenefer recalled as a stab of pain pierced through his side. "She even dressed up as a boy to get in."

"She disguised herself as a man?" Finnian asked.

"Yes, she loved words and books, and nothing would stop her." Ankhwenefer recalled the moment on the balcony when his love for her had become crystal clear. "She vowed she wouldn't grow old weaving my blankets and clothes. Rather she was a weaver of words and spells."

Finnian tilted his head and smiled. "She was a magician until her last breath. I don't think she would have made a good queen, my lord. Goddesses don't do well under such controlled conditions."

"No," Ankhwenefer said. "I suppose they don't."

The two men looked at one another in silence. They weren't friends, and yet they shared a very special bond.

When he couldn't take the silence any longer, Ankhwenefer spoke, "It's been a pleasure to spend time with you Finnian. Thank you for delivering Natasa's final letter to me personally. It was important we meet. I know it pleases her."

Finnian nodded. "Yes, Your Majesty, she is very pleased."

Ankhwenefer held out his hand and the scribe shook it. The boy's handshake was steady and sure. "Safe travels, Finnian of the North."

"To you as well, Lord Ankhwenefer."

Ankhwenefer turned and left the golden boy in his temple.

☥

The next morning, the pharaoh and his entourage boarded the royal flotilla to Behdet. His arrival in Behdet was celebrated with parades, dances, singing, and festivals. Ruia had insisted upon it. As he approached the palace of Behdet on his white horse in his pharaoh's crown and phoenix collar, his people lined the streets singing his praises. In the royal garden stood his queen, dressed in their mother's collar and crown, her back straight and chin held high. Weret was now the high queen of Behdet, and therefore all of Egypt. At her side stood their sons: Ankhmaat, who was now seven, and Khenefer, barely three. Ruia and Silus were there with their children, as well as Alexa, Ennaeus, and Iu-Amon. Ankhwenefer dismounted Biriq and walked to his family, his cape fluttering in the slight breeze. Ennaeus stepped forward to greet him.

"Lord and Pharaoh, Ankhwenefer, Good Being of Isis and Golden Eagle King, the city of your birth welcome you. You have been away many long years and you have fought bravely. We thank you for your service."

Ennaeus and the entire court bowed before him. Ankhwenefer gazed at them, his heart heavy like a stone tablet. He had no desire to be near them. He turned to address the crowd, "I have returned, but only for a little while. I call my queen and sons to Thebes. King Silus and Queen Ruia shall rule Behdet in my stead. We may be at peace with Ptolemy right now, but never for a moment think this war is over. We have united with Nubia and Kush, and now control a vast empire; with time, however, the Lower Kingdom will try to take it back, and when they do, we must be ready. For this reason, Behdet will remain the center of our military and support the nation in a critical way."

The crowd applauded. There were many soldiers in attendance. Ankhwenefer bowed to them and then turned to Weret. Her eyes were lined not only with kohl and ground lapis but also the beginnings of wrinkles. He kissed her lips, pursed and unwelcoming. How was he going to live the rest of his life with this woman? He bent down to his eldest son, and his heart swelled as Ankhmaat looked him in the eye. To the boy, the pharaoh was a stranger, so much time had passed. He picked up little Khenefer and held him close.

"Come," he said to Ankhmaat and Weret, offering his arm as was protocol. "We must greet our people in the great hall."

☥

Hours later, Ankhwenefer found himself alone in his chambers, reading *The Goddess of the South*. He'd practically memorized the text, but there was one picture of a naked woman dancing under the moon that always held him spellbound—Finnian had captured Natasa's image so perfectly, Ankhwenefer felt as though he held her in his hands. He poured himself another goblet of wine and rose from his seat. Without thinking, he left his apartments and walked toward the home Natasa and Helena had shared with Hecataeus and Corinna.

When he arrived, he found it in disarray. Woven panels had been tied across the windows, and he opened them to let light in. Dust covered the furniture. Clothes, shoes, toys, and other personal items were strewn across the floors and hanging from overturned chairs as if someone had gone through the home looking for something. He entered the room Natasa and Helena shared. In a corner sat the pandura he'd kept there and beside it, a toy cat he'd given his little girl. He picked up the toy and held it to his chest, sniffing it and imagining the smell of horses and rosemary, as if his daughter had just held it. He lay down on the musty bed, cradling the toy and curling up in a ball. As he clutched the dirty blankets, he recalled the last time he'd been in this bed. It was the night Natasa had called for him after his recovery and they'd made love. His body ached as he recalled the taste of her warm, jasmine-scented flesh.

A sound from the main room made him jump up. He ran toward it, expecting to see an intruder. Instead, he found the cat, Princeling, blinking at him with bright blue eyes. The beast meowed and then dashed away, jumping out the window. Ankhwenefer stared after it, frozen at the spot, still clutching Helena's toy to his chest.

"Your Majesty?" a female voice asked from behind him.

He spun and found Eleni standing in the doorway. She was a grown woman now, at least sixteen, and about the same age as Natasa when they'd fallen in love. Her brown and golden hair fell over her full breasts to her waist, and her blue eyes were brimming with tears.

"Eleni," he said, placing the toy on the table. He took her into his arms and squeezed her in his embrace. He stepped back to look at her, hands still clutching her shoulders. "Is it you? How did you know I'd be here?"

"I saw Min standing outside and assumed you were here," she replied, tugging away from his grip. She held a cedar box under her bosom. Ankhwenefer recognized it.

"Bastyre gave this to me before she left," Eleni continued. "She said it was important I give it to you and no one else. I've kept it all these years."

He took the box from her hands and turned to set it on the dusty table. "Thank you, Eleni."

Ankhwenefer opened the box and peered inside. Just as he expected, the two Wands of Horus sparkled in the sunlight streaming in through the door. He touched one and felt a shock of energy pour through him. He drew back his hand in fear. This was Natasa's energy; he could feel it. He started to close the box when a glimmer of gold and lapis caught his eye. His heart splintered as he took Natasa's ring and placed it on his smallest finger. It fit.

"I will never take this off," he whispered, noticing one more item in the small chest—the bloodstone from his brother, and the color of red filled his vision. "Chanax," he shouted, holding the necklace up for Eleni to see. "He killed Helena and thus he killed Natasa."

Eleni trembled. "Oh, Ankhwenefer, I'm so sorry." She fell into his arms, and he squeezed her body closer to his own. Her jasmine scent filled his nose. She gazed up into his eyes and whispered, "Is there anything I can do for you, anything to take away the pain?"

Ankhwenefer trembled at her beauty. She looked so much like Natasa when she was younger.

"I know you're hurting," she continued, as she pushed a lock of his hair behind his ear. "Let me help you."

She drew his face close and placed her lips upon his. He dropped the bloodstone to the floor and tried to step away, but Eleni held him in her embrace. Her desperation and pain were real, and they matched his. She understood his agony. Ankhwenefer drew her closer and returned her kiss, his fingertips tracing the small of her back. He hadn't felt the arms of a woman in years, not since he'd last been with Natasa before she'd left him. He needed to forget her touch and her death, if even for a moment. The heat swirled between them, and the pharaoh lost his mind.

Just as he gave in, Princeling the cat landed beside them on the table. Startled, Ankhwenefer jumped up and back, jerking himself from Eleni's warm, sweet lips. He took in her eager face and a wave of nausea churned through his innards.

"Eleni, this is wrong."

He backed up from her and put the length of the table between them. She stumbled closer. "My lord, I thought you wanted me to please you. The way you kissed me, I assumed you needed me."

"The way I kissed you?" Ankhwenefer replied, running his hand through his hair. "You were the one who offered yourself to me. I was trying to console you."

"I was trying to console *you,*" she yelled, wringing her hands, tears now streaming down her round face.

He wanted to hold her and comfort her and tell her everything was fine, but he didn't dare. There was something in her gaze that scared him. While she looked like Natasa, she wasn't. What was wrong with him for letting it go so far? He was a grown man, and she barely a woman yet.

"Eleni," he said, trying to sound calm, "I am the lord and pharaoh of this land. I do not have the luxury of taking advantage of young girls. I'm to be a model, not a scoundrel."

"But I want it. I've always wanted it," she whispered, her wet, full lips parted ever so slightly.

He grabbed the cedar box. "I'm sorry, Eleni," he replied, holding his hand in the air, "but I don't."

As he made to leave, he stepped on the bloodstone and picked it up. He wanted to throw it across the room and scream with all his might. Instead, he put it in the box next to the wands. If Natasa had kept it all these years, so would he. He turned to Eleni.

"I'm sorry," he said, softer this time. "I apologize for my actions. I must go now. I have business with the court. We ride out the day after tomorrow and you're to join us. Your father will be in Thebes later this month to collect you."

Eleni hugged herself, squeezing her nails into her forearms, her lower lip trembling, and Ankhwenefer wanted to comfort her but refrained. She was no longer a little girl sitting on his knee while he told her tall tales and charmed her with gifts. She was a woman, and not one he could be trusted with.

"I won't go with you," she said, her voice now hissing like a cobra's.

"Your father expects me to deliver you," Ankhwenefer explained.

"No," she yelled, pointing a finger at him. "You can't show up after abandoning me for years and tell me what to do. Neither of you can."

She sprinted past him and out the door, leaving him alone with the cobwebs and the cat.

23

Proposals and Refusals

"He says to his heart: "O come, my heart that I may speak to you,
And you shall answer me my verses,
Explain to me what is throughout the land,
How the once bright ones are cast down!"
~ The Words of Khakheperreseneb, Late Twelfth or Thirteenth Dynasty

Behdet, Egypt, 196 BCE

On his last day in Behdet, Ankhwenefer walked to the temple of Isis to visit the high priestess, dragging his feet in the sand as he approached. It was here he'd given Natasa her first rites. His own chambers also held memories of her, which was why he no longer wished to live in Behdet, but the temple of Isis had been her true home.

Alexa, the high priestess of Isis, met him in the courtyard. She wore a light green dress and golden bands around her upper arms. Atop her head was the golden circlet he'd often seen Neferu-ankh-maat wear. When she bowed, his knees weakened. This wasn't going to be easy.

"Lord Ankhwenefer, welcome. Come, let us take shelter from the heat of the day."

She led him to a small pool upon which stood a statue of Isis. At the goddess's feet floated lily pads and white lotus flowers. Alexa took a handful of dried herbs from a pot and threw them into the water.

"May Our Lady oversee our conversation and lead us to wisdom," the high priestess sang in hushed tones. Then she beckoned him to sit on a bench beside the pool in the shade.

"Yes," Ankhwenefer said, picking his nails. "I could use some wisdom. What is it you wish to discuss, Lady Alexa?" He sat on his hands.

"Your plans for the temple of Isis," she replied. "I wish to know whether or not you want to continue the development of Anit-Shadya in your kingdom, for the sake of your sons and the line of kings, as well as the nobles with whom you aspire to cultivate loyalties."

"Yes." He nodded. "I've been giving it some thought."

"I know," she answered. "I've read some of your proposals. I take it you think Anit-Shadya is important and want the men of the court to participate?"

"Yes, but the priestesses should have a say in whom they pair with. They are to be in control."

She tossed her hair over her shoulder. "I've discussed it with the other priestesses, and they agree."

"In addition," he continued, his pulse now rising, "you may not re-assign a pair without agreement from both parties. Never shall a king, or a priest, or priestess, have the right to tear apart that which the goddess herself has bonded together."

"Are you willing to give up such power?" she asked. "Because Zethus and the priests of Horus are not."

"They are not the pharaoh of the land," he answered, crossing his arms.

"You feel very strongly about this, and while I agree with you, I must also warn you. Be careful with the priests. Isidor was the one who hurt you, and he's no longer here. The men who remain grant you your power."

"I will not deviate from this. You should agree with me. After the way Queen Keket assigned Natasa to eleven men? What would have happened if Iu-Amon hadn't stepped in? No man or woman shall ever tell one of your priestesses what they must do with their bodies. Is this clear?"

Alexa frowned. "Yes, my lord."

"What is it?" he asked, noting her discomfort.

"I was thinking about how wrongly Natasa was treated. Not only by your mother but by my own spiritual companion and her best friend."

"Chanax was *not* Natasa's friend," Ankhwenefer replied, his body tensing at the mention of his brother.

"Oh, but he was," Alexa argued. "The three of us were inseparable growing up. He adored her. I spent years in his arms, showing him the Way of the Goddess. Where did it lead him? To betray her. My Lord and Pharaoh, please forgive me for not noticing the darkness in his heart."

She lowered her head, dabbing her eyes with her sleeve. Ankhwenefer sat closer to her on the bench.

"It's not your fault," he said, rubbing her shoulders. "It's mine. I should have waited until I wore the crown to take Natasa into my embrace as my lover. It's my own fault she and Helena are dead."

Alexa shook her head. "We all had a hand in their deaths."

He rose from his place. It had been a long day and he desired solitude. "I must leave. Is there anything else?"

"Yes," she replied, her gaze drifting to the statue of Isis. "Now, for the difficult part."

"What?" Ankhwenefer asked.

"You are the pharaoh of Upper Egypt," Alexa said, still looking at the lily pool and wringing her hands, "and I am the high priestess of Behdet. The law states I'm to be your spiritual companion."

He jumped back and gasped. "What?"

"Your Majesty," she continued, rising from her place and taking his hand in hers, "Shadya is vital. Your health and spiritual wellness are critical for the kingdom. I know you haven't taken ceremony in many, many years. Since the horrible day your father reassigned our dear Natasa to your brother, your Anit-Shadya has been sporadic and done in secret when the two of you thought no one was looking."

His head began to throb and hot flashes swarmed across his skin.

He wanted nothing more than to flee the conversation.

"When were you last touched by the goddess?"

"Just before Helena was killed," he whispered. "Over three years."

"When did you last take proper ceremony in the temple?"

Ankhwenefer thought back. He couldn't remember. How long ago had it been since his father ripped Natasa from his side and banned him from the temple? Helena had been two. She would be ten now if she were alive. His chest seared with pain as if sliced with a sword. He feared falling apart in front of his high priestess.

Alexa stroked his cheek. "My lord, you must consider it. I offer myself to you of my own free will. Not only because it's my duty, but also because Natasa would want me to do this."

Ankhwenefer contemplated her offer. "I don't know if I can do it. I can have sex, but to be in a place of bliss without her, I have no idea."

"Don't worry," she replied. "I will show you, and you will remember."

The pharaoh drew away and wrung his hands. The answer wasn't clear, but he needed to decide, for the high priestess of Isis was waiting. He turned to face her. Alexa was a beautiful woman and quite desirable. He considered the handsome Finnian, and a pang of jealousy flashed through him, causing his throat to contract—Natasa had spent the past two years in the arms of another man, why should he refuse the sex of his high priestess?

"Yes," he agreed. "I accept your offer and am willing to bond with you. It is right that the pharaoh has his high priestess of Isis. We'll relocate your cult to Thebes. The temples there are splendid, there is one in Karnak that should suit your needs. I'm sure we can work with the Theban priesthood to create a sacred space for Our Lady and her priestesses."

"Thank you, Lord Ankhwenefer," Alexa answered, placing her palms together over her chest and bowing stiffly. "When would you like to begin? I can take ceremony this evening if you wish."

"No, not here," he said, shaking his head and looking up at the temple. "Too many memories. Besides, I have one more thing I must attend to. You head out to Thebes with your women as soon as possible. I'll send word to High Priest Setep and will meet you there when I'm ready."

"What is it you must do?" she asked.

"I must visit the temple of Seti I, in Abdju. I have a promise to fulfill."

24

The Wall—Revisited

"I wish I were your mirror so that you always looked at me.
I wish I were your garment so that you would always wear me.
I wish I were the water that washes your body.
I wish I were the unguent, O woman, that I could anoint you.
And the band around your breasts, and the beads around your
neck."

~ Egyptian Love Poem, New Kingdom

Abdju, Egypt, 196 BCE

Ankhwenefer led Khaleme and Min into the Osirian, forcing his every step. He was afraid, but he'd promised Natasa he'd use the wands in the Resurrection Bath. He had to at least try.

When they entered the quiet womb of a room, Khaleme inhaled and stretched out his arms. "This is a holy place. I can see why she wants the wands to be used here."

"I'm not sure I can do this," Ankhwenefer admitted, handing the small cedar chest to Khaleme. "Natasa should've been the one. I don't have her skill."

"You're her divine pair," Khaleme said. "Your intention and sincere effort will be enough. It's not about skill, it's about being open to love and your power."

Ankhwenefer took off his shoes, sword, clothes, and simple golden crown, the one he wore for casual affairs. He laid them in a pile near the entrance and shivered.

"I'm not sure I'm open to very much anymore. Nine years of war and the loss of one's lover and beloved child will do that to a man."

"Which is why you need this," Khaleme replied, opening the lid and holding out the box to his king. "Now, take the wands into your proper hands and walk into the pool."

Ankhwenefer glanced at his right hand and noted Natasa's ring. It gave him a bit of courage, but not much. He took the wands into his hands and felt her energy swirl through him. It made him feel ashamed and unworthy.

"I can't," he said, placing them back into the box.

"You must," Khaleme demanded.

Ankhwenefer clasped the wands again and this time allowed her energy to flow through him. Focusing on the Flower of Life carved into the wall, he walked toward the pool. It felt as though Natasa stood before him, drawing him closer with each breath.

"Come to me," she spoke to his heart.

He shivered as his feet entered the warm, spring-fed water. He walked into the pool until he was submerged up to his neck and closed his eyes.

A humming and vibration pulsed throughout his whole body as his muscles contracted and trembled all on their own. His hands, legs, arms, and feet tingled, and then he felt the tug at his abdomen and found himself in the realm of light. The Way of the cosmos still swirled around him, but now new events loomed on the horizon and old possibilities were long gone. Ankhwenefer sensed her even before she was there, for, in death, she was everywhere.

Natasa surrounded him, not as Natasa herself, but as a being of light. She swirled about his head and melded into him. It was not unlike when he'd traveled out of the body with her. Their Ba grew in size and pulsed. Relaxing, he allowed himself to fall into their light body, and their consciousness spread out across the universe. After years apart, they were now together, out of time, and the peace of the

All-One poured into his heart. This was what it felt like to be whole, and he wanted nothing more than to stay there forever, yet the pain of being so close without touching was excruciating. It burned him, like fire on his skin.

"*I love you,*" she said.

"*I love you,*" he answered, speaking to her without sound. "*I never want to leave this place.*"

"*I know,*" she replied, "*but you still have work to do in your body. You can come here often and renew yourself in this way. If you do this, you will live forever, like our ancestors of old.*"

"I can't," Ankhwenefer begged. "*I can't connect to you in this way over and over. I must move on, Natasa.*"

"*You must uncover the ancient mysteries of Egypt,*" she argued. "*We can still do it together, even though I'm no longer in my body. The Old Kings built the Osirion for such a connection. The ancients knew they could work with the whole of life, even the dead, from this place. This is our mission, why we were born, and why I left you the wands. Death need not stop us. In this place, you can renew your body and seek the answers to the universe. You can create the circumstances in the Way for you to succeed. Anything you desire, you can have, and I will be by your side.*"

"*All I want are you and Helena in my arms.*"

"*My love...*

They remained silent. Their love grew stronger, yet so did the pain and grief of their physical separation.

"*This is not a true Resurrection Bath if you are still dead,*" he declared. "*I do not wish to live forever if you aren't by my side.*"

"*Ankhmakis, don't do this.*"

"*Natasa, when I first used the wands in the apiary, I saw the two of us as a couple, defying mortality and creating a new Egypt with Helena at our side. All three of us together—the perfect trinity. They killed her and now the Way is slipping in a new direction. The story is different.*"

Her spirit didn't respond. He spoke the truth—the entire cosmos mourned the loss of the Golden Child, for, in her death, the course of history had been altered. His desire to be near Natasa was too much to bear. His soul burned in agony. He needed to let her go.

"I'm sorry, my love," he continued, this time out loud, his words echoing in the chamber, "but a man needs his woman's arms to be able to accomplish what we set out to do. You should have lived. You should have come home to me."

"*Ankhmakis, please, listen to me,*" she begged.

Ankhwenefer forced open his eyes and stepped out of the tub. Khaleme held the cedar chest open in his hands, and Ankhwenefer dropped the wands on top of the bloodstone in the box and shut it, closing one of Khaleme's hands over the top, as if to protect the contents from himself. Min wrapped him in a warm blanket. Ankhwenefer was shivering as the salty water dripped from his body, yet in spite of his grief, he felt as if he could run the entire way home to Thebes.

"I saw her," Min whispered, pointing to the pool. "Her image stood before you. Like a specter."

"I heard you speaking to her," Khaleme said. "You can connect to her even in death. How splendid."

"No," Ankhwenefer replied, still shivering, "it's not splendid. I can't bear it, Khaleme. Can't you see? How can I be near her and yet not touch her? How do I get over her?"

"She left you the wands so you could renew yourself like the kings of old," Khaleme admonished. "You should see how you glow right now."

"He's right," Min added, poking Ankhwenefer's chest as if to prove he was still alive. "You look like you did before the war. All of your scars are gone."

Ankhwenefer looked at his chest and rubbed it. He inspected his thigh and found the butterfly scars from his arrow wound had vanished. Min was correct; his skin was that of a twenty-year-old man.

"What if I don't want to renew myself?" he said, his jaw so tight he thought his eyes would burst out of his head. "What if I want to live only long enough to pass the crown on to one of my sons?"

"Well, this seems like a good way to do it," Min advised.

"No," Ankhwenefer said. "I need Natasa, not her magic."

"No man in his right mind would reject such a gift," Khaleme said.

"I'm not *in* my right mind," Ankhwenefer growled. "I'm grieving her. She left me behind, Khaleme. She chose death over me."

"What are you suggesting?" Khaleme said, stepping closer, cradling the cedar chest as if it held the keys to the kingdom.

"Natasa was a great healer. She wove the muscles in my thigh back together. She saved me from death's door when I was poisoned. Why did she let herself die?"

Ankhwenefer panted as the love he'd felt for Natasa melted into molten anger. His heart pounded in his chest and pain seared in the center of his back as if someone had stabbed him between the shoulder blades.

"Don't say such things," Min demanded.

"It's true. If Natasa wanted to be with me, she would have returned," he shoved past Min toward the exit. "I lost a daughter, too. Yet here I stand, alive and well." He nodded to the cedar box in Khaleme's hands. "We need to keep them safe. Natasa was right, in the wrong hands, the wands are dangerous. I'm sure others could use them in the same way, and not every king deserves such power. It's not merely about renewing the physical body. The wands grant the ability to co-create the events of time."

He put back on his clothes, fastened his sword around his waist, and placed his crown upon his head. His friends waited in silence, Khaleme glowering from beneath his painted brow, Min shifting back and forth on his feet, gaze darting between the other two men and the cedar box.

"I'd rather die than live forever without her," Ankhwenefer said. "Natasa abandoned me. My goal is to live long enough to hand my son the crown and then join her in death."

The pharaoh of the Upper Kingdom turned and marched out through the dark tunnel, torch in hand. As he did, he closed himself to Natasa, to their power, and to his heart. It hurt too much to think of her. Rather than live with her spirit close by, he built a wall and cut her off, even though such an act would make it harder to ever find her in this lifetime, or any other.

For now, it was easier this way.

25

Sweet Nothings

"Behold! It cannot happen—yet it happens! Hidden are the counsels of god."

~Fragment from the Tale of the Eloquent Peasant, Middle Kingdom Egypt

Memphis, Egypt, 196 BCE

Chanax,

I write to you, not out of pity nor duty, but rather to inform you that have won a great battle against me, for Natasa has died. Yet do not think this is victory, for it is I, not you, who sits on the Golden Throne in Thebes. It is I, not you, who wears the crown of Ramesses the Great while you rot away in darkness, cowering behind Metakryon in your temples in Memphis.

No, you are not victorious, yet you have won. For the light of this world has gone out, and of all people, you understand the pain of losing her. May that pain destroy you, knowing she died at your hands.

Signed,

Lord Ankhwenefer, Good Being of Isis and Golden Eagle King, Pharaoh of Upper Egypt

Chanax let the letter slide from his grip, spinning as it fluttered to the floor. He stared into the fire, searching for her Ka out of habit. Yes, this time she was dead.

A lump formed in his throat, his pain strangling him as if Ankhmakis had a physical hand around his neck. Chanax gripped the wooden arms of his chair and screamed out at the top of his lungs, howling like the jackals in the night. When he could scream no more, his gaze settled on the letter, blurry through his tears. It had been unsealed when they delivered it. Anything from the pharaoh of Upper Egypt was investigated. That meant Isidor knew what information it held and had allowed its delivery unto Chanax's hands.

His bastard father wanted him to know this agony.

Chanax rose from his chair and grasped the letter, crumpling it in his fists. He chucked it into the fire and relaxed the muscles on his face as he stared at the burning papyrus. For a moment he considered casting himself in along with it. Yet death by flame wasn't appealing. Instead, he poured himself a mug of wine and made his way to his desk. Picking up his reed and a piece of papyrus, he responded to the fiend.

Dear brother,

> *You will live alone, and you will die alone.*

> *That is victory enough for me.*

Chanax, Beloved of Set and Prince of Behdet

PART TWO

CIVILIZATION'S END

"When you know the song of your own being, you are able to communicate with every other being of life. Behind the matter you can see with your eyes is a frequency, a tone, a vibration. Both a sound and a symphony. You know this; it's in your music and your art. It is sacred geometry and it sings the universe into being. It is time, and it is unique for each living thing. Yet you are part of a greater song both infinitely small and infinitely large. If you can find it in yourself, if you can find the tone that has created the form you inhabit, you can begin to shape your body, heal your body, and grow your body with choice. You can work with the conductor who is already conducting, and that conductor is you.

Once you have done this, you will see that every form has a song, and everything that lives is of consciousness, and you can communicate with it, shape it, and create with it. Humanity has concentrated only on destruction, which requires no work. Creation is discipline. Creation is interest and interest is love. There is an equation for this force called love, but the mind of man cannot see it.

~ "The World," by Finnian, Scribe of the North

26

A Most Important Mission

The war with Syria raged for years, and Ptolemy's army lost many lands, including Judea. However, once Antiochus III gained this territory, he sought peace with the Ptolemaic Empire, and offered up his daughter, Cleopatra the Syrian, to the young pharaoh as his queen. Thus in 193 BCE, at the young age of twelve, the first Cleopatra found herself in Alexandria married to the seventeen-year-old pharaoh. So it would be that Ptolemy V Epiphanes would grow to become a man and king in his own right.

Ten Years Later

Memphis, Egypt, 186 BCE

Chanax strode down the long hall toward Metakryon's chambers. He'd never wanted to linger this long in Memphis, but thanks to his banishment by his brother from the Upper Kingdom, he now found himself a middle-aged man who'd squandered thirteen years in the one place he'd sworn he'd never return.

Thank goodness for the free-flowing opium and loose women, or he wouldn't have survived.

As he approached the high priest's chambers, Chanax froze. Several royal guards from Alexandria were stationed at the doors. His heart pounded in his chest and sweat formed upon his brow as horrible memories of childhood flooded his mind. Not a night passed that he didn't wake from a nightmare, fearing these same royal guards were in his room, summoning him to Philopater's late-night games.

"Gentlemen," he said with a flourish of his long, dark robes, "I believe High Priest Metakryon is expecting me."

"Yes, Lord Chanax," one of the men replied. "They await you."

He gulped down the bile forming in his mouth as the men opened the doors and he entered his master's chambers. Metakryon sat in his usual seat by the fire, and beside him lounged Isidor. Standing in the center of the room was none other than Ptolemy V Epiphanes, no longer a boy, but a grown man. He was built like a warhorse. His brown gaze glittered above his long, crooked nose. He wore the traditional white robes of the pharaoh, a golden circlet of olive leaves set in the brown curls framing his olive-skinned face. A golden cape was slung over his shoulder and his sword handle gleamed in the firelight.

At twenty-four years of age, Epiphanes reminded Chanax of a young Ankhmakis.

"Your Majesty." Chanax bowed low. "Forgive me. I didn't realize you'd be here."

"Or what?" Isidor snapped. "You would have been on time?"

"Of course, Lord Isidor," Chanax answered, giving his father a forced smile.

"No matter," the pharaoh of the Lower Kingdom of Egypt replied. "Let's begin. We have much to discuss."

Chanax took the empty seat next to his father. Isidor's face was untouched by age, his skin smooth and unwrinkled, even after all these years. While Chanax felt like an old man at thirty-seven, Isidor, who was approaching sixty, appeared as youthful as the young pharaoh who stood before them. Perhaps it was time to explore whatever dark arts the man employed to prevent aging. Chanax knew Metakryon's secret was the blood of young sacrifices in the temple, but such barbarity wasn't Isidor's style. The man had mastered other techniques. If Isidor knew Chanax was his son, perhaps he'd share his wisdom.

"Well," Ptolemy V began, "we're here because your brother has something of mine, and I want it back."

Chanax stared at the young man and chuckled. "I assume you're referring to the entire Upper Kingdom?"

"From Abdju down to Aswan," Ptolemy V replied. "We managed to take Lycopolis back from him seven years ago, but we can't get past that damn fortress he built."

"Which is why there hasn't been much going on at the border in a while, correct?" Chanax asked.

"I was busy fighting my father-in-law," Ptolemy V answered, gaze narrowed, and mouth drawn into a thin line. Chanax saw the form of anger surround the king and inwardly grinned. Epiphanes was untrained in the mysteries, and thus, an open book. "I lost many men against the Seleucids and was forced to create a new army of soldiers. I've also put down several rebellions in the Delta. How I hate the filthy natives. The time has come for me to take back what is mine—the rest of the country, stolen from me when I was a boy. Stolen by your brother."

"Technically," Chanax clarified, raising his index finger, "my father started the war, and you've kept Ankhmakis from finishing what they started. He hasn't gained an inch since he took the throne ten years ago."

"His name is Ankhwenefer, and he's stayed behind the line in peace because we've left him alone while *I* rebuilt our army," Ptolemy V yelled, his voice booming off the stone walls. "I am a man now, I have troops of my own loyal to me, and I will no longer leave the rebel king in peace. Why your brother never surged forward when he had the chance amazes me. It's as if he gave up."

"I don't think he gave up, my lord," Isidor suggested. "I think he's satisfied being pharaoh of the Upper Kingdom only. It is considered the birthplace of our nation, and he controls at least eighty percent of the lands your father once held."

Epiphanes stormed to Isidor's side and leaned over him, his hand on the hilt of his sword.

"In addition," Isidor continued, rising from his seat and placing his skilled hands on the king's shoulders to calm him down, "he's managed to secure Nubia and Kush as his allies. They're practically one kingdom. I hear Prince Senui is to marry a Kush princess this month."

"Ankhwenefer also controls the Nubian gold supply," Ptolemy V growled, shrugging Isidor's hands from his body. "He charges us absurd taxes to use the Nile to trade with the countries south of him. Between the cost of the war and the loss of taxes and grain from the south, I'm barely able to launch another attack."

"Yet it appears you're prepared to do so," Isidor noted.

"Yes," Ptolemy V answered. "We have begun fighting in full force along the border. We hope to destroy the fortress and advance along the river while Ankhwenefer is still in Kush celebrating his nephew's wedding."

"However, you're not sure military action will win out, are you?" Isidor asked. "Which is why you have come to visit us."

The young pharaoh blinked at Isidor. "Yes, I need another plan. A backup. My general, Conanus, he doesn't like this idea, but what must be done must be done. Even though I've married his daughter and we have two children, I believe Antiochus the Great will strike us. He controls the entire Syrian peninsula. I need the rest of Egypt. I need Nubian gold, I need the Wadi Hammamat, and I need the fields for grain. I can no longer be the pharaoh of Lower Egypt. I must have all of it if I'm to survive."

"I see," Chanax mused. "This is why you've called for me. To help you find another way to destroy my brother."

"We need you to go back to Ankhwenefer's court," Isidor explained. "Beg his forgiveness and try to find a way to corner him so we can arrest him. If he falls, the kingdom falls. Silus won't try for the crown. He's always been weak and will negotiate with us, I'm sure of it."

Chanax glared at the man. All these years he'd been led to believe he'd be the pharaoh. That he'd have Ankhwenefer's title and Memphis would crown him king. But Ankhwenefer never took Memphis. He never took anything again after he'd built that damn fortress. Rather than finish what their father started, the bastard had spent the past ten years living as a false king and enjoying his life without a care in the world, while Chanax slaved in Memphis, a place he hated, working for men he hated even more. It had all been in vain.

"Chanax?" Isidor asked. "Why do you hesitate?"

"You know why," he said, his throat tight.

Isidor nodded and gave him a conspiratorial look. "Those plans of our youth are long gone. Nothing turned out as we'd hoped."

"No, they didn't, did they?" Chanax said, fists curling into balls. "Helena's death was supposed to have driven Ankhwenefer insane. He was supposed to curl up and die after taking Lycopolis, wasn't he? What about Natasa? She died in Gaul. Wasn't her death going to be the end of him?"

"The man has proven more resilient than we'd thought," Isidor answered. "It appears nothing can kill him. Not the loss of his lover nor a child. Not even battle. He didn't lie down and die. Instead, he built a successful kingdom, rich with Nubian gold and trade with Greece, Syria, and Macedonia through the port in Coptos. They have plenty of food, and he's built an army out of Behdet rivaled only by the Romans, whose sole purpose is to guard the border and keep Pharaoh Epiphanes out. We can no longer wait for him to fail. We must take him down, and you're the only one who can do it."

Chanax rose from his seat and paced the room.

"You hate him, Chanax," Isidor continued. "Why would you hesitate?"

"What would you have me do?"

"Go back to his court, beg forgiveness, and infiltrate the priesthood. We believe they will be useful. It's the priests who gave him his title. If they wish to remove it, and crown Epiphanes their pharaoh, the rest of the kingdom must follow, no matter what they feel for Ankhwenefer."

"Why would his priests betray him?" Chanax demanded.

"Because," Isidor replied, "Ankhwenefer is not very religious. Our sources tell us he no longer worships the gods and goddesses. He participates only in ceremonies that include the public in order to appear devout. He's made his high priestess his representative with the priesthood of Thebes, and she struggles to keep the diplomatic relations between Ankhwenefer and his priests cordial."

"His high priestess?" Chanax frowned. "You mean Alexa, don't you?"

"Yes, I believe she was your spiritual companion?" Chanax nodded. "She's been your brother's companion for a decade."

Chanax grasped his robes over his heart and shrank back.

"You see, Chanax?" Isidor's lips curled into a sneer. "He banished you and took your lover. He took your sons as well. Made your wife a servant. Ankhwenefer has done nothing but destroy your life. I know the plan is different now than when we set out…"

He stopped talking and eyed the pharaoh, who was trying to follow the conversation. Isidor sent a current of befuddlement to the royal, causing his gaze to glaze over a bit. In spite of his anger, Chanax appreciated the little bit of practical magic.

"…but we must end this. It was a mistake on our part, and you can remedy it. Go to your brother's court. Use your relationship with Alexa to get in with the priesthood there and help us end this war."

"How can I work with Alexa now that she's his lover?" Chanax asked. "How do I go back and face them?"

"Well," Isidor answered, "our sources tell me that while the first years of their relationship were quite romantic, after she gave birth to their daughter seven years ago, things soured between them. She's more of his counselor than anything else. Alexa is now intimate with Setep, the high priest of Thebes. She loves him, not your brother."

Chanax struggled. Was it any better to hear she pleasured Ankhwenefer as a duty if she still performed the duty?

"I believe she is the key. If you can get back in her good graces, she will introduce you to Setep. He's the one we want."

"She'll never betray Ankhwenefer," Chanax replied.

"No, but she doesn't have to know. It's Setep we need."

"Priests," Epiphanes interrupted, "your politics irritate me. I don't have time to sit here listening to you bicker. Either you do this, Chanax, or not."

"If I do," Chanax answered, "what do I get in return?"

"Your life," Ptolemy V said, his hand once more at his sword.

"Now, Your Majesty," Isidor replied, wagging his finger as if Epiphanes were still a child, "that's not what we agreed to. Chanax will be rewarded for his work in Thebes."

Ptolemy V looked Chanax up and down, and Chanax extended his Ka around the pharaoh, finding nothing but anger and malice in the young man. This was a person who believed he'd been robbed of something precious and would stop at nothing, now that he was a man, to get it back.

"If you succeed," Pharaoh said, "you shall be my high priest in Alexandria and I'll give you all the gold and riches you can imagine. My city is more beautiful than any in the entire kingdom."

"What if I refuse?" Chanax asked.

"Then I will kill you," Ptolemy V replied.

"I have no choice, do I?"

"No, you don't." Epiphanes looked to Isidor and Metakryon and shrugged. "This is how I work, gentlemen. Do as I wish or suffer the consequences."

The pharaoh turned and stormed toward the doors. His royal guard opened them, and he walked through without a backward glance.

"He doesn't treat his priests very well," Metakryon said as the doors slammed shut. "It's a shame we didn't get Ankhwenefer to take the kingdom when he could have, years ago."

"Metakryon," Isidor said through clenched teeth, "you keep changing your mind. First, you wanted the rebellion, but when Ankhwenefer took control, you wanted him to fall."

"So we could crown Chanax," Metakryon replied, smiling at Chanax. "A prince with loyalties to Set. Instead, we have two pharaohs who don't care about the gods and thus don't care about us. Epiphanes was raised poorly. He's had too many generals as his regents, but I blame you for Ankhwenefer's lack of devotion."

"Please, not this again." Isidor walked to a desk and poured himself a glass of wine. "I had the opportunity to kill the Golden Child and I took it. I refuse to discuss it any further."

"You promised that upon her death we'd be able to connect to Ankhwenefer and destroy him with our magic," Chanax said in a hard voice. "Why do you need me to go to Thebes and do it myself?"

"I misjudged her abilities," Isidor admitted.

"What do you mean? Does Helena still protect him?"

"Yes." Isidor sighed. "I should have seen this, I know, and I am ashamed. She was protecting the couple long before she was born so of course, she continues to protect her father in death. The golden shield of hers is gone, but in its place is something even more powerful, an insurmountable energetic wall, one even I can't breach. The Golden Child is the only explanation I can think of. Unless Ankhwenefer himself is an adept, though he's never shown any promise in the energetic arts."

"Then we killed the child for nothing," Chanax said, his shoulders sagging under the weight of his guilt.

"No, we killed her for Our Lord Set, and now we must kill her father for the same reason."

"She would be twenty now," Chanax murmured. "If she were alive that is."

"Yes, yes." Isidor waved his hands as if swatting at a fly. "Now, back to your assignment. Seek Alexa once you get to the court. Don't let your jealousy of her station get in the way. Trust me when I say she finds your brother lacking. He isn't religious enough. He liked her sex, and her company, but I believe he failed at Anit-Shadya."

"How do you know this?" Chanax asked.

"I have a spy in the palace," Isidor admitted, a crooked smile forming upon his face. "Several for that matter. I can only speculate what split them up, but in the end, she fell in love with Setep. A king can't satisfy a priestess. Only a priest can know her heart. You and I both know this to be true."

"The issue will be getting back into the court," Chanax argued, throwing his hands in the air. "I can't saunter in and say, 'Hello brother, sorry I killed your daughter, can I come to stay?'"

"No, you can't," Isidor agreed, "but we know Ankhwenefer is in Kush for his nephew's wedding. To tell the truth, he's been away from Thebes for most of the past five years."

"What?" Chanax exclaimed. "Why didn't you tell me this before?"

"Does it matter? The point is he's not there and won't be for several more months."

"What has he been doing?"

"Traveling the kingdom and south to Nubia and Kush. He took all seven of the princes, including your sons, in addition to his most trusted men and generals. He set out with them once Khenefer, his youngest son, turned nine. The official line was a diplomatic trip to show the young men the kingdom, introduce them to the land and administration, and strengthen the relationships with Nubia and Kush. I have no idea what they've been doing. I don't have any spies on board their ship."

"He didn't ask any women to join?"

"With the exception of a few of the soldier's women, no," Isidor replied. "Your brother won't keep concubines and of course refused his queen a place in his entourage. He left her in Thebes to represent the crown to the public, but not in policy. His vizier, Ennaeus, is the one who's in charge."

"No concubines? That's crazy."

"He wants to set a good example for his men," Isidor replied. "That doesn't matter to us. What you need to pay attention to is the fact he left Weret behind."

Isidor now paced the room in front of the fireplace. "They too have a strange relationship. In public, they show a united face. My sources tell me that when the court first arrived in Thebes, he often visited her chambers, but like Alexa, he stopped spending time with her. He appears cordial with her in public, but Queen Weret has different interests than he does. While he enjoys evenings within his study with music, games, and conversation, she prefers parties in her chambers with young men, lots of drinking, opiates, and her palatial indoor pool. Consider Weret's private life to be extravagant with a heavy dose of debauchery, and it has become more so in the pharaoh's absence."

"Ankhwenefer doesn't like to have a good time?"

"I don't think he can," Isidor answered. "Some say he's like a man waiting to die."

"Then perhaps Natasa's death did affect him." Chanax twisted his mouth.

"Yes, I think it did, but not in the way we'd hoped. It's not unusual for a man to close his heart after such a loss and find himself unable to connect. I should know," Isidor replied with a faraway gaze upon his face. "Women don't like closed men."

Who was he thinking about, Neferu-ankh-maat, or his own mother, Keket, who had died a few years prior?

"Weret is my target," Chanax said. "I need to get her to invite me to the court while Ankhwenefer is still away."

"Invite yourself," Isidor replied, his face still hard. "Send her a letter. Tell her you're on your way to visit. She loves to stir things up in the court. You'd be just the thing to vex her husband when he returns, and he will return now that Ptolemy V has launched his campaigns in earnest."

"Is that part of the plan? Fight along the border to draw Ankhwenefer out of his hiding and back into battle?"

Isidor tapped his lip. "His army is good enough to hold Ptolemy back without him. He doesn't need to return, but he will, for Ankhwenefer feels most alive in battle."

"No," Chanax argued, "he was most alive in Natasa's arms."

"Well, in absence of her touch, the sword will have to do," Isidor replied, snapping his head toward the table and pouring himself another glass of wine.

As the priest drank his wine, Chanax felt the urge to tell him the truth—that he was his son. Now that the crown could never be his, what did he have to lose? He might never see Isidor after this; Ankhwenefer would most likely kill him.

"Isidor," Chanax began, "there's something I must tell you before I go."

"What is it?" Isidor asked.

Chanax extended his Ka and felt his father's energy. It was cold, like the chill of a tomb. He searched for warmth and found none. Isidor was completely empty of emotion.

"I wanted to thank you," Chanax said. "For all you've taught me."

"It's been my pleasure," Isidor answered. He gazed at Chanax, one eyebrow raised. "Is that it?"

Chanax considered confessing but realized there was no use in telling the man the truth. Isidor could care less about him.

"Yes, sir."

"Well, don't you have a letter to write to your sister?"

Chanax spun away from his father and left the two priests. As he walked back to his chambers, his stomach churned, stewing as if he'd eaten rotten meat. He had to use Alexa, a person he loved, to end Ankhwenefer, or Epiphanes would kill him. This was his path now, a familiar path, for he'd loved Natasa and used her in the same manner. Killed her daughter even, to no use. Natasa lay in a grave somewhere far away and his bastard brother still lived, ruling his golden kingdom, making love to Alexa, and raising Chanax's sons.

What was another betrayal?

27

The Company of Men

The baths of Egyptian Royalty were renown across the ancient world. Legend has it that Cleopatra VII Philopater held her first audience with Julius Caesar from her bath. Of course, had the royalty of Behdet accomplished what they had set out to do, Julius Caesar never would have had that infamous meeting, for Cleopatra VII wouldn't have been born.

Nile River, north of the Aswan Cataract, 186 BCE

Ankhwenefer took a deep breath, inhaling the warm Nile Valley air. Ra was high above the palm trees lining the muddy banks, and the river sparkled like diamonds. Eight young men, all of the princes plus Min's son Djau, wrestled on the deck, their dark bodies glistening with sweat and river water. Their raucous laughter filled the air. Ankhwenefer turned and looked behind him to the upper deck, where Maharet, Min's wife, sat beside Abana, her twelve-year-old daughter, and Durame, the Kush princess and Senui's new wife. They were a young couple; Senui was twenty years of age and she herself eighteen. They'd fallen in love in the temples of Kush, and there was no stopping their union. Silus had joined them for the wedding in Kush, and Ruia would meet Durame when they arrived in Behdet to drop Silus off and pick Ruia and the princesses up for an extended visit to Thebes to get to know the newest member of the court.

The pharaoh smiled at the women and felt a stirring in his heart. It had been a good five years. What had started out as a diplomatic trip for the men turned into an exercise in uniting the princes behind Ankhmaat as their future king. There would be no question of inheritance; his son was already capable at seventeen, wiser than his father, and just as brave. Ankhmaat would be the one to carry the pharaoh's crown, and the princes would follow him unto their death. This had been the main goal—to form a cohort, a loving group of brothers, cousins, and strong males to lead the country, and this could only be done away from the court—in the company of men.

He'd chosen his best companions to attend to this task. Khaleme and Min, as well as Ansel and Tsui. Sebastos, the royal falconer, had also joined them for part of the several years-long journey. There were a hundred other men and guards in their retinue, but Ankhwenefer's friends were the ones who spent time each day with the boys, training them in the Way of the Warrior, swords, xystons, and other fighting techniques. Even Sethe, Chanax and Alexa's son, had joined them. His life was destined for the priesthood, which made it important he respected Ankhmaat. Loyalty, rather than jealousy, was the true purpose of their work together.

When they'd arrived in Kush two years ago, Ankhwenefer decided they should stay for a while. It would be there, in the pure temples of Meroe, untouched by the Ptolemy dynasty and the worship of Set, where the boys would learn the Alchemies of Horus and be initiated into Anit-Shadya. All of them, with the exception of Khenefer, had received their first rites at the hands of the goddess, the way love was meant to be. This was how Senui met Durame, and he begged to marry her, claiming he could never touch another woman, and Durame felt the same about him.

Ankhwenefer knew full well what Senui felt for the woman. It's difficult to let go in any other arms once you've tasted the touch of the goddess. While he and Weret had come to an agreement, one in which he could seek her out when he was in need, their sex never meant more than release. He hadn't missed her once the five years he'd been gone and knew full well she didn't spend any time thinking about him. She'd given him two male heirs and left the parenting to Ankhwenefer without complaint while she frolicked in their riches.

"Those young men are amazing." Khaleme laughed as he approached.

"Yes," Ankhwenefer agreed. "I think we've done well."

"Quite a passel of them," the Kushman continued. "You were very busy in the years of your youth."

"It's amazing we managed to create these children, given the war and everything else going on," Ankhwenefer replied. "Silus's sons, Senui and Horpais, are only one year apart. Chanax's first son, Sethe, was born the same year as Senui, and then Panas and Hor, a few years later. They're also a year apart. Bithiah was pregnant for five straight years. Each of my brothers also has daughters mixed in there. I'm anxious to meet them when Ruia comes to court. Perhaps one of them will be a fit for Ankhmaat?"

"I thought you said your son didn't have to marry a sister?" Khaleme asked.

"They're his cousins. Ankhmaat doesn't have any sisters." Ankhwenefer let out a long exhale. Helena's image flashed in his memory. No matter how hard he'd tried to forget her, the child's laughter and the sweet sound of her singing crept up in his memory without warning, and there was no stopping the pain in his heart. The starlight that was once Helena was impossible to forget, even more difficult than her mother. Always the girl haunted him. He clenched his teeth and forced her out of his mind.

"What about Meryt?" Khaleme answered.

Ankhwenefer stepped away from the general, glancing at the deck. "Yes, there's Meryt, but she's only seven. That'd be a long time to wait for love. He'll need a queen sooner than later."

"My lord," Khaleme began. "I know her birth was hard on you—"

Ankhwenefer rounded on his friend. "I'd told Alexa I didn't want any more children. I knew she wanted a female heir and gave her permission to seek others to sire the child. As the high priestess, she can have as many lovers as she wants, but she wanted her daughter to be born of the pharaoh and conceived the child with me against my wishes."

"Why does this still bother you? The two of you were so compatible at first, I thought she might be able to heal you and open your heart once more."

Ankhwenefer grimaced and swatted the air with his hand. "Heal me? Even though I adored Alexa, even though the sex was wonderful and the conversation just as good, I could never let go. I never entered a state of bliss with her. It was Anit-Shadya without the magic, and it made her resentful. I can't surrender to the All-One with her. There's something in the way."

He glanced at his right hand and touched the gold and lapis ring on his small finger. He was still furious with Natasa for dying, but he'd never removed her ring from his hand.

"She has been dead ten years, my lord."

"Don't I know it? The anniversary of the day in which Finnian delivered her final letter was last week. While I can manage to keep her out of my mind most of the time, I seem to remember that horrible moment, year after year." He placed his hand on Khaleme's shoulder. "A part of me died when I read her last letter. Besides, you're one to talk. How long ago did you lose your wife and child?"

"Eighteen years." He sighed. "Just before I became the General of the Kush army."

"How many lovers have you taken since her death?"

"Very few. I have found no other woman as of yet that makes me feel the way she did."

"I haven't met anyone either, even after our long travels," Ankhwenefer admitted. "I was open to finding a second queen on this trip, but I believe you're the one who told me it's better to be alone than to have sex without love." Khaleme nodded. "Alexa was aware of my issues, and thought she could help, which is why she put up with me for so many years."

"Then why deny her wish to create an heir to the temple with her king?"

"Because, Khaleme, children are liabilities. I have many enemies, inside my own court as well as in the Lower Kingdom, and I've already lost one daughter to their spite and anger. Children are the only weapons they have against me. My twin flame is dead, and I care not for my own life. I refused Alexa's request to conceive a holy child because I thought her daughter would be safer if she were born unto another man."

He looked to his sons as they shoved and jostled one another, slipping on the wet deck while wrestling their cousins. Horpais, Silus's second son, picked Khenefer up over his head and flung him over the side of the boat. Within moments, all eight young men were in the river, swimming, throwing mud, and calling each other impolite names.

"She conceived the child with me anyway," Ankhwenefer said, "and I found I no longer desired her. It was a betrayal, and I'm tired of being betrayed by those who claim to love me."

Khaleme stood beside him, looking out at the raucous in the river. "Meryt shouldn't suffer because of her mother's misjudgment."

"I know, but I'm not long for this world, my friend. In the end, she is her mother's child."

Khaleme's eyebrows lifted. "What do you mean? I thought this trip healed you of your melancholy."

"Oh, it has." A smile touched the pharaoh's face. "These have been the best five years of my life. No war, no court politics, visiting archeological sites, learning the intimate details of my kingdom, meeting my subjects and other nobles, planning and creating a strong nation, and of course, spending time with my best friends and these young men. This trip was perhaps the best idea I've ever had, but the war returns, and I'm forty-one, not a young man anymore. Time runs out for everyone, Khaleme. I will fight as best as I can, but Ankhmaat is ready to take the crown. If I fall in battle, you must make sure that happens."

"I do not think you will fail," Khaleme said. "You are the golden eagle king. You can't be killed. You know this is true."

Ankhwenefer eyed his friend and laughed. "You don't believe those legends, do you?"

"Of course I do," he answered. "You have the Wands of Horus."

"I sent those back to Eleni in Behdet years ago for safekeeping," Ankhwenefer admitted. "I have no use for them."

"I delivered the silver wand to your kingdom for a reason," Khaleme answered, grasping Ankhwenefer tightly on the arm. "Your refusal to use them causes me great distress."

"Natasa told me the goddess instructed my father to never let any of his sons have the wands. That only a priestess of Isis could inherit them," Ankhwenefer answered, his jaw hardening. "I am one of Hugronaphor's sons, am I not?"

Khaleme sighed and let go of Ankhwenefer's arm. "You are correct. The goddess said the same to me. Natasa was to use them and then hand them down to Helena."

"Well, they're both dead, aren't they? There are no other priestesses of Isis worthy of them."

"I think they should go south to Kush," Khaleme advised. "Let my people keep them safe in the vaults of Meroe. I sense this is very important."

Ankhwenefer considered his friend's words. "Yes, I agree. I'll discuss it with Eleni when we return to court."

The pharaoh turned back to the river. Min stood by the railing, heckling the boys as they played in the water. Silus walked up to join him, throwing in his own taunts.

"Halt the boat," Ankhwenefer commanded to the captain as he dropped his loincloth. Better to swim naked than with a wet blanket around your waist.

"Excuse me, my friend," he said to Khaleme, "but I have some fun to attend to."

He ran across the slippery deck and grabbed Min in his arms, hoisting him up and over the railing and into the water, and jumping in after him. Silus laughed and followed suit. Within moments, several other grown men joined in the play, and the river was filled with princes, soldiers, generals, and the pharaoh, wrestling, splashing, and throwing mud and wet reeds at one another. The people on the shore laughed and waved, and the women on the upper platform cheered.

Khaleme stood by the railing, arms crossed, wearing a huge, white-toothed grin on his painted face.

Ankhwenefer swam to his eldest son and hugged him close while kissing his cheek. The young man slipped out from his grip and climbed on his father's back. Ankhwenefer laughed and dove under the water, feeling the precious Nile wash away his fears. He was the pharaoh of Upper Egypt. He'd done his duty, raised his sons, and now, he was free to live and die as the fates allowed.

28

Weret's Welcome

Egyptian royalty lived lavishly in palaces built to their exact desires. From the glyphs on the walls to the gilded floors, their world was stunning. For when the priests granted the kingship unto a man, all the gold, riches, and people of the kingdom were his, and by association, they were also his queen's.

Thebes, Egypt, 186 BCE

Chanax squinted at the palace entrance, a brilliant set of golden doors shining in the sunlight behind twenty guards. After his journey down the Nile, it was quite clear to him that his brother's kingdom was well fortified. The fortress south of Lycopolis stretched for a half-mile in either direction along the river, halting every boat that passed, and surrounded by an army compound. Even more interesting was the land that followed for at least twenty miles—barren, empty fields, and cities lying in ruin, inhabited by nothing but troops. Archers lined the banks, battleships at the ready, and men dwelling there for one sole purpose—to keep Ptolemy V out. There was no way, even if he breached the fortress, the pharaoh of the Lower Kingdom could get his army to Abdju and beyond.

Chanax needed to create a plan in which they took Ankhwenefer by surprise, but how to do it? Even if he convinced Setep to crown Ptolemy

V the pharaoh, Epiphanes could never sail the Nile this far south to claim his prize. Unless Ptolemy's general arrested Ankhwenefer, only then would the army agree to lay down their arms and parley.

It was an impossible mission.

"Who are you, stranger, and what is your purpose?" Ankhwenefer's guard called out.

"I am Prince Chanax, younger brother of Pharaoh Ankhwenefer and High Queen Weret."

The guard looked back at who must be his superior because the other man nodded and said, "Her Majesty said her brother would be arriving any day. Escort him to the great hall."

"At midday?" Chanax asked. It seemed a strange time to be in the great hall, normally used for evening feasting and revelry.

"Any time of the day is a good time for the great hall," the main guard said. One of the others smirked. "Especially for Queen Weret."

The men gave each other a wink, and Chanax saw the forms of disrespect shimmer amongst them. Perhaps Ankhwenefer had left her alone too long? The fool had a way of underestimating the impact of the negative aspects of others.

Chanax followed a pair of guards down the opulent hall toward a stunning courtyard. A statue of Ankhwenefer rose tall in the center, flanked by bubbling fountains and fragrant flowers. Birds flew in the open air, and members of the court lounged in various alcoves, hiding from the midday heat. Chanax stopped before the statue and read the stele at its base.

In the third year of his reign, our Lord and Pharaoh Ankhwenefer, the Good Being of Isis, took Thebes into his own hands and remade it into the capital of Egyptian civilization. Hail the golden eagle king.

Chanax clenched his fists so hard, his palms bled as he glared at the statue. His brother's form had been fashioned in Horus's image. Chanax swallowed a sour taste in his mouth.

"Come," the guard commanded, "this way to the queen."

They led him to another pair of golden doors towering at least forty feet high. It took four men to open them. The moment he stepped inside the hall, he was greeted by revelry. Not a feast, but a few dozen people indulging in food, wine, and entertainment. There were fire blowers, jugglers, acrobats, and dancers. Musicians played traditional songs. Weret lounged in the King's Corner while a serving boy fed her grapes and figs. At her feet sat several men and women, each much younger than her. Bare-chested women fanned the royal entourage while they laughed, drank, and smoked. It was loud and a bit distasteful, yet it lifted Chanax's spirits. After all he'd been through, he needed a good party.

"Chanax," Weret said, jumping from her place and startling the other guests, who turned to peek at the object of her attention. He looked down at what he was wearing and felt the fool in his leopard skin robes and bald head. It was time to dress like a prince once more and grow out his hair.

"Sister," he cooed, arms held wide as he made his way toward the small gathering.

She trotted to his side and squeezed him as if he'd returned from the dead. He could smell the wine on her breath and see her gaze was glossy, yet she appeared quite happy.

"Oh, Chanax," she gushed, "I'm so glad you're here. When I received your letter, I jumped for joy. I've been telling my friends about you. Come." She dragged him toward the group and flicked her hand, forcing a man out the spot next to hers. "Have a seat, right here, by me." She patted the silken pillows of the divan, wavering a bit as she sat, her voice slurred. "Chanax, these are my friends. Friends, this is my little brother, Chanax."

He waved to them and most of them held up their goblets to toast him. A servant placed a cup full of wine in his hand. He returned their gesture and took a sip. Even the wine was splendid here.

"Little?" he asked her. "I believe my mother gave birth to me only ten hours after your mother, and I'm at least a foot taller."

She giggled and rubbed his bald head. "Now that you're here, we must do something about this sullen priestly look. I want you in wigs and tunics and golden collars."

"Thank you, Weret," he said, his gaze lowering, "I would appreciate that very much."

The musicians resumed their tunes, a plate of food arrived, and a young woman sat behind him, massaging his shoulders.

"If you like her," Weret whispered in his ear, "you can take her to your chambers. She's my gift."

"I thought your husband didn't keep concubines?" he challenged her.

Weret waved her hand. "He doesn't, but he's not here, is he? As queen, I need to keep the men of the court happy, don't I?"

"Tell me, sister," Chanax asked, leaning in as if already her best friend, "how do you keep yourself happy?"

She threw back her hair and smirked at the man she'd shooed away for Chanax. He crawled back to sit at her feet, gazing up at his queen, a hand over his heart. Weret stroked the man's hair and said, "There are concubines for women as well. My close friend Adma keeps me company, don't you, dear?"

The concubine, who was at most in his late teens, grinned, eyes fluttering under fake eyelashes. "I will serve you for as long as you allow, my queen."

She turned to Chanax. "You should have returned much sooner. Ankhwenefer has been gone so long, you could have spent years here playing with me, rather than praying in your boorish temples." She glanced over her shoulder as if searching for someone and giggled. "I'm so glad there aren't any priests nearby to hear me speak such things. Then again, I never invite them to these soirees. It doesn't fit their station."

"What will you do about your playtime when your husband returns?" Chanax probed. "I hear he's on his way home now."

Weret frowned. "Yes, he is, which is unfortunate. He's always allowed me this lifestyle. I even had a huge indoor pool constructed for my play. I doubt he'll ever join me. He rarely did, even before he left. He stays out of my business." She gazed at the woman massaging Chanax's temples. "Though I'll have to let the concubines go, which is such a shame. Take advantage of them while you can, brother. Ankhwenefer arrives within a fortnight."

A fortnight? That was sooner than Isidor had suggested. Chanax didn't have much time to get to Alexa and Setep. He grinned at his sister. At least this part had been easy, as Isidor had hinted. The man did have accurate intelligence on the ground in Thebes. This was both comforting and terrifying, for if Isidor could spy on Weret, he'd make sure to assign someone to spy on Chanax. Everything he did would be watched.

"Oh, sister, believe me, I will take advantage of your hospitality," Chanax said as a servant refilled his wine goblet.

He ate and drank to his heart's content, and when he was full, he rose from his place, stretched, and yawned. He was exhausted. Weret snapped her fingers and two guards arrived.

"Take Chanax to his rooms," she commanded, winking at the concubine at Chanax's side, "and anyone else he'd like to join him."

Chanax turned to the girl who'd been massaging him. He looked to Weret, smiling as he spoke, "Have a spare? I'd like two. Thirteen years in Memphis was difficult."

"I can only imagine, dear brother," the queen replied, running her hands through the young Adma's hair. She snapped her fingers and a second young woman appeared before him. "My cup runneth over. Return to the great hall when Ra sets. I'm throwing you a party, and everyone will attend." She winked. "Including Alexa."

☥

Later that evening, dressed in a prince's clothes and wearing a borrowed wig, golden collar, and crown, Chanax entered the great hall, the room now packed with nobles from Thebes and Luxor, as well as priests, soldiers, and their mates. The women were dressed in gold, fur, and silks, the men also in their finest. Fires blazed in copper braziers scattered about the hall, musicians played, singers sang, and dogs chased one another. Ankhwenefer's banner, the phoenix rising from the ashes, hung from every window and each waved in the evening breeze. Weret had granted him noble treatment, but what would Ankhwenefer do when he arrived? What sort of a man was he now? Would his brother allow him to keep his station? Or would he make him a servant?

As if to answer his question, someone grabbed him and spun him around.

"Bithiah," Chanax said, almost fainting at the sight of his wife.

She put her hands on her hips. "Why didn't you seek me out when you arrived?"

"I didn't know you were here," he stammered. "I thought you were in Behdet."

"No," she said. "After you abandoned me, the children and I traveled south with Mother for a few years until she passed. Then I was forced to send my sons here to Thebes to be raised by Ankhwenefer and my daughters to Ruia in Behdet."

"They didn't let you raise your own children?"

"No," she replied, shaking her hair around her head and clasping her hands over her breasts. "It was horrible, Chanax, I became nothing more than Ruia's handmaiden. For some reason, she took pity on me and sent me to Thebes. Iu-Amon needed a royal midwife. Since I was husbandless and no longer bound to marrying a man of the court, I realized my lifelong dream had come true, and now I find myself in the service of Iu-Amon like I'd wanted as a young girl."

Chanax felt a tingle in his throat. They had four children together, and he hadn't even said goodbye when he left.

"Does Ankhwenefer approve of your station?" he croaked, trying to keep from tearing up in front of her.

"Iu-Amon claims the pharaoh approved my assignment. That in exchange for taking my sons away for five years, the least he could do was grant me this position. Weret wasn't too happy, but Ruia has always been able to convince Ankhwenefer of the right course of action."

"Ruia?" Chanax asked. "Interesting."

"Chanax," Bithiah said, her lips pursed as she stepped closer, "why are you here?"

"To reunite with my family," he replied. There was some truth to his statement.

"That's it?" she demanded, poking him in the chest. "You and

Isidor aren't up to one of your schemes, are you? Because we know how well your last plans turned out, don't we? Ankhwenefer is immune to your treachery, and the people are happy. Even Weret's happy. No one needs trouble. Let our brother rule and fight off the threat in the north."

"What if he dies in battle? He's not immortal, you know."

"Then Ankhmaat will become pharaoh."

Ankhmaat. Chanax had forgotten about him. "How old is that boy now?"

"Seventeen, going on eighteen," she answered, crossing her arms. "Chanax, I know that look. Please, if you're here to seek revenge, turn around and go back to Memphis. We've made peace with the past. Why can't you?"

"Weret's games and lechery don't bother you?"

"She's excessive," Bithiah admitted, wrinkling her nose at the queen as their sister partied it up in her corner. "Some of the subjects love her for it, others dislike it, but she's kept them happy for the most part, with Ennaeus's help. He rules with the law, she throws parties, and the subjects remain loyal to Ankhwenefer. It works."

Chanax looked away from her, knowing she could read him, even after being apart so long. It would be hard to hide his mission from Bithiah. He considered the legions of soldiers between him and Ptolemy V. Perhaps he was safe from the man's threats?

"Bithiah," he said, speaking in a softer tone, taking her arm, "I'm here to reconcile with my brother. I wish to make peace and return to the court."

"If that's true, you should get on Ruia's good side," she advised.

"Ruia?"

"Yes, she's the one the pharaoh listens to. She will join Ankhwenefer on the boat when he stops in Behdet. She wants to spend time in Thebes with her new daughter-in-law and introduce the princesses, including our two daughters, Baktre and Shesh, to the court."

"Baktre and Shesh?" he asked, his heart beating fast. "Why, Shesh wasn't even born when I was banished."

"I was pregnant with her at Natasa's trial," Bithiah said, mouth twisted for a moment before turning into a genuine smile. "She's now fourteen, and Baktre is eighteen and eligible for marriage. She hopes to meet a nobleman while here."

"Much has happened while I've been in exile."

"Yes," Bithiah replied. "Not everything has been easy, yet I seem to have found a way to thrive. I don't wish to be a princess anymore, nor your queen. I'm happy as a midwife and freer than I ever was under Father's reign. I hope you understand."

He nodded, swallowing his pride. It seemed everyone but him had made the best of things.

"Now," she said, placing a firm hand on his shoulder and turning him toward the Royal Corner. "You're expected to sit at the queen's table. I suggest you take your place."

"Thank you, Bithiah."

"Chanax," Bithiah called as he walked away. He turned to meet her gaze and she gave him a little smile. "It *is* good to see you."

Then she was gone in the crowd, making her way toward a table of friends. Slow anger festered within him. They'd moved on, even Bithiah, who'd been as guilty in Helena's death as he had. Yet Ankhwenefer had forgiven her.

As Chanax approached Weret, now dressed in her formal queen's attire with the crown of the high queen displayed upon her head, she stood and clapped.

"Attention, everyone," her voice rang out in the great hall. "This is my brother, Prince Chanax, returned after a long time away. Please, make him feel comfortable. Soon my sister, Queen Ruia, and my husband, your Lord, and Pharaoh and the Good Being of Isis, will return to Thebes, and after a decade, our whole family will be together."

Chanax looked out at the crowd and noted their contentment and ease while he fought the anger swirling like a whirlpool in his soul. His gaze fell upon Alexa, and his heart sputtered. She sat next to an elegant older man who had his arm around her shoulders. Chanax assumed he was the high priest Setep. She glanced away for an instant before meeting his gaze, raising her goblet, and toasting him. Yes, everyone was thriving, except him, and yet he was the one who held the power.

He could yank their stable life right out from under them, or he could let the mission go and hope Ptolemy V left him alone.

His decision depended on the two pharaohs—would Ptolemy V forget about him down here, holed up behind thousands of troops and ships? Would his brother forgive him and keep him safe, or would Ankhwenefer spite him? That would be the true test.

Yet, there was one small thing Chanax wanted more than anything else but had no idea how to pursue.

For more than revenge toward his brother, or fear of Ptolemy V's threats, Chanax was in Thebes for a higher purpose—to find the Wands of Horus and take them to Abdju. He'd heard what Natasa told Ankhwenefer years ago in the apiary. He understood what she was talking about and never forgotten it. Time spent in the Resurrection Bath of the Osirian, and he'd be free from both of the pharaohs.

He would rule them instead.

29

A New Adventure

"May I walk every day on the banks of the water, may my soul rest on the branches of the trees which I planted, may I refresh myself under the shadow of my sycamore."
~ Egyptian tomb inscription, ca. 1400 BC

Behdet, Egypt, 186 BCE

Eleni stood on the royal docks gripping her six-year-old daughter's hand. Her luggage rested beside them. All of their small family's belongings fit in three wooden trunks. She rubbed her nose and trembled. Change was never easy but moving from Behdet was the hardest thing she'd done in a while. For twenty-six years Eleni had lived in the city of her birth. Yes, she'd seen many loved ones go, some in death, some to escape death, and others on new adventures, but always, this had been her home. Now, it was her turn to leave.

Her husband, Pamu, had been selected to be a part of the new royal guard in Pharaoh's court in Thebes to protect Prince Ankhmaat and serve him for the duration of his life. It was a great honor, as Ankhmaat was to be the pharaoh when his father died, but it also meant Pamu would have to go to war with him, and sooner than Eleni wanted. Battle had broken out in the north, and Pharaoh Ankhwenefer was sure to travel to the front line in order that Ankhmaat complete his first battle under his expert guidance. Eleni hated war. She'd spent her adolescence tending wounded men, sewing them back together, or worse, helping them die. The past ten years had been so wonderful without it.

She looked up at the ship's masts and watched as Ankhwenefer's banner flew in the wind. The boat was enormous; there was room for hundreds of people, a small banquet hall, private chambers for the officers, and Pharaoh himself had several rooms. It seemed strange to have such a large ship on the Nile, but everything the royals did was larger than life. Her father had told her that to be royal was to be grander than everyone else.

Hecataeus, oh how she missed him. He'd come to visit after she gave birth to her son, Khui. It had been a healing reunion, but also hard on both of them. He'd never understood her refusal to leave Egypt and join him in Greece. Back then, it had been important for her to remain in Behdet. She'd been angry at her father, yes. She'd been angry with Ankhwenefer as well. Tired of men telling her what to do. Yet there had been another reason she'd wanted to stay—Pamu. He'd asked Queen Ruia for permission to court her, and Eleni had chosen to remain by his side.

She'd taken her father to Corinna's grave and Helena's tomb during his visit and visited the apartment to collect the last of his belongings. Every day he'd sobbed in her arms as he told her of the pain in his heart, of how horrible it had been to choose between his daughters and begged her to forgive him.

Eleni knew Hecataeus loved her and found it in her heart to let go of her anger, but she never told him of her part in the event, of how she'd been the one who'd shown Chanax the peephole that allowed him to spy and turn her sister in for breaking her vow of celibacy. It was easier for Eleni to forgive her father for leaving her behind than it was to forgive herself for betraying her sister.

After her father's visit, the two kept in touch. He now lived in Athens and even had a new wife and a son the same age as Eleni's own little girl. Never a day passed by when Eleni didn't think of Hecataeus and wish he'd stayed in Egypt, but she understood this land had never been his home. He was Greek through and through, and needed the sea, not the languid Nile, to make him happy. Besides, Behdet reminded him of his failure to save his family, and Eleni was sure he'd never forgive himself. Better to start over somewhere far away. That was Hecataeus's way.

Her husband strode by, leading several men carrying supplies onto the ship. Pamu winked as he passed, and she fluttered her fingers at him. From the moment he'd first kissed her, Eleni had been in love. True, she'd faltered once early in their relationship and offered herself to another man, but that was an event best forgotten. Unfortunately, forgetting her indiscretion would be hard to do, given her ride to Thebes was on the same man's flotilla.

"Our Lord and Pharaoh approaches," a young servant called out.

Eleni turned and saw him walking toward the docks, wearing his white tunic, pharaoh's collar, and blue crown. His people knelt before him as he passed by, his gaze set upon Eleni. He was still as handsome as ever, and Eleni blushed when she recalled that horrible day when she'd misunderstood his kiss and offered herself. She'd been sixteen, heartbroken about the loss of her mother, sister, and of course, Helena. After being left behind for years unaware of what was happening to her family, Eleni had been confused, hurt, and scared. She'd grown up in Ankhwenefer's company and found herself attracted to him, but that day, she'd gone too far. Even as a grown woman, she regretted it.

Worse, they hadn't seen or spoken to each other since. Ankhwenefer rarely visited Behdet, and Eleni left the palace when she married Pamu to live in the city with the soldier's families. Back then, she'd thought Ankhwenefer refrained from coming to Behdet to avoid her. Now, after loving Pamu for so many years, Eleni understood what kept the pharaoh from Behdet—every inch of the palace and city reminded him of Natasa and the horrible event that led to Helena's death. Something Eleni had been responsible for. As he now approached her, all these memories and more overwhelmed her, and her throat stung. Her lower lip trembled, and she gripped her daughter's hand a bit tighter before bowing to the pharaoh as he stopped before her.

"Eleni," he said, as she rose to face him, placing his hands on her cheeks, "my, you are a wonder to behold."

He hugged her, and she wrapped her arms around him, surprised by his public display of affection.

"Your Majesty," she answered. "It's been so long."

He noticed her little girl. "Why? Is this Rai?" he asked, kneeling down to the child's eye level.

"Yes, it is."

"Hello, Rai," he said, shaking her hand, so small in his. "Your father has told me much about you. I'm grateful he will be serving my son as captain of his guard. There is no better man."

The little girl curtsied to the king, and Ankhwenefer patted her on the head. He stood and smiled at Eleni. "It's appropriate that you and your family join us in Thebes. We need a soldier like Pamu, and it will be an honor to know you as a woman and mother, Eleni."

She wiped her eyes, now unable to control her tears.

"Did you get the package I sent you long ago?" he asked her.

"Yes, my lord," she replied. "I have kept it safe."

"You will need to continue to do so," Ankhwenefer instructed. "There are many things that need to be done when I return home, and once I'm settled and have been to the front line, I plan to send the cedar box to Kush. In the meantime, guard the Wands of Horus well in your home in Thebes, should I need them after the battle."

"Yes, Your Majesty," Eleni agreed.

"Eleni," he said, "please call me Ankhwenefer. You will always be family to me." He kissed her on the cheek and then walked toward the boat.

Pamu approached her, a grin the size of the sun on his face. "I'd forgotten how close you and Pharaoh Ankhwenefer were."

"We're not that close," Eleni said, her chest swelling. "I remind him of someone very dear. Someone he lost long ago."

"Your sister was his true love, wasn't she? That's what the songs and stories about him say—that the river god Hapy took his beloved from his side, and he's been alone ever since."

She glanced up to the boat where Ankhwenefer now stood giving his men orders. "Hapy did take my sister from this land, and he never returned her to us."

"I'm sorry, Eleni." Pamu drew her close and kissed her lips.

Eleni felt light as air every time her husband embraced her. "Pamu, you have given me so much joy, I'm no longer sad about the loss of my birth family. You and our children are my family now."

"Good. Now, are you ready for our new adventure in Thebes?"

"Of course."

"Then get on the boat. We leave as soon as Queen Ruia and the princesses arrive."

Eleni grabbed Rai's hand and walked up the plank and onto the deck. Her son was already on board, gathered with the other boys whose fathers were also being reassigned to Thebes. The war made it necessary for many men, including entire regiments, to make their way to Thebes, and onward north. Behdet had been a military training center the past decade, but it would now also be a hospital again, and Eleni was glad to be gone from it. Though Thebes had a Houses of Healing as well, and she imagined Iu-Amon would call upon her if the need arose.

Trumpets played and the queen of Behdet arrived in a litter with the three princesses. The young women stepped from their ride, each wearing crisp white tunics and finely made leather sandals, and walked toward the boat, giggling and pointing at the vessel. Their golden bracelets glowed in the sunlight and the beads in their hair glittered like diamonds against their thick, black braids. Ruia followed behind them and a smile graced her face as she met Eleni.

"My dear," Ruia exclaimed, "I'd forgotten you'd be on this trip as well. I'm so glad you're here. Let us spend every moment together. It's been so long."

Eleni grabbed Ruia and held her close. This was the woman who had saved her and ushered her out of her melancholy, taking her in as one of her ladies-in-waiting and helping her to meet Pamu. Ruia had been both her mother and big sister and had taught Eleni how to be a lady as well as how to forgive her father for leaving her behind. Ruia was everything to Eleni.

"Yes, Ruia," Eleni agreed, grateful to be near her guardian. "I want to spend every moment I can with you."

☥

Later that evening when Eleni and Pamu arrived for dinner with the pharaoh, they found the royals' quarters loud and boisterous. Ankhwenefer sat in between his sons, wearing a big, goofy grin. Eleni gasped as she gazed upon Ankhmaat, now a young man. He looked exactly like Ankhwenefer had when the same age. Surrounding the pharaoh's sons were more princes and young men, laughing and telling jokes while drinking their ale. Ruia sat across from Ankhwenefer with the three princesses at her right side. There were two seats open on her left.

"Eleni," Ruia called out, yelling to be heard over the noise of the young men. "Come, sit next to me."

Pamu led the way, and Eleni took the seat next to Ruia. She looked across the table at Ankhwenefer, who held his younger son's head under his arm, tickling him.

"You'll have to excuse them," Ruia said. "I believe this is how men bond. They wrestle with their sons, like puppies in a pack."

Ankhwenefer laughed and released his boy. Eleni hadn't seen him so happy since her childhood before the war when he showered her with presents and serenaded Natasa. His gaze glowed and his hair was long and thick—even his skin looked wonderful as if he hadn't aged. She glanced at Pamu and thought perhaps they looked the same age, yet Pamu was at least thirteen years younger than the pharaoh.

"She's right," Ankhwenefer agreed, a wicked look gleaming in his eye. "We've been without women so long, we might have forgotten our manners."

"Yes," Ankhmaat added, his low voice sending shivers down Eleni's spine, "but Princess Durame has set us straight, hasn't she, Senui?"

Senui, who had his arm around an exotic Ethiopian woman, raised his glass and cheered his cousin. "I don't think she's set anyone straight, except for me."

The crowd laughed, and the young girl glanced at Senui from under her thick eyelashes as he kissed her on the cheek.

"Durame is Senui's wife," Ruia explained to Eleni.

"Oh, yes, I'd heard you married," Eleni said to the young prince. "Congratulations, my prince."

It was so strange, for she remembered him as a child. He'd spent hours at the apartment playing with Helena. The two had been inseparable, and back then, Eleni often thought that when they grew up, he would marry Helena. She would have been a young woman now if she had lived. A sorrow overtook Eleni's heart, and she grabbed her wine glass and took a big gulp. She sensed a pair of eyes on her and looked up to find Ankhwenefer watching her, his mouth turned down.

"Yes," he said as if reading her mind. Then he glanced down at his hand and fingered one of his rings. Eleni recognized it as Natasa's, and she took in a sharp breath. So much hurt still lingered. So much left unsaid.

Eleni raised her glass. "Thank you very much, Queen Ruia and Pharaoh Ankhwenefer, for inviting us to dine with you. My husband and I appreciate all you have done for us."

"Hear, hear," Ruia exclaimed.

Pamu planted a kiss on her cheek, grounding her with his love. Yes, she shared a painful event with these people, but she'd let go of the past, and it appeared, they had as well. There was much to celebrate. She glanced at Ankhwenefer's hand once more, the lapis phoenix glimmered under the candlelight. Perhaps not everyone had healed.

30

The King-in-Waiting

"In Egypt, consciousness was seen as a power of life that seeks its final liberation through all possible expressions of Nature."
~ The Temple of Man, R.A. Schwaller de Lubicz, 1949 CE

Thebes, Egypt, 186 BCE

"Thebes ahead," the sailor announced. "We disembark in five minutes."

Ankhmaat rose from his chair and took a deep breath. He felt the weight of the golden collar around his neck. It had been his father's when he was the prince of Behdet. Now Ankhmaat, the Crown Prince of Upper Egypt, wore it. There were many firsts on the horizon—his first battle, and his first spiritual companion.

His stomach tightened as he considered where life was now taking him. After the trip from Behdet, he was no longer sure he wanted a spiritual companion from the House of Isis. His thoughts drifted to Anen, King Silus's daughter. He'd fallen under her spell the moment they'd met in Behdet, and Ankhmaat longed to know her in a more intimate way. She wasn't a priestess, but was part of their royal line and thus qualified for the position of high queen of Upper Egypt, a role he'd have to eventually fill as well.

Ankhmaat opened the door to his quarters and made his way

toward the stairs. The royal entourage was lining up below, his father and Ruia at the front, followed by his little brother, Khenefer, the rest of the princes and Sethe, and the princesses at the rear; all dressed in their finest tunics, golden crowns, and collars, their eyes painted with kohl and lapis, lips with red ochre, and hair braided. The princes wore swords at their waists with golden cuffs upon their upper arms while the princesses' arms jangled with golden bangles. In the distance, throngs of people gathered on the docks of Thebes, eager to see the return of their pharaoh and his sons. At the end of the promenade sat High Queen Weret in a decadent litter, the golden pillars sparkling in the sunlight, held in the air by eight slaves.

On several occasions, Ankhmaat overheard the sailors on the boat imply his mother was a loose woman. He hated the idea and wondered why his father allowed her to throw such indulgent parties—parties even the sailors would comment upon. She was quite beautiful to behold, but Ankhmaat felt nothing for the woman. He'd never known her. She'd left his nursemaids to the task of raising him and Khenefer until their father swept them up into his care and took them far from the court.

Ankhmaat still wondered why his father had chosen to leave Thebes, but as the events of the past five years replayed in his head, he found himself approving. It was the best education a prince could have, and he now had six faithful companions in his life. All of them, from Senui down to Khenefer, were a team, well prepared to run the country, and if things turned out as planned, take the Lower Kingdom from Ptolemy V.

Anen looked up from her place in line and waved before turning away from him and whispering in her cousin's ear. Ankhmaat grinned and strolled down the steps to the deck, stopping beside her.

"You look very handsome," she said, peeking out at him from under her thick eyelashes. Her cousins giggled.

"Of course," Baktre, the eldest of the princesses teased, "he *always* looks handsome."

Ankhmaat felt his face flush. He bowed to Anen and then winked. He'd taken a risk and stolen a kiss from her the previous evening. He could tell by the way she smiled she was still pleased.

"I would love to stay and chat," he replied, "but my place is at the front, near father." He touched Anen's cheek with the back of his hand. "Soon, you will take your place next to me, like Durame next to Senui," he said, noticing the other girls' eyes grow wide. "If you so wish."

It was a hasty thing to do before he'd asked his father, but something in his heart told him Ankhwenefer would grant him any woman he wanted. Always his father had been clear Ankhmaat's queen would be his own choice. Well, Ankhmaat had chosen. No woman, not even the high priestess of Meroe, with her delightful Anit-Shadya techniques, made his heart sing like Anen did. The taste of her kiss still lingered on his lips.

"If I wish?" Anen replied, placing her palms on her cheeks. "Of course, I wish."

Ankhmaat grasped her hand and kissed it. "Then I will discuss it with Pharaoh." He looked to Baktre and Shesh, both of whom were turning red while trying to hold back their laughter. Silence was difficult for the pair of sisters. "Good day, ladies."

The three girls chattered in high-pitched squeals as Ankhmaat continued past his male cousins, each of whom slapped him on the back. This wasn't only a moment of return; his father planned on announcing him as his successor in front of the kingdom. Ankhmaat's stomach turned circles. He didn't want his father to die anytime soon, but naming his successor was important because it meant the throne would remain intact should the pharaoh die in the upcoming battles along the border. Ankhmaat shook the idea from his mind. His father would not fall to the sword—Ankhmaat would make sure of it.

As Ankhmaat took his place at his father's side, Ankhwenefer put an arm around him and drew him close to his side. His father kissed his forehead and nodded toward the docks. "My son, these are our people, we defend them and honor them, and in return, they grant us our power. Never forget that."

Ankhmaat looked out to the noisy crowd. Several dozen of Ankhwenefer's banners waved in the wind. Throngs of people cheered and threw flowers and palm leaves on the ground. Musicians played drums and trumpets. Their golden royal ship glided along the slow, smooth Nile River and docked. Several men threw ropes to men on the deck and they tied the boat steady. The plank was lowered, and Ankhwenefer led the party of royals to the landing.

"My people," Pharaoh yelled in a deep, booming voice, arms raised above his head.

The crowd roared, cheering his father's name and welcoming him home with various cries: "Hail to the golden eagle king," "Hail to The Good Being of Isis," "Our Lord and Pharaoh has returned."

"It has been several years since I set out to survey the Upper Kingdom," Ankhwenefer continued over the din. "I bring my people many blessings. Treaties with Nubia and Kush, jewels, gold, and supplies from the south, and seven strong royal men to lead this country."

On cue, the seven princes stepped forward, and Ankhmaat shivered as he took in the elated smiles and tears forming on the people's faces. They clapped their hands above their heads, jumped up and down, and hugged each other. Ankhmaat glanced to either side at his cousins and brother, his chest tight, as if the goddess were gripping his heart.

"They have been trained in war, diplomacy, and politics," his father continued. "They have met the nobles of our kingdom and dined with them. They were present when I signed our treaties with Kush and Nubia. They know the kings and queens of our great nation by face. These are good, honorable men, who have pledged to uphold a standard of dignity and protect our lands from the Lower Kingdom. Have no fear, as long as these princes live, so will the Upper Kingdom of Egypt."

Ankhmaat's knees buckled as the crowd's enthusiasm washed over him in a frantic wave. His father turned and held out his hand. "And now I present to you, the Crown Prince Ankhmaat, my eldest son, and king-in-waiting."

Ankhmaat stepped forward and bowed low to his father, with his hand upon the handle of his sword. Sucking in a deep breath, he rose and faced the sea of faces as his father continued to address them,

"Ankhmaat will be my successor. I am proud of this young man and trust he will keep you in his heart when he rules with truth and justice."

The crowd cheered, this time calling out his name. "Prince Ankhmaat, the future king."

Most of the court stood near his mother, with the priests beyond them and then the soldiers. The commoners were so far away, there was no way they could hear anything other than the cheering, yet they danced about and threw palms and lotus flowers into the air. Ankhmaat looked to the priests and soldiers and understood these were two groups he needed to impress, for the priests would be the ones to give him the crown and the soldiers would give him their arms. Without them, he was nothing.

While the priests stood still, arms folded behind their backs as if reserving their judgment, the soldiers bellowed, swords raised above their heads to salute their future pharaoh. Ankhmaat knew he looked like the young Ankhwenefer, and his youth inspired them. He hoped he'd be a good enough man for them when he took the crown. His father was a renowned strategist, but Ankhmaat was as of yet untested. A sheen of sweat formed on his brow as he considered going to war within the month.

"I am grateful to be home," Ankhwenefer said. "Please join us in the throne room and meet these fine men. All are invited to tonight's feast."

The pharaoh strode toward his wife, who had left her litter to stand at the front of the dock, clapping for her eldest son and surrounded by beautiful young men and women, some not much older than Ankhmaat himself. Ankhmaat and Khenefer followed their father to greet her.

"My word," she said, her eyes glistening as she wrapped her thin, bangled arms around Ankhmaat first. "Where has my little boy gone?"

Ankhmaat cringed as he replied, "It's good to see you, Mother."

"Khenefer," she exclaimed, now tugging his little brother into her arms. He was fourteen years old yet towered over her. "I'm so glad you're okay. My, how I've missed you both."

She appeared genuine in her compliments, her smile wide and face eager, and while it made Ankhmaat uneasy, it comforted him to know she cared. "We're glad to be home as well," he answered, kissing her hand. "It has been a long time."

His mother looked to his father, biting her lower lip. Ankhwenefer cocked his head, but his gaze was hard and cold. Ankhmaat didn't understand why they were so uncomfortable in each other's company, but it had been this way his whole life.

"My queen," Ankhwenefer said in a low voice, placing an arm around her and kissing her lips in front of her courters. The crowd cheered at his affectionate embrace. "You are radiant to behold."

Ankhmaat thought there was a bit of adoration in his mother's gaze, but it vanished as she spoke, instead replaced with a grin that looked more devious than loving. For some reason, she looked like a viper ready to strike, and it gave Ankhmaat pause.

"Come," she said, grin still plastered on her face as she clasped the pharaoh's arm and waved to the crowd, "we have many guests to greet."

Several litters transported the royal entourage to the throne room where they would spend the day greeting the Theban nobility, priests, soldiers, and peasants. The pharaoh and his queen stood in the center of the line in front of the throne. Ankhmaat was to the right of his father and Khenefer next to his mother. On Ankhmaat's other side stood Senui, his wife Durame, and then his brother, Horpais. His other cousins, Panas and Hor, stood next to their mother, Bithiah. Queen Ruia and the three princesses rounded out the group. Sethe was nowhere to be seen, having gone straight to the priests after their arrival. Ankhmaat missed him already. The two were close, his cousin was like an older brother, but Sethe was the high priestess's son and had his own role in the court to fill.

The nobles entered first. After what seemed like hours, the priests entered, led by High Priest Setep and High Priestess Alexa. Sethe was beside his mother, wearing his dark, priestly robes and looking very formal, a lopsided grin on his face in spite of it. At his side stood his little sister, Meryt. As Ankhmaat greeted them, he recalled Meryt was also his little sister, a holy child between High Priestess Alexa and his father. The little girl had been a toddler when they'd left five years ago, and Ankhmaat's stomach tightened as he considered how he'd have to bond with the high priestess upon becoming pharaoh. What if he didn't want to be so close to anyone other than Anen? Wasn't a queen enough? He looked at his father as the man greeted Alexa and watched the pharaoh take the woman into his arms, lingering as he held her. What did his mother think? Five years from court, and Ankhmaat had forgotten about the intrigue. He'd rather steer clear of it. Simple seemed better.

His father stiffened and dropped Alexa from his embrace, his hand flying to his sword as if to draw it. Ankhmaat searched for his father's source of concern and saw a man, a bit shorter than himself, standing before them. He wore a wig, prince's collar, and clothing, full makeup on his face, as well as a crown, yet stood among the priests. Ankhmaat looked closer and noticed a clear resemblance to not only his father and Ruia but his cousins as well. He racked his mind. Who was this man?

"What are you doing here?" his father growled. Alexa placed a hand on Ankhwenefer's arm, but he shrugged it off as he took a step closer to the stranger. "I thought I'd banished you from my court, Chanax."

"Dear brother," Chanax replied, dropping his gaze to the floor and executing a bow, "good to see you as well. I assume the queen neglected to tell you I was here?"

"Chanax?" Ankhmaat asked, the grimace on his father's face giving Ankhmaat much concern. The pharaoh gasped as if struggling to breathe, and his face was turning red. Ankhmaat feared he might make a fool of himself. "Are you Sethe, Panas, and Hor's father?"

The brothers once told him their father lived in Memphis, but Ankhmaat hadn't thought much of it, until now.

"Yes," Chanax answered, turning and bowing to the prince. "Very nice to meet you, Ankhmaat. The last time I saw you, you were barely walking."

Ankhwenefer grabbed Chanax by the collar and heaved him from the ground. "Get out."

The crowded room grew silent, and everyone stared at their

pharaoh as he held Chanax's neck in his grip. Choking a relative on the day of their return wouldn't bode well, and Ankhmaat knew he needed to do something before his father murdered his own brother in public.

"Father," Ankhmaat said, glancing at his cousins, who were staring at the scene, mouths hanging open. Ankhmaat placed his arm on Ankhwenefer's bicep and spoke in a low voice so the crowd wouldn't hear. "If this is my cousins' father, I welcome him. They are dear to us, and we wouldn't insult them."

The pharaoh released his brother and took a step back, rubbing his hands along his tunic. Ankhmaat offered his hand to Chanax, who shook it, still shaking from the encounter. Ankhwenefer gripped the hilt of his sword but left it in its sheath.

"Excellent counsel, son," Ankhwenefer said, his voice hoarse and trembling as he struggled to contain his rage. "I'm sorry. Please forgive me. It's been thirteen years since I last saw my brother, and while you may have changed during that time, I'm certain he hasn't."

Chanax rubbed his neck as he gazed at the king from under lowered lids, "Believe me, brother, much has changed."

Ankhmaat felt a chill run down his back.

His uncle turned to Weret, who hugged him and stroked his cheek while inspecting the red marks on his neck, and then he passed on down the line to greet his sons and daughters. Weret avoided Ankhwenefer's cold, penetrating gaze, and Ankhmaat knew she had tricked his father. After the priests and priestesses filed by, the soldiers arrived, and his father's jaw relaxed. The royal party spent the rest of the long morning in this way, greeting the people. Ankhmaat's feet were on fire when the last peasant left and the doors to the throne room slammed shut. The moment they were alone, his father turned on his mother.

"How dare you allow him back into the court," he screamed, his angry tone echoing off the gilded walls.

"Ankhwenefer, please," Weret shushed, "not in front of the children." Ankhwenefer grabbed her by the arms, and her mouth twisted as she begged, "Stop it, you're hurting me."

Ankhmaat turned to Panas, who was running his hands through his hair, staring at his younger brother, Hor. Their sisters, Baktre and

Shesh, gazed at their feet, hands folded behind their backs. Khenefer wrapped an arm around Shesh's shoulders as Ruia stepped forward, her mouth opening to speak. Rather than letting his aunt handle things, Ankhmaat decided to take control.

"Father," Ankhmaat said, stepping closer to the couple, "may I have a word in private?" Ankhwenefer's grip on his wife's arms loosened, and Ankhmaat saw bruises already forming. "Now."

Ankhwenefer let her go and spoke without looking at his son. "Yes. I need to rest. Meet me in my chambers. The rest of you are dismissed."

He stormed toward the golden doors, and the guards opened them as he approached, allowing them to bang shut behind him.

The queen turned to Ankhmaat, rubbing her arms. "Well, you *are* a grown man now, aren't you? I've never seen anyone handle your father with such ease."

"That's not true," Ruia challenged as she walked up to Ankhmaat's side, her arms crossed.

"I suppose you think you're the only one who can make him see reason?" Weret said, placing her hands on her hips.

Ruia shook her head. "Oh no. I can't talk sense into that man. Natasa was the one he listened to most."

Queen Weret jumped back as if stung by a bee. "How dare you speak her name?"

"Natasa?" Ankhmaat asked.

"There's no need to tear open old wounds," the high queen continued, shaking her finger at Ruia.

"The boy needs to know," Ruia snapped.

Weret flinched as her sister spoke.

"What do I need to know, Mother?" Ankhmaat asked, trying to be careful with his words. He needed the truth and wasn't sure how to get it from this woman.

"Just this—your father broke the law years ago, and he still won't admit his failure. Instead, he blames his misfortune on Chanax and me, and it is unfair."

"Broke the law?"

"Yes." Her nostrils flared a little. "You'll see."

She spun on her heel and sprinted from the room, her small entourage steps behind. Ankhmaat let out a held breath. This was not the homecoming he'd imagined.

"My Lord Ankhmaat," his aunt Bithiah said, falling to her knees at his feet as she approached him, bowing low, her face prostrate on the floor. "Please forgive me."

"Get up," Ruia said, tugging at the back of Bithiah's collar, but she wouldn't budge.

"It's true, your father did break the law, with Natasa, a healer," Bithiah continued, speaking at the floor, her shoulders now shaking. "She had taken a vow of celibacy, yet the two continued to be lovers, which is a crime."

Ankhmaat looked to Ruia to see if this was true. His aunt nodded to him.

"But it wasn't your mother who betrayed them," Bithiah explained, now sitting up on her knees, hands clasped over her heart. "It was Chanax and I. We spied on your father and his lover and turned them in to the authorities. She and their daughter were condemned to death. Please believe me, I never would have—"

"Daughter?" Ankhmaat interrupted. "What do you mean, daughter?"

Bithiah again bowed low before him, grasping at his feet. "My lord, they had a child of the temple, Helena. She was taken as a proxy for your father's sins as he was too important to lose during the great battle with the Greeks." She paused and looked up again, grasping at the hem of his tunic. "I never ever would have testified if I'd known they'd kill the child."

"Why did you testify at all?" Ankhmaat demanded.

Bithiah bit her lip. She ran her hands through her hair. She rubbed at her eyes, smearing her kohl all over her cheeks.

"I did it because Chanax wanted me to, and he was my husband."

"Lies," Ruia said, rushing up to her sister's side and yanking her from the floor. "You did it because you wanted to be queen. With Ankhwenefer out of the way, you thought you could steal the throne for yourself."

"No," Bithiah replied, sobbing now into her hands. "That's not true."

"You and Chanax betrayed your own brother, and as a result, my sister died?" Ankhmaat asked. The thought was unimaginable. He glanced at Khenefer, who now held Shesh tightly in his arms. Never would Ankhmaat do such a thing to his little brother.

Both his aunts looked to one another, and then Ruia nodded. "Yes, that's what happened."

"Then why are you here, Bithiah, as the pharaoh's royal midwife? Has he forgiven you of your betrayal?" Ankhmaat asked.

"He has forgiven me, my lord," she answered, looking to her feet.

Ankhmaat took a step closer and her head jerked to attention. "Tell me, Aunt Bithiah, should we trust Chanax as we've trusted you?"

Her lower lip began to tremble. She glanced at her daughters, then at Ruia, and last at her sons, holding Panas's gaze a bit longer than the others. Finally, her eyes snapped to Ankhmaat.

"No, my lord, I would not trust him."

Still trembling, Bithiah turned and fled the room.

31

A Father's Pain

"Organization is impossible unless those who know the laws of harmony lay the foundation."
~Proverb from The Temple of Luxor

Thebes, Egypt, 186 BCE

Ankhmaat stormed into his father's study. The king stood by the fire, his crown, collar, and sword removed. He'd tied back his long dark hair, exposing his tired face. Ankhmaat had never seen him look so frail.

"Why didn't you ever tell me about my sister?" Ankhmaat demanded as he crossed the room to stand at his father's side.

"Who told you about Helena?" Ankhwenefer replied as he fingered the ring on his pinky. "Your mother? I imagine she enjoyed informing you of my crimes."

"It wasn't mother, though she did mention you unjustly accuse her and Chanax for my sister's death."

"She would say such things," he said, his lips curled. "Your mother is a dim-witted woman."

"Father, please, I don't care what you think about Mother. I want to know about Helena."

Ankhwenefer walked to the table and poured himself a glass of wine, which he downed in one gulp. Then he poured himself another and held the bottle out to his son. "Would you like a drink?"

Ankhmaat shook his head.

"Come, sit beside me," Ankhwenefer commanded.

They sat on a leather divan by the brazier, Ankhmaat's body tight and alert, while his father sagged into the cushions. Ankhwenefer drank his wine and stared into the fire.

"First," the king began, "I want to know who told you."

"Aunt Bithiah."

Ankhwenefer raised an eyebrow. "Interesting, since she was my brother's accomplice."

"Yes, she told me she'd witnessed you having sex with a healer. Why would you do such a thing?"

"When I was twenty," his father began, "I bonded with the priestess Natasa, daughter of the high priestess, Neferu-ankh-maat. I loved her more than anything and during our first year as spiritual companions, she gave birth to our daughter, Helena. Under the law, I had to take a sister as my wife, and your mother hated the love I had for Natasa. Her jealousy corrupted her, and when she found herself without child while each of her sisters was pregnant, even though I was doing all I could to help with the situation, she accused me of treason."

"Treason? What for?"

"She accused me of plotting to use the army to take the throne from my father. It was nonsense, but she was willing to put the kingdom at risk in order to punish me for not loving her as I loved Natasa. Imagine it, demanding love from someone? My father believed her and banned me from the temple of Isis and her priestesses. He reassigned Natasa to Silus, and I was sent off to battle without even a chance to say goodbye."

"What a terrible thing for a king to do," Ankhmaat said, clutching his chest as he considered how he'd feel if his father assigned Anen to Khenefer.

Ankhwenefer rubbed his temples. "Tired of kings and priests telling her how to use her body, Natasa retired from the temple of Isis and entered the Houses of Healing. She took a vow of celibacy, as is protocol, and healed many during the civil war."

"Natasa the Healer?" Ankhmaat asked, remembering her from a legend about his father. "Is she the same one they sing about in the song where the love of your life rescues you from death?"

"Yes. I'd arrived from battle in Behdet dying and returned to the battlefield stronger than ever, and that was Natasa's doing. She was my twin flame and my partner in life."

A grimace crossed his father's face. "We became lovers in secret. We knew death was the punishment for our crime, and each of us was willing to die for the other. I was often at war, but every year or so I'd return to Behdet, and we'd fall into one another's arms. Until the day when Chanax and Bithiah spied on us and turned us in. I was away at battle, and rather than send the police to arrest me, they took Helena instead, as a proxy for my crime. Somehow she was killed during the arrest."

"What happened to Natasa? Did they hang her?"

"No," Ankhwenefer answered, shaking his head. "She escaped with her parents. They took the Nile north, into the heart of the battle at Coptos, and then rode the Wadi Hammamat to the Red Sea before eventually sailing to Gaul, where she died of illness, though her mother insists Natasa died of grief."

Ankhwenefer's head fell into his hands. Ankhmaat placed a hand on his father's back and remained silent. His mind reeled from the revelations. Which adult could he trust in a court filled with such corruption?

After a moment, Ankhwenefer spoke, his voice clearer, "I banished Chanax from my kingdom and have spent the past thirteen years raising my sons and trying to forget it ever happened."

"Where has my uncle been all this time?" Ankhmaat asked.

"In Memphis, serving the Cult of Set. Training to be their high priest, no doubt."

"The Cult of Set? They're evil, the priests in Meroe warned me about them."

"Yes, and since I banished the cult from the Upper Kingdom, they now serve Ptolemy V. I am certain of it."

"Then he's here to spy on us."

"Yes," the pharaoh agreed. "Your mother has again risked the security of the kingdom in order to punish me. What do you think my options are, son?"

Ankhmaat considered his answer carefully. The question was his was his father's way of testing him. "You can't let him return to Memphis."

"No, I can't. The way I see it, I either have to kill him, or let him remain here, kept under constant watch."

"You can't kill him, at least not right away. That would drive a wedge between myself and his sons. You've worked so hard to bring us together, and for the stability of the court, we need to wait and see."

"I agree." Ankhwenefer rose to refill his cup. "The high queen has let him roam free for weeks. He's sure to have already sent letters to Memphis detailing any weaknesses, daily rituals, and habits in the court, such as the changing of the guards, the number of troops in Thebes, and any openings for invasion. He will not be free anymore. I will set four of my best men on him. Chanax can never be alone, not even when he's sleeping. I want his comings and goings reported to me daily, and his correspondences monitored. We must cut him off from Memphis."

"That's a good idea," Ankhmaat agreed.

"I'll have Alexa keep tabs on him as well. They were spiritual companions before his banishment, I'm sure he'll try to rekindle something. Anything else, son?"

"Yes, there is," Ankhmaat said. "You should have told me about Helena." He rose from his seat and took his father's hands. "If I die, I don't want you to forget about me."

"You're right, son, I'm sorry," Ankhwenefer replied as he wrapped his muscular arms around Ankhmaat, squeezing the air out of the boy's chest. When Ankhmaat coughed, the pharaoh released him, yawning as he did so. "If there's nothing else, I need to retire before the banquet. I must rest before facing that scoundrel."

Ankhmaat cleared his throat. "There is one more thing."

"What is it, son?"

"I wish to request Anen's hand in marriage."

Ankhwenefer smiled, and the light seemed to dance in his eyes. "Is that so? You've only just met."

"I fell in love the moment I arrived in Behdet," Ankhmaat admitted. "I want her to be my queen, and I don't want to take a spiritual companion. Anen will be enough."

"She's not trained in Anit-Shadya."

"It doesn't matter," Ankhmaat said, his heart racing as he considered what he was asking. "I will teach her. I'm more than qualified, as the high priestess of Meroe can attest."

Ankhwenefer slapped him on the back and laughed. "Someone is a bit sure of himself, isn't he? King Silus must approve the marriage, but there's no reason you can't take ceremony before we head out to the front line."

"Thank you, Father. Truly, thank you." Ankhmaat said, hugging his father. "This is the best gift you could give me."

Ankhwenefer returned the hug, lifting his son from his feet. "The two of you will make a fine pharaoh and high queen of Upper Egypt. Now go get some rest. It's going to be an exhausting month."

Ankhmaat nodded and jogged to the door. He turned to check on his father, who was staring once more into the firelight, his jovial grin replaced with a stony expression.

"Father?"

Ankhwenefer's head snapped to attention. "Yes?"

"I'm sorry you've lost so much."

"Thank you, son."

32

A Priestly Agreement

We are awake, I must believe it. Evil cannot win. Any other truth will destroy me. Love must reign and we are all called to learn to fly above this darkness.

~ Natasa's notes, found in her study by Iu-Amon in 197 BCE

Thebes, Egypt, 186 BCE

Chanax blew a kiss at the four men who stood at his door. They looked past him as if he didn't exist. They didn't even speak. They were the perfect guards. Damn his brother. It'd been days since Ankhwenefer had returned, and the bastard still hadn't called to see him. Instead, he sent four guards to spy on Chanax's every breath. Weret complained when he attended her parties in the evenings to indulge in her lifestyle. The usual protocol was for their guards to stand outside of the queen's chambers to enable the guests to let go and feel fancy-free, but Chanax's bodyguards had different orders. It was maddening. Weret's noblewomen were starting to avoid him, they didn't like to be observed while cheating on their dear husbands in his bed.

He should have expected it. Ankhwenefer knew Chanax was there to spy, but Chanax himself wasn't even sure this was his purpose in Thebes anymore. Life was good in the golden city, especially with the arrival of his children. He was safe from Ptolemy's threats. Perhaps in time, he'd prove to his brother he no longer wanted to harm him but rather desired to be a member of the court.

He'd visited his children several times, and while their various reunions had been tense, progress was happening. His sons were remarkable young men, and his daughters were charming. It stung that they considered Ankhwenefer and Ruia to be their parents, but at least the children hadn't suffered for their parents' sins. It surprised Chanax that Ankhwenefer had taken such a generous approach, given Chanax and Bithiah's hand in his own daughter's death.

"My lord," one of his guards said. "High Priest Setep has arrived."

Chanax rose from his settee and made his way to his parlor. Weret had given him an exquisite set of chambers. She insisted they'd been unused since her arrival in Thebes a decade ago. Chanax glanced at the artwork and thought they favored a distinctly feminine touch yet could not think of any woman whom Ankhwenefer would keep here. Perhaps he had a mistress in the beginning of his Pharaonic rule? Or had planned on a second queen? Both seemed unlikely, and Chanax hadn't heard any rumors of such a thing.

He strode into the parlor, head held high, where the high priest stood at the window. Setep turned and nodded to Chanax. "Thank you for seeing me."

"It's my pleasure," Chanax lied. He couldn't stand the man. "I've been meaning to call upon you myself but found re-entry into the court a bit busier than I'd expected. Please, join me for some refreshments."

The men took a seat at the table and servants brought wine, cheese, bread, and figs. Setep poured himself a drink and gazed at Chanax over his goblet as he took a sip.

"What is it you wish to discuss?" Chanax asked.

"Alexa," Setep replied.

"Alexa?"

"Yes," Setep continued, "your return has upset her very much."

"I'm sorry to hear that," Chanax offered. "What can I do to make it easier on her?"

"I understand you've been seeking her out. Why is this?"

"Certainly you know why, my lord," Chanax replied, painting a pleasant grin upon his face. "We were quite close before my brother banished me from the Upper Kingdom." Setep winced, and Chanax shrugged as he continued, "It appears my sorrow has led to your joy, and you must understand that while life goes on, my heart still longs for her friendship. From her response to my visits, it appears she still desires my friendship as well."

Setep cracked his knuckles. "Yes, she longs for you in some strange way. Yet she also cries herself to sleep every night, and our ceremony has been filled with the forms of her sadness and grief."

The high priest paused to eat a fig, never breaking eye contact, and Chanax sensed the man attempt to penetrate his Ka. Chanax sent out the form of contentment and put up his defenses. He'd been around Weret and her foolish friends for so long, he'd forgotten how tricky the priests were with their energetic manipulations. It was both irritating and refreshing to be playing this game once more.

Setep sensed his response and smiled. "I hear you are a very powerful magician. In line for the high priest role in Memphis, should your masters ever die. This is the problem with dark power—those who are adept at it use it for immortality, affecting the very balance of life."

Chanax considered what the priest was suggesting, and the image of Metakryon slurping his elixir of blood and wine flashed through his mind. Setep raised an eyebrow, and Chanax closed himself even more. This man was a master.

"I'm here to ask you to leave Alexa alone," Setep declared. He glanced at the four guards in the corner. "I wanted to demand you leave Thebes, but it appears your brother has decided you're now a prisoner in his palace. Thus, the way to bestow peace upon my lady is for you to refrain from calling upon her."

"I will come to the temple as I wish," Chanax argued. "I have the right to visit my son and his mother."

Setep's brow wrinkled. "Lord Ankhwenefer and I raised Sethe, not you."

"You *do* have some loyalty to the pharaoh," Chanax suggested, sensing his opening to discuss the potential of betraying Ankhwenefer.

"Why wouldn't I?" Setep replied, waving his hand, but Chanax sensed he was hiding his disdain for the pharaoh and decided to nudge him further.

"We heard in Memphis that your pharaoh doesn't respect the gods and goddesses anymore. If this is true, why do you lend your support to his crown?"

"Do you consider Ptolemy Epiphanes devout?" Setep parried.

"Yes and no," Chanax admitted. "He's cruel and undisciplined, but he follows our customs and takes part in our rituals. He takes our counsel. As I understand it, Ankhwenefer put Alexa in that role and has ignored you, with the exception of the public rituals he must attend for the people's sake."

"What you speak of is true," Setep replied, raising his folded hands to his face, his two long index fingers resting on his lips. "Our relationship with the royals is tenuous. Neither the pharaoh nor his wife, are devout. It was obvious from the beginning when Ankhwenefer forced us to share our secrets with the Northerner."

"The Northerner?" Chanax asked. It was the first he'd heard of it.

"Yes, a scribe from the north, named Finnian. He'd been close to Natasa during her time away," Setep explained. "Our pharaoh never explained the nature of their relationship, but Finnian arrived from Gaul, claiming to have known the Lady Natasa and bearing her final letter to Our Majesty."

Chanax felt a clench in his stomach. A man from Gaul who had been close to Natasa?

"Why did the pharaoh force you to share our secrets with the man?" Chanax asked, moving closer to the edge of his seat and grasping a cluster of grapes into his palm from the table.

"It appears Natasa channeled the goddess Isis while in Gaul, and the Northerner scribed it," Setep explained, his brow furrowed as he recalled the story. "The book contains many of our mysteries. The pharaoh commanded Finnian to read it aloud in its entirety, and in exchange, Finnian requested access to our most important steles, temple inscriptions, and monuments. He took notes and copied our artwork. It was blasphemous, but we had no choice."

"This book of Natasa's, did you ever read it?" Chanax asked.

"Of course," Setep answered. "Finnian made the pharaoh his own copy before he left."

"His own copy? You mean I could read it?"

"If you wish. Pharaoh Ankhwenefer kept it for years in his study, until one day he gave it to me and asked me to keep it in the temple library. He'd said it haunted him, and he no longer wished to have the book near him."

"May I borrow it?" Chanax begged.

"Yes. I'll let my page know you have permission."

Setep drank his wine in silence while Chanax digested the revelation. A book existed, something Natasa had left behind, something to let him know of her suffering. He had to read it. Chanax glanced at Setep and smirked.

"It is a shame the pharaoh allowed a northerner to know our religion. I feel your pain."

"He and his wife have been a disgrace to the religion from the beginning. It is a scandal the way he allows her to participate in inappropriate behaviors while he ignores her, locked away in his study with his men."

"Yet you allow it when you could take the crown from him and give it to Epiphanes."

Setep remained silent and unreadable. He was on high alert and Chanax knew it.

"That is treasonous talk," Setep said in a low voice. "We've long supported the rebellion. Better to have a native king than a Macedonian fraud. Ankhwenefer has been good for Upper Egypt. As you can see, the people are thriving. A change of command would destroy our peace and prosperity, for Ptolemy Epiphanes would not come here in kindness for the crown. We decided long ago that until Ankhwenefer died, we would support him, even with his failings."

"If he dies on the battlefield? Will you consider returning the country back to Epiphanes and allow the Egyptian Empire to be whole as it should be?"

"I must be honest with you, until the pharaoh's return from his southern travels, that had been the plan," Setep replied. "Ankhwenefer and his queen have made many in our priesthood angry. We tire of their irreverence, and we long for a united Egypt under a pharaoh who will partake in the mysteries. We've assumed that when the man died, we'd send for Ptolemy Epiphanes and make an offer in peace, but no longer."

"Why? What has changed?"

"Prince Ankhmaat."

Chanax's pulse quickened. "His son?"

"Yes," Setep explained. "The entire priesthood has spent the past week interviewing the king-in-waiting before they leave for battle. Ankhwenefer hasn't fought with the blade against his foe in ten years. The likelihood of him dying is high, and he wants us to crown his son pharaoh upon his death, so we had to see if we agreed. After many deep discussions with the young man, we find him to be everything his father is when it comes to diplomacy, and even more. He is religious, devout, loving, and honorable. He has altars in his chambers to various gods and goddesses and has pledged himself to Horus and our mother Isis. He was trained by the priests in Meroe and has a complete understanding of our faith, as well as a yearning to practice it. Crowning Prince Ankhmaat will ensure our stability should the pharaoh fall and perhaps even usher in the next golden age."

Isidor had said they needed to strike before the eldest son grew unto manhood. It appeared they'd tarried too long.

"He will turn eighteen next week," Setep continued. "He is also trained in Anit-Shadya and has given his cousin, Anen, first rites. The two will be married when he returns from battle in the north and then we will have not only a king worthy of the temple but a queen as well, for she too is a being of pious perfection. Do you know of the Golden Child prophecy?"

Chanax nodded, his heart going cold. Images of Helena running with Sethe in the palace halls flashed through his mind.

"The priesthood of Thebes has officially recognized Prince Ankhmaat as that being, the promised one who will drive the

Macedonians from our shores. Thus, we no longer have the need to parley with Ptolemy Epiphanes. Should his troops manage to kill our pharaoh, who is very loved by his people, we will crown his son, Ankhmaat, who is very loved by his priests."

Chanax felt his spirits deflate. There was no way he could carry out Ptolemy's request. Managing to find an opening to arrest his brother was impossible at best, but also killing Ankhmaat in the process? His gaze shifted to the four guards, and he grimaced. He hated them, but they'd probably keep him safe. Perhaps he should resign to failure and find a way to live in peace with his brother.

"Setep," he said, his voice soft, "I agree with you. The young man is worthy. That's why I'm here. I want to be with my children. They've done well, and Egypt is better for it. Why can't I be a part of that? I've paid a high price for my mistakes."

"Yes," Setep replied, "Alexa has told me how you betrayed your brother and her best friend in an act of greed for the throne yourself."

"Ankhwenefer committed a crime when he slept with that woman," Chanax answered through clenched teeth, now wishing the conversation was over.

Setep's lips curled into a slight smile. Using Chanax's anger as a means to penetrate his Ka field, he slid into Chanax's unguarded mind. The high priest's eyes grew wider as he searched Chanax's soul. "You loved her, didn't you?"

Chanax rose from his seat, closing himself off to the energetic attack. How could he have been so sloppy? "No. I didn't. She was my playmate as a child, but Alexa was the one I loved."

"Ah," Setep answered, "we've come full circle. Leave Alexa alone."

Chanax paced around the table. "Fine. Anything else?"

"Yes," the high priest continued, "I want to know if you desire to join our priesthood. You're a trained master at energy work and would be an asset, if you denounce Ptolemy Epiphanes and the Cult of Set."

Chanax paused. Did he want to be a priest? He searched his heart and then looked to Setep. "I no longer wish to wear the priest's robes. I was forced to enter the temple in Memphis. I never wanted it."

Setep rose from his seat and nodded. "I see. Well, thank you for this, Chanax. It has been a most fruitful conversation."

The priest let himself out, and Chanax fell into his chair, exhausted. He poured himself a glass of wine and nibbled on a piece of thick, coarse bread. It was clear he'd have to drop the mission to help Ptolemy end his brother. This was a battle between the pharaohs, and Chanax no longer wanted to be a part of it. Instead, he wanted to party in Weret's chambers, take strolls in the gardens with beautiful noblewomen, and get to know his children. Moreover, he wanted to read Natasa's book. Since his father had offered him as tribute in Memphis, Chanax had been living someone else's life. He drank down his wine and let any thought of betrayal leave his mind.

It was time to be a prince again.

33

The Front Line

In Alexandria, Cleopatra I was known as the Syrian. By the year 186 BCE, she'd born Ptolemy V two children, a boy, and a girl, and was pregnant with a third. In 187 BCE she was named her husband's vizier. In court life, as well as politics, the young woman showed great promise, which is why she would become the first Ptolemaic queen to be a sole ruler over all of Egypt.

North of Panopolis, Egypt, 186 BCE

"They've breached the fortress, my lord," the soldier announced.

Ankhwenefer clapped his hands as if pleased with the news. "It was only a matter of time. Nothing we can't fix once we've finished them off."

A mile north, after months of relentless fighting, the Greeks had taken control of the fortress his father had built years prior and were on their way toward them, yet Ankhwenefer looked like he was on his way to a festival. He held his bow in his hand and gestured to his son, grinning from ear to ear. "Prepare to fight. This will be a battle between ships, trust me."

Ankhmaat had spent years under his father's instruction learning to shoot the bow and arrow. He extended his Ka and connected to the pharaoh. Together they saw more than alone.

"That's it, son." Ankhwenefer plucking at his bowstring. "Focus on the space around us in all directions. Their boats will arrive in moments. Remember there are at least twenty of my own ships following the attack. The fleet Ptolemy has sent is small. We will crush them."

"Why would they send so few boats?" Ankhmaat asked.

"Because, they're not prepared for a full invasion just yet," his father said. "Consider this a test run, each side getting a close-up of the other."

"What about the hundreds of men on horseback who now ride along the shore?" Ankhmaat replied, pointing to the dust clouds on the horizon to the north.

"My cavalry has been released as well," his father answered, glancing to the south where the dirt swirled like a summer storm brewing to strike.

Ankhmaat felt caught between two sandstorms—his heart raced, yet his mouth was dry as if his body couldn't decide if it should fight or flee. Ankhmaat swallowed hard and planted his feet firmly on the wooden deck. He would fight.

"Aim for the horses as they ride past along the shore, but also focus on the boats," Ankhwenefer instructed. "When their ships arrive, we will attempt to board them. Any cavalry that slips past us will be shot by my men farther south. As we attack their ships, we will sail downriver toward the Greeks and force them to retreat to the fortress. They won't pass us and continue south, for there is no way into my kingdom with this small of a force."

There was a fire in his father's gaze as he spoke. Senui, Horpais, Panas, and Hor stood at the pharaoh's side. The time had come for all of them to be tested in battle. Only Khenefer had been left behind in Thebes. At barely fourteen, his father still wouldn't let him fight beyond the training ring. Besides, if the worst happened and both Ankhmaat and his father died in this battle, Khenefer would take the throne under the regency of Ennaeus. For his part, Ankhmaat had no intention of letting his father fail today. Victory would be theirs.

The first of the cavalry approached as a noisy din of screaming men and galloping horses. Ankhmaat pulsed out even further with his Ka, sensing the excitement amongst his soldiers, and nocked an arrow in his bow. He drew back and aimed at the horseman leading the Greek charge. He sensed the golden stream between the tip of his arrow and the horse's chest and let the weapon fly. It met its mark and the horse fell, throwing its rider into the oncoming traffic, and stampeding him.

It was Ankhmaat's first kill.

"Good job, son," Ankhwenefer shouted as he released his own arrow. The megau formed a line behind them along the deck as he commanded, "Fire."

Hundreds of arrows soared from the portside of the ship and into the Greek riders. Ankhmaat drew another arrow and, keeping his connection to his father, shot one after the other. Several met their target, and as he took a moment to reload, he glanced at his king. Ankhwenefer fought like a jaguar along the ship's deck, climbing on railings and booms, aiming and firing arrows at lightning speed. Ankhmaat had never seen anything like it, not even in training. The man was dancing with death and thriving in its embrace. Soldier after soldier fell along the shore and while some of the cavalries flew past them, by the time the Greek ships had arrived from the north, hundreds of men and horses lay dead in piles along the shoreline, the Nile River lapping over the bloodied bodies.

"To starboard, men," Ankhwenefer called out.

They obeyed their leader's command and shifted into a new formation, grabbing full quivers from the center of the ship and taking their places on the riverside. Five huge Greek vessels loomed in the distance. Across the river were three more of Ankhwenefer's ships at the ready as well, and farther south, another set of six ships docked along the shoreline, three on each bank. This formation continued for miles. The Greeks were sailing into a slaughter.

"Why send so few?" Ankhmaat murmured. "I still don't understand."

"Conanus has an enormous fleet waiting in Lycopolis, as well as thousands of men, hiding behind the fortress walls. Now that he's driven us from the fortress, he's testing the situation, seeing for himself what our army has been doing south of the border, offering up soldiers for information. The cavalry that slipped past us will report back, and he'll know I've been preparing for this very moment. They will not be granted entry into our country."

"Who is Conanus?" Ankhmaat asked.

Ankhwenefer wiped the sweat from his brow. "Ptolemy's general. After a decade, Epiphanes finally has a commander of his army worthy of meeting me in battle. Conanus is experienced and a renowned strategist."

"Shouldn't that give you pause?"

His father threw back his head and laughed. "It will be a pleasure to fight him."

The Greek ships fired at their position and one of their arrows took down an archer to Ankhmaat's left. As the man fell to the deck, screaming like a cornered beast, Ankhmaat connected to his father and followed his movements, ducking and getting out of the way, as well as firing arrows himself. The front boats on either bank sailed toward the Greek ships. His father had every intention of boarding one of their ships. Ankhmaat held steady, continuing to launch arrow after arrow, as the distance between the boats decreased with every minute.

Time stood still as the two ships collided, Ankhmaat's vessel's bowsprit tearing a gaping hole in the Greek ship's side. The crushing sounds of wood splintering and men screaming filled Ankhmaat's ears.

"Swordsmen at the ready," Ankhwenefer yelled over the din.

Ankhmaat slung his bow across his back and removed his sword from its sheath. It glimmered in the bright sunlight, and again his mouth felt as if he'd swallowed a handful of sand. Now he would face his true test and fight real men, looking them in the eyes as he killed them. Of all his firsts, this was the one he would have loved to avoid. Yet no man can be king without blood on his hands. This was the way of the world.

A group of Kushmen appeared on the deck behind him, screaming and yelling their battle chants. They sprinted toward the enemy with their spears and xystons held high and leaped from their boat onto the Greek's deck, scattering the enemy archers and clearing a way. Ankhwenefer was right behind them, and Ankhmaat followed his father. He leaped from the boat up, over the water, and landed with a thud upon the slippery, wet deck. Taking a deep breath, Ankhmaat approached the nearest enemy. The man was as wide as the mast of the ship, much bigger than Ankhmaat would have liked.

Ankhmaat struck the man, but the soldier blocked it with his shield. After taking many hard blows to his own shield, Ankhmaat remembered his father's lessons and calmed himself, seeking his mind's eye. Extending his energy in all directions, he sensed the soldier's arm moving before it physically did. Knowing that the man would expose his left side, Ankhmaat spun to his right and drove his sword deep within the man's ribs while blocking the man's sword from taking off his own head. His shield vibrated along his arm from the force of the hit, and there was a crackle and a pop as his sword broke through the man's bones and blood squirted everywhere. His enemy's eyes opened wide, and Ankhmaat found himself caught in the man's death gaze. This was what it meant to kill. He wrenched his sword out of the man's body as his victim fell to the ground. Ankhmaat's blade no longer glimmered, instead, it dripped in thick, red blood.

Rather than scare him, his bloodied blade invigorated his soul, and Ankhmaat allowed himself to fall into the battle frenzy and be swept away in its violence and madness.

An hour later, they sailed the Greek ship under their command toward the broken fortress. Behind them, the rest of the Egyptian fleet followed, snaking their way around the Greek vessels' torched corpses as they burned and sank in the river. Ankhmaat stood at the bridge, covered in blood and sweat. His skin smelled of death, and he longed to wash himself clean. The soldiers piled the dead Greeks on the deck in a heap of blood and flies. Ankhwenefer lost several of his own men, but in the end, the Egyptians held the upper hand, and the outnumbered Greeks were either killed or taken prisoner.

As they approached the fortress located between Lycopolis and Abdju, Ankhmaat's heart sank. Behind the wall, thousands of men lined the shores, and Greek ships barricaded the river as far as his eye could see. Ptolemy hadn't sent even a sliver of his army into the battle. Their ship glided toward the fortress docks, where a Greek vessel, bearing Ptolemy's crest, was anchored off the shore. This would be where General Conanus had sat out the battle.

Ankhwenefer strolled to the bow as the Egyptian ships at the lead turned around to go back south. The pharaoh raised his bloodied sword above his head and called out, "General Conanus."

A tall man strode forward to the bow of his unsullied ship. He was well built with a mess of blond, curly hair on his head. He wore a red cape and held his sword and shield at the ready. Fires burned along the top of the fortress walls, and much of it crumbled into the Nile, rendering the river impassable.

"Yes, traitor?" the Greek general answered. Ankhwenefer was bare-chested and covered in blood, sweat, and dirt. He looked like a heathen compared to the pristine Greek general. "I see you have stolen yet more of the true pharaoh's property."

"Not stolen, borrowed," Ankhwenefer replied. "I return it to you with a warning. As many men as you have, I also command, lining these shores all the way to Thebes. These lands are forsaken to you, and your military may not pass."

One of the Egyptian ships now lined itself up along their starboard side, facing the south as their vessel faced north. Only a dozen Egyptians were with the pharaoh aboard the Greek ship. They waited on the bridge for Ankhwenefer's signal.

"It appears you have conquered my fortress," Ankhwenefer continued. "Now that you control it, you will need to fix it, if you hope to let any of your merchant ships travel through our lands. However, given your behavior these past months, my megau have orders to fire at and capture any merchant vessels headed south to Nubia until we come to another peace agreement. Is this clear?"

Conanus placed his hands on his hips. "I will deliver your message to Ptolemy Epiphanes," he said, his lip curled. "However, let me warn you, my lord and king is no longer a child. He will ride to the border himself if need be to kill you and remove your traitorous followers from the face of the earth."

Ankhwenefer threw his head back and taunted, "Tell him to withdraw his troops and stay behind the border, or so help me, there will be no trade between our kingdoms allowed on these shores."

The pharaoh turned back to the bridge and nodded to the captain, who let out the sails, causing the boat to sail faster toward the general's ship. As the ship gained speed Ankhwenefer yelled, "*Now.*"

Ankhmaat launched himself from the stolen vessel and onto the Egyptian craft as it passed by. As they sailed south, the now-abandoned Greek ship, bearing the dead, glided into the dock where Conanus's ship was tethered, crushing the dock and everyone standing on it. The general's ship itself was spared, and Ankhmaat watched as the man observed the destruction. Conanus shrugged as if he had allowed it to happen and glanced back at Ankhmaat. Their gazes met as the young king-in-waiting sailed away with his father. Ankhmaat saw the form of fury surround Conanus, as well as regret.

☥

Later that evening, they docked in Panopolis and made camp with the soldiers. A messenger arrived with a scroll bearing the official Ptolemy seal.

Ankhwenefer read the letter before rolling it back up and playfully hitting Min over the head with it. "Well, that didn't take long. They've agreed to keep to the terms of the original peace treaty set ten years ago, in order that we allow their merchants to continue their trade with Nubia."

"Why do we grant them such a luxury?" Ankhmaat asked.

"Because I tax them in Aswan, and a second time at the fortress downstream from Lycopolis."

"They now have the fortress," Ankhmaat noted.

"Which is why I'll double the tax in Aswan," his father replied, tossing and catching a fig. "They need gold and taking the river through our kingdom is still the easiest route for them to get there. The desert is treacherous, and they lose more to bandits than they pay in taxes to me. Looks like we've bought ourselves some more time."

"Will they make another attempt to attack?" Ankhmaat asked as his father popped the fig in his mouth.

Ankhwenefer swallowed before continuing. "I'll destroy any of their merchant ships en route and take their gold and goods the instant they try anything else, so we'll see when they strike next. Trust me—Ptolemy will never stop trying to take back the south."

"Then why don't we finish him and take Memphis?" Ankhmaat demanded. "Why not drive the Macedonians from our land?"

"The Greek Surge at the beginning of my reign revealed to me how difficult it is to fight this war along the river. The enemy held out in Thebes, surrounded by my army on all sides, for nearly two years. I lost many men, as well as civilians. I've not wanted to risk another surge like that one. Now that Ptolemy has peace with Syria, he has more troops than we do. We're well stationed in our kingdom and can manage to keep them out for several generations, perhaps forever, but if there's a way to surge upon Memphis with the troops we have, while also protecting our people from unnecessary death and onslaught, I'll honor any plan that makes sense."

Ankhmaat nodded at his father across the fire. He noted how the men sat around the pharaoh, hanging on his every word. It was obvious they loved him. Ankhmaat smiled at the scene and envisioned himself surrounded by such loyal men, when he looked to his right and left and saw his cousins, all of whom were looking to him, waiting to hear how he would respond.

"I will set my mind to it, Father. I promise."

"Wonderful. Now, who wants music and ale?"

34

Dangerous Threats

The energy field of those who practice dark magic is forever damaged. They carry their darkness with them, from lifetime to lifetime, and wonder in their ignorance why life is such a struggle.

Thebes, Egypt, 186 BCE

The season of Perit ended, and the farmers harvested their crops as the country fell back into a state of watchful peace. The king-in-waiting married his true love Anen, and the court celebrated for months. While Ankhwenefer spoke with Chanax at public events, he still hadn't called him for a private conversation, acting as if Chanax didn't exist, yet Chanax knew his brother received daily reports detailing his every action. Chanax didn't mind the neglect. His life in Thebes was a party compared to Memphis, even if he was Ankhwenefer's prisoner.

Chanax enjoyed visiting the Valley of the Kings and spent hours gazing upon the monuments of his ancestors. One day it occurred to him that Ankhwenefer wasn't building himself a tomb. The pharaoh's image dotted the cityscape on the various monuments made in his name, but no royal funerary had been commissioned. Didn't he want to be buried properly when he died? At Chanax's next visit with his eldest son, Sethe, he asked him about it.

"That's an interesting question," Sethe answered. "I asked Setep the same thing after I returned to Thebes. It seemed odd to me that such a great pharaoh, the one to regain control of the entire Upper Kingdom after over three hundred years of occupation, would refrain from building himself a tomb so that all would remember him. Setep said the pharaoh has no desire for his Ba to return to Egypt after death. He'd rather face the underworld alone and let his spirit soar the cosmos. He's not very religious you see."

"Ah," Chanax replied, "now I understand."

Natasa. She'd died overseas and was buried in a foreign land. Her soul was no longer Egypt's, and Ankhwenefer would want to be free to find her when he died. It was a romantic, if not morbid, gesture.

With each passing day, Chanax felt renewed, as if the pain and disappointment of his life had fallen away, and he was left with a new set of possibilities. Returning to his brother's court was the best thing he'd done in his entire life.

It was unfortunate then, that as Shemu grew to a close, and the farmers began preparing for the wet season of Akhet, Chanax awoke one night to a knife at his throat.

"Guards?" he whimpered, to no answer.

"They're not awake," a low voice hissed in the darkness. "Their ale was easy enough to tamper with."

A hood covered the assassin's face, and his cool blade glittered against Chanax's skin in the moonlight.

"I have a message," the stranger whispered, shoving the weapon against Chanax's Adam's apple, causing him to choke. "From Isidor." Chanax attempted to break free, but the man held him down. The knife cut into his throat. "He wants you to know his informants have told him about your sweet family reunion, and it warms his heart. However, it appears you have forgotten your true purpose in Thebes. If you don't send a plan to Memphis by the end of this month, I will return to kill you.

Chanax struggled and croaked, "How dare he threaten me?"

"You made a promise to Ptolemy V, and if you think your brother's armies and guards protect you from his hand, you're mistaken. Assassins are easy enough to come by in Thebes."

"Then why not assassinate Ankhwenefer yourself?"

"They want him arrested and alive. They also need Setep to crown Ptolemy pharaoh. I may have a knack for murdering people in the dark of night but shackling a man like Ankhwenefer and slipping past dozens of guards through miles and miles of guarded territory will take an act of the gods. Which is why a magician's services, not an assassin's, are needed."

The man withdrew the blade and let him go. "I hope I don't have to return."

"Guards!" Chanax screamed, but it didn't matter, the assassin had disappeared.

He ran to the window and found no sign of the devil. Had it been a dream? He returned to his bed and found a scroll bearing Isidor's seal. Chills ran down his spine as he opened it with shaking hands.

Yes, that man will slit your throat. Now finish your job, you fool.

Chanax tore the letter into pieces. Just when Chanax's life had turned for the better, Isidor had to take it all away. His vision blurred, and he ran to the table and poured himself a goblet of wine. He drank it down and then took some herbs to calm his nerves, chasing them down with more alcohol. He sat on the edge of his bed, cradling his head in his hands. Not even Ankhwenefer's guards could save him from this terrible fate.

He was utterly alone in the world.

The herbs did the trick, knocking him out cold. When Chanax awoke in the morning to the sounds of his concerned guards as they rose from their drugged condition he knew what he must do. He was done with the pharaohs of Egypt. It was time to end both of their reigns, which meant he needed to pay Eleni a visit. She lived in Thebes with her husband, who now protected Ankhmaat. Other than himself and Ankhwenefer, she was the only one who was aware of the Wands of Horus. Perhaps she could tell him where they were?

He bathed and put on his best tunic as well as wig. He wanted to look the part of the handsome prince, for Eleni had long adored royal attention. However, she was now a married woman, with children of her own. Perhaps Chanax's charm would no longer be enough? There was nothing for it. Only the wands would help him find a solution to this impossible mess, and Eleni was the one who could help him.

His guards followed him at first through the busy city streets, but Chanax lost them when a litter carrying several noblewomen rode by and he climbed inside, scaring the ladies. He remedied their fears with his charm, inviting them to Weret's next party, and leaped away from the giggling group a few blocks later, his guards far behind, searching for him in confusion. They'd tell Ankhwenefer he snuck away, but he didn't want them to hear his conversation with his old friend.

Eleni lived in a comfortable house in the soldier's quarters, near the north side of town. Several young children played in the street outside, tossing a ball through a ring. One of them looked so much like the young Eleni, with her lighter skin and golden highlights in her dark hair, Chanax knew he'd found the correct house. He strode to the door, knocked, and extended his Ka out in all directions. It was time to surround her and read her mind.

Within moments, Eleni appeared. Her face bore no delight—rather fear radiated from her.

"Chanax," she said, stepping back from the door clutching her chest.

"Hello there, Eleni," he said, looking her up and down. She was no longer a girl, but a woman, her bright blue eyes blinking at him, a frown upon her round, beautiful face.

"What are you doing here?" she asked.

"Visiting an old friend. I'm sure you were aware I'd returned to court?"

"Yes, Pamu told me."

"I haven't seen you at the palace," he said, holding out a bundle of magnolias he'd picked from Weret's garden. "I'd hoped to run into you there.

"Well," she replied, her gaze darting away as she took his offering, "I have two young children to care for, and I've never liked parties. My daughter and I visit Iu-Amon quite often. It appears you and I don't enjoy the same crowd."

"I see," he replied. "May I come in, or will you leave me standing at the door?"

"Oh," she answered, turning over her shoulder to glance at the room behind her. She tucked her hair behind her ear and shrugged. "Fine, but not for long. I have many things to do today."

"I understand."

Chanax strolled into the small apartment and marveled at how much it looked like the one she'd grown up in. There was a large open room with a long wooden table and a cooking fire, as well as two small bedrooms. It was built from sturdy mud bricks, which kept them cool during the hot days. Evidence of children was strewn about the place, and it felt homey and safe.

"So," he began as he sat at the table. She placed a mug of ale and a loaf of bread before him. "You married a soldier?"

"Yes," she replied, taking a seat across the table from him. She clasped her hands and faced him, biting her lower lip. As he peered into her eyes, he discovered he wanted her—she reminded him of Natasa, only taller and bustier. A heat passed through his body. "I met him while I was Ruia's lady-in-waiting."

"You were raised by Ruia?" he asked. "Both of my daughters were as well."

"Yes. I know Baktre and Shesh."

"Of course you do. It's been wonderful meeting my children. They're the reason I returned to Thebes. I no longer wanted to be away from my family. You can understand that, can't you Eleni?"

Her face pinched as her fists balled on the table. "I'd love to have my mother, sister, and dear little Helena here with me, but I'll never get my wish, thanks to you."

"Eleni," he answered. "How can you say such things?"

"You tricked me. You asked me to show you the hole in the apiary wall. I thought you were going to close it up, but you didn't, did you? Instead, you spied on them and turned them in the moment you got the chance."

The conversation wasn't going as planned, and Chanax realized he'd have to change tactics. It would be fear and guilt, not charm and adoration that would allow him to get what he wanted here, which was a shame because he'd liked Eleni, even more so now that she was beautiful and tempting.

"They broke the law," Chanax retorted, "and in the end, I thought it best to follow the rules and report them."

"You were her friend."

"I know," he said, lowering his voice and allowing himself to slump a bit for effect. "I feel terrible for hurting Natasa the way I did, and now I want to do something in her honor. Something in return."

"What could you do to make up for such betrayal?" Eleni asked.

"Help Ankhwenefer take Memphis," he lied.

"What?"

"Yes," he continued, "I fled that horrible place, and I have much information to give to my brother. Together we will create a new plan of attack, but first, I need those wands Natasa used to work within the apiary."

Eleni froze and gripped her hands even tighter. "The wands?"

"Yes," he continued, "with the wands, I can craft a plan to grant my brother success and rid Egypt of the illegitimate Macedonian kings."

"Have you spoken about this with Ankhwenefer?" she asked.

"No, I wanted to surprise him. Do you know what happened to them after she died? I know Bastyre inherited them, but she traveled south long ago and perhaps she confided in you before she left?"

"Why would she give them to me?" Eleni asked, rising from the table as if to flee. "Bastyre and I weren't close."

Chanax surrounded her with his Ka, sensing her and reading her emotions. She knew something, and she was going to try and hide it.

"I know you know, Eleni," he whispered, covering her in a blanket of fear. Her emotions followed his energetic caress as if she were a puppet, and sweat formed along her brow. "No one can hide from me."

She pointed to the door, her arm shaking. "Get out."

"Eleni, there's no need for this. Just let me know where the wands are, and I'll take it from there. Are they in Behdet?"

She remained standing and crossed her arms. She didn't speak, but her gaze darted to the back of her house. They weren't still in the apiary. He'd play with her a bit before going in for the kill.

"Does Ankhwenefer have them? Because if that's true I will ask him."

"Yes, he does have them. Now get out."

Chanax encircled her energy field tighter and knew she was lying. He probed further and deeper into her Ka, and he opened her unskilled mind, like a scroll in a scribe's hand.

"You have them," he said, taking a step toward her. "That's wonderful. Now all you have to do is give them to me."

"No," she begged, holding out her hand to keep him at bay. "Please, go away."

Chanax turned to the window. Several younger boys, at most nine, played with the little girls. They ran after each other in the streets, kicking a leather-bound ball with their dirty bare feet.

"Children are precious, aren't they?" he asked, his voice flat. "It would be a shame for anything to happen to yours."

"What?" she squeaked.

He turned and inhaled her fear as he continued to approach. "I wanted this to go differently, Eleni. I wanted us to be friends, but it's more important I get those wands. Here's how it will be instead—you give me the cedar box and I'll leave your children alone."

"What if I refuse?"

"Then there are accidents that can happen."

She continued stepping away, and he sensed the form of terror pulsating from her in all directions, its energy infecting her own ability to think. He continued to crawl closer and soon backed her into the wall.

"Chanax," she begged, "no, don't do this. I promised Ankhwenefer I'd keep them safe."

"It's always about him, isn't it?" he replied, running a finger along her soft cheek. "You admire him so much, and it's obvious he adores you. Trusts you so much he's given you the most powerful items in the kingdom. Would he hold you in such regard if he were aware of the truth?" He leaned into her face and she turned away, refusing to meet his gaze.

"What are you suggesting, Chanax?"

"I wonder how much he'd care for you if he understood your role in Helena's death?" Chanax grinned, enjoying the form of terror now surrounding them. Threats against her children scared her, but Ankhwenefer knowing the truth horrified her. "I haven't told him, you know. He's still ignorant to your sins."

"Chanax, don't tell him. *Please*. He'll hate me, and I couldn't bear it."

"True, he would hate you, like he hates me. Give me the wands, and your secret remains safe with me."

"Chanax, please go away."

Why did she continue to resist? He wanted to strike her. Never had she made him so angry. He grabbed her close, tugging her from the wall and nuzzling into her neck as she struggled, inhaling the scent of her sweaty flesh. Her large breasts were soft against his chest, and the fear in her eyes aroused him.

"Go get me those wands. Now."

He stepped back, and she fell away from him. Tears poured down her cheeks and she glanced out the window at the children, struggling with her choice. He sent a wave of anger over her, and she ran to the back room. When she returned, she held a cedar box in her hands. He ripped it from her grip.

She stumbled back, wiping the tears from her eyes. "Please don't tell Ankhwenefer I gave them to you."

He opened the box, and the two wands shone in the afternoon sun, their energy surrounding him. It was Natasa's energy, and a thrilling surge of power coursed through his body. He brushed them aside to see what else was in the box, and his heart froze at the sight of the bloodstone necklace he'd given her lying next to the wands. She'd kept it, even after their friendship ended.

Chanax looked to Eleni, unable to keep himself from grinning. "Of course I won't tell him. You and I are good at keeping secrets from the pharaoh, aren't we?"

"Please, leave me alone and never come back."

"Don't worry, you won't be seeing me any time soon," he replied as he walked to the door.

He'd find his guards waiting at the palace, but no matter, there was a trip to Abdju to plan with them. They were going on their final journey. Isidor wasn't the only one who knew how to hire assassins. It was time to inform Weret he was heading to Behdet to visit Silus. She'd tell Ankhwenefer the lie and no one would even think he'd gone north, to the temple of Seti I, where he'd take the bath of a lifetime.

35

The Return of Natasa

"In Pharaonic Egypt, the king symbolizes human perfection for the cycle in which he is active."
~ *The Temple of Man, R.A. Schwaller de Lubicz, 1949 CE*

Abdju, Egypt, 186 BCE

Chanax woke in Natasa's bed to Ra's early morning kiss and rolled over to look out the window, recalling how he'd climbed through it at sunrise the day he set sail for Memphis. It was here, at her father's house in Abdju, where he'd first shown her his love, a love she'd come to reject. He remembered her warm lips and the way her green eyes sparkled in the new day's sun. He'd thought she loved him. Had imagined her waiting faithfully in Behdet while he endured his torture in Memphis. What a fool he'd been. He glanced at the leather-bound manuscript laying on the bed beside him and opened to the page where he'd dozed off the night before. A picture of two lovers stared out at him, the woman looking so much like Natasa. A sharp stab of pain flared in his abdomen when he considered the man who had drawn the picture—Finnian.

After acquiring the book, he'd asked Weret about Finnian and his relationship to Natasa. Weret had been quite eager to tell him juicy tales of the golden-haired man from the north who had captured

Natasa's fancy. Chanax often wondered while he read the book if the rumors were true that Natasa had found it in her heart to love someone other than his brother. Part of Chanax hoped it had been so, yet another part of him was in anguish. If Natasa could replace Ankhwenefer with another, why hadn't she chosen Chanax? Why had she rejected his pure love, yet accepted the embrace of a foreigner who knew nothing of her people?

He snapped the book shut and rose from the bed. Leaving Thebes had been easy. Weret had arranged the entire trip to Behdet, and his guards joined him. Chanax had contracted a band of river bandits to attack his boat in the middle of the night, killing his guards and burying the bodies in the desert for the jackals to feast upon. Once the guards were disposed of, the bandits forced the captain to turn their course north. Thus, Chanax arrived in Abdju, alone for the first time in almost a year, and went at once to Hecataeus's house. The man still kept it, but the inch of dust on every surface made it apparent the Greek hadn't been there for years.

All of the maps and excavation notes were still in the man's study, and after a night's rest, Chanax felt ready to try to find the Osirian—nothing like the present to begin anew. He fingered the bloodstone he now wore around his neck. He'd given it to Natasa as a means to remember him, but now he found it a wonderful way to remember her as they were in Abdju, before the Cult of Set had taken him and Ankhwenefer had stolen her. How intoxicating their kisses had been, her eyes full of delight as they'd explored the town together. She should have been Chanax's, regardless of what Isidor felt. That man and his pureblood nonsense had ruined Chanax's entire life.

He took a quick meal and dressed in a simple gray tunic, a similar wrap woven around his head. He grabbed the cedar box, the leather-bound book, map, and a torch and headed to Seti's temple. It was as mysterious as the last time he'd been there, and while more had been uncovered, it appeared that when Hecataeus abandoned the dig, so had everyone else. The building was silent as a forgotten tomb as the sun made its full ascent in the morning sky.

Chanax strode through the crumbling courtyard to the location of the tunnel, remembering his steps from long ago. Even as a boy, Chanax had found the ancient pool fascinating. He lit his torch and followed the tunnel down below the earth, not even bothering to look at the hieroglyphs on the walls, instead, aiming his fiery torch in front of his body and seeking the end. As he entered the sacred, circular room, he inhaled the deep and ancient silence. Out of instinct, he muttered a few prayers and incantations for protection as he put his torch in a ring on the wall. Then he walked to the spot where the Flower of Life was engraved, and placed Natasa's book below it, running his fingers along the words engraved with gold into its cover.

"The Goddess of the South," he murmured as he removed his clothes and opened the cedar box. Chanax brushed the golden rod with his fingers.

Her soul greeted him. He recalled watching her in the apiary, standing among the bees, the sunlight shining on her face. She'd stand for hours, holding the wands, her eyes moving back and forth under closed eyelids as if storing the entire contents of the universe into her small body. He grasped the silver wand with his left hand, as she'd seen her do, and took the golden one in his right. She was both in and around him, somehow everywhere at once.

"Come to me," she sang to his heart.

Chanax trembled as he entered the salty pool, each step cool and refreshing, yet also painful to the skin, as if he were on fire. He ignored the sensation and continued until his entire body was submerged within the ancient spring water. His hands vibrated and his muscles pulsated. He felt a tug at his navel and found himself in an unfamiliar realm. In all his work with Isidor, they'd never been able to access this place, and yet there he was, open to the entire cosmos. Light swirled and danced before him, and he allowed his Ba to connect to it. At first, Natasa's energy surrounded him, but he didn't trust her and swept past it, blocking her and searching for others who might have used the wands. After a moment, his Ka connected to an ancient source, one of the great elder kings of Egypt, from the time when the Osirion had been crafted deep within the belly of an even older temple, now long turned to dust. The being was so ancient, there were no numbers for the age in which this king had lived.

Chanax rested in the dead king's protection and explored the realm of light, watching the requests and actions, the events and potentialities. Every possibility, past, and present, stretched out before him. How long he stayed in this trance, he was unaware, but the entire time his body shifted and renewed itself. His desire became clear in his mind, and in a deep, ethereal voice, Chanax called out to the cosmos.

"I seek to aid Ptolemy V in arresting my brother, Ankhwenefer, and uniting the Upper and Lower Kingdoms of Egypt. There can be no heir left to claim the throne in Thebes. I also seek the path that will include the end of Ptolemy V and his death, that I might be freed from both men's treachery."

A pulsing sensation grew in his solar plexus, causing him much distress as if someone was sitting on his chest, and he found it hard to breathe. The form of panic surrounded him, orange-red and insistent. Yet the light around him swirled and possible events shifted from one place to another across the All-One, like pieces on a game board. The plan came into view before him, the series of events that needed to occur to bring Ankhwenefer to his knees. The simplicity of the solution was breathtaking, and he committed it to his memory.

Chanax's heart pounded like a mob of horses charging toward an army in battle, and darkness clouded his vision.

"*I see you...*" a voice whispered.

He tried to stand and leave the pool, but a force beyond his control surrounded his body and held him back. He recognized her, for Natasa was at once inside his very cells and outside of him, woven into his Ka like an energetic blanket and holding him tight. He'd let down his guard, and she'd discovered him.

"*...and I know what you do in secret.*"

His body was paralyzed. Her anguish was a hand squeezing his heart, and her grief was his grief. Helena laughed in the distance, and his throat tightened. "Natasa, I didn't mean to kill her."

"*No, you meant to kill me,*" she accused. Her energetic grip seared into his skin like flames.

"You betrayed me, Natasa. I loved you, don't you understand?"

Chanax felt her confusion and guilt and cast out with his Ka, weaving his own spell, attaching himself, and hoping to break her. She blocked him and wound her Ka deeper into his.

"Why do you seek to destroy the pharaoh?"

"They'll kill me if I don't. My children as well. Natasa, Isidor is evil, you know this. It was he who plotted to kill Helena because she was the Golden Child and he feared her. Now he works for Ptolemy Epiphanes. Please, you must believe me."

He forced open his eyes and found the room filled with light particles, dancing over the water like fireflies. The scene was a thing of beauty, and Chanax wanted nothing more than to surrender to Natasa's light, as he let his own Ba bond with hers. The instant he connected to her spirit, his skin burned. His hands felt on fire, and he struggled to keep a hold of the wands. He howled in excruciating pain.

The pain flamed across his body, yet he continued to cast his Ba further into hers. He wouldn't let her go, not ever. She was hurting him, but he was determined to bond himself to her in this way while he had the chance. If he connected a cord to her Ba, she'd love him instead of Ankhwenefer for all eternity.

As if sensing his perfidy, she released him and he sprung from the tub, tossing the wands into the cedar chest as if they were hot coals. His body was red and raw, and there were singe marks on his palms where he'd held the wands. He glanced around the room, which was now dark, lit by his dying torch. He'd been in the Resurrection Bath for hours.

Chanax glanced back at the pool and again at the wands. They glowed. He placed a finger on the golden one and winced in pain.

"I see you," Her words echoed through his mind.

She'd somehow cursed them. How did she get past his shields? In his moment of glory, he'd forgotten her, yet in her moment of anger, she had also forgotten him. Chanax tugged at the cord he'd connected to her Ba, firm, and coursing in darkness. No matter where he was in any lifetime, he would find her, and she would mistake him for her twin flame. It was advanced magic, even for him, but he had no doubt he'd been successful.

He rubbed his skin and while the entire surface of his body stung, his skin and muscles were also firmer and more taught. Gone were scars and wrinkles accumulated through his years of hard living. He ran his fingers through his hair and found it longer, thicker, and more luxurious. He dressed and fled the room, making it out of the tunnel mere moments before the torch extinguished. He surfaced in the upper temple, shocked to see the sun god Ra setting in the west. He'd been in the pool for the entire day, yet his skin wasn't pruned nor waterlogged. Other than the burning Natasa gave him, he felt fantastic.

He cradled the cedar box in his arms and hoped he'd be able to use the wands again; there were other desires he wished to manifest, but he wasn't sure he could. Even though she was dead, Natasa had found him in the world beyond the world. Which made sense, for that was where she now existed. He fingered the bloodstone around his neck and tugged at the chain.

No matter. He'd gotten what he'd come for—a renewed body, an eternal energetic connection to Natasa, and a plan to end the pharaohs' lives. He had no idea why the series of events he was about to set in motion would lead to both Ankhwenefer and Ptolemy's demise, but it didn't matter. If the plan was executed to the last detail, they'd be dead, and Chanax would be free. He walked to town and sent a letter via horse to Isidor. He paid extra for the rider to expedite delivery, for there was less than a month to act. He also contracted a boat to Thebes the next morning.

It wasn't until he was sailing back toward Thebes when he realized he'd left Natasa's book in the Osirion. No matter, he'd read it several times over. There were plenty of lifetimes ahead of him to return and reclaim it, and the Resurrection Bath, for himself.

36

The Song of the Sunrise

Ankhwenefer spent the first half of his reign as pharaoh of the Upper Kingdom rebuilding his cities after the Greek Surge and making them whole again. He spent the second half raising his sons and nephews, in an attempt to ensure the kingdom would remain whole forever.

Thebes, Egypt, 186 BCE

Ankhwenefer chuckled at the jugglers as they dropped their props on purpose, only to pick them up while bumping into one another and making fools of themselves. His study was crowded with the people he loved most in the world, as well as many others reveling in the celebration. It was his birthday, and Ruia had insisted they throw him a party. The event was held in his gaming room, for he'd refused a large gathering. No more than one hundred nobles, as well as his family, were in attendance.

Ruia and the princesses had been with the court for nearly five months and the time had come for her to head back to Behdet. While Anen would stay behind with Ankhmaat, Silus needed his wife. Managing the military operations of the entire kingdom wasn't easy. He'd grown to be a much better man than he'd been in his youth, but he still drank too much and often had trouble sleeping. It pained

Ankhwenefer to know that his dear sister had to suffer such a marriage, but they understood each other, for both of them knew what it meant to be unmet by their spouses.

Anen's laughter filled the air, and Ankhwenefer turned to find his son nibbling on her neck. Face aglow, she grabbed his arms and wrapped them around her body, as she leaned in for a passionate kiss. Durame, her belly large with child, sat on Senui's lap, stroking his hair while he drank his ale and called out to the rhapsodist, who was now taking the stage to sing. The rest of the princes played dice at the game table, challenging each other to outrageous bets. Even Shesh joined them, her girlish smile beaming at Khenefer as he taught her the rules. To Ankhwenefer, this was the most important gift he'd bestowed upon the kingdom—a close and loving royal family.

Chanax entered the room, and a sheen of sweat broke out on Ankhwenefer's brow. He turned to Weret, who sat beside him clapping her hands and drinking her wine, oblivious to their brother's arrival.

"I imagine you invited him?" he said to his wife.

She turned and looked to the door. "Of course, he's family. Besides, you haven't addressed him since he arrived home weeks ago from his ordeal. Some brother you are."

Ankhwenefer had heard the reports, but he wanted to hear from the man directly, and this was the perfect time. Public conversations with Chanax were better than private. It forced a bit of civility upon the situation. That Chanax had managed to survive a bandit attack, while all four of his guards went missing, screamed of wrongdoing. Ankhwenefer rose from his seat and strode to his younger brother, eager to speak while everyone else was distracted by the entertainment. As he approached, he noted how much younger and vibrant his brother appeared. He wasn't wearing a wig, his natural hair now fell well past his chin, yet he'd arrived at court bald five months prior. His skin glowed in the firelight, and he was more handsome than ever. A group of women fawned over him, fluttering their eyes and tossing their hair as they listed him weave his tales.

"Chanax," Ankhwenefer interrupted, breaking up the hen party. "Welcome home."

"Why thank you," Chanax replied, gaze lingering on a youthful, dark-haired beauty as the women scattered to clear a path for the king. "And happy birthday to you, brother."

"I understand your boat was attacked on the way to Behdet. Are you okay?"

"Showing concern for me? That's a switch," Chanax replied, eyebrows raised.

"Please, Chanax," Ankhwenefer insisted, "four of my men were killed in the attack, and I need to know what happened."

"It's simple, yet tragic. One day into the trip, bandits struck in the middle of the night. The guards fought them off, as was their duty, but failed. Just after the first one fell, I jumped overboard, taking nothing but my coin purse and sword. I swam to the opposite shore, using the moonlight to guide me. The next day I found myself walking north, stumbling upon the small town of Esna, where I was able get some food, clothes, and a boat to come home. Your men have checked the vessel I arrived in. It was a fishing boat for goodness sake."

Ankhwenefer folded his arms over his chest. Something didn't add up. Chanax was lying, Ankhwenefer knew it, but he couldn't put his finger on why. "Well, you don't look worse for the wear. Rather you look better, younger even."

"Perhaps I thrive in adversity," Chanax suggested.

Ankhwenefer looked his brother up and down, noting the necklace Chanax wore around his neck, and a distant sense of fear filled his heart. "That's a very nice stone," he said, touching the bloodstone with his fingertip. "I believe Natasa owned one just like it."

Chanax smirked. "I gave her that necklace when we were in Abdju before I left for Memphis as a boy. I'd bought one for each of us."

"Why?"

"Because, I hoped it would keep us connected while I was away," Chanax admitted, his proud smile turning to a frown. "I'd hoped it would help her remember me." He glared at Ankhwenefer. "It didn't work, did it? She forgot me."

"Hecataeus told me he'd caught you climbing out of her window during that trip," Ankhwenefer continued probing. "What were you doing?"

"Saying goodbye, if you know what I mean."

"You were twelve, Chanax."

"Twelve-year-old children know their way around the bedroom, brother," he replied, tilting his head while fingering the bloodstone. Ankhwenefer stepped back as if he'd been slapped and Chanax laughed. "Don't worry, I didn't steal her maidenhood, but you weren't the first to kiss her. Nor were you the first to love her."

"If you loved her, why did you betray her?"

Chanax answered, his face hard, "I stopped loving her the day I found her in your arms."

"Are you sure that was the reason?" Ankhwenefer challenged.

"What do you mean, brother?" Chanax demanded, his eyes widening.

Ankhwenefer hadn't told anyone of Natasa's revelation about his mother's affair. By the time he'd settled down in Thebes and made to call for his mother to verify the rumor, she'd died. Yet from the look on his brother's face, Ankhwenefer knew Chanax was well aware of his parentage.

"You killed my lover and my child to silence Natasa, didn't you?" Ankhwenefer accused. He squeezed his fists at his side, recalling the moment he'd choked the villain, years ago, when he'd found Helena dead. The rest of the room ignored them, enjoying the party, with the exception of Ruia, who watched them, perched on her throne as if ready to take flight if things got out of control.

"Why would I have needed to silence Natasa?"

"Because she had threatened to tell everyone the truth—that you're nothing but the queen's bastard. Isn't that right my dear little half-brother?"

Chanax shook his hair and waved a hand. "I don't need to stand here and listen to your mad ravings. Natasa broke her promises, Ankhwenefer, and you know it. She promised she'd never forget me. She promised me with a kiss. It was the sweetest kiss I've ever tasted. I imagine the man from the north would say the same, wouldn't he?"

Ankhwenefer grabbed his brother and thrust him against the wall.

Chanax cackled like a hyena, causing several others in the room to notice the two men interacting.

"She broke her promise to you as well," Chanax continued in a high pitch. "She promised to return, but she didn't, did she? She left you behind for death."

"*Enough,*" Ankhwenefer yelled, squeezing his forearm into his brother's neck. "Don't speak of her that way."

"I'm not saying anything you haven't already considered." Chanax coughed and gasped, struggling against his brother's hold. "I know well the dark thoughts that have haunted you since her passing."

Chanax's guards as well as Min and Ansel drew closer to intervene, and Ankhwenefer stepped away. The rhapsodist stopped playing, and intense silence filled the room as the guests stared at the pair of panting men. Ruia now stood beside them, as well as Weret.

"Is everything all right, brothers?" Ruia asked, placing an arm on Ankhwenefer's shoulder. He relaxed at her touch and turned to Chanax.

"No," he admitted, "it will never be all right between us."

Weret rolled her eyes, and Ankhwenefer swallowed down the numerous insults upon his lips.

"Come, Chanax, sit with me," she said, taking the man's arm unto hers to lead him away. "We have to endure this gathering only a bit longer and then the real fun begins, doesn't it?"

"You are free to leave anytime, Weret," Ankhwenefer said, gesturing his hand to the door. "I care not if either of you is in attendance." He turned to the guests and apologized, "I'm sorry, we're always at each other's throats, my siblings and me. Please, rhapsodist, sing us a song."

"As you wish, Your Majesty," the entertainer replied. He was Egyptian but trained in the Greek forms of musical entertainment. His songs were stories, legends, and even current events. Ankhwenefer was considering offering him a place in his court, and the man was trying very hard to earn that cherished position.

The singer began with a story about their recent battle at the fortress up north. He called the tune "The Fortress of Nowhere," for that's where it was. Nowhere. Not Lycopolis, not Panopolis, but in between the habitable zones. Nowhere. Ankhwenefer smiled at the rhapsodist's cleverness and forced himself to appear relaxed as Weret and Chanax chatted, their heads touching, thick as thieves. Several songs later, the rhapsodist paused to drink down some ale and asked for requests.

Ankhwenefer was guzzling down his fifth goblet of wine when Ankhmaat called out, "Sing a song about the golden eagle king's lover."

Ankhwenefer looked to Ankhmaat and fought the urge to deny him his request. The young man shrugged, held up his wine goblet, and winked, swaying with drunkenness. Ankhwenefer had already made one scene already. He didn't feel like making another.

"No," Weret demanded. "There will be no songs sung of her in my court."

Ankhwenefer petted his wife's hand, relishing this moment to make her cringe in public. "My dear," he said, in a sing-song voice, as if she were a child. "This is *my* court, not yours." He turned to the rhapsodist, who waited, lute in hand. "Sing it."

The man nodded and plucked the strings. Melancholic notes filled the air, and Ankhwenefer wondered if he had the courage to listen. Yet the chance to force both Weret and Chanax to hear how the rest of the kingdom sang of Natasa was too good to pass up, even if hearing her story hurt beyond belief. He snapped his fingers and a servant filled his goblet and he allowed the wine to soothe his nerves.

"Where is the king's green-eyed girl?" the rhapsodist crooned, *"Why does she fly away?*

The black-eyed cobra attacked her they say, and her terrible sorrow has led her astray.

Our king fell in love with the goddess you see, and as a youth, he lived in her arms.

She sang to him and danced for him and pleasured him with her charms.

His green-eyed girl was at his side when he was slain in battle.

She brought him back from the edge of death and his injury she did unravel.

He loved her so, she was his light, and he her rising sun.

But one day jealousy struck them both, and their love affair undone.

Why did she fly away?

They ask. Why did she leave his side?

The black-eyed cobra attacked her they say, and she had to run and hide.

Far to the north, the god Hapy took her, to shelter her from the storm.

Why hasn't she returned to him, her lover to whom she's sworn?

The tears of Isis, that what did it, they flooded her heart with grief.

The black-eyed cobra not only stung the king's lover, he was also an evil thief.

He took their child into the night and into death she passed.

The sting of the cobra has no equal, and evil has no rest.

And in the end, she will not return, the king's beloved one.

For she followed her daughter into the night, and he is the rising sun."

As the last of the notes passed over them, the room remained silent. Ankhwenefer turned to Weret and Chanax, neither willing to meet his gaze. He had no pity for them. The rhapsodist sat by the fire, wringing his hands as he awaited his king's assessment. Ankhwenefer raised his goblet to the man. "Excellent song. What do you call it?"

"'The Lament of the Golden Eagle King,'" the entertainer replied, his gaze shifting to the queen, who clutched her breast.

"It's a good song, and quite true," Ankhwenefer continued, now rising from his seat to address the entire room. "It impresses me how such a song can be written by a person who wasn't even a part of the story." He looked to the man and waved his finger. "However, you got it wrong on one count. Natasa, not I, was the rising sun."

The rhapsodist looked to the floor, defeated even though he'd done everything right.

"Don't fret," Ankhwenefer assured him. "Here, I have an offering for you. Can someone please fetch me a pandura?"

The rhapsodist stood and offered his stool by the brazier, which roared with fire, providing warmth in the cool desert night air, as well as illumination for the room. Within moments, Ankhwenefer held one of his favorite panduras in his hand. Sometimes, it was good to be the king.

He looked to the audience. His sons sat tall at the edge of their seats. Weret looked up to the ceiling as if reading the inscriptions etched into their surface, and the grimace on Senui's face caught his attention. He was still feeling the sadness of the previous song—he'd known both Helena and Natasa. Well, this next one wasn't going to make him feel any better.

"Ankhmaat," Ankhwenefer began, "you asked for a song about Natasa. Well, here's one right from the source. I call it 'The Song of the Sunrise' and I wrote in on my way home from a trip to Alexandria, more than twenty years ago, on the day I fell in love with her, and knew I wanted nothing more than to spend the rest of my life by her side."

He turned to Chanax, who sat, arms and legs crossed, watching him. Ankhwenefer could sense the form of envy between them. "I didn't get the chance to grow old with her, for the black-eyed cobra of jealousy infested the court of my youth, but at least our love still lives on in song."

He filled the room with the beautiful notes of the pandura, but this time, the tune was romantic and bouncy, like the heart of a young prince in love. "*Time abandons me when I'm in her arms, and my heart is always seeking her.*

Time abandons me when I'm near her charms, and my body is always longing for her.

She moves like the wind, she dances like wine, she is the goddess and I need her to be mine.

The sunrise comes and bathes the Earth in her beauty, but she is the one for me.

For under her gaze, she sees my light and makes me feel passionately.

I will have her, I must, as the sun has the sky.

She will be the bride of my heart, and her name I will glorify.

The songbirds sing when she appears, and only her kiss will satisfy this man's heart, this man's soul, that woman is my life.

I will only be happy in her arms, for she is the song of the sunrise."

As Ankhwenefer played, his heart opened, and Natasa's essence filled his mind and body. His fingers danced along his pandura, note after note, and he was no longer singing, but allowing the notes to tell the tale of his heart. As he played, it was as if Natasa danced for him as she had in their youth, following his lead, and drowning in her desire. His heart pounded as his Ba left the room and surrendered to the All-One, blending with his beloved in eternity. It had been so long since he'd been whole, so long since he'd seen his true self. Deepening into their Ba, he drank in the experience and played his heart out. Ankhwenefer rested in the knowledge of his divinity and his truth. Underneath the human shell, the illusion of life, he was love.

After a while, he knew the song must come to an end, so he turned away from the All-One and entered his body. Sensing the marble walls of the room, the movement of his guests, the warmth of the fire, and the vibration of the strings beneath his fingers, he sang with all his heart and soul, "The songbirds sing when she appears, and only her kiss will satisfy, this man's heart, this man's soul, that woman is my life. I will only be happy in her arms, for she is the song of the sunrise."

He allowed his Ka to expand and felt the awe and trepidation in the audience. Many of his courtiers had never heard him play the pandura, much less sing. He'd kept this part of him locked away for none to know. He sought out Khenefer's eyes, which were glowing with tears in the firelight. Then he found Ankhmaat, who held Anen to his chest as if afraid she too might be plucked out of his life. When his gaze settled upon Chanax, he found a knowing smirk upon his brother's youthful face. Instead of anger, a cold dread passed through his body. Chanax was the dark-eyed cobra in his court. It was time to get rid of him, no matter the cost.

The pharaoh rose from his seat and the crowd applauded. Many proclaimed the song was beautiful and gushed over his talent. He was a warrior king with a heart, and they loved him even more. He bowed to their compliments and called the paid entertainment back on stage.

"Play something livelier." He raised his glass to his guests. "No more songs about my Natasa, at least, not tonight. Let's celebrate those who are alive, and still breathe upon this good Earth."

The crowd cheered and wine flowed once more. A servant took his pandura. The pharaoh spoke with his guests, and when he sought out Chanax, he found two empty chairs—for both his little brother and Weret had left.

37

A Warning

To the ancient Egyptians, the rise of Sirius marked the new year and the coming of the all-important Nile flood. They called the star, Sopdet, or the star of Isis. She is the brightest star in the sky and heralds the chance to renew oneself and become nobler in one's actions.

Thebes, Egypt, 186 BCE

Ankhwenefer slept in his bed, the warm desert air blowing through the room, caressing his hair.

"Ankhmakis," a charming, familiar voice called.

He opened his eyes and found himself in his chambers in Behdet. It felt so real he bolted upright and discovered Natasa lying naked beside him, smiling at his reaction.

"Hello, handsome." She winked.

"What?" he asked.

She tugged him down upon her chest and kissed him, sending flames of delight down his spine. "Is this a dream?" he asked.

"Yes," she replied, kissing his neck, "but now that you've called for me, I will try to make it feel as real as possible." She wrapped her legs around him, and he grew hard against her soft, warm body. "Of course, dreams aren't any less real than the things you do in your body when you're awake. Everything is happening all of the time in the All-

One. What we do when we leave our bodies to dream is real in the book of life. Separation is an illusion."

"I called you?"

"Yes," she murmured as she continued to kiss him. "When you sang my song, you called upon me and enabled me to approach you. The dead are ever near and ready to help, but we can't connect without your permission."

"You mean, I could have been making love to you in my dreams all these years?"

Natasa kissed him, rubbing breasts upon his chest as if to emphasize her point. He grew harder, and she responded by slipping him inside her. Ankhwenefer let go, not caring that his bliss was happening in the world behind the world, and embraced her as his pleasure exploded. She groaned and he thrust deeper inside. It felt so real—he tasted the salty sweat of her body. He fell upon her chest and breathed in her scent.

"I love you," she whispered. "Always and forever."

"I miss you," he replied. "My heart is breaking being so near to you and yet so alone."

"You've created a beautiful kingdom, my love, and are a remarkable pharaoh."

"I want to join you in death," he begged.

"Ankhmakis," she continued, using his old name—it was the only one she'd known. "That's why I'm here. You're in danger."

"Ankhmaat is ready for the throne."

"Everyone is in danger. Chanax has used the Wands of Horus in the Resurrection Bath of Abdju."

"*No*," he exclaimed, popping up to sit. "That can't be true. I gave them to Eleni."

Natasa sat up as well and grasped his hands. "I saw him use them. He took them to the Osirion and seeks to destroy the kingdom. Ankhmaat is also in danger, as well as every member of your family. You must try to save as many as you can, my love."

"How can I stop him?"

"I don't know. You need to get the wands and use them yourself.

No one but you will be able to use them now. I cursed them in my anger with Chanax. You must try and see for yourself."

"You're dead. Don't you know everything?"

She lay down, placing one arm above her head. Her breasts were exposed and her nipples hard. The hot flash of desire swirled like a cyclone in his groin, in spite of the dangerous warning she spoke.

"My love, the dead can access the Way, but I see only what has happened and what might happen, not what will. The choice is up to the living."

"Why didn't you come to me sooner?"

"Because, as I already told you, I can't interfere. You must ask for my help. You've never called for me, until tonight."

"What might happen?"

"Chanax works to have you arrested and all of the heirs killed. How he plans to do this, I don't know, but that was the request he issued to the Way. I think there's a way for you to at least enter the All-One and look for yourself."

"How?" he asked.

She lay him back down on the bed and settled herself in between his legs, kissing his stomach as she made her way toward his manhood. "Bliss," she answered as she put him in her mouth.

He arched his back, calling out her name in ecstasy. When he was hard enough, she climbed on top of him. This time, when she rode him, they fell into their realm of bliss. The ecstasy grew in his groin and then snaked along his back. As he climaxed, he guided the energy into his ankh channel, and fell into her soul as they merged into one. He gazed up at her as she rocked her hips, bearing down upon him, her head back and mouth open in delight. A field of light surrounded them.

"*I love you,*" she whispered to his heart. "*I am always near.*"

Ankhwenefer was no longer beside Natasa, nor in his bedroom in Behdet. Instead, he stood in the realm of light and watched as the actions of humanity swirled and twirled around him, like golden ribbons. He sought to see what Chanax plotted, and the image of Behdet burning filled his vision. He ducked, shielding his eyes from the flames, and in the next instant, he was on the shore of the Nile, standing among his soldiers. They stood, shoulders slumped, their weapons dropped to their sides, and their right hands on their chests as one of his naval ships passed by flying Ptolemy V Epiphanes's banner. He saw himself chained to the prow, bloody and torn, while Greek soldiers whipped him on the deck.

Ankhwenefer fought against the visions, asking to see more, but instead, he woke, gasping for air and alone in his bed in Thebes.

"My lord," the guard on duty, Ansel, said as he approached. "What's wrong?"

Ankhwenefer looked around in confusion, patting the empty bed. Natasa was no longer beside him. "Nothing," he said, still dazed from the nightmare. "It was only a dream." He made to lie back down but called Ansel back. He needed to be sure. "Ansel, please send a letter at dawn to Eleni, Pamu's wife. Tell her I need her to fetch me the cedar box."

"The cedar box?" Ansel clarified.

"Yes," Ankhwenefer answered. "She'll know what you mean. It's important."

"Yes, Your Majesty."

Ankhwenefer tried to sleep but found he couldn't. He stared at the frescoed ceiling in his elegant chambers and waited for Ra to return to the sky.

38

Secrets and Cover-ups

To fail the pharaoh of Egypt was to commit a grave crime, punishable by death. Many people fail their kings, and Eleni was no exception. Yet she loved her king, so her failure hurt all the more.

Thebes, Egypt, 186 BCE

Eleni bit her fingers as she stood beside her husband in the hallway outside of Chanax's chambers, her gaze shifting up and down the hall, terrified he might discover her there.

"I can't believe I'm doing this for you," Pamu hissed. "How could you put me in this position?"

"I need to get them back," Eleni said, tugging on his leather cuff. "Please. The pharaoh will punish us if I don't."

"Why in the world did you ever let Chanax have the box?"

She didn't dare tell him. He already had so much on his mind. If he knew Chanax was threatening them, it would cause him a great amount of trouble. Pamu was a guard of one prince and speaking out against another would put him in a tight spot. Moreover, she couldn't bear the thought of her husband knowing how she'd been the one to reveal Natasa and Ankhwenefer's affair to Chanax. Pamu would never forgive her for such a thing.

"I didn't think Ankhwenefer wanted it anymore, and Chanax said he'd use the contents to help him win the war," she lied. "Now the pharaoh wants the box back, and he never gave me permission to let others have it."

Pamu's jaw tightened, but he walked toward the two guards stationed outside Chanax's door. The other two were missing, which meant Chanax was out.

"Hello, men," Pamu began, chest puffed out. He glanced over his shoulder at Eleni and then back to the guards. "I'm here on Ankhmaat's orders. He left something in the prince's room and would like me to retrieve it."

He spoke a bit of truth. Ankhmaat had been to see Chanax a few days prior to discuss a possible courtship between Baktre and one of the noblemen of Thebes. Chanax had blessed the union.

"Go ahead," one of the guards answered, and the man opened the door. Eleni and Pamu walked into the prince's chambers and closed the door behind them.

"What are we looking for?" he asked her.

"A small cedar box, about the size of two hands," she replied.

The two scoured the room. Eleni found clothes, jewelry, many scrolls, and an altar, upon which sat a creepy, crystal skull. Only Chanax would worship something so evil. She shivered and continued to look for the cedar box. After fifteen minutes, it became clear he wasn't keeping it out in the open. She walked through an archway and into his baths, gasping at the opulence. The tub, which was empty, was a large as her house and covered in beautiful tiles made from gold, jade, and onyx.

The tiles on the wall depicted the story of Osiris's resurrection. She gazed at the image of Isis, singing her dead husband back to life. Eleni hugged herself, her throat beginning to sting; it reminded her of Natasa. She and Helena would sing the "Song of Isis" often, and it had given Eleni peace when she was a child. She glanced around the room, and to her delight in the far corner stood a desk similar to the one Natasa once had in her room in the apartment in Behdet, the sort that allowed for containers to be hidden under them.

She ran across the bath to the table, upon which sat towels, oils, herbs, and copper bowls. Eleni searched under the table and felt in the corners, finding her prize latched in the far right-hand side. She fiddled with the wooden locks that held it in place and released the cedar box, opening it. Inside sat the two wands, safe and sound. She exhaled and turned to her husband.

"This is it," she said, running back into the main room. "Now, I need you to take me to the pharaoh."

A moment before she entered Ankhwenefer's chambers she considered what might happen when Chanax discovered the box missing. How often did he use them? How long did she have before he'd notice them missing?

"Eleni," Pamu said, his voice short. He was still disappointed in her. "You need to focus. We're here."

The guards opened the doors to the pharaoh's study, and they entered with careful footsteps. Ankhwenefer sat behind his desk, High Priestess Alexa standing at his side. When they were a few steps into the room, the pharaoh glanced up from his work at Eleni and Pamu, and a huge smile covered his handsome face when she held out the box in her hands.

"Thank the goddess," he said as he strode to her side and took the box. "I knew it was just a dream."

"A dream?" Eleni asked, gulping down a wave of terror.

"Yes," he explained, "Natasa visited me in a dream last night and warned me we were all in danger because Chanax had used the Wands of Horus, but as you can see, that's not possible, because you've had them." He walked to his desk and placed the box down to open it.

"The Wands of Horus?" Alexa gasped, rushing to Ankhwenefer's side and peering into the box. "I thought they were all lost."

"Natasa gained possession of a pair," he answered, "but that is a story for someone else to tell. What you must know is those who possess the wands have the ability to command the Way of the universe. Their effects are even greater when used in the Osirion in Abdju.

"When Natasa died, the wands went to Eleni, who has guarded them for over a decade, but I feared Chanax had stolen them from her and used them for himself."

"That is a serious accusation," Alexa said. "I've been watching him for months, ever since you assigned me to the task, and he's shown no signs of malice or ill will. Why can't you accept he's different?"

"Because, the dream felt so real," Ankhwenefer replied. "Natasa said she found him in the Osirion with the wands, and he plans to destroy us. She begged me to save as many of you as I could."

"A dream?" Alexa laughed. "You take that seriously?"

"I thought you were the high priestess of Isis," Ankhwenefer challenged. "You know dreams often contain omens and meanings."

She cocked her head over her shoulder, chin held high. "You have a blind spot when it comes to Natasa."

"You have a blind spot when it comes to Chanax," he replied. Alexa turned away, unable to meet his gaze.

Eleni looked to Pamu, whose face begged her to tell the truth. She shook her head. It was best to let Ankhwenefer think she'd done as he'd asked.

"No!" Ankhwenefer roared, causing both her and Alexa's heads to whip around. "Eleni, are you sure this box has been in your possession this entire time?"

She shivered as she squeaked, "I don't understand the question."

"Natasa used this box for many things," he explained as he walked toward her. His eyes were wide as if he'd seen a monster. She stumbled back into her husband's arms. "She used it to keep items she considered precious. Like this ring I wear." He held up his hand to show the phoenix signet. "When I gave you this box, there was a bloodstone necklace inside with the wands. Do you remember that amulet?"

Eleni knew she was discovered. The bloodstone, Chanax must have taken it. What was she to do? She looked to Pamu for help, and he cleared his throat, "Your Majesty," he began but the pharaoh held up his hand to silence him. Ankhwenefer towered above Eleni and searched her face.

"Eleni, I saw Chanax wearing the same bloodstone at my birthday. He told me he'd purchased one for himself when he gave Natasa hers. He lied, didn't he? He did have these wands in his possession, and he's wearing her amulet as his prize. I'm sure of it."

Eleni whimpered and nuzzled into her husband's chest as if to escape the king's disappointment. "Oh, Pamu. I'm so sorry."

The captain of the prince's guard held his wife and glanced up at his pharaoh, his voice cracking as he spoke. "My lord, I'm sorry, but it's true. Eleni did give Chanax the wands, and I helped her steal them from his room before returning them to you. I have failed you and accept any punishment you think is proper."

Ankhwenefer backed away from Eleni and Pamu as if they were hot coals. He ran his fingers through his thick, black hair and watched Eleni shake in her husband's arms.

"Eleni," the pharaoh said, his voice low, "look at me." She glanced up from Pamu's chest and faced her king. "Why did you let him have them?"

"Because," she sobbed, "he showed up at my house, about a month ago, demanding them. He knows of the wands because he watched Natasa use them when he spied on her in the apiary."

She paused as a darkness like a moonless night fell upon Ankhwenefer's face. It scared her.

"He spied on her while she worked?"

"Yes," she said, "and I did too. That's how I learned of the wands. I loved to watch Natasa use them, and would do so for hours, as did Chanax."

Ankhwenefer clutched his chest as if someone had stabbed him. Alexa walked toward Eleni, shaking her head as if she didn't believe it.

"It was I who told Chanax about the hole in the wall. I'm the one who killed Helena and my mother, not you," Eleni admitted, unable to stop talking. She dropped her face into her hands and sobbed. Her husband rubbed her shoulders and drew her closer.

"Eleni," Ankhwenefer replied, his voice now cracking, "you were a child. I'm sure Chanax deceived you."

"He did," she said in between sobs. "He told me he wanted to fix the wall, to keep her safe, but instead he spied on her for months, and then used it to witness your crime. I hate him."

She was panting now, surprised at how angry she was at Chanax.

She'd never allowed herself to feel this way before, and even though the kingdom was in grave danger, she experienced a great relief telling the truth after hiding in the dark for so long. She'd laid bare her soul, and would accept her punishment, grateful she no longer had to lie.

"Did he trick you into giving him the wands, even though you are now a grown woman?" he asked.

"No," she answered, "he threatened Rai and Khui. He said he'd hurt them if I didn't give him the wands. I'm so sorry. Please don't hate me."

"How dare he," Pamu grumbled.

Ankhwenefer rubbed his eyes. "This is worse than I thought. Pamu, I want to place guards on each of your children. We can't let Chanax know I've got the wands. I have a few things to put in place first, one of which is the successful evacuation of Queen Ruia and the princesses."

"Evacuation my lord?" Pamu asked.

"Yes," the pharaoh replied, walking to his desk and tugging out a piece of parchment, "they're to leave for Behdet in a few days. It's already scheduled, but instead, I will send them to Coptos, where they will take the Wadi Hammamat to Quseir and wait in safety with Pistias, the same man who took your father and Natasa to Pelusium. I've kept him on retainer in Coptos since fighting began on the border. Perhaps nothing will happen, and Chanax failed to use the wands properly. If this is the case, they can return, but if he was successful, he's already put into action events that can't be stopped. I want the women far away until this is sorted out."

He turned to Alexa. "That includes Meryt."

Alexa shook her head. "No, you can't take her. I won't let you."

"You can join her," Ankhwenefer offered.

"No," Alexa said, crossing her arms over her chest. "I'm the high priestess of the Upper Kingdom of Egypt. The new year is in eight days, one of our holiest times. I'm needed in the temple. I will not abandon my station because you have a bad feeling."

"I won't allow another of my daughters to be murdered in my name," Ankhwenefer replied banging his hands on his desk. Alexa cowered before him. "I told you to choose another man to father your heir, but you refused, and now you understand what it means to be the mother of my child. Meryt will go to Quseir with Ruia. Maybe she will return, maybe she won't, but if I'm to die, I want to die knowing she escaped, unlike Helena all those years ago."

Alexa covered her mouth with her hand, her shoulders shaking as she sobbed. Eleni burrowed deeper into Pamu's arms. She'd never seen Ankhwenefer so angry, and it was her fault.

Ankhwenefer turned away from Alexa and made his way to Eleni's side, speaking to the high priestess over his shoulder. "Pistias's ship will leave before sunrise in three days. If you don't escort my daughter to the docks, I will take her from you myself."

Ankhwenefer placed his hands on Eleni's shoulders. "You and your children are welcome on the boat if you wish."

Eleni trembled. Leave Pamu's side? She wasn't sure she could do it. "How long would we be gone?" she asked.

"I have no idea," Ankhwenefer admitted. "When I sent Natasa away, I thought she'd be home in a year at most, but that's not what happened. It could be a few weeks. It could be forever."

"No," Eleni answered, "I will not leave Pamu. We will stay, but I appreciate guards for my children. Chanax will be angry when he discovers the wands missing."

"Yes," the pharaoh agreed. "I have a feeling he doesn't use them very often, so we have some time. I don't want him to know he's been discovered until Ruia and the princesses are far away."

"My lord, what is our punishment for failing you?" Pamu asked, gaze to the floor.

"Nothing, Pamu," Ankhwenefer replied, peering into Eleni's face. "Eleni has suffered enough already."

☥

In Memphis, Isidor opened the letter from Chanax. He read it and then called for General Conanus. A few hours later, the soldier arrived looking harried and annoyed.

"What is it, priest?" he asked.

"It's time to act," Isidor answered.

"You want me to take him without warning, like a coward? I should meet him on the battlefield."

"You had your chance at The Fortress of Nowhere and well, got nowhere. You know the pharaoh's wishes. Arrest the rebel and deliver him to Lycopolis. Make sure his heirs are dead. Chanax has provided a plan to make it so, and you will do it."

Conanus swallowed hard and squeezed his fists. "Fine. What must I do?"

"Procure an Egyptian battleship," Isidor began. "Shouldn't be too hard to do. Every crew is for sale, particularly those who have been stationed in the uninhabitable zone for years. Buy the ship and enough Egyptian soldiers to sail it. Stuff the hull with two hundred of your men, including yourself, and sail to Coptos. There you will hide in plain sight and wait for Chanax's sign."

"What will the sign be?"

"The rising of Sopdet before dawn. It's eight days away, so you must do this with haste, or you will lose your window of time and return to Memphis empty-handed." Isidor handed the scroll to the soldier and then turned his back to the man. "The exact details of your operation once you're in Coptos are written there. You can see it's quite simple."

"So, this is it?" The general croaked after he read the letter. "This is how I will be remembered."

Isidor didn't turn around and instead gazed into his cup of blood-colored wine. "Better than Ankhwenefer, for he won't be remembered at all."

When the general left, Isidor called for his servant once more. He'd seen the future and knew that he'd best not be the sole Egyptian-blooded priest in Memphis when the event was over.

"Yes, my lord," the servant said.

"Make plans for me to take the next boat to Alexandria, and from there to Massilia in Gaul. I have a dear friend there whom I'd like to pay a visit."

The servant left his chambers, and Isidor stood alone drinking his wine. "I'm coming for you, Neferu," he whispered to no one.

☥

Hecataeus strode into the parlor where his young wife, Phile, sat at a loom, weaving a blanket.

"Where's Macarius?" he asked.

"Out in the yard, why do you ask?"

"Because I received a letter from the pharaoh of Upper Egypt, and we need to discuss it. I don't want our boy to be worried."

She looked up from her work and frowned. "What does the pharaoh want?"

"Trouble is on the way," Hecataeus replied. "I need to go to Alexandria and investigate. Wait and be at the ready. Eleni might need me."

"I see," Phile said.

"I'm not sure how long I'll be gone."

"You must do what you believe is right."

"I can't leave her to the Greeks. I need to be there if the worst happens."

"How will you know if the worst has happened?"

"Trust me, bad news travels fast. I might not be able to save her, but if I can, I will. Her children as well."

"You're a good man."

He kissed her and picked her up in his arms. "I leave on the next ship for Alexandria, in a few hours. How about a proper goodbye?"

She scratched his beard and returned his kiss. "I'd love nothing more."

As he carried her to the bedroom, he asked. "What do you think of visiting Paros after I return from Egypt? I'll need to see an old friend there."

"Paros?" Phile asked. "Why, I hear it's quite beautiful."

"Yes, my love, it is."

39

Too Late

Anen was sixteen when her husband sent her away. Within her womb, she carried his unborn son. Always her beloved child would remind her of the greatest love she'd ever known.

Thebes, Egypt, 186 BCE

Three days later, before Ra rose in the east, Ankhmaat led Anen down to the docks. They wore the plain clothes of peasants in order to blend in with the other workers. He shivered under the pale moonlight and cursed himself for being such a fool for failing to let his father kill Chanax when they had the chance. Because of his desire for peace among the princes, he now had to send his precious Anen away into the great wide world. They approached the ship, not a royal flotilla, but an old, sea-worn vessel that had seen too many years. He heard his wife suck in her breath.

"That is our transport?"

"It's a bit rickety, I know," Ankhwenefer said from behind them. "However, you must flee undercover. Trust me, the chambers below are fit for the future high queen of Egypt."

Ankhmaat smiled at his father, grateful for the bit of humor, and added, "A fishing boat is not the worst way to flee into the night. You could be setting out on foot."

"Or in one of our cramped, smelly naval ships," Senui said, patting his sister on the back. "Trust me, those men stink way worse than this guy."

Senui nodded to the deck where a pale-skinned man stood, hands on his hips and chest puffed out, his curly brown hair tossing in the pre-dawn breeze. Upon his shoulder sat a mongoose. He descended the plank and greeted them in a hushed voice.

"It's good to see you, my lord," the sailor said, grinning as he addressed the prince, and Ankhmaat noticed several of the man's teeth were gold. Pistias looked the crowd up and down. "Is this my new crew?" The women gazed from under the lowered hoods but said nothing. "My, my, you're as quiet as mice. Don't worry, ladies, I'll take good care of you. Andara, the mongoose, doesn't bite and neither do I."

Meryt stepped forward, dragging her mother behind her as she gripped her hand. "What is a mongoose?"

"The perfect animal for me, little girl," he said as he took the creature from his shoulder and let the little girl hold her. "Trust me, passengers often find my pet very comforting. I know Natasa was quite fond of my Belladonna, Zeus rest both of their precious souls."

Ankhmaat caught his father's gaze and cleared his throat. "I'd like to say goodbye to my wife in her chambers if you don't mind."

"Her chambers, yes," Pistias said, chuckling. "Go on board. Hurry now. You'll find your quarters down below. Men, say your goodbyes quickly, we need to set sail before the sun rises. The fewer dockworkers who see the specifics of my ship, the better. Get comfortable ladies, you won't be allowed up on the decks until we arrive in Coptos. Understand?"

Everyone nodded, and Ankhmaat saw his father kiss Ruia on the forehead. They whispered something to one another, and he handed her the cedar box.

"Take it," he overheard his father say, "and throw it into the Red Sea."

Ruia nodded and turned to say goodbye to her sons. Ankhwenefer picked up Meryt to kiss her before setting her down. Alexa carried her child on board to get her settled with Bithiah, and Senui followed with Durame.

Ankhmaat turned to Anen and pointed toward the ship. He was afraid to speak, so he let her lead him onto the boat and down the steps to where the group was to hide. Her chambers were nothing more than a small room with a porthole. Her eyes widened as she took in her surroundings.

"Don't worry," Ankhmaat whispered in her ear, his stomach churning. His throat stung. "Your mother will be with you, as well as Shesh and Baktre. I'm sure you'll be home before our baby is even born."

She slumped forward, weeping into his chest. "My love, my heart tells me I will not return."

"Don't say such things, Anen," he answered. "I will send for you, I promise. Father and I will go to Chanax's chambers once you're far away and set everything right. When we have him in our custody, we will take care of the matter."

"I hope so." She sniffled. "I truly do."

Ankhmaat grabbed her and kissed her. They'd made love through the night, and still, he craved her. How could the fates take her from him like this? He'd known her a mere five months, not nearly enough time. A child, the heir to the kingdom, was on the way. There was so much life left for them to live.

"I will send for you," he promised, his voice thick.

"What if you don't?"

"Only death will keep me from you."

They clung to each other until they heard a pounding on the door. Khenefer opened it and peeked his head in. "Off the ship. We must set sail."

Ankhmaat kissed his beloved wife goodbye and made to leave with his brother, who was to accompany the women. Ankhwenefer didn't want both of his heirs in harm's way, so the younger of the two would be sent away. Ankhmaat turned to look at his wife one last time. "If I should die, please don't forget me, Anen."

"I will never forget you," she answered as tears poured down her cheeks.

Khenefer dragged Ankhmaat into the narrow hallway as Ruia rushed past and into the room with Anen. Ankhmaat heard his young wife wail behind him, and Khenefer grabbed him before he could run back.

"Let her go," Khenefer advised. He dragged his older brother to the ramp. The sky was beginning to lighten as the young man spoke. "We have to leave now, Ankhmaat. I will take care of her, I promise."

Ankhmaat grabbed his little brother and squeezed him.

"You must take care of Father," Khenefer continued. "He needs you until the very end. Do you understand?"

"Yes, brother, I do."

"This is not our fault, Ankhmaat. This story began long before we were even born."

"It falls to us to rectify the situation."

"I'm not sure that's even possible, but if it is, I will do what I can to see it done."

"Thank you, Khenefer. I love you." Ankhmaat said.

"We go now," Pistias hissed from behind. "Get out of here. We can't have a crowd seeing the ship off."

Ankhmaat left his younger brother standing on the deck of the ship. As the sailors released the vessel from her captivity, the king-in-waiting walked away down the docks, each footfall heavier than the other. The boat carrying his beloved, along with his brother and unborn child, slipped along the Nile current from the harbor and to the north.

Ankhmaat watched his father across the harbor, standing in front of the royal ship, where hundreds of workers were preparing the craft for departure. He'd thrown off his peasant cloak to reveal his royal adornment. They were to pretend they were seeing the women off on the royal craft. Ankhwenefer looked alone and small, even though Min and Khaleme now stood by his side. His face was pale and gray in the dawn light, and his mouth was set in a firm line. Ankhmaat wasn't used to seeing the man so frail and fragile. He recalled Khenefer's words to take care of him and now understood what the boy had meant. Always Khenefer had been the observant one; nothing ever escaped his watchful eye.

"Well," Senui said as he approached with Panas, Hor, and Horpais, they too no longer dressed in their disguises. "I guess it's time to act the part of the prince. Come, let's join your father and see the women off."

Ankhmaat looked into his cousin's eyes and noted the tear stains in his smeared eyeliner.

"You look horrible." Ankhmaat laughed. "I imagine I don't look much better, do I?"

Senui shrugged as he fought back new tears, and Ankhmaat put an arm around his cousin. "It's going to be fine, Senui. We'll take care of Chanax and this will be over. Okay?"

"Sure, Ankhmaat," he replied. "Whatever you say."

They took their place next to the pharaoh as the great Ra rose high in the sky, pretending to see off the royal ship on its way to Behdet. Chanax was nowhere to be seen, but High Queen Weret saw the ship leave the dock and was heard uttering, "Good riddance," under her breath as her slaves carried her litter back to the palace. Chanax's guards reported to Ankhwenefer that the prince had remained in his chambers the previous evening in a deep meditative state before his altar but planned to visit Weret's chambers later in the day.

Ankhwenefer's response was curt, "Fine, let the villain have one more evening of debauchery, but set two more guards upon him."

☥

The next morning, after they knew both boats were long gone, Ankhmaat joined his father to face Chanax. As they approached his uncle's chambers and found the doors open and unguarded, it was obvious they were too late.

"Where are his guards?" Ankhmaat asked, his heart sinking at the sight of the abandoned doorway.

His father strode across the empty hall and thrust open the golden doors to Chanax's chambers, revealing a parlor in disarray, as well as six guards passed out around a table, covered with food and drink.

Ankhmaat ran to them and felt for their pulses—his own heartbeat quickening when he found none. Their flesh was still warm.

"They died only moments ago," Ankhmaat said.

"Yes," his father replied, sniffing the clay mugs on the table, the remains of their morning meal still half-eaten on their plates. "Poison."

Min and Ansel swept past them, leading several other guards, as well as Senui, Horpais, and Panas, deeper into the chambers. Ankhwenefer followed the group of men to help them search the chambers. "Come," he said to Ankhmaat.

They entered the posh bedroom, and Ankhmaat noticed his father's shoulders tighten. Animal pelts, woven blankets, and silken pillows were strewn upon the floor. It was obvious Chanax had left in a hurry. His storage chest was open and leather sandals, white spun tunics, colorful scarves, dark beaded wigs and jewelry lay scattered, all unnecessary for whatever perfidy Chanax had fled the castle to accomplish. His crown and prince's collar shone in the sunlight on their wooden stand near the window.

"Chanax murdered six people before breakfast," Ankhmaat said, his voice rising. It was unimaginable. "What have I done?" He sat on the bed and rubbed his temples.

"What have you done?" his father asked. "How is any of this your doing?"

"I'm the one who convinced you to let him stay," Ankhmaat said. "You wanted to kill him when he arrived at court, and I begged you not to." He looked over his shoulder at Senui and Panas, who stood still in the doorway, unwilling to enter the tainted room. "I did it for you, Panas," Ankhmaat screamed, tearing the bed curtain down and throwing it at his cousins. "For you, and Hor, and Sethe." He turned to his father and pointed an accusing finger. "You never should have listened to me."

The pharaoh walked to a simple set of table and chairs in the corner, upon which sat several pitchers of wine and ale as well as bundles of herbs scattered near a mortar and pestle. He ran his fingers over the fine wood.

"These were her chambers," he said, his voice soft.

"These were Natasa's chambers?" Ankhmaat asked, his heart pounding even faster.

"Even after I learned of Natasa's death, I had the builders finish the apartments and brought some of her furniture from her apartment in Behdet." He shrugged. "Sentimental I know. The chambers were to remain unoccupied, but Weret gave them to Chanax when he arrived, and she mocked me when I'd argued, claiming ten years was too long to keep a museum to a dead lover."

Ankhwenefer turned and stormed about the room, stopping abruptly and pointing to an altar in the corner, covered in shadow. Three thick, black, unlit candles, cooled wax running down their sides, surrounded a crystal skull. Darkness filled Ankhmaat's soul as if he'd seen a ghost.

Ankhwenefer grabbed the crystal skull and flung it across the room. It crashed into the marble wall, breaking the fresco in two, before falling to the floor with a thud. He stomped into the bath, and Ankhmaat followed with the rest of the men. The tiles and artwork surrounding the tub were even more opulent than the ones in his chambers.

"Father," he said, gazing at the carved and decorated ceiling, "this is divine."

Ankhwenefer wasn't listening. Instead he was inspecting a broken wooden table shattered across the tile floor. Broken jars of oil, copper bowls once filled with soap stones, and linen towels were strewn amongst the debris.

"The evil snake," Ankhwenefer yelled, kicking a broken leg so hard it struck the far side of the room and shattered into pieces, its demise echoing across the empty pool. "This was Natasa's table and underneath the desktop was a hiding place where she'd kept her cedar box filled with the items she'd considered treasures. He's sure to have known how the table and small box worked together, she'd have told him her secret hiding place when they were young.

"The poisoning of the guards tells me he'd planned on leaving this morning, and when he went to collect the wands and found them missing, he broke the table in anger."

"And then he fled," Panas finished, his voice trailing off. "I'm so sorry, my lord. I had no idea my father was this evil."

"Son, don't bear this guilt," Ankhwenefer interrupted. "I am the king of these lands, and I'm the one who has failed. It's my fault a murderer now walks our city streets. Min, Ansel, call up the guard. I want several troops scouring the city for the criminal. Warn Pamu and tell him to go home, Chanax is sure to have gone there to punish Eleni for taking the wands. Leave no stone unturned. I want him returned to my court as soon as possible. His plans for my undoing must be in motion if he chose this day to flee."

"What will you do to him, Father?" Ankhmaat asked, scared to see the man so angry and yet comforted at the same time.

"I will hang him for the murder of his guards and feed his body to the crows. Now go and find him, Min. We must hurry."

"Yes, sir." Min bowed and sprinted from the room, Ansel and the rest of the guard hurrying behind him, the sounds of their footsteps and clanking of their swords thunderous in the tiled room.

"You're dismissed," Ankhwenefer said to the princes. His voice sounded preternatural as if he were already dead.

"Father?" Ankhmaat asked, fearing the cold, lifeless stare in the man's gaze.

"Leave me, son," he answered.

Ankhmaat turned to go. As he crossed under the arch of the tiled bath and into the bedroom, he stopped to gaze at the image of Isis on the wall, singing her husband back to life. It reminded him of his own young wife, Anen, and their unborn child, now sailing away from his side to an unknown land, as Natasa had long ago.

Ankhmaat turned to his father, the man's head hung low to his chest.

"I'm not going to see Anen again, am I?" the young prince asked, tears now pouring down his cheeks, knowing he should show more restraint but unable to find such control within him. "We're too late, aren't we?"

Ankhwenefer lifted his head, his gaze softening yet still cold and distant. "As long as we breathe, there is hope," he answered. Then he turned his back and Ankhmaat saw the man's shoulders begin to shake. "Now please, leave me."

40

Hidden

There is no harmony in the energy field of the dark ones. Every time they participate in darkness, they tear their Ka, bit by bit. Often, a dark magician is one who shines bright when in the company of others and does great evil when alone—as if two people live in one body.

Thebes, Egypt, 186 BCE

Chanax peeked through Eleni's window. He'd paid her guards more gold than they could carry to take the children to the market, and she now worked alone at her table, sewing the straps back onto her son's sandals. A wave of desire hit Chanax full force. It was time to punish her.

He walked to the door and kicked it in, startling her. She sprung from the table, her work falling to the floor.

"Chanax," she said. "I have two guards and they'll be back any moment."

He stepped into the room and slammed the door behind him, advancing toward her with ease.

"Why do the pharaoh's guards protect you and your family, Eleni?" he asked, cocking his head to one side.

"You know very well why," she replied, holding her chin in the air. "You threatened me and my children. Why wouldn't I ask for protection?"

"You told your husband of our encounter?" Chanax asked, walking closer. She backed away. "I told you not to tell anyone." He continued to walk forward until he backed her up against the wall. It was a familiar dance between them—she was nothing more than a little animal, and he the bird of prey ready to strike. "Eleni," he whispered, his face inches from hers. "My wands are missing."

"I returned them to Ankhwenefer."

"Did you tell him I used them?"

"I didn't have to," she answered, looking him in the eye. "Natasa came to him in a dream. He knows everything, and now you won't be able to hurt him."

"He knows nothing," he said as he grabbed her arms and shoved her against the wall. Her head banged against the stone from the force of his thrust. The fear in her eyes turned him on, and he wanted her, needed her. Having his way with her would be both her punishment and his reward.

"Chanax," she begged, "stop it, you're hurting me. The guards will be back soon."

"No they won't, Eleni," he whispered into her ear like a lover making soft promises. "I sent them to the market to watch a puppet show with your children. I have plenty of time to discipline you for your actions."

"Discipline?" she quivered as he pinioned her against the wall with his hard body. "Chanax, please. Don't hurt me. The pharaoh asked for them, I had to oblige."

"Why, Eleni?" Chanax asked, rubbing his hips against hers. "Why does everyone choose to follow him? There's a price for loving Ankhwenefer. Consider Natasa's fate. Now you too will pay that price."

He dragged her into the bedroom. She struggled, and power surged through him. He ripped her tunic from her body and relished in her naked body as he threw her on the bed.

"You are so beautiful, Eleni," he murmured as he hoisted up his skirt. She flailed, but he slapped her and held her beneath his knees, forcing her legs apart and thrusting himself inside her warmth. "This is the perfect way to teach you a lesson, don't you think?" Eleni screamed as he pleasured himself with her unwilling flesh. He put his hand over her mouth. "Hush," he cooed, "I don't want to worry the people in the street."

Tears streamed down her face, and he licked them from her cheeks as he continued to have his way with her. When he climaxed, he let go of her mouth and brushed his lips upon hers. She was no longer struggling; instead, her body shook beneath him as she continued to sob. It was pitiful, which made it even more enjoyable. When he was done, he yanked himself from within her and stood. She rolled over, hiding her breasts from his gaze.

"Eleni," he said, grinning while straightening his skirt. "I knew you'd grow to be a desirable woman. I hope you remember this sweet encounter the next time you think of betraying me. I punish those who disappoint me."

Chanax turned and left the house, not even bothering to close the door behind him. He didn't care if she told Pamu; he'd wanted to dominate her before he ran away. It was powerful taking someone's sex against their will, and he wondered why he hadn't thought of it sooner.

He needed to stay in Thebes until Sopdet rose in the morning sky. Four days and then it would be over. He walked to the alley down the street from Eleni's home, where he'd stored his rucksack. He put on a simple brown tunic, discarding his princely clothing in a pigsty as he passed by. He no longer wore makeup, gold, or jewels. He'd left his sword in the palace and carried only a knife and the onyx wand his true father, Isidor, had given him long ago. His short-lived time as a prince had ended. He made his way to the worst part of the city and paid an outrageous amount for a room in the hovel of an old woman who had a look in her eyes as wild as his own and was missing most of her teeth. The place smelt like piss, but Ankhwenefer would never think to look for him there.

As Chanax sat in his small, filthy room, he leaned his head against the wall. Images of the plan kept flashing in his head, and yet all he could see was Behdet burning. His daughters were on their way to the city of his birth. Were they safe? Would his sons survive this? Why would Behdet burn? He banged his head on the wall to stop the flow of information. He was tired, yet he couldn't leave the room until the eve of the event. Until then, he was alone with his evil thoughts, for his mind had become a jumbled mess of anger, fear, lust, and hate. Chanax had no idea who he was anymore, except that if he did as he'd promised, both Ankhwenefer and Epiphanes would die, leaving Chanax free from the plots and plans of royal men.

He hated kings. They'd done nothing but control him and use him his entire life. From his father offering him up as tribute to Memphis, to Philopater's sexual abuse, to his brother stealing Natasa's heart, to Epiphanes demanding he destroy his entire family—all kings had ever done was hurt him. It was time to show them who held the power of the universe in his hands.

Ankhwenefer's troops covered Thebes like ants, searching for the missing Chanax. Yet when they arrived at the old woman's house, they barely gave her a glance. Her home was so small, and she was frail, ugly, and a bit insane. Everyone knew she lived alone because she was a witch. Her neighbors, crooks and thieves each one of them, testified that they hadn't seen any stranger in the area in a long time. Chanax wasn't the first criminal with a purse full of gold to be her guest, and they knew the drill when the authorities came looking. She shoved food into his room at regular intervals, and the two never spoke.

As Ra sank beyond the horizon on the eve of the rising Sopdet, Chanax rose from his place in the corner and swung his rucksack over his shoulder. He was numb inside, for there was nothing left to care about in the world.

It was time to end it.

41

The Star of Isis

"Believe the liar up to the door of his house, and no further than that."

~ Ancient Egyptian Proverb

Thebes, Egypt, New Year's Day, 185 BCE

Ankhwenefer entered the silent Temple of Luxor. The ceremony would begin before dawn, as the star, Sopdet, rose in the east. This was their sacred celebration of the new year, and he was required to attend. It was one of the few ceremonies Alexa forced him to do each year. She claimed it made the priests happy. Beside him walked Ankhmaat and the four other princes. Min, Pamu, and Khaleme strode behind, trying to appear alert and reverent despite the horrible hour of the day. Being awake before the dawn had a way of making a man yawn.

He'd stationed sixty guards around the outside of the temple. If an assassination attempt was going to happen, this was a good time. The Temple of Luxor was located across the river from Thebes. Ankhwenefer hadn't bothered to place permanent troops on this side of the river—other than the priests' comings and goings, nothing happened in Luxor. The ceremony would be small, only the pharaoh and his entourage, the high priest and priestess, some singers, and a few lower ranked priests. This formality was bearable—quiet, private, and quick.

He stopped before the altar and looked around the room, taking in the spiritual splendor. Even if he hated the gods, he still found the temples soothing.

"The ceremony takes place in the inner sanctuary where the light of the bright star will shine through a hole in the roof at the precise time of its rising," he explained to Ankhmaat, who had never attended a Sopdet rising before. "The room was built centuries ago for this single event. When the time is right, the high priest will call us to order and we follow his lead. Once we're dismissed, we head out north to join the troops. Given we still haven't found Chanax, we'll be safer surrounded by miles of our soldiers. We're here only to please the priests. We'd have left yesterday if I had my way."

The pharaoh glanced around the empty temple, lit by dozens of torches hanging on the wall. The priests weren't there yet, and they were alone. Ankhwenefer felt a strange longing as he gazed at the intricate hieroglyphs.

"I feel like walls are trying to tell me something," Ankhwenefer admitted. "As if they contain a secret message. Natasa told me each picture was a symbol that contained a spell, and those who know the language of Isis can speak the words needed to activate the spell. This entire temple is a storehouse of wisdom from our ancient ancestors. They built this here to pass down our knowledge, power, and mysteries, but I can't access it. I feel my forefathers call out to me but do not have the ears. I know Natasa and Helena would have shown me the way back to our country's wisdom."

"I miss them both so much," Senui said. "Sometimes I still wake from my slumber, thinking the horrible night when they murdered her was a dream, and instead Helena will come running through the door, her blue eyes alight and ready for adventure."

"They were taken from us too soon," Min agreed.

"Helena would have been twenty-one by now. A grown woman." Ankhwenefer wished he could've seen her grow up. "Not a day goes by I don't think of her."

Noises near the altar signaled the arrival of Setep and Alexa. Behind them, Sethe and their retinue walked in silence, arms folded like an X over their chests, bald heads shining as if polished. They took their places, and Ankhwenefer and his men approached the altar.

"Are you ready to begin?" the high priest asked.

"Yes," Ankhwenefer replied, kneeling at the altar, Ankhmaat beside him.

The chantresses formed two lines, one on either side of the altar, singing not with words, but guttural, unearthly chants. Their voices rose and fell, echoing in the chamber. Setep and Alexa stood before the statue of Isis, their arms held toward the small opening in the temple roof.

"I call upon Our Lady Isis," Alexa sang in a low voice. "Renew our hearts. Usher in the rains and make the crops abundant. Bless our pharaoh and grant him wisdom. Bless the royal infants as they are born this year. We thank you for your gifts, dear mother of us all."

As the woman continued to chant, starlight poured in through the ceiling and illuminated the statue of Isis behind the altar. Her golden image shone under the golden beams, and Ankhwenefer felt a sense of peace, in spite of his conflicted feelings about the gods.

The sounds of doors slamming and latches drawing closed filled the air, tearing him from his reverie. The singers halted, and everyone turned to look at Setep.

"What was that?" Ankhwenefer asked. The hair on his arms rose as a chill ran down his spine.

The high priest shook his head. "I have no idea."

Dozens of Greek soldiers poured into the room from the alcoves, and Ankhwenefer sprung from the floor, his heart racing as his mind processed the situation. The enemy soldiers must have been hidden in the catacombs beneath the temple before Ankhwenefer's arrival. They slashed the priests out of the way and rushed toward the pharaoh, like ants streaming in from all directions. Ankhwenefer drew his sword but lacked a shield or armor; he hadn't been ready for battle. There were only the nine of Ankhwenefer's men to fight back against the Greek invaders, but he'd prepared for this.

Ankhwenefer called out for the soldiers he'd stationed outside the temple. "To me. The sanctuary has been breached."

As the Greeks fell upon Ankhwenefer, Min yelled out in the distance, "My lord, they've locked the doors from the inside and are defending them. Our soldiers can't get in, and we can't get out."

Ankhwenefer's blood raced faster as the form of fury began to build around him. They would be slaughtered. He rushed a Greek and slashed his arm off before stabbing three more of them. Yet most of the soldiers ran past him as if he didn't exist. He jumped on the back of one passing soldier and drew his sword across his throat, yet still, the others rushed the princes rather than defend their fellow comrade. Khaleme roared as he defended the young men. Min's voice disappeared mid-battle-cry from the noisy din.

Ankhwenefer grabbed another soldier and spun him around, screaming, "Fight me, you coward."

"I'm sorry," said a voice from behind, "but that's not going to happen."

He turned and found General Conanus standing at the altar. Soldiers held Setep, Alexa, and the chantresses tight, but the other male priests, including Sethe, lay dead in a pool of their blood on the floor. Ankhwenefer sped toward the general, his sword at the ready, but as he made to strike, he was tackled from behind. He fell at the general's knees, his crown flying from his head. Ankhwenefer struggled to get up, but several Greek soldiers held him down as they tied his hands together. They weren't there to kill him, they were there to arrest him.

The soldiers dragged Ankhwenefer from the floor to face the general. The men inside the temple were panting, but no longer fighting, the booming sounds of his soldiers outside pounding on the doors, trying to get in, reverberated across the room. He imagined them scaling the outer walls, trying to find another way in, but they'd never consider the catacombs below. No one but the priests knew they existed.

"Father," Ankhmaat moaned. His son was still alive.

"Bring him to me," General Conanus commanded.

Ankhwenefer turned to see two soldiers drag Ankhmaat to the altar. He was hurt, a huge, bleeding gash across his chest. From the silence behind him, Ankhwenefer knew his nephews, as well as Khaleme, Pamu, and Min were dead.

"Go," the general commanded his soldiers, "return to the boat via the catacombs and join the others at the palace. The changing of the guard has begun, and our soldiers will need help with their mission. Kill every man you stumble upon. Ptolemy wants the rebel's queen alive, and she's bound to try and flee, so take every woman you come across as insurance. Avoid engagement with the Egyptian soldiers outside. I want to keep their attention on trying to break into the temple a bit longer to give us time to leave with our prize."

The men filed past him and back into the shadows from whence they'd come.

Ankhwenefer struggled against his captors like a bear in a trap, but their grip held strong.

"I'm sorry it had to be this way," General Conanus continued. "I'd wanted to meet you in battle, like real men, but my pharaoh tires of this war. He sent your brother to Thebes to finish this, and thus you and I are both left disappointed."

Conanus looked around at the dead princes on the floor and then to Setep. "Priests," he murmured, "they're so damn good at stabbing others in the back. Even those they claim to love."

"You can have me, but let the others go," Ankhwenefer begged. He caught Ankhmaat's gaze and felt as if someone was breaking his chest open with a blunt blade. After committing his life to the raising of the boy, he'd still failed him as a father.

"No," General Conanus replied, his voice lowering, "there can be no one left alive to claim to the throne. That is my mission."

He nodded to the soldiers, and one of them drew his sword and thrust it into Ankhmaat's chest. The young man groaned, his mouth open and jaw lax. Somewhere in the distance, Alexa screamed, but she sounded like she was on another world.

Ankhmaat held his father's gaze as he collapsed, eyes blazing before they fell lifeless and dark. While his son bled on the stone floor before him, Ankhwenefer understood how Natasa had felt when Helena bled to death at her feet. As the breath left Ankhmaat's lungs, the breath left Ankhwenefer's lungs; as the life left Ankhmaat's body, the will to live left Ankhwenefer. He stumbled to his knees in silence, unable to cry for anyone anymore.

"I meant it, Lord Ankhwenefer," General Conanus said, his voice barely audible above Alexa's wails. "This isn't the way I'd wanted our relationship to end."

The general turned to Setep, standing in silence next to Alexa as she sobbed, the priest's hands tied behind his back. The blue crown of the pharaoh lay at the high priest's feet.

"It's a strange thing," Conanus continued, picking up the crown and holding it before Setep's face. "So much bloodshed for a crown. Many men have died trying to claim it. Thousands of soldiers offered up to this singular task. Yet it's a matter of one simple sentence, spoken by you, Setep. You're the one who decides who will rule and who won't."

He held the crown above his head waved it back and forth. "It's time for you to crown Ptolemy V Epiphanes, Amon-Re, Pharaoh of Thebes and of Upper Egypt."

"Why should I?" Setep asked, the corner of his mouth twitching.

"I will kill you if you don't," the general warned, "and I'll keep killing until I find a willing priest."

"You've already killed several of my finest priests," Setep challenged, looking to the men lying dead by his feet. "How do I know you will let me live if I do this?"

"I'm sorry about that," Conanus said, gesturing to the bloody pile. "My men were overzealous in the thrill of the moment. The priests of Thebes will not be punished—my pharaoh wants as many of you alive as possible."

Ankhwenefer, still on his knees before the altar, unable to peel his gaze from his dead son, felt Setep's gaze upon him as the priest spoke, "I'm so sorry, my lord. I had nothing to do with this betrayal. Chanax worked alone, in the shadows. He is an evil man, and my heart is breaking, for your son would have been the greatest pharaoh of our age. A legend. I curse the ones who were behind his undoing. May the Lord of Death take them when they least expect it." Ankhwenefer heard the priest spit at the floor. "Including you, General Conanus. Now, unbind me, and I will do as you say."

They did as he requested, and in a matter of moments, after twenty years of waiting, Ptolemy V Epiphanes was crowned the pharaoh of the whole of Egypt.

"Wonderful." Conanus nodded to his remaining guard, holding the crown under his arm. "Bring the rebel to the ship. Send word to Ptolemy to meet us in Lycopolis and take the women prisoners."

His men rushed toward Alexa and the priestesses.

"You swore you wouldn't hurt the priests of Thebes," Setep demanded, stepping in front of Alexa.

"That is correct, your men are safe," Conanus replied, tossing his cape over his shoulder and sheathing his sword. "The priestesses are mine. We know what magic they practice, and my lord despises the temple whores. The time has come to shut down the temple of Isis."

A pair of guards ripped Ankhwenefer from the floor, but he lacked the will to stand, and they were forced to carry him as he stumbled out of the room. Everywhere he turned, the face of someone he loved gazed up with dead eyes; Min, Khaleme, Senui, Horpais, Panas, Hor, Sethe. He took one last glance at Ankhmaat, who lay lifeless beside his cousin Sethe at the base of the altar and found himself unable to feel. How could it be that he, the one so willing to die, was the only one who had lived?

☥

Eleni woke to the sounds of rushed footsteps outside her room in the Houses of Healing. Within moments after Chanax raped her, her husband had arrived and found her huddled in the corner of their room, naked and in shock. He'd delivered her to Iu-Amon, who had given her a royal room where she could be alone to recover from the violence. Her daughter slept in her arms.

"Eleni," Iu-Amon exclaimed as he burst into her room. "Get up. Something terrible has happened."

"What?" she asked, rubbing her eyes. The sun hadn't even risen.

"We're under attack. Greek soldiers have infiltrated the palace. They're killing everyone."

That meant only one thing: Chanax had struck, and he'd been successful.

Eleni climbed out of bed and followed Iu-Amon out of the room, carrying Rai over her shoulder. The little girl was seven and as heavy as a sack of grain. Iu-Amon turned a corner, and they found Ennaeus sprinting toward them.

"It's no use," Ennaeus said, panting and pointing over his shoulder. "They're coming, Iu-Amon. We're surrounded."

Several Ptolemaic soldiers appeared before them in the hall. Eleni turned to flee the other direction and found Ennaeus spoke the truth— more soldiers arrived in the hall behind her. They poured into the sick room, slaying every male, even though they lay injured in their beds.

"Iu-Amon," Eleni whimpered, unable to breathe, "what do we do?"

The old man leaned in and kissed her on her forehead. "Always I have loved you, Eleni. You are so precious to me. Don't forget that."

The soldiers were upon them. Two of them grabbed her, one ripping Rai from her arms. Another stabbed Ennaeus while his partner thrusted his sword into Iu-Amon's back. The soldiers dragged her down the hall as she screamed.

"Why are you arresting me and my daughter? Where are you taking us?"

"To Alexandria," the soldier laughed, "to be sold into slavery."

42

The Defeat of the Rebel King

By 184 BCE the rebels of the south formally surrendered to Ptolemy V Epiphanes in hopes of bargaining for their lives. Instead, the young pharaoh showed his cruelty, and slaughtered them in large quantities, to ensure another rebel king would never again rise from the ashes of Egypt.

The Nile River, Egypt, 185 BCE

Chanax crouched in his small quarters, the ship rocking side to side. He'd been squatting in silence since he'd met the Greek soldiers in their stolen Egyptian naval vessel on the shores of Luxor and snuck them into the temple under the cover of a dark moon, showing them where to hide in the tombs below the temple floors, and pointing the way to the specific room where the ceremony would take place.

Once his part in the deed was complete, General Conanus had ordered him to the ship and locked him in this small room. They supplied food and water, a place to relieve himself, and a hammock. No one, except the servant who delivered his meals, had visited in what seemed like days. Where in Egypt they were by this point, he had no idea.

The door thrust open and a bit of sunlight shone upon him, causing him to squint.

"Get up," a soldier said. "The general is ready to see you."

"It's about time," Chanax answered, his legs hurting after sitting for so long.

He rose and followed the man to Conanus's chambers on the upper deck, behind the bridge. There was nothing on the shoreline but desolate fields, abandoned villages, and Egyptian soldiers, their weapons at their sides, as the ship passed along the river. The sound of a flag fluttering in the wind caused him to look up, and he beheld Ptolemy's banner shimming along the breeze.

Chanax entered the cabin, and General Conanus rose to greet him. "Zeus, you look terrible and smell worse. I suggest you use my chambers to wash up. There's a fresh priest's robe from Alexandria already set out for you, compliments of Our Majesty."

Chanax did as he was told. He felt much better when he returned to the general's desk.

"There," Conanus said, a smile on his face as he tapped his fingers on the desk, "now we can talk. The Lord and Pharaoh of this great land, Ptolemy V Epiphanes, wants me to say thank you. The mission was successful. The palace was caught off guard, the rebel king captured, Ankhmaat slain, Ptolemy V named pharaoh in Thebes, a quick escape before the entire city was alerted, and we now have dozens of women to sell into slavery, including Queen Weret herself. She will make a nice prize at the market in Alexandria. As a matter of fact, she's already making a nice prize for several of my officers. We heard she enjoys male attention."

Chanax cringed, knowing the agony Weret was experiencing at the hands of the filthy Greeks. She'd welcomed him home with open arms, and this was how he'd repaid her. Guilt flooded his heart, but he swallowed it down. The woman was a fool for putting her trust in him. She was getting what she deserved.

"It was my pleasure," Chanax replied, voice steady. "My family was not worthy, and Egypt will now be one whole kingdom, not divided in two."

Did he believe his words? Of course not. Chanax realized nothing but lies would now fall from his mouth, for the truth was forever lost.

"Come," Conanus said, rising from his seat, "I want to share a moment with you."

He walked out of the cabin, and Chanax followed him to the bridge. They stood next to the captain as several soldiers dragged a man out onto the deck. It was Ankhwenefer. He'd been lashed, and his body was covered in long, red-hot wounds oozing blood onto his dark brown loincloth. They were fresh, not even beginning to scab. The soldiers led him to the bow, where they chained him to a post. Chanax heard cries from the Egyptian soldiers, who now lined the banks of shore in droves, placing their right arms over their hearts as they recognized their king. These men had been stationed here for years, protecting the Upper Kingdom from the Greeks, and now one of their own ships sailed by, flying not Ankhwenefer's phoenix, but the banner of the enemy himself.

Conanus stepped forward and thrust the blue crown above his head, signaling to the soldiers that the priesthood had crowned a new king. He grabbed a papyrus cone, put it to his mouth, his voice booming across the great river, "Soldiers of Egypt, look at your false king. See how he has failed you. We have him in our custody and will kill him in Lycopolis for all the world to see." Shouts and cries rose from the men on the shores, and Conanus continued, "Lay down your weapons. Go home to your women and children. The Great Egyptian Revolt is over, and the rebel king will pay for his sins. Do not try to avenge him, for Ptolemy V Epiphanes, your true lord, and pharaoh, will not show mercy to anyone who is against him. There will be no more rebellions in Egypt. Long live Epiphanes."

The Greek soldiers on the ship cheered, and the men on the shore continued to scream their disbelief and anger. The Egyptian troops fired a few arrows, and two of Conanus's soldiers fell on the deck of the ship as they were struck.

"Unwise," Conanus admonished, yelling into the cone and pointing downriver where several dozen Greek ships were now in view. "Do you see those ships to the north? They're heading this way to cleanse the land, and they will not be merciful, you heathens."

The Egyptian soldiers scattered from the shoreline as the Greek fleet glided closer along the river. Smoke lined the banks behind them as they burned their way toward Thebes. The purging of the rebellion had begun, and Chanax had been the cause. A sense of pride swelled within his breast. Chanax, the great magician, had single-handedly taken down an entire kingdom. Perhaps his work in the Cult of Set hadn't been useless after all.

"Would you like to speak to your brother?" Conanus asked.

Chanax looked down at Ankhwenefer. The man trembled as the whip struck him, his head hung low upon his chest. Only his chained arms kept him standing. He was pitiful in his weakness.

"No," Chanax replied. "I have no need to speak to that man."

☥

"Failure. Won't you even try to fight back?"

"It was so easy to destroy you, like taking a toy from a child."

"Your people will suffer for your crimes."

"Who did you think you were, oh great Rebel King? What right did you have to claim Egypt as your own?"

"Idiot, we'll show you how useless you are."

Ankhwenefer lost track of time, each moment a blur of pain as the Greeks beat, whipped, and mocked him. Their words no longer stung, for they spoke the truth—he was useless, a false king whose fate had caught up with him. It was worse when they left him alone to lie in his blood and filth in the small room at the bottom of the ship, for in the silent absence of their torture his own mind kicked in, and he recalled his son, slain on the altar of his gods, while he, the pharaoh, stood by and did nothing.

He had failed, and because of his incompetence Egypt would burn, and all that was beautiful and true about her would fade out of time and memory as if their great civilization never existed. He was the last in a line of kings to save her—there was nothing left for any of them now.

The door burst open, rousing him from his twilight consciousness. He turned his bloodied face from the wooden floor, but his body remained still—he was in too much pain. A guard stomped toward him and tugged him to his feet.

"Get up, filth," the guard hissed. Ankhwenefer struggled and found he had no strength as he tumbled back to the floor into a bloodied heap. The guard kicked him. "This is the great warrior our pharaoh was so afraid of he resorted to trickery to have him arrested?"

"Watch your tongue," a second voice warned. "It's best not to speak of Lord Epiphanes that way. Carry him if you have to, he has a meeting with the general."

Ankhwenefer winced as the guard grabbed him around his broken ribs and dragged him to the door. The newly formed scabs on the oldest of his lacerations rubbed against the guard's rough leather vest and broke open, making the walk up a short set of stairs excruciating. He knew the layout of his ships and understood they weren't headed to the general's apartment behind the bridge. This meeting would take place in the bowels of the ship, where no one else would see. He could only imagine the torture he would endure. They wouldn't kill him. Ptolemy wanted him alive so he could have the honors himself. No, death wasn't on the table tonight, no matter how much he begged for it. They would hurt him because there was one last bit of information they needed—the whereabouts of Khenefer.

"In here, scum," the guard said as he shoved Ankhwenefer into a large room in which several greedy-looking men, captains of the highest rank, stood around the impeccably dressed General Conanus, who looked as if he were on his way to a royal banquet. He smiled as Ankhwenefer entered the cramped room.

"Good evening, Lord Ankhwenefer," Conanus said. "I say, you looked much better in the temple than you do now. A king isn't much without his crown, is he?"

Ankhwenefer cocked his head to get a better look. His eyes were swollen to slits, and everything was blurry. The wounds on his skin burned. In the corner of the room was a large bed covered in dirty, used bedclothes. Why in the world were they meeting in here?

"Ankhwenefer," a female voice wailed.

He turned and swallowed down the bile in his mouth as a set of guards tugged Weret into the room. She wore a torn skirt around her waist, abuse evident in the scratches on her face and bruises on her arms and hips. They'd bound her hands behind her back, causing her to arch her back in discomfort, but allowing the men a nice, full view of her bare chest.

"What have they done to you?" She gasped as she looked him up and down.

Was he that unrecognizable? He was going to respond when his mind wandered to Ankhmaat's death, and rage rose within him. There were no words for the woman—it was her fault as much as Chanax's that his son was now dead and the kingdom lay in ruin.

"Good evening, dear queen," Conanus said as the men ushered her closer. "I hope you've been enjoying your journey to Alexandria. I hear my officers have been enjoying you." She winced at his words, and Conanus licked his lips as he continued, "We're delivering your husband to the true pharaoh in Lycopolis tomorrow morning, so I thought it'd be nice to include him in tonight's festivities." He turned to Ankhwenefer and winked. "You must wish to say goodbye to your wife, yes?"

Ankhwenefer cleared his throat. "Before me stands my queen, that is true. However, my wife died long ago."

Weret shook her head. "Ankhwenefer, how can you say that? Please, you must help me."

He grinned at her foolishness and winced from the pain; they must have broken his jaw as well. "What is it, darling? Are they mistreating you?"

Conanus snapped his head to Ankhwenefer, raising an eyebrow. He must have thought Ankhwenefer would beg him to spare Weret from whatever torture they had in mind. Instead, he giggled like a mad man before he spat blood on the floor.

"Are you surprised at this treatment?" Ankhwenefer continued, his mood now bordering upon raw insanity. He could feel everyone, including Weret, step away from him. "You didn't believe Chanax's revenge would hurt me but leave you unscathed, did you?" Her shoulders shook as tears poured down her swollen cheeks. "I knew you were ignorant, but my dear, the queen is linked to the king's fate.

I warned you, but you ignored me and let that traitor back into the kingdom."

His voice rose to a howl as Weret cowered in a corner and the others stood back. He considered trying to flee and attempt to make it to the upper deck to throw himself in the river, but at that moment, two more guards arrived and blocked his way, this time dragging Alexa, who was also naked, bound, and scratched. He recalled the bed in the corner and his heart sank as he understood what Conanus was going to do to get the information he sought.

The general gathered his composure as Alexa entered. "We invited your high priestess as well."

Ankhwenefer looked away. Alexa had let him down, for she'd also chosen to believe in Chanax, yet he couldn't bear watching them hurt her. He hoped she had her wits about her and would recall their last conversation before Chanax struck and destroyed their entire world.

"Well," Conanus continued, "this is very simple, Chaonnophris. We've searched Thebes high and low and have found no trace of Khenefer. You know my assignment is to leave no heirs behind, so this is a problem for me. I need you to tell me where he is."

Ankhwenefer shrugged. "What if I don't?"

"My men like your taste in women, so you will watch as they indulge in your queen and your high priestess. One by one they will take turns until you tell me where your son is."

"No, please," Alexa begged, struggling to break free.

Ankhwenefer stared out from under his swollen eyes and tried to astrally connect with her. He needed Alexa to stay focused. He gulped as he spoke the words, knowing they would sound harsh, but hoping she would hear the message behind them. "I care not what you do to these women," he lied, for he didn't have the strength to watch the show Conanus planned. "They are yours to do as you wish. I will not tell you where my son is."

Both women gasped, and Weret screamed, "You bastard," but Conanus continued to wear a false smile like a wolf caught in the chicken coop.

"You're colder than I thought," Conanus murmured. "I'd heard a rumor you didn't love your queen, but you'd abandon your high priestess as well? Don't you consider her your spiritual companion? After a decade of sexual servitude, I'd think you'd be a bit more respectful."

Ankhwenefer took another deep breath, wincing as his broken ribs crunched as they moved. He looked at Alexa and saw not her terrified face, but Natasa's, and for the first time he was at peace about his beloved's death. If she'd returned from Gaul, it would be her standing before him, naked and violated. The idea of Natasa being raped by these men was too horrible to consider. Perhaps if she'd lived, none of this would have happened, but if this betrayal had been in the cards, it was best she'd never returned.

"My true spiritual companion lies dead in Gaul," Ankhwenefer declared, "and for once I am grateful." Alexa glared at him. *Good,* he thought, he had her attention. He couldn't see her clearly through the crust of blood and pus now sealing his eyes shut, so he extended his Ka, nudging hers, hoping the connection they'd created through Anit-Shadya was still intact. She raised her eyebrow, nodding ever so slightly. She'd heard him. She would deliver the information as he'd instructed her days prior.

He exhaled and continued, "I warned you this might happen, Alexa, but you didn't believe me. I offered you safe passage with the children, and you refused, instead choosing to believe in Chanax. Whatever happens now is by your own choice, not mine. My part in this is over."

"Safe passage?" Weret said, her voice high and unsteady. "What safe passage? Ankhwenefer, where is our son? If you knew Chanax was going to betray us, why didn't you warn me of any danger?"

"Because, my dear," he said, slurring due to the pain in his jaw, "you would have told Chanax my plans, and then both of our sons would be dead. There was never any plan to save you, the one so eager to put the entire kingdom at risk just to punish me for my indifference."

"Enough," General Conanus demanded. "Tell me where the prince is, and I'll let the three of you spend the night in peace."

"Never," Ankhwenefer answered, setting his jaw in anticipation of the blow he was about to receive.

Conanus stepped forward and struck Ankhwenefer so hard his legs gave out in agony. His entire face felt on fire as his head crashed with the floor.

"Beat him," the general commanded, and feet struck his ribs as the men kicked him from all directions. It hurt beyond words, but at least they weren't raping the women. Ankhwenefer wondered if he had any bones left to break and as if in answer, heard his wrist shatter as one of the men stepped on his bound hands with all his strength. He wailed as the room spun around him.

"Stop," Alexa yelled in the background. "Stop hurting him and I'll tell you where the boy is."

The men paused, and Ankhwenefer panted in a pool of his own blood. "Alexa, please don't."

"Well?" Conanus asked, hands on his hips. "Where is Prince Khenefer?"

"Ankhwenefer put him on the boat to Behdet with Queen Ruia and the princesses. Silus plans to send them to a western oasis and into hiding. They left a little over a week ago." She lied with such conviction, Ankhwenefer almost believed her himself.

He sighed, grateful, and mumbled with a weak groan, "How could you? You promised."

"Take the priestess back to her cell," Conanus commanded his men. "She's been a good girl and deserves some rest. You will not touch her for the remainder of the trip to Alexandria. Do what you want with the queen, it's obvious her husband lays no claim. Send word to Lycopolis, I'll need a boat readied to take me to Behdet as soon as we deliver Chaonnophris to the pharaoh."

"Please," Alexa begged. "Leave Ankhwenefer alone."

"Indeed, my lady," Conanus laughed as he stood above his broken prey, "I think we're done for the evening."

The next thing Ankhwenefer knew, Conanus administered one more swift kick to his temple, and his world faded to a merciful black.

43

The Halls of Amenti

"The Ancient Egyptians believed that upon death, they would be asked two questions and their answers would determine whether or not they could continue their journey into the afterlife...The first was, 'Did you bring joy?' The second was, 'Did you find joy?'"
~ Leo Buscaglia, twentieth century, CE

Lycopolis, Egypt, 185 BCE

Ankhwenefer hung from the cell wall, his arms tied above his head in shackles. Blood dripped down his face, arms, chest, back, and legs. His dark hair matted in sweat and pus from his head wounds, a thin beard beginning to grow in. The complimentary scourging and beatings on the boat were only the first of many tortures the young Ptolemy king would bestow upon him before his life was over. Of this Ankhwenefer was sure.

A door opened at the end of the hall, and the noise of the rowdy Greek crowd echoed down the chamber. They were hungry for justice. The long civil war had come to an end. The Greeks would keep Egypt, and the Egyptians—along with their magic, knowledge, and power— would fade into history.

He had failed.

How many had died in this venture? How many at his own hand?

He'd lost count years ago. There was only one murder that mattered, one that had weighed upon his heart his entire reign—Helena's. He closed his eyes and saw her playing in the sunlight down by the river, her unusual blue eyes shining.

He had failed to protect her then, and now his beloved son and nephews were dead as well.

"Natasa," he choked, finding the courage to call upon her, "I'm so sorry, but I need you."

He let his head hang. Since the day the handsome messenger from the north had set the final blow upon his heart and shattered it into pieces, Ankhwenefer had built a wall between his spirit and his twin flame. Yet he needed her, and she wouldn't fail him. He took in a deep breath and raised his head. Standing before him, shimmering in white light, stood Natasa.

"Are you a phantom?" he asked, his voice hoarse.

"Don't tell me Ankhwenefer, the last native pharaoh of Egypt, is afraid of ghosts," she teased. There was a lightness in her voice, despite the serious circumstances.

"It is you." He gaped. "How can that be?"

"You called for me."

He stared at the specter, knowing he couldn't touch her. She smiled, and peace flowed through his being. His cells hummed, and his heart beat a steadier pace.

"My love," he continued, "why aren't you in the Halls of Amenti?"

"You know I can't go there without you."

"What? How can that be?"

"You and I are bound to each other, one Ba in two bodies. Have you forgotten?"

"You don't deserve such a curse. I'm not worthy of your love."

"Why would you say that?"

"Have you no idea what I've done? How many people I've killed? How I led Ankhmaat to his death?"

"Yes, I know these things, for you and I are one. Nothing can be hidden between us."

"You can't allow this. You must keep yourself separate from me."

"That is impossible, and you know it. Stop struggling against your true self. Let me help you, please."

"I am broken," he admitted. "I can't face my brother, Thoth; my heart is too heavy. I will not pass Maat's test."

"This is true. You and I will not remain long in the Halls of Amenti. We have too much regret."

"Then what will happen to us?"

"We will be sent back, to live out another life on Earth."

"Dear goddess, no," he asked, panic inflating his chest. He breathed through it, but his heart continued to flutter.

"As many lives as it takes until we've healed, and our hearts are as light as a feather," she replied. She sent him a wave of peace, and his body responded.

"It could take a few lifetimes before we're whole," he said once he'd calmed down.

"Thousands of years," she agreed.

The sounds of guards entering the hallway startled Ankhmakis. He wanted to vomit.

"My love, it's time for you to join me in beautiful death," she said. "Come rest with me in sacred union, in the bliss of the All-One, in the place where you and I are one in our ecstasy."

"That doesn't sound so bad," he replied.

She paused for a moment before continuing, "They will take you to the stadium and put you to death. You must be strong."

"Will it hurt?"

"Death? Yes, it hurts, but you are no mere mortal, remember?"

He gazed upon her shimmering, ghostly form and found strength entering his body. He stood straighter as she continued to speak. "You will walk out there, head up and look at these people one last time, without hate. Let the story go. Then, when they tie you to the horses—"

"That's how they plan to kill me?" he interrupted.

"When they tie you to the horses," she continued, "close your eyes and enter our Ba. You know you can do it by remembering how much I love you. Travel out of your body to me, as we did years ago." The guard's footsteps grew louder. "In that moment, when we are one, we will cut the cord connecting the Ba to the body, and the two of us shall leave this plane and return to our true nature. This madman will not kill you. Instead, you will depart by your own choice."

She moved closer, placing a shimmering hand to his heart. "I am you, and you are me. I will be the keeper of our light for all time. Look for it, and you will find me."

Natasa merged with him, entering his body. They were one soul, complete, if only for this final brutal moment, no longer of two minds, but one being, whole and unified in the physical body.

The perfect female. The perfect male.

As the guards approached, Ankhwenefer felt he could fly.

"The time has come to pay for your crimes, rebel traitor." One of them laughed. "Let's watch the four directions tear you into pieces."

They entered the cell and unlocked his arms. He should have fallen, given the severity of his injuries, but instead, he stood strong. They tied his hands behind his back and slapped the blunt edge of a sword into his side.

"Walk, slave," the guard hissed.

Ankhwenefer did as he was told. Each step leading him closer to public ridicule and shame, each moment escorting him closer to death, yet he'd never felt more alive. He could see the energy of fear and distaste encircling each of the guards. As the door to the arena flew open, he was greeted by the jeers and cheers of thousands of Greeks, and some dark Egyptians, throwing stones and glass into the arena and calling him names.

He scanned the crowd, looking at each one of them. He wanted to hate them but now saw them as a part of the cosmic dance, each one playing his or her part. Light permeated the space and dancing particles filled the air. Soon, he'd be a part of that dance. The guards escorted him to the stand where Ptolemy V Epiphanes sat wearing a golden robe and white tunic, his sword at his hip. Upon his head, he wore the blue Khepresh crown of Thebes. His light brown hair and skin shone under the sun.

To the pharaoh's right sat Chanax, and at the sight of the traitor, Ankhwenefer's heart pounded beneath his chest. His strength faltered.

"Let it go, my love," Natasa advised. *"It is finished. You can't enter our Ba with rage in your heart."*

"Lord Chaonnophris." Ptolemy Epiphanes curtsied in mockery. The crowd jeered. "We finally meet. You, who caused twenty years of war and strife in this great country, will now face punishment for your crimes. What is it you have to say, Rebel King of Egypt?"

The crowd cheered with shouts of, "Kill the rebel king. Kill the rebel king," filling the air. It was a song of joy and victory to their cruel and ignorant hearts.

"Egypt will never be yours," Ankhwenefer said, his voice even and steady "Her secrets, her power, and her magic die with me"

Ptolemy snorted. "Bold words from a man who shall be torn apart. Do you have anything to say to your brother, who thought Egypt would be better off in my hands than yours?"

Ankhwenefer tilted his swollen face to Chanax, and a vision flashed before him—Chanax's head rolling on the dusty ground. Treachery was in the heart of Epiphanes, and even this great betrayal would not save Chanax from the fate of their house.

"Be careful, my brother, I fear you will be joining me in the Land of the Dead quite soon," he said. "Do not follow me into the dark."

"Kill him," the pharaoh of Egypt commanded.

The guards yanked Ankhwenefer toward the four horses standing at the center of the arena, each wearing a single chain and shackle—one for each of his limbs. He walked without fear and stood at the center of the ring. He closed his eyes and breathed in the hot, turbid air. Dust filled his lungs as the soldiers struggled to put the chains on him. He fell backward into their arms and surrendered.

"Now, beloved," Natasa whispered.

He sent his consciousness out in the six directions across the universe. The form of unconditional love surrounded him, and he allowed his Ka to connect with it. The rhythm of Natasa's heart filled his soul. In this place of light, a deep silence quieted his mind. His heart stopped pounding in his ears and found a steady beat. It was time to leave his body and cut the connection. His time as king had ended.

As the horses tugged at his limbs in anticipation, he began to sing, "Time abandons me when I'm in her arms, and my heart is always seeking her…"

Ankhwenefer, the last native king of Egypt, took one final deep breath and allowed the song of his soul, of her soul, to enter into every cell. Natasa's face beamed amidst the colors of the universe. The streams danced within and around his body. His Ba lifted itself from its physical chamber and followed the music to where she was, in the realm of the All-One. His body fell limp as he cut the silver cord that kept his spirit connected to life, and the energetic field that was his Ka scattered, like dust in the wind. Without this life force, his heart stopped beating, and his broken, tortured physical body hung like a ragdoll in the chains as it died.

Ankhwenefer never looked back, so sweet was this kiss of death. He returned to love and bathed in the bliss of the divine pair. After forty-two years of physical life, he was now whole.

☥

Chanax knew something was wrong the moment his brother's body fell lifeless at the chains. There was no struggle, no crying out for mercy. The guards gave the command to send the horses off in the four directions, but the man didn't scream in pain as his body was torn apart, for he'd already died. Somehow, he'd avoided this last, final punishment. The crowd knew something was odd and grew quieter, their jeers and cheers directed toward the pharaoh now.

"How?" Ptolemy asked, turning to Chanax. "Did my eyes trick me, or did he die on me prior to his execution?"

"You're not mistaken, Your Majesty," Chanax replied. "It appears he departed into the All-One before the horses took off."

Ptolemy V pinched his eyebrows together. "How is that possible?"

"Only our highest initiates know how to do it, my lord," Chanax explained, knowing the man was too dull to ever comprehend what had happened.

The pharaoh raised his hand to silence him. Then he turned to his guards. "Take him to the dungeons. I despise his nonsense and babble."

"What?" Chanax exclaimed. "We had an agreement."

"Yes, we did, but you were too eager to give up your brother for your own safety. That makes you much too dangerous to keep alive. Besides, there can be no heirs to the Upper Kingdom left alive."

"I'm not even a true heir to the throne," Chanax confessed.

Pharaoh crossed his arms. "What do you mean?"

"Isidor's my real father," Chanax explained, his heart now racing. He needed to get out of this predicament, and fast. "He was my mother's lover at the time of my birth. Just ask him."

Ptolemy V placed his hands on his belly and chuckled. "This is wonderful. You're Isidor's bastard? Fabulous." He was laughing so hard tears were forming in his eyes.

"Ask him," Chanax begged.

"I would, if I could, but he left Egypt weeks ago, and I don't think he'll ever return."

"What?" Chanax asked, his heart sinking. Isidor had abandoned him?

"Yes," Ptolemy explained, laughter still in his voice. "He set out after he delivered your letter unto Conanus's hands. I received word yesterday they experienced ill weather and the ship sank, taking Isidor and many goods with her to the bottom of the sea. No one survived. My merchants lost much in that storm."

Chanax couldn't believe his ears. Isidor, his father, was dead. Ptolemy V continued speaking, "It doesn't matter if the rebel wasn't your father, anyone associated with the House of Haronnophris shall die. I've sent Conanus to Behdet to take care of Silus. Your city is burning as we speak. Guards, get him out of my sight."

The guards grabbed Chanax and hauled him to the cell where Ankhwenefer had lived out the last moments of his life. They chained him to the wall, and the shackles cut deep into his wrists as he struggled against them.

"He can't do this," Chanax screamed at the guards. He flinched as the door to his cage clanged shut behind them.

Chanax leaned back against the cold, stone wall and looked to his sandaled feet. He was standing in a puddle of his brother's blood. Chanax closed his eyes and recalled Natasa as a little girl, singing to him in the fig tree, and wept.

44

The Slave Yards of Alexandria

Thus ended the reign of Ankhwenefer, the forgotten Rebel King of Egypt, and last native to rule the land of Kemit. No mention is made of him in Greek texts, and all of his own scribes' work was destroyed. His name chiseled from every stone surface in the Upper Kingdom, his monuments destroyed, and the city of his birth burned to the ground, left to the elements and buried under the sands of time. He controlled eighty percent of Egypt for twenty years, yet no one beyond the borders of his country ever knew his name.

Alexandria, Egypt, 185 BCE

Eleni stood before the rowdy crowd, wearing only a skirt, her chest exposed, and hands tied in front of her. Below the stage stood a cage, about ten feet by ten feet, crammed with small children. She had no idea what happened to her son after Thebes fell, but little Rai was in that cage. Eleni sucked down her panic. She'd experienced some of the worst abuse she'd ever known and lost her son and husband, yet this moment, the moment when she was to be forever separated from her little girl and knowing Rai would live on as a slave under someone's cruel care, was something she couldn't endure.

"How much for the rebel's whore?" the auctioneer bellowed. "I know she's got some wear on her, but she was his high priestess. She'll make any man happy for a long time."

Eleni glanced to the stage where Alexa stood naked, her hands chained behind her back. The bidding began.

"Thirty drachmae. Do I hear thirty drachmae?

"Thirty."

"Forty."

The numbers kept climbing. Within moments, Alexa was worth five hundred drachmae.

"Five hundred. Do I hear five-fifty?" the auctioneer continued.

"I'll take her for one thousand," a low voice called in the crowd.

Eleni strained to see what sort of man would pay so much for a woman. He was tall and cloaked in a brown robe. She couldn't see his face, but his beard was white.

"One thousand?" the auctioneer proclaimed. "Well, you must have a thing for high priestesses."

"I do," the man replied.

"Sold to the man in brown."

The men dragged Alexa from the stage and Eleni was next. The crowd whistled as she was shoved onto the platform.

"Yes," the auctioneer began, "she's a good-looking one, isn't she? A captain of the guard's wife, we believe. Got some Greek blood in her, and a body guaranteed to leave a smile on your face. This one will start at two hundred."

"Please," she begged, "my daughter. Let me have my daughter."

The man swatted at her. "She will be sold independently."

Eleni collapsed to her knees, and the crowd jeered as the auctioneer yanked her to stand.

"Two hundred. Do I hear two hundred?"

The value rose and soon she found herself worth eight hundred drachmae. She looked to the faces bargaining for her like a horse or a dog to be trained. This was a cruel game to them. Her head hung over her chest, and she dug her nails into her palms, silently begging the Lady Isis to help her.

"One thousand drachma," someone yelled over the crowd. Eleni jerked up and saw the hooded man had bought her as well. Was he cruel, this man who would dare to own her?

"My, my," the auctioneer replied, "you like young Egyptian women as well as priestesses?"

"I'm in need of new staff for my house in the country," he answered. "These women will suffice."

"Sold."

"Wait," the robed man continued, "I want her daughter as well."

"Whatever for?"

"Women are useless if you separate them from their children," her owner answered. "If I take her without the girl, she will die of grief within three years at best. I want to protect my investment."

"You have a point there," the auctioneer replied. "Fine, but you must pay me another 300 drachmae for the child."

"It'll be worth it," the man agreed.

Eleni's head throbbed as they dragged her from the stage and left her next to Alexa. She couldn't believe her child would remain by her side and vowed to repay the man, no matter what he asked.

"At least we're together," Alexa said, wincing as she spoke. There was a large gash across her cheek. "We will take care of one another, no matter what happens."

Their bonds were cut, and a man threw a rough robe at each of them to put on. They turned to see their owner approach them, holding her little girl's hand. Eleni gazed under his hood, and she bit her lip to fight back her tears as she saw the man's face.

The impossible had happened.

"Hush," Hecataeus whispered as he dropped his hood. "It's best to pretend you don't know me until we're on the boat."

Eleni grabbed Rai to her side. "You came for us," she said, chin trembling, her father's face blurry as tears stung her eyes.

"I promised I'd return if you were in trouble," her father answered. "Now, let's go."

As they made to leave the slave yard, Eleni heard the auctioneer call out over the noisy crowd, "Here she is, the one you've been waiting for, the Rebel Queen."

A pair of men dragged Weret onto stage, wearing a fake crown and nothing else. The slave yard lit up with catcalls and jeers. They had tied a rope around her neck, her skin red where it rubbed her, her hands bound behind her back. While all of the women suffered at the harsh hands of the soldiers on their way from Thebes to Alexandria, none had been dealt worse treatment than Weret. She cowered like a rabbit in an open field before the rough crowd. Hecataeus looked at Ankhwenefer's sister-bride and paused.

For a moment, Eleni thought her father would buy Weret as well. Instead, he shook his head at the last native queen of Egypt and turned away. "Come," he said to them as he led them toward the docks. "It's time to leave this place."

"Father, any word about Pamu or Khui?" Eleni asked as they walked away from the scene in the slave yard.

Hecataeus took her hand. "Pamu was killed in the temple, as were Min, Khaleme, and all the princes except Khenefer, who escaped on the boat with Pistias."

Eleni looked to the ground, her throat tight. "I thought so, but still I hoped."

"I have better news about your son," her father continued.

"Khui?"

He nodded as they approached his ship. "The guards taking care of him had strict orders from Ankhwenefer to flee the city if the palace fell. They're on their way to Paros right now."

"Paros?" Eleni asked him.

"Yes, Paros," Hecataeus replied, looking at Alexa, "where I believe there's also a little girl waiting for you."

Alexa placed a hand on his arm, her body beginning to shake as tears ran down her dirty cheeks. "Thank you, Hecataeus."

"Where is Paros, Father?" Eleni asked, now eager to get there and find her son.

"Far away from Egypt," Hecataeus answered. "Far, far away."

45

A Job Well Done

"The villainy you teach me, I will execute, and it shall go hard but I will better the instruction."
~ *The Merchant of Venice, William Shakespeare, 1598* CE

Five Years Later
Hermopolis, Egypt, 180 BCE

The assassin moved like a shadow through the stone hallway, dressed in black pants and shirt, his face covered with a dark mask. He was grateful the pharaoh was vacationing in Hermopolis; a villa was much easier to penetrate than a palace. As he turned the corner, he found the five soldiers he'd been expecting, guarding the king's bedroom.

"There aren't any more inside his chambers," his partner's voice sounded in his mind. *"Only five more to kill, and then you're done."*

"Six," he answered without speaking. *"Don't forget the pharaoh."*

He'd already killed many to get to this point, what was a few more? He drew his knife from his belt and took aim, striking the first guard in the chest. The assassin was on the back of a second guard before the first even hit the floor, breaking the man's neck as if it were dry kindling. The last three guards drew their swords as the assassin made his way toward them.

He knew their every action, even before they did. His Ka filled the room and combined with his partner's, they were everywhere in the entire villa, monitoring and tracking every movement. One of the men struck first, and the assassin ducked down below the enemy sword, his own knife out and slicing his opponent's leg, cutting through the bone. The man collapsed, screaming in agony, and the assassin flung his knife in his throat to silence him.

Whipping out his own sword, he faced the last two guards, who fought like gladiators from Roma refusing defeat, and the assassin found himself struggling to take them down. Within moments, however, he'd stabbed one through the heart and the second in the middle of the back, kicking the dead man with his thick boot in order to dislodge his bloody sword. The killer retrieved his knives from the other two corpses before turning to the bedroom door.

He paused, taking in a deep breath and then exhaling, giving blessings to the goddess. He'd been training for this moment for five years, and now success was close at hand.

"*Go now,*" his partner warned him.

The assassin opened the doors as if an expected guest. The pharaoh lay naked in his bed flanked by two young, wide-eyed, naked women.

"What is the meaning of this?" the pharaoh demanded.

The intruder strode to the bedside and drew open the king's bedcurtains, gesturing to the women. "You like your whores in pairs. I've noticed that's a habit amongst nobles."

The concubines stumbled out of bed and scurried out the door and down the hall, their footsteps echoing in the distance. He needed to work fast—their panicked flight would alert the second guard.

"Whoever sent you must have paid a pretty price for my head," his target said, sitting up taller in his bed. "I am the pharaoh of the Egyptian Empire, and I will pay you even more to spare my life."

The assassin gazed at the pharaoh, fighting hard to keep the emotion out of his voice as he replied, "No one sent me, I come on my own accord."

The pharaoh tossed back his covers and launched himself out of bed to fight, kicking the intruder hard on the side. The assassin countered by throwing the naked king to the floor, sitting on the man's back as if the pharaoh were a pony and smashing the king's face into the marble tile. Gripping the pharaoh's scalp, the killer yanked the king's head to expose his neck.

"What did I ever do to you?" Epiphanes begged, struggling under the weight of his captor.

The assassin spat on the floor as he drew his knife and placed it on his victim's throat. "You stole the Upper Kingdom from my family, you Macedonian fraud."

He carved his knife across the pharaoh's throat, and in the blink of an eye, Ptolemy V Epiphanes was dead.

The assassin wiped the blood from his blade on the dead man's bare back in the form of a cross, and rose from his position, sheathing his weapon in his boot. Footsteps approached in the main hall.

"*They're coming,*" his partner warned. "*Ten of them. Get out.*"

Quick as lightning, he made his way to the window and jumped two stories down, landing and rolling to his feet before dashing off into the night toward the river. He thanked the goddess the villa was on the outskirts of town so he'd be able to avoid the city streets. When the coast was clear, he slowed down, allowing himself to relax. He made his way through thickets of olive and cypress trees, pushing through the tall reeds along the river's shore to the rendezvous point, where a small fishing boat awaited him.

As he climbed into the boat, Khenefer tugged his mask from his face and felt the warm Nile air on his sweaty skin. He smiled at Shesh, who stood to embrace him.

"You did it," she whispered into his ear.

"As did you." Khenefer smiled.

They kissed, the heat rising between them. After a few moments, Khenefer pulled back and gazed into his wife's face. She was the most perfect thing in his whole wide world.

"What next, my love?" she asked, bouncing on the balls of her feet.

He considered her request. The other men responsible for his father's downfall, Chanax, and Conanus, were also dead. Epiphanes killed Chanax years ago, and Khenefer had murdered Conanus in

Alexandria before heading to Hermopolis. The pharaoh was the final target in their mission.

"Good question," Khenefer replied. "We could go back to Paros with the rest of our family. Pistias and Ruia's home on the island is never boring."

"Yes," Shesh laughed. "I've never seen Aunt Ruia so happy. They make a wonderful couple, the proper Egyptian queen and the unruly Greek sailor. Their home will always be a safe haven for us."

"Yet you and I both long for life along the Nile," Khenefer noted. Shesh nodded, and Khenefer kissed her before continuing, "I could use my title to wage a rebellion. Now that Epiphanes is dead, and leaves young children behind, there is an opening to do so."

"More war?" she asked, cocking an eyebrow.

She would do whatever he asked, but Khenefer wasn't sure war was the answer. He raised his gaze to the sky, the stars shining above as he considered his choices. After a moment, he shook his head.

"No more war. Our people have suffered enough. Let's go south, to Kush. That's there where my heart lives."

He'd grown up in Kush and loved the men and women of Meroe. They'd welcome Ankhwenefer's heir with open arms. Who knows, perhaps they needed a husband and wife assassin team as well? Their skills would come in handy in any court.

"Yes," Shesh replied, "Let's start anew in the south, now that we've completed our revenge."

"Dandue," Khenefer called to the man who owned the boat.

"Yes, my lord?" the fisherman replied.

"Take us to Coptos. We'll catch a ship to Meroe from there."

"As you wish, my lord."

The boat sailed south under the moonlight, and Khenefer lay back, Shesh in his arms, gazing at the stars, and imagined his father and brother were looking down upon him, praising him for a job well done.

Epilogue

The Game

The sages and gods of ancient Egypt were under no illusions respecting the possible future of the tradition, which they confided to the intelligence and virtue of future generations. It was a great thing to give the people a book which they could adore respectfully and always guard intact, but to give them a game which would enable the tradition to live, was yet better.

~ Papus, "The Tarot of the Bohemians," 1892 CE

Marseilles, Francia, 627 CE

"My word, child, slow down," Hanzi exclaimed. It was summer in southern Francia and sweat dripped down his back like mist on a foggy night. He was a large man, barrel-chested and well over six-and-a-half-feet tall. Upon his back, he carried a tent, food, candles, flint, a slingshot, sword, and enough coins for months on the road with his ambitious daughter. He rubbed his thick, dark curls that were matted to his forehead with dirt and perspiration and called out again. "Ragnetrude, I told you to slow down."

The child was at least twenty feet in front of him, and he'd lost sight of her in the thick woods just north of the town of Marseilles.

"Tata," he heard Ragnetrude call out from within the trees, "I've found a road."

Hanzi pushed through the dense brush beneath the ancient trees and discovered his daughter standing on what appeared to be an old Roman road in the middle of a clearing. She placed her hands on her hips and smiled, her white teeth glowing against her copper-colored skin.

"Just like the lady in the dream told me, Tata," she proclaimed. "We need to follow this road to Marseilles." She turned over her shoulder, swinging her long dark braid across her back for effect.

"We want to go to Marseilles?" he asked, not for the first time during this journey. He still wasn't sure why he'd journeyed to the south with her. This was a land of warring kings and priests. No place for a wandering entertainer like himself.

"Come, Tata," she said waving down the road. "We must go now. If we get there by sunset, we can spend the night in safety."

"I still can't believe I've allowed this," he grumbled as he followed behind. The road was Roman, built at least three centuries prior, and in ruin. The earth had eaten through the structure and large broken blocks spread out before him like a jigsaw puzzle.

"Dagobert, the king of Francia, needs us to find this book, Tata," she insisted.

"Dagobert is king of Austrasia, darling."

"He is now, but by the time we meet him, he'll be the king of the Franks."

"Let me see if I understand," Hanzi began. "The goddess came to you in a dream telling you we had to find a long-forgotten book, filled with the ancient secrets of our people, and she wants us to give it over to the future king of Francia, a man who won't allow us to entertain at his court? What sort of man denies the Wanderers? We're the finest in entertainment. We tell the stories of old, we sing, and we pass on information. If we find anything, child, we are *not* giving it over to the king of the Franks. You know how I feel about royalty. They can't be trusted."

Ragnetrude didn't turn around; she skipped along the path, springing from flat brick to flat brick, humming a little tune.

"Girl," Hanzi called again, "you never told me we were going to give this relic to King Dagobert."

"We won't have to give it to him," she answered, still moving forward, her arms now swaying to some rhythm only she could hear. "We need to find it, study it, and then make a game of it."

"A game?"

"Yes, like a card game. Only this game will contain the wisdom of Egypt."

"Yes, Egypt." He sighed. "You've said that. Tell me again how this is connected to Egypt?"

"The beautiful woman in my dream said that long ago, the goddess of Egypt came here, to these very lands. She mated with the Stag King, the god of the forest, and together they gave birth to the wisdom contained in this book. It was written by the hand of the Stag King himself."

"And why did the goddess of Egypt do this?" Hanzi asked.

"Because," Ragnetrude explained, "her lands were under attack by the god of chaos, and she'd lost the battle. She knew that Egypt would fall into ruin, and Rome would instead conquer the world, killing all knowledge of the Way. She didn't want that to happen, so she came here, to Marseilles, only it wasn't called that back then, and gave the people of Gaul this most precious gift."

"If it's so precious, then why is it hidden away in some forest way far north from the city?"

Ragnetrude paused mid-movement and turned around to face him. Hanzi saw tears in her green eyes as she whispered, "The lady said that a great priest and priestess were supposed to have shared it with the gods of Britannia, but instead they hid it in a grave."

"Why would they do such a thing?" Hanzi asked.

"Maybe they didn't trust they were the goddess's words?" she continued. "Now it falls to us, and we must find it, Tata. Come, we need to arrive in Marseilles before dark. It isn't safe on this road."

Hanzi gazed at her. His daughter was known to have the sight, all the Bunica of the troupe agreed. Ragnetrude was of the old blood. Older than their roots in Punjab. As old as Egypt herself, from where their people had first fled a thousand years ago as their lands fell to the Persians. They'd spent centuries in Punjab before moving on to Europe, integrating into the culture, mating with the people, learning of the Way, and synthesizing it with what they knew. What more could they learn now? Why would the goddess send his daughter out here, five hundred miles from Paris where their troupe was currently living? And why had he gone along with this wild goose chase?

They walked in silence for an hour, each one deep within their own thoughts. Hanzi reached out with his awareness and tried to connect to the child's emotions and discern her inner thoughts, but Ragnetrude blocked him. She was an adept at the arts of subtle energy. Hanzi had heard that the kings of Francia and Austrasia, called the Merovingian, were also adepts at the ancient magic. He shivered as he thought of their upcoming audience with King Dagobert. He wasn't sure he wanted to introduce his little girl to the court. In preparation for their journey, Ragnetrude had been sent into a trance to discover how they might be granted safe passage from the king so that they would be able to work their magic, storytelling, and entertainment throughout the Frankish kingdom. As a result, Hanzi now found himself in the middle of nowhere, talking about Egypt, goddesses, and games.

When they arrived in Marseilles, Ragnetrude led him along several winding roads, past beggars, street musicians, and many taverns, out past the town walls to an old cemetery. At the entrance was a rusted gate, hanging off its hinges, and the grove was covered in vines, trees, blackberry bushes, and other plants that had long ago made it their home. No one had been buried here for centuries. All that remained were ancient family tombstones, the names and dates long ago washed away by the rain. A stone fence crumbled around the property and what looked like an ancient orchard surrounded the northern side.

Hanzi stood, pulled out his sword, and began to chop at the brush that blocked their path. "Did the lady in your dream tell you where exactly it was hidden?"

"She said it would be in the center, for that's where wisdom lives."

"Of course," Hanzi said as he cleared the way to the center of the cemetery, where a larger tombstone stood, the image of the Egyptian ankh still visible.

"Well," Ragnetrude said, her face glowing like the full moon, "this must be it. Now we dig."

"We are *not* digging up someone's grave. That is against our way," he admonished.

"No, it isn't near her body. The priestess left it under the tombstone. Knock it over for me."

He shook his head. "Knock it over?"

"Yes, you're strong enough. It's why I asked you instead of Maman to take me here."

His daughter's honesty never ceased to amaze him. Hanzi yanked the hatchet from his supplies and began to hack away at the ancient rock, apologizing to the poor soul who was buried beneath it. A few strikes and the tombstone was on its side. He handed his daughter a shovel. Ragnetrude began to dig like a woodchuck preparing for winter.

Within moments she held a huge package wrapped in thick linen in her hands, sniffling as she brushed away the dirt. She unwrapped the linen, dropping it to the ground, and held up a leather-bound book, golden letters embossed across its front above a delicate trinity knot.

"This is it. Just like the goddess said."

Ragnetrude gazed up at her father's face, clutching the book to her bosom as if it were a precious child. She held it out for him to see. Burned across the cover was a set of Greek letters. Hanzi didn't know how to read Greek, but his daughter knew a little.

"It says, 'The Goddess of The South,'" Ragnetrude whispered, tears now streaming down her ruddy cheeks. She traced the words with her fingers and sighed, the corners of her mouth turning up as she spoke, "After centuries, what was lost, has now been found."

"Little hawk," Hanzi said, his own throat tight, "this is a very old book. It has to be at least five hundred years old."

"The lady in my dream told me it was eight hundred years old."

"How did it survive?"

"Ancient magic."

"Are you sure she wants us to give this to Dagobert? Will it encourage him to be our patron and let us work in his lands?"

"We can't give it to him." She tapped at the cover as she wiped her tears. "We're to make a game from it. Nandal, the smithy, he knows Greek, yes?"

"Yes, he does."

"He will translate it for me, and then I will tell you all about it, and you will make it into a card game."

"I'm not sure I understand," Hanzi complained.

"You're a gambler, Tata, so think harder. Think of cards and how we might use them for play, but also for teaching wisdom. Think of how we might have suits and—" she broke off and began to page through the book. There were beautiful pictures with pages of writing following them.

"Trumps," Hanzi said, understanding what was being asked of him.

"We'll hire the best artist in the troupe to paint the pictures on the cards," she continued, bouncing from foot to foot.

"And present the game, not the actual book, in Dagobert's court."

"Yes."

"This is a good idea," he agreed as he began to pack up his supplies.

"Tata, Our Lady told me that this wasn't the only book. Another copy is hidden in the deserts near Seti's lost temple in Egypt. And yet another made it to a Persian prince, whose people will bring this same knowledge to Francia as well. We must teach the wisdom to the Merovingians, and then the king of Francia will let us sing for him and remind the people of these lands of the Way."

Hanzi laughed as he picked her up into his gigantic embrace. "You have saved the mission of the Wanderers."

"No, Tata," Ragnetrude answered as she wrapped her arms around her father's shoulders, "the goddess saved us."

Character List

Alexa: High priestess of Isis. Daughter of Tyia. Mother of Sethe with Chanax. Mother of Meryt with her spiritual companion, Pharaoh Ankhwenefer. Also the spiritual companion of the high priest of Thebes, Setep.

Anen: Daughter of Silus and Ruia. Married to Ankhmaat.

Ankhmaat: First son of Pharaoh Ankhwenefer and Queen Weret. Crown Prince of Upper Egypt. Married to Anen.

Ankhwenefer: Pharaoh of Upper Egypt from 199-186 BCE. Second son of Horwenefer and Queen Keket. Father of Helena with his spiritual companion, Natasa. Father of Ankhmaat and Khenefer with his sister-wife, Weret. Father of Meryt with High Priestess Alexa. Known to the Greeks as Chaonnophris. Known as Ankhmakis before becoming pharaoh.

Ansel: One of Ankhwenefer's guards. Greek heritage.

Aurelia: Witch of the North. Mentor to Natasa in Massilia.
Baktre: Eldest daughter of Bithiah and Chanax.

Bastyre: Royal midwife of Behdet. Teacher of medicine and herbalism.

Bithiah: Second daughter of Horwenefer and his second queen, Mafuane. Promised to Nefermaat but forced to marry her half-brother, Chanax. Mother of Baktre, Panas, Hor, and Shesh.

Ceana: Gaelic. Friend of Finnian's.

Chanax: Is brought up as the third son of Horwenefer and Keket but discovers later that his real father is the High Priest Isidor. Priest of Set and father of Sethe with his spiritual companion, Alexa. Father to Baktre, Panas, Hor, and Shesh with his sister-wife, Bithiah.

Cleopatra I: Daughter of Antiochus III of Syria. Married to Ptolemy V Epiphanes.

Conanus: Ptolemaic general who arrests Ankhwenefer in 186 BCE.

Corinna: Nursemaid of Nefermaat and Natasa. Mother of Eleni with her husband, Hecataeus. Murdered by Nefermaat when trying to save Natasa and Helena.

Durame: Kush princess. Married to Senui.

Eleni: Natasa's younger half-sister. Daughter of Corinna and Vizier Hecataeus. Married to Pamu. Mother of Khui and Rai.

Ennaeus: Vizier of Ankhwenefer, beloved of High Priest Iu-Amon. Appointed by Ptolemy III Euergetes.

Epiphanes: Son of Ptolemy IV Philopater and Queen Arsinoe III. Fifth Ptolemy to take the throne. Married to Cleopatra I.
Finnian: Gaelic scribe of the druid Taran. Penned "The Goddess of the South" with Natasa during her time in Massilia.

Hecataeus: Greek Vizier of Behdet, originally assigned by Ptolemy III

Euergetes to spy on the royals of Behdet. After the death of Euergetes, betrays Ptolemy IV Philopater and helped Horwenefer procure an army and launch the rebellion. Father of Natasa with High Priestess Neferu-ankh-maat. Father of Eleni with his wife, Corinna.

Helena: Holy child of the temple. The first daughter of Pharaoh Ankhwenefer and his spiritual companion, Natasa. Killed as a proxy for her parent's crimes.

Hor: Second son of Chanax and Bithiah.

Horpais: Second son of Silus and Ruia.

Horwenefer: Pharaoh of Upper Egypt from 205-199 BCE. Father of Silus, Ankhwenefer, and Senmen with Keket. Father of Ruia, Bithiah, and Weret with Mafuane. Father of Nefermaat with his spiritual companion High Priestess Neferu-ankh-maat. Launched the rebellion against the Ptolemaic Empire in 205 BCE. Known to the Greeks as Haronnophris. Also known as Hugronaphor.

Ikui: Weapons trainer and master smithy for Upper Egypt.

Isidor: High priest of Set in Memphis. Mentor to Chanax. Spiritual companion of High Priestess Neferu-ankh-maat. Had a decades-long affair with Queen Keket.

Iu-Amon: High priest of the Houses of Healing. Beloved of the Vizier Ennaeus.

Keket: Married to Pharaoh Horwenefer. Mother of Silus, Ankhwenefer, and Senmen. Had a decades-long affair with High Priest Isidor.

Khaleme: General of the Kush (Ethiopian) army. Sent by King Adikhalamani to support the Egyptian Revolt.

Khenefer: Second son of Pharaoh Ankhwenefer and Queen Weret. Marries Shesh.

Khui: Son of Pamu and Eleni.

Latharna: Druid high priestess of Massilia.

Maedoc: Gaelic. Friend of Finnian's.

Mafuane: Priestess of Isis. Second queen of Horwenefer. Mother of Ruia, Bithiah, and Weret. Died giving birth to Weret.

Maharet: Theban nobility. Wife of Min and mother of Abana and Djau.

Meryt: Holy child of the temple. Daughter of Pharaoh Ankhwenefer and High Priestess Alexa.

Metakryon: High priest of Memphis and the Lower Kingdom of Egypt. Head of the Cult of Set and training in Memphis.

Min: Son of the priest Zethus and a royal nursemaid. Twin brother of Pontius. Pharaoh Ankhwenefer's captain of the guard. Father of Abana and Djau with his wife, Maharet.

Natasa: Daughter of High Priestess Neferu-ankh-maat and Vizier Hecataeus. Mother of Helena and spiritual companion of Ankhmakis.

Neferu-ankh-maat: High priestess of Isis in Behdet. Spiritual companion to Horwenefer and High Priest Isidor. Mother of Nefermaat with Horwenefer. Mother of Natasa with Vizier Hecataeus. Also known as Neferu or Neffa.

Nefermaat: Son of High Priestess Neferu-ankh-maat and Horwenefer. Member of the royal guard. Had a years-long affair with Bithiah. Executed by Ankhwenefer for the murders of Corinna and Helena.

Pamu: Captain of the guard to the Crown Prince, Ankhmaat. Married to Eleni. Father of Khui and Rai.

Panas: First son of Chanax and Bithiah.

Pistias: Greek sailor commissioned twice by Ankhwenefer to help his family flee the country. Married to Ruia.

Pontius: Son of the priest Zethus and a royal nursemaid. Twin brother of Min. Executed by Ankhwenefer for the murder of Helena.

Philopater: Fourth king of the Ptolemaic Empire. Reigned from 221-204 BCE. Pharaoh when the Great Revolt of 205 BCE was launched. Died shortly thereafter. Father of Epiphanes with his wife, Queen Arsinoe III.

Rai: Daughter of Pamu and Eleni.

Ruia: Eldest daughter of Horwenefer and his second queen, Mafuane. Mother of Senui, Horpais, and Anen with her husband and half-brother, Silus. Marries Pistias after fleeing Egypt with the royal daughters and Khenefer.

Sebastos: Horse trainer and master falconer of Behdet.

Senui: First son of Silus and Ruia. Married to Durame.

Setep: High priest of Thebes and the Upper Kingdom of Egypt.

Sethe: Holy child of the temple. Son of Chanax and High Priestess Alexa.

Silus: Eldest son of Horwenefer and Keket. Father of Senui, Horpais, and Anen with his sister-wife Ruia.

Shesh: Youngest daughter of Chanax and Bithiah. Marries Khenefer.

Taran: Gaelic druid priest. Friend of Hecataeus's. Helped the family find shelter in Gaul. Goes to Avalon with Neferu.

Weret: High Queen of Upper Egypt. The youngest daughter of Horwenefer and his second queen, Mafuane. Married to Pharaoh Ankhwenefer. Mother of Ankhmaat and Khenefer.

About the Author

Nicole Sallak Anderson is a Computer Science graduate from Purdue University, and former CTO for a small Silicon Valley startup, turned novelist and blogger, focusing on the intersection of technology and consciousness. She currently lives in the beautiful Santa Cruz Mountains in California with her husband, where she raises goats and bees. She enjoys spinning, knitting, playing the bass, and dancing, particularly the tango. You can keep up with all her latest writing by following @NSallakAnderson on Facebook, Twitter, and Medium or her blog, nicolesallakanderson.com. Feel free to contact her; she almost always answers any query or comment!

www.ingramcontent.com/pod-product-compliance
Lightning Source LLC
Chambersburg PA
CBHW030807200726
48285CB00015B/1561